# the summer of broken things

## ALSO BY MARGARET PETERSON HADDIX

**CHILDREN OF EXILE**

*Children of Exile*

*Children of Refuge*

*Children of Jubilee*

**UNDER THEIR SKIN**

*Under Their Skin*

*In Over Their Heads*

**THE MISSING**

*Found*

*Sent*

*Sabotaged*

*Torn*

*Caught*

*Risked*

*Revealed*

*Redeemed*

*Sought* (an eBook original)

*Rescued* (an eBook original)

**THE SHADOW CHILDREN**

*Among the Hidden*

*Among the Impostors*

*Among the Betrayed*

*Among the Barons*

*Among the Brave*

*Among the Enemy*

*Among the Free*

**THE PALACE CHRONICLES**

*Just Ella*

*Palace of Mirrors*

*Palace of Lies*

*The Girl with 500 Middle Names*

*Because of Anya*

*Say What?*

*Dexter the Tough*

*Running Out of Time*

*Full Ride*

*Game Changer*

*The Always War*

*Claim to Fame*

*Uprising*

*Double Identity*

*The House on the Gulf*

*Escape from Memory*

*Takeoffs and Landings*

*Turnabout*

*Leaving Fishers*

*Don't You Dare Read This, Mrs. Dunphrey*

# the summer of broken things

MARGARET PETERSON HADDIX

SIMON & SCHUSTER BFYR

NEW YORK LONDON TORONTO SYDNEY NEW DELHI

SIMON & SCHUSTER BFYR
An imprint of Simon & Schuster Children's Publishing Division
1230 Avenue of the Americas, New York, New York 10020

Also available in a SIMON & SCHUSTER BFYR hardcover edition
Cover design by Lucy Ruth Cummins
Interior design by Hilary Zarycky
The text for this book was set in New Caledonia.
Manufactured in the United States of America
First SIMON & SCHUSTER BFYR paperback edition April 2019
2 4 6 8 10 9 7 5 3 1
The Library of Congress has cataloged the hardcover edition as follows:
Names: Haddix, Margaret Peterson, author.
Title: Summer of broken things / Margaret Peterson Haddix.
Description: First edition. | New York : SSBFYR, 2017. | Summary: Fourteen-year-old Avery Armisted and sixteen-year-old Kayla Butts, once good friends, begrudgingly travel to Spain together for a summer vacation where they uncover a secret their families kept hidden from them their entire lives.
Identifiers: LCCN 2016055583| ISBN 9781481417648 (hc) | ISBN 9781481417662 (eBook) | ISBN 9781481417655 (pbk.)
Subjects: | CYAC: Vacations—Fiction. | Families—Fiction. | Secrets—Fiction. | Spain—Fiction.
Classification: LCC PZ7.H1164 Su 2017 | DDC [Fic]—dc23
LC record available at https://lccn.loc.gov/2016055583

*For Meredith*

## How It Begins for Avery

**"We need to talk," Dad** says.

He's got his hand on the door to the garage when I walk into the kitchen for breakfast. He's wearing his Important Business Deal suit, with the power tie I gave him last year for Father's Day. (Mom picked it out. Of course she wouldn't trust my fashion sense.) And, yes—*there*—he glances at his watch.

I translate: Body language + watch consultation + four terse words = He doesn't want a conversation. He's going to talk; I'm supposed to listen.

"Oh, sorry," I say, flipping my messy just-out-of-bed ponytail over my shoulder. I add an eye roll for effect. "I didn't get the memo from your administrative assistant. Did we have a meeting scheduled this morning?"

"Avery," Dad says, and I've succeeded. There's an edge of helplessness in his voice, a hint of *How is it that I can negotiate multimillion-dollar deals practically in my sleep, but I can't get my fourteen-year-old daughter to treat me with respect?*

I just have to be careful not to push him into *You know, my parents spanked me when I was a kid, and that kept me from back-talking them . . . and I did three hours of farm chores every morning before school . . . and even though we didn't have two pennies to rub together, we had one another, and that's all we needed . . .*

Blah, blah, blah.

For the record, my parents have never spanked me, and never would.

And Mom would never allow Dad to force me to do farm chores, even if we lived on a farm.

I don't think.

"About this summer," Dad says, and I regret the eye roll.

"Yes?" I say cautiously. I can hear in my head how my friends would tell me to play it: *Beg. Or go over and kiss your daddy on the cheek and throw your arms around his shoulders and tell him, "You're the best dad in the world! You decided I can go with Lauren and Shannon to soccer camp for the whole summer, right?" And then he's got no choice. He has to agree.*

That kind of thing doesn't actually work very well with my dad. It's like my friends' fathers were all stamped out from some generic Business Executive Father mold—some Easy-to-Wrap-Around-Their-Daughters'-Little-Fingers mold—but mine wasn't. I think it's from the spankings and the farm chores and the being born poor.

"Where's Mom?" I ask.

"She had an early meeting," Dad says. "Important new client."

Mom's an interior designer. Dad and I secretly make fun of the slogans she's been trying out for her new business. Her latest is "The things around you can set the tone for your entire life."

Dad glances at his watch again.

"But your mother and I talked last night, and—"

"Don't you mean, 'argued'?" I ask. I reach into the refrigerator for a yogurt. I pretend I really care whether I get blueberry or pomegranate. "I heard you when I came downstairs to get my phone charger. What was Mom saying? 'Fourteen is the worst age for a girl to be unhappy'? And 'Three months with Avery furious and miserable, and you'll *wish* she were a thousand miles away'?"

Dad has pretty good posture to begin with, but I see his back stiffen.

"What else did you hear?" he asks.

*You think I stuck around to hear my own parents trash-talking me?* I want to ask. But we don't ask questions like that in my family.

I open a yogurt and slide a spoon into it.

"Nothing," I mutter. I only skim the surface of the yogurt. Then I change my mind and dig the spoon in deep, flipping it to bring up the blueberries hidden on the bottom. "Dad, you know I want—"

He isn't listening. He holds up his hand in that way he has, all *Wait your turn. I'm talking now.*

"We figured out a compromise," he says. "You get one week at soccer camp. Then you come to Spain with me."

That's a compromise?

"But, Dad, you'll be away working all the time, and I won't have any friends there, and even Mom wouldn't be able to come for very long, not that I'd want to spend the whole summer just with *her* anyway, but . . ."

There's a word I can't quite bring myself to say, because it'd be too much like groveling, or admitting a weakness: *Lonely. Don't you know how lonely I'd be? Or how much that would wreck me?* Dad wouldn't understand how the summer before freshman year has to be all about building up confidence, getting ready to start strong. Lauren has an older sister, and she's told us about girls who messed up their whole high school careers the first week of ninth grade.

I switch tacks.

"And you know soccer's my *thing*, and I have to get really, really good at it this summer if I'm going to make varsity in the fall, and . . ."

*And what if Lauren and Shannon make varsity, and I don't?*

Dad has been talking about Spain for weeks, and it's like we've developed rules for this argument. At some point, I'm supposed to say, *Look, I know it's a big deal, you offering me the chance to go to Europe for a whole summer. I get it. I'm not a spoiled brat. It's just, this isn't the right summer.* And whenever I bring up varsity, Dad is supposed to say, *You're already an amazing soccer player. You'll make the team no matter what.* He's supposed to be my biggest cheerleader.

But Dad doesn't say any of that now. It's like he's deaf. He keeps talking, like I haven't said a thing.

I realize I haven't heard what he said either.

"What?" I ask.

"I said, this is what we came up with: You can bring a friend to Spain with you."

"I can?" I take a step back. This is new. This is . . . well, acceptable. Maybe.

"You mean Lauren and Shannon could come with me?" I ask. "Or Maya or . . ."

Suddenly, I'm picturing my whole eighth-grade soccer team with me in Spain. We'd play soccer in some really cool Spanish park. (Or *fútbol.* I know they call it *fútbol* there.) We'd shop in a pack, grabbing up all sorts of European fashions. We'd flirt with really hot European boys. We'd sightsee just enough that we could drop a casual *Oh yes, when I was at the Alhambra . . .* into conversations when we went back to school in the fall.

We'd go back as the coolest freshmen in the history of Deskins High School.

"*One* friend," Dad says. "One. And it has to be someone responsible and trustworthy and, preferably, older. I thought of the perfect person. Kayla. I checked with her family last night, and they're thinking about it, but it's probably going to work."

"Kayla?" I repeat blankly. "Don't you mean Kennedy? Or Kylie?"

I can't decide which is more annoying: that he thinks he can pick a best friend for me, or that he can't even remember the names of the friends I already have. Not that Kennedy or Kylie are such close friends. I'd call them second-string. Maybe third.

"No, I mean Kayla," Dad insists. "Kayla Butts."

I almost drop my yogurt.

"Kayla Butts?" I repeat. "She's not my friend! When was the last time I even saw her?"

Kayla Butts is this girl whose mom was best friends with my nanny when I was little. They live out in the middle of nowhere, an hour or two from Columbus, so it was always a big deal when they'd visit. Angelica, my nanny, always wanted to show me off, so she'd put me in some frilly dress. And then Angelica would bribe me to be good by letting Kayla and me do things that weren't usually allowed: drinking chocolate milk, not white, with lunch; climbing to the top of the jungle gym at the park, instead of having to stop halfway up . . . I can remember Kayla's mom laughing and saying *she'd* catch us if we fell. But we never fell. I almost always cried when it came time for Kayla to leave, because I'd gotten the frilly dress dirty, or Angelica was extra-mean when she went back to enforcing rules—or I just didn't like having to stop playing what I wanted.

But my crying when Kayla left made everyone think Kayla and I were BFFs.

Back then, maybe we were.

But for years after that, Kayla and her mom would still swing by at the holidays and drop off Christmas presents for me. Which was silly, because I'm pretty sure Kayla's family is kind of poor.

Maybe Kayla and her mom even came this past Christmas, and I just don't remember.

"You and Kayla always played together better than any of your other friends," Dad says. "That's what Angelica always said."

"You mean when I was *five*?" I ask. "And she was *seven*? Dad, news bulletin—five- and seven-year-olds, fourteen- and sixteen-year-olds—it's not the same! I don't play with Barbie dolls anymore either. I bet I couldn't even pick Kayla out in a crowd. You really want to make me spend the whole summer with a total stranger?"

"No," Dad says. "With a whole country full of strangers. Some of whom might become friends. It'll be good for you."

And then he opens the door and walks out, like the conversation is over.

I grab my phone and immediately text Shannon and Lauren: **My dad is crazy! He IS going to make me go to Spain!**

Shannon texts back, **Nooooo . . .**

Lauren texts a bunch of frowny face emojis, along with the one that's crying so hard the tears flow upward. Then she writes, **You have to talk him out of it!**

**I can't**, I write back. Then I just stare at the words on the screen. I can't bear to send them.

But it doesn't matter. I know my dad.

This is really going to happen.

## When It Registers for Kayla

**"I am a girl who's** going to Europe," I whisper to myself in history class. "I am a girl who's going to Spain."

I'm trying out the idea, trying to make it seem real. I'm carrying the words around the way Grandpa carries a lucky penny everywhere he goes.

But maybe I'm a little too loud, because Stephanie Purley turns around in front of me.

"What'd you say, Butt-girl?" she asks.

Kids started calling me "Butt-girl" in kindergarten, because of my last name. The nicknames got worse over the years, so it's like she's bringing back a golden oldie. Maybe she thinks she's being nice.

But it's crazy how nobody forgets anything in Crawfordsville. Roger Staley is still the kid who ate paste in kindergarten. Jayden Allen is still the kid who peed in the principal's office in second grade.

I'm still "Butt-girl."

Stephanie Purley was Little Miss Snowflake for the whole town of Crawfordsville in first grade. She's always on a float in the annual Christmas parade for something. She was "Prettiest Girl" in eighth-grade superlatives. She was freshman-class homecoming attendant last year. She's been a cheerleader forever.

She's wearing her cheerleader uniform now, even though I kind of thought sports to cheer for were over for the year.

Maybe it's just one of her outfits that look like her cheerleading uniform.

Most of them do.

The rules of Crawfordsville High School—the rules that let people like Stephanie Purley tolerate people like me—are that I'm supposed to mumble, "Nothing," and look down at the study guide on my desk. The one I'm supposed to be filling out. And then Stephanie Purley will go back to flirting with Ryan Decker in front of her, and I'll be like an annoying fly she shooed away, or an ugly cockroach she squashed flat.

But today I am not just Butt-girl. I am also a girl who's going to Spain.

Someplace not even Stephanie Purley has been.

"I was talking about what I'm doing this summer," I tell her. I look her straight in her pretty blue eyes. "I'm going to Europe."

"You?" Stephanie asks, and there's everything in that one word: *How would someone like you afford that? People like you, it's a big deal just to go to Dayton or Toledo or Columbus. You are* not *going to a whole other continent!*

Truth is, it's kind of a big deal for anyone from Crawfordsville to go to Dayton or Toledo or Columbus.

Truth is, even Stephanie's not so dumb that she can't find her way to the natural conclusion: that I'm lying. Kind of like back in fourth grade, when I had that unfortunate episode of making up stories that nobody believed.

"I have a job," I say quickly. "I'm traveling with a family that wants me to be, like, kind of a nanny."

And even though this is Stephanie Purley I'm talking to, not anybody I'm remotely friends with, I suddenly want to spill everything. How when Mom got off the phone last night with Mr. Armisted, she had tears in her eyes, and she kept saying, "Oh, Kayla, you are going to have opportunities I never had! This is, like . . . a godsend!" How she'd been worrying that everything *I'd* been dreaming of for the summer—getting my driver's license, working at the Crawfordsville Dairy Queen—wouldn't happen because the car insurance would cost too much. Because the nursing home cut her hours *again*.

But I can already see the smugness flowing across Stephanie's face.

"Oooh," she says. "Should have known. You're the type who'd go all the way to Europe and still do nothing but change diapers. Only, baby's diapers this time, not old people's."

"I don't change diapers at the nursing home!" I protest, outraged for Mrs. Hudson and Mr. Lang and, well, certain other people I care about who have to live in nursing homes.

Like my dad.

Before Stephanie can say anything about him, I go on.

"The girl I'm 'babysitting' in Europe is fourteen," I say. "Almost as old as me. So there. No diapers. Her dad has to go to Spain for a business trip, and he wants her to go along. For the experience. But her mom can't go, because of her own job. So they want me to go with Avery instead. To keep her company."

If I were talking to almost any of the old ladies at the nursing home, I would have added, *It's like I'm a paid companion. Like in those regency romances you're always reading.*

But I have learned something since kindergarten, when I thought I could talk to other five-year-olds the same way I talked to my best friends at the nursing home—all of whom were over seventy.

Metamucil jokes—not a big hit in the kindergarten set.

To Stephanie, "paid companion" would probably sound like something dirty.

And suddenly, I'm not so thrilled with the comparison myself. In the regency romances Mrs. Lang, Mrs. Shrivers, and Mrs. Delaney are always urging me to read, the paid companions are mostly there to find lost gloves and tell the hero that the heroine truly is in love with him, no matter how much she pretends otherwise.

The "paid companions" never get to be the heroines themselves.

They might as well be maids.

*This is not the 1800s*, I tell myself. *Nobody's expecting you to be a maid. Nobody will even know you in Europe. You can be anyone you want.*

But I can feel my face settling into the patented how-Kayla-Butts-gets-through-the-school-day empty expression. The one that pretends that nothing anyone says can hurt me.

Stephanie snorts.

"Whate*ver*," she says. "Even in Europe, you'll still be Butt-girl."

Stephanie turns back around. But I can't bear to pick up my pencil and start filling in blanks on the answer sheet about all the European explorers who came to America, and what two hundred forty years of American history have done to us all.

What if the whole world outside Crawfordsville is just full of Stephanie Purleys, there to put me down?

What if *Avery* is like that now too?

## Avery, Leaving Home

**"You know you're going to** miss me," I tell Mom.

We're standing in my bedroom, my suitcase between us—packed, zipped, and ready to go. I know how Mom will play this: She'll ask if I'm sure I packed enough underwear, or remind me that if my clothes are wrong for the European scene, I have to make Dad let me go shopping.

She won't say anything about missing me.

But Mom surprises me by wrapping her arms so tightly around my shoulders that I fall forward, my knees banging against the suitcase, its telescoping handle digging into my ribs. For a moment, she's the only thing holding me up.

Instinctively, I push her away.

"Mo-om!" I protest. "I can't breathe!"

She lets go, and I right myself, solid on my own two feet again. But there's a weird moment where our eyes meet. Hers have gone all watercolor, a flood of tears kept penned in place by her eyelashes and perfectly applied mascara. On her face—with her blue eyes, her straight nose, and her gently framing ash-blond hair—the effect is really pretty. Of course, everything's always pretty on Mom. She works hard to keep it that way.

"Oh, no," I say. "You are not doing that to me. *I'm* not going to cry."

*Anymore*, I think.

Mom's gaze slides away. She still hasn't said anything. She swallows hard.

I ignore the lump forming in my own throat.

"I was going to be away this summer regardless, remember?" I ask. "Only, soccer camp would have been a whole lot closer. You could have even come to visit some weekends, if you'd just . . ."

Mom keeps her face turned to the side. I see the first tear escape the mascara corral and slip daintily down her cheek. Then her face quivers and twists. The pretty crying has gone ugly.

"Mom?" I say uncertainly. This isn't like her. But I've never traveled so far away from her before. It's not like I have hope anymore, but I still seize the opportunity. "Mom, really, you could stop everything right now, if you just tell Dad—"

Mom's shaking her head hard. *No, no, no . . .*

"Don't you see?" It's like the words are ripped from her mouth. She's almost snarling, which is *so* not like my mom. Not with me. "I can't stop *anything*. I don't have *any* control over . . ."

She spins around and sprints toward my bathroom. This is *totally* not like her. I've never seen her move so gracelessly.

"Avery? Celeste? The car service is here," Dad calls from downstairs.

I step out onto the landing.

"Mom's in the bathroom," I say. "Um, crying."

Dad stares up at me from the foyer, the front door open before him. Even at this distance, I can see a muscle twitching in his jaw.

"I'll come up and get your suitcase," he says. "You go tell the driver I'll be right out."

I pick up the backpack I'm using as a carry-on and walk over to the bathroom door. I knock.

"Mom? Dad and I are leaving now," I say.

There's a muffled sound from behind that door that might have been a good-bye, or might have been just a sob. I back away from the door.

Down in the car Dad's company sent for us, I slide onto leather seats. The driver holds the door for me and points out complimentary water bottles and mints. He's so formal it's almost funny. Mostly, Dad likes to drive himself to the airport, and he's only ever taken Mom and me on shorter trips where that makes more sense. So this is my first experience with a car service.

*Maybe someday I'll be in the corporate world like Dad, and I'll travel in style like this all the time*, I tell myself.

The thought of Mom's weird sobbing upstairs makes it so I can't enjoy that fantasy.

*Or . . . probably my friends and I will get a limo for proms and homecoming dances in high school, and the limo will be like this*, I tell myself, seizing on something a little more immediate.

That's if I still have friends, after I'm cut off from everyone this summer.

I hear the driver shutting the trunk behind us, and the sound makes me jump. A moment later, Dad climbs through the open door across from me.

"Is Mom okay?" I ask.

He raises an eyebrow.

"She said she flashed ahead in time, and the emotions caught her by surprise. . . . I mean, it's only four years until you leave for college," he says. "Probably your mother and I will both cry that hard, on that day."

"Remind me to sneak out without telling anyone, then," I mutter.

I want to make Dad laugh—I want to be able to laugh myself. But it's like he doesn't hear me once again. He's staring so fixedly at the seat back in front of him that the driver has to say three times, "The airline you're flying is United. Is that correct, sir? Sir? *Sir?*"

We're not even out of our neighborhood when my phone pings with a text from Mom: **Sorry about that!!! That wasn't how I wanted to say good-bye. Have an incredible time in Spain!! This IS an amazing opportunity for you!!!!**

I analyze the text like it's a passage on a language arts test. The multiple exclamation points show Mom is trying way too hard. The "incredible" and "amazing"? Hyperbole.

And she still hasn't said she'll miss me.

## Kayla: A Journey of a Thousand Miles Begins with . . .

**"Excited?" Mom asks, glancing over** at me from the driver's seat of our ancient Chevy.

"Or are you nervous?" Grandma asks from behind me. "You shouldn't be nervous. There's nothing to worry about. You get a nervous stomach, it will just make you throw up."

I should feel grateful that Grandma and Grandpa wanted to come to the airport with us, to see me off. But—and this is assuming I manage not to throw up, and embarrass myself that way—I kind of feel like we're going to look like the Clampetts from *The Beverly Hillbillies* when we get there and all pile out of the car.

I remind myself that at least we don't have a rocking chair strapped to the roof of our car.

Then I remind myself that I can't make *Beverly Hillbillies* references around Avery. She doesn't need to know that most of the people I normally hang out with remember watching shows like *Beverly Hillbillies* and *Green Acres* when they were new. Not reruns.

"It's more like none of this seems real," I say. I watch the cornfields whip by outside the car window. The leaves sway like they're waving good-bye. "It feels like a dream."

"A good one, I hope," Grandma says.

"Now, why is it," Grandpa asks, "that there's a special word for a bad dream—a nightmare—but there's not any word for a really, really good dream?"

"Maybe there is in Spanish," Grandma says.

*Oh no, Spanish*, I think. And despite Grandma's warning about nerves, my stomach twists. Starting tomorrow, if I want anyone besides Avery and Mr. Armisted to understand me, I'll have to speak Spanish. I've had two years of it at Crawfordsville High, but it's not like my teachers ever expected any of us to really use it. Spanish is one of those classes they make easy on purpose. The tests are usually open notes.

Grandpa taps the back of Mom's headrest.

"You gave Kayla the good-behavior run-down, right?" he asks. "Told her she's not allowed to fall in love with any of those Spanish boys? Told her if they start talking to her in their fancy Spanish, all *boo-wane-us dee-uss seen-your-rita*, they're just trying to—"

"Dad!" Mom says, at the same time that Grandma says, "Roy! Stop it!"

"What?" Grandpa says. "Isn't anyone going to be impressed that I learned Spanish?"

He's probably the only person on the face of the earth whose accent is worse than mine.

"I trust Kayla," Mom says, and she shoots me a little glance that kind of apologizes for Grandpa.

When Mom was born, Grandma was forty and Grandpa was forty-five. They thought they'd never be able to have children, so even now they call her their "miracle baby." That's when they're not just agreeing with the rest of Crawfordsville that Mom's a saint for how she's handled everything since Dad's accident.

When I was born, Mom was only twenty. I guess to Grandma

and Grandpa, twenty years is nothing. So sometimes they act like Mom and I are sisters, not mother and daughter.

We don't look like sisters.

Mom is tiny and perky and constantly in motion, like a hummingbird. She has this cap of dark curls that she dyed orangey red once when she was in high school, so she could play Annie in her senior-year musical. She did that even before she got the role. I've seen her high school yearbooks—I think she was kind of the Stephanie Purley of her graduating class. The one who won everything. Only . . . nice. A future saint.

I look more like my dad. He was a linebacker back when, well, you know. Back when he could walk. Back when he was himself. Grandma says I'm just big-boned, and there's nothing wrong with that. The Stephanie Purleys of the world say there is something wrong with that—they say I'm fat. (The word pairs so well with my last name. And its synonyms.)

Maybe I could get away with being one of those fat girls who at least has a pretty face, except that I don't. I have dirt-colored hair that just kind of hangs there. My eyes are the color of sludge. My nose and my mouth and my ears are all too big.

One time when I was in middle school I burst into tears talking to Mrs. Carvis, one of my favorite old ladies at the nursing home. I told her it wasn't fair that I was so ugly. She said, "Honey, you're beautiful. Everyone young is beautiful. But I guess no one realizes that until they're old."

I pretended to cheer up, for Mrs. Carvis's sake. But all I could think was, *Great. That means I'll be even uglier in the future.*

Mrs. Carvis is dead now. When all your best friends are in a nursing home, you get used to losing people.

"That's the next highway you want, right?" Grandma asks, pointing to a sign by the side of the road. "Two seventy?"

Mom squints off into the distance. I think she probably needs new glasses, but she says she doesn't have time to go to the eye doctor.

I know it's really that we don't have the money.

"Yes, two seventy," she says. "Then the next exit we take will be the one to the airport."

She slows down and turns her blinker on, and the car behind her honks. Even I can tell she's not driving right for the big city. I look around and wonder if I missed seeing some sign that said, NO PICKUPS OR OLD CARS ALLOWED. All the cars I can see around us are new and shiny and expensive-looking, straight out of a TV commercial.

Behind me, Grandpa whistles.

"Kayla, look quick—is that a Maserati?" he asks. "Red car, two lanes over? Never thought I'd see one of those with my own two eyes."

"Whose eyes were you going to see it with?" Grandma asks. "Roy, it's just a car. Four tires, an engine, steering wheel . . . It's not that different from any other car. Settle down."

She gives him a playful punch on the arm, and they grin at each other, and that makes it so I don't have to answer. I'm grateful. This is just Columbus, just an hour and a half from home, and already I'm overwhelmed. Why did I ever think I could fly in an actual airplane, cross an entire ocean, step onto a completely different continent? People like me don't do that.

*Is there some way to get out of this?* I wonder. *If I really did throw up, if I fainted, if . . .*

The car gives a jerk and there's a sound like gunfire.

"Mom!" I cry.

I look over and she's gripping the steering wheel like her life depends on it—like suddenly the car has a mind of its own and it wants to smash into every car around us. The car bucks and veers into the next lane. My head slams into the window. Mom jerks the wheel back and my neck wrenches the other way.

And then somehow we're stopped by the side of the highway, the other cars whizzing past us at top speed.

For a moment we're all totally silent. Just being able to breathe feels like a miracle. Then Grandma says, "Was that . . ."

"Tire blew out," Grandpa says. "Right side on the front."

Only then do I realize the whole car's tilted in my direction.

Mom lets out a shaky breath.

"I knew that tire was bad," she whispers. "I just thought it could wait. . . . I could have killed us all."

"But you didn't," Grandma says firmly. "You saved us all, steering out of that. You and the good Lord watching over us."

A semi passes by, seemingly just inches from Mom's door. The whole car shakes.

"Kayla, remember how I keep promising to show you how to change a tire?" Grandpa says. "Guess you'll get that lesson now."

Mom glances at her watch.

"I'm going to miss my flight, aren't I?" I ask. And it's weird how I can't decide: Would I be delighted or devastated? Would I be relieved or distraught if this one little tire blowout meant that I never get to go to Spain at all?

Before I can figure myself out, Mom says, "Of course not. You know we left way early. I just have to let Mr. Armisted know it will be . . . oh, what do you think? One thirty before we get there?"

Mom reaches into her purse for her phone, but she doesn't flip it open to call right away. I see how she bites the inside of her lip and does her smile-frown-smile routine, the same way she does at the nursing home to steel herself for ordering some difficult resident to stay in his room all night or eat strained carrots or be ready for a sponge bath.

"Back in the day, I could change a tire in five minutes flat," Grandpa brags. "Won a contest once at the trucking company, you know."

"Roy, that was thirty years ago," Grandma says. "Nowadays it takes you five minutes just to stand up."

"Let's prove her wrong, Kayla," Grandpa says, winking at me.

We all pile out of the car through the passenger-side doors. Mom has to scramble over the emergency brake. I don't time anyone, but it feels like it takes fifteen or twenty minutes for Grandma and Grandpa to maneuver their way out. Grandpa wobbles a little once he's on his feet. He and Grandma both put on their church clothes to see me off, and her skirt and his thin cotton pants whip around in the stiff wind from the passing cars. Grandma's beauty-parlor-perfect curls quake, and the extra-long clump of white hair Grandpa usually combs over his bald spot flaps around like a tattered flag. It kind of looks like the breeze might knock both my grandparents flat to the ground.

I wonder how long it's been since Grandpa changed a tire.

"*I'll* change the tire, after I call Mr. Armisted," Mom says, as if it's all decided. "Kayla, you help Grandma and Grandpa down into the ditch, where no one will get hit."

I'm surprised Grandpa doesn't argue. But it's like stepping out of the car made him smaller and older. Defenseless. Carefully, I thread my arms through my grandparents' elbows and lead them downhill. Mom follows us down into the ditch, the phone to her ear. I can hear what she says: She turns the whole scary blowout and veering into other lanes of traffic—and right now having our hair whipped practically off our heads with every car that passes—into "just a minor problem."

She pauses. Then I hear, "No, no, you really don't have to do that. I'm sure we—" Another pause. "Oh, okay." Her voice has gone stiff and unnatural. "We certainly would not want to make you late."

Mom snaps her phone shut. Somehow there's a break in the traffic just now, and so that one sound seems unnaturally loud, as extreme as the tire blowing out.

"He insisted on sending a taxi to pick you up," she says. "And someone to change the tire for us. Even though I said we were perfectly capable."

"Well, that was nice," Grandma says soothingly. "See, honey, this is proof that Kayla's going to be with kind people all summer long. . . ."

She pats Mom's back. Mom looks around dazedly, as if she's just now noticed how deep this ditch is.

"But this is where we'll have to say good-bye to Kayla," she says. "The last place we'll see her for the next eight weeks."

*Mom's like me*, I think. *She's kind of wishing we could cancel everything, and I could go back home. I could stay in Crawfordsville with Mom and Grandma and Grandpa for the rest of my life.*

For a moment it feels like I have all the power. The words are on the tip of my tongue. I could say, *You know what? Forget this. I don't want to go to Europe. I don't want to go anywhere. I don't need anything I don't already have in Crawfordsville.*

But that would be a lie.

The moment passes. In no time at all, a yellow car with the word TAXI on the side is pulling up behind our tilted, broken-down Chevy. And then Mom and Grandma and Grandpa are hugging me, and we're all crying . . .

And then we're all letting go.

And I'm leaving.

## Avery at the Airport

**"I told you this is** a bad idea," I say.

Dad ignores me. I have to stop myself from tugging on his arm like a little kid, to get him to really *look* at me. It seems like if he just looked into my eyes, he would understand that I don't just mean it's a bad idea to take Kayla Butts with us to Spain. It's a bad idea for me to go to Spain. It's probably even a bad idea for him to go to Spain.

Today, especially after that weird moment with Mom saying good-bye, everything feels like a bad idea.

Why doesn't Dad understand that already?

Dad stabs his finger at his phone screen, lifts the phone to cradle it against his shoulder.

"Yes, I can hold," he says into it.

We're sitting on a bench right inside the doors for departures at the airport. The doors keep whooshing open and shut, and it's annoying. People stare at us. It's weird that the bench is even here; nobody else needs to sit down. You're supposed to come in and go to the counter and check your luggage and then go to your gate right away. That's what normal people do.

I've already had enough abnormal for the day. I can't handle any more.

"We could go on through security," I suggest. "Kayla can just meet us when she gets here."

*If she gets here*, I think. Maybe she'll totally miss the flight.

That would be okay. And since Dad would have to reschedule her plane ticket, anyhow, maybe I could talk him into making it for one of my actual friends, instead.

Or maybe not.

Dad's shooting me one of those looks that makes me feel about three inches tall. It's like he's thinking, *What's wrong with you? Didn't we raise you better than this?*

Can't he understand how much Mom's crying threw me off?

"That would be cruel," he says. "Kayla's never flown before. She wouldn't know what to do."

"Right, because it makes so much sense that you're taking me to a foreign country with someone who's never even flown before, who doesn't know what she's doing. You're even *paying* her to go with us, and she—"

Dad's not listening. He's saying into the phone, "I need you to send someone to change a flat tire. Look for a blue Chevrolet Aveo off on the shoulder. It's on eastbound two seventy between thirty-three and the Sawmill Road exit. . . ."

Now he's giving his credit card number.

"How do you know that tow truck will even show up?" I ask, as soon as he's off the phone. "It's not like you're going to miss your flight to check on them. I bet they'll just charge your credit card and not do anything."

"You sound like your mother," Dad snaps. "Stop it."

"You sound like yourself," I snap back at him. "That's worse."

And *then* Dad looks at me. I try to make my face into a hard mask, one that says, *You know I'm right.* And, *You can't hurt me.* And, *I don't care what you say.* I can do that at school, on the soccer field, anywhere I'm with my friends. There was that one nasty boy I stared down at Morgan Perez's end-of-eighth-grade party when Shannon wanted him to leave her alone. I got him to go away just with a *look*. My friends thought I was practically a superhero after that.

But it's like I can't get Dad to see my mask. He's staring into my eyes, and his eyes are so sad, so . . . old. For a minute it's not like he's David Armisted, successful business executive, so important his company wants him to fly to a totally different country to save the world for capitalism. He's someone who can be hurt and disappointed and confused and scared.

He's someone who can fail.

I want to say something to cheer him up. Like I do on the soccer field with a friend who's lost her confidence: *You can do it! Go for it!*

But Dad's talking. He's saying, "When did we forget to teach you to be kind? To care about anybody but yourself?"

## Kayla: Traveling with Strangers

**I am a girl who's** riding in a taxicab to the airport. Me. Kayla Butts.

My mood flips, and I want to giggle. I want to call Mrs. Lang back at the nursing home, the person I know who watches the most soap operas. *People really do ride in cabs, in the world outside Crawfordsville*, I would tell her. *Some of the stuff that happens in soap operas really does happen out in the real world. For real.* I want to call Harley Seitz, who's the closest thing I've ever had to a best friend who's actually my same age. We're still friends, I guess, but it's like 99.999 percent of her brain and her time has been taken up with her boyfriend, Gunnar Graves, ever since they got together last fall.

*Guess what?* I would tell her. *There are other fun things in the world besides kissing Gunnar. Maybe I'm going to have a better summer than you. Maybe* I'm *going to fall in love with a hot cabdriver and . . .*

This thought almost makes it so I can't even look at the man driving my cab. I peek out through lowered eyelashes—because what does it matter? A hot guy wouldn't like me, anyway—and it turns out that my cabdriver is old. He's got white hair.

I know how to talk to old people. I lean forward.

"Do you like driving a cab?" I ask him. "Have you been doing this for a long time?"

He looks at me in the rearview mirror, and I realize he also has dark skin and the darkest eyes I've ever seen. I'd been too emotional and then too giddy to notice that before.

He is not anything like the old people I know back in Crawfordsville.

But he's answering my questions. I think. He opens his mouth and sounds come out, but it's not a language I recognize. Or maybe it is—maybe it's even English—but his accent is so thick I can't make out a single word.

"What?" I say. "Can you talk slower? Please? My ears are a little clogged, so I can't hear very well."

I flush, because I've automatically given one of the excuses I always use with Mr. Wicks back at the nursing home. He had a stroke last year that garbled his speech, and it really bothers him when people can't understand. So I always make it seem like it's my fault, not his.

The cabdriver must not understand: Now he seems to be talking faster. Straining hard, I catch the words "Somalia" and maybe "professor."

Is there a place called Somalia? Maybe in Africa? And was this cabdriver maybe a professor when he lived there? No way could he be a professor here. Who would understand him?

The cabdriver gestures at the passenger-side front seat, where books slide around. The only book cover I can see holds a bunch of curlicues and dots—is it written in some language so foreign they don't even use the same alphabet?

The driver pats the books, and his hand lingers in a way that makes me think of Grandpa pulling out old maps and photographs in the spring and fall, when he misses planting and harvest. Some of Grandpa's pictures are so faded now that I can barely make out ghosts of images, but he claims he can still identify the model numbers of every John Deere tractor and combine; he can remember the reason for every little bend in the otherwise straight rows of corn.

Suddenly, I miss Grandpa so much. The cabdriver and I don't understand what the other person is saying, anyway, so I let Grandpa's story spill out of me. It's like talking to Mr. Angstrom or Mrs. Lyles, two of the nursing home residents who aren't ever conscious, so it's safe to tell them anything I want. It's weird how comforting it can be to sit in their darkened rooms and hold their hands and whisper things I don't dare tell anyone else.

I do this with my dad sometimes too.

"My grandfather used to be a farmer," I tell the cabdriver now. "His farm was in our family for five generations, but the way the economy went, that wasn't enough. So he borrowed money to buy more land. And then in the 1980s, the interest rates got really bad, and lots of farmers went bankrupt and lost everything, and Grandpa was one of them. He had to take a job as a truck driver. But he would never clean his floor mats, because he said maybe some corn or soybean seeds might accidentally fall there and sprout, and then he could say at least he owned that much of a farm. He carried around dirt in his truck the way you carry around books. It's kind of the same thing."

The cabdriver answers, talking faster than ever, his words even more incomprehensible. No, wait, there is one word I can understand: "war." The cabdriver says it again and again: *War . . . war . . . war . . .*

Was there a war in his home country? Is that why he ended up here?

My face reddens even more. Somalia . . . Maybe I have heard of that country before. Maybe I have heard of a war there. Sometimes when we go visit my father at the VA nursing home, the other patients tell us their stories. Some of them are older than the Iraq and Afghanistan veterans, but not as old as the Vietnam vets. Maybe some of those men talk about fighting in Somalia.

You have to be respectful to people who survived a war. Maybe this cabdriver fought in a war and I'm babbling away to him about dirt.

The cabdriver takes his hand off his books and gestures at something rubber-banded onto the sunflap over his head. Maybe he's saying, *This is my family*. He pulls down a picture of lots of people with dark skin. Grandparents and parents and children. The women and the girls wear coverings over their heads, letting just their faces show, not their hair. I guess that means they're Muslim. I don't know anyone like this family back in Crawfordsville. But this is like all the old people at the nursing home whipping out pictures of their families.

"They look like nice people," I say politely, just like I say to all the people in the nursing home. I tell old people this even when I know for a fact that their kids and grandkids never bother visiting. Even when I know for a fact that their grandkids or great-grandkids are some of the worst bullies at Crawfordsville High School.

I don't know the cabdriver's family. Maybe they really are nice people. Maybe people outside Crawfordsville are nicer than people in it.

Can I dare to hope that that's true?

Now the driver points out the window—we're almost to the airport. My stomach twists a little and I rehearse the instructions Mom relayed from Mr. Armisted: *The cab ride was already paid for, so you don't worry about that. The cabdriver will get your suitcase from the trunk, and then you can go on into the airport. Mr. Armisted and Avery will watch for you—remember, I sent that picture so they'd be sure to recognize you—but if you don't see them right away you can always call . . .*

The cabdriver pulls up to the curb. He gets out and goes around to the trunk, so I do too. He puts my suitcase down on the sidewalk, then leans toward me.

"Good-bye, granddaughter of a farmer," he says, and it seems like he's trying hard to pronounce the words the same way I would. "Have a good trip."

He understood what I was saying. He understood me better than I understood him. Maybe he even understood every single word I spoke.

I feel a little like I'm standing here naked, my ugly, blobby body on display for anyone to see.

*But he's saying nice things*, I remind myself.

I stammer out a "Thank you." I want to apologize, too, for not understanding him. But someone's calling my name behind me: "Kayla? Kayla?"

I turn around, and Mr. Armisted and Avery are walking toward me.

Mom said they wanted to arrange a meet-up for Avery and me before we were actually leaving for Spain. But Avery had soccer tournaments every weekend, and then she had soccer camp, and Mom got stuck working a lot of nights and . . . it never happened. Avery was also really busy last December, and the only time Mom could take her her Christmas present was one Saturday morning when I had driver's ed. So I haven't seen Avery since two Christmases ago. She had braces back then, and she'd gotten tall in a way that reminded me of a baby giraffe just learning how to use its long legs. (Mr. Lang at the nursing home likes to watch nature shows, so I've seen a lot of baby giraffes taking their first steps.)

Avery doesn't have braces anymore. She has such straight, white, perfect teeth that it reminds me how much my dog tooth sticks out on the left side. I pull my lip down to hide it.

Avery also isn't baby-giraffe gawky and awkward anymore. She's dancer graceful, or maybe teen-model graceful. She moves like she knows people are watching her, like she thinks they *should* watch her. (I mostly move like I'm darting from shadow to shadow, hoping nobody notices me.) Avery's got stretchy black leggings on—yoga pants?—and they cling to her legs just right, and her long blue shirt blouses out just right, kind of like a minidress, but classy, not slutty, because of the leggings underneath.

I pull my shirt down to cover the label on my jeans. I hope if Avery saw it, she doesn't know that Faded Glory is a Walmart brand.

Avery doesn't seem to be wearing any makeup, and that makes me feel like the eyeshadow and mascara I put on is too dark and heavy. She flips her long, thick ponytail over her shoulder, and it's like the practiced moves girls have on YouTube.

Mr. Armisted grabs my hand and shakes it.

"Kayla!" he says heartily. "You made it! With plenty of time to spare."

"I . . . guess so," I mumble.

It always throws me off to talk to other people's fathers, but this is worse than ever. I mainly recognize Mr. Armisted from the annual Armisted family Christmas card, where they all looked so glossy and glowing and happy. I used to study those photos so carefully; I knew I would seem awkward and weird if I stared like I wanted to when we would go visit Avery and he was there.

"The cabdriver didn't have any trouble finding your mom's car?" Mr. Armisted persists.

"No. I mean, I don't think so."

I have to hold myself back from asking, *Do you know how much you look like a dad on a TV sitcom? Only real?*

Seeing Mr. Armisted in person again reminds me of a game I used to play when I was little. I'd look through the sale circulars that came in the mail, and Grandma and Grandpa would tease, "Oh, Kayla, are you in the market for a new chain saw?" or "Kayla, you looking for a new pickup truck?" when really I was just looking at the ads that featured male models so I could pick out the one that looked like the best dad.

Even at three or four years old, I already knew that my own father would never again be able to do anything but lie in a bed. He would never again be able to pick up a chain saw. He would never again be able to steer a truck or build a pole barn or cast a fishing line.

He would never again be able to hug me.

Or just shake my hand.

*Even if your dad hadn't had that accident, he would never have been like Mr. Armisted,* I tell myself. *He wouldn't have worn shirts with polo pony logos on the pocket. He wouldn't have flown around the world making millions. He wouldn't have wanted to. He was proud of being a marine. Proud to serve his country.*

I look away from Mr. Armisted, but my brain is still churning out *wouldn't haves*: *Even if your dad hadn't had that accident, he never would have hired some other teenager to be a "paid companion" for his daughter. He wouldn't have needed to. He would have taught you to take care of yourself.*

"Were you talking to the cabdriver just now?" Avery asks. She doesn't put out her hand to shake, but she kind of smiles. It looks like she's trying to, anyway.

"Yes," I say. Did I break some rule I didn't even know about?

"Do you know him?"

*Better than I know you*, I want to say.

There is no way I'm telling *her* about Grandpa. Or anyone or anything else that's important to me.

"Just being friendly," I say, attempting a failed smile of my own.

"Oh," Avery says.

And then it's like none of us knows what to say to the other two. We stand awkwardly for a moment, until Mr. Armisted grabs my suitcase and says, "Well, let's go, then. Off to Spain!"

I notice that he leaves Avery to carry her own suitcase. Or pull it, I mean—unlike mine, hers is on wheels. But is that fair when she's the daughter and I'm just the paid companion? Should I offer to carry hers?

I don't think I can say anything. It might make me cry.

Forget worrying about speaking Spanish. Forget worrying about being in a foreign country. How am I supposed to live with total strangers for the next eight weeks?

Why do the Armisteds want me to?

## Avery: Complications

**"Avery, put your phone away,"** Dad says.

We've checked our luggage and gone through security, and now we're sitting at the gate. Our flight is delayed fifteen minutes—because of thunderstorms in Chicago, or something like that. Dad's been explaining to Kayla that the whole airline system is interconnected, and the plane we're supposed to fly on might be coming from Dallas, and still be delayed by Chicago weather.

I don't care. I'm texting back and forth with Shannon and Lauren, who are on their after-lunch break at soccer camp. They claim the drills they ran this morning were harder than any I did there. I think they're just being wimps, but I don't say that. I'm telling them about Kayla, and how embarrassing she's been ever since she got here. I want them to know exactly how much I wish one of them were with me instead.

**Then K stared at Auntie Anne's like she's never seen one before,** I write.

**Never eaten a cinnamon pretzel? Too sad,** Lauren writes back.

**Maybe she hasn't,** Shannon writes. **Didn't you say she lives in Nowheresville? Maybe she's never even been to a mall.**

**Maybe that's y your dad is taking her to Europe. B/c K's disadvantaged,** Lauren writes.

She must be texting five or six other people at the same

time she's texting me. You can always tell with Lauren. She starts using abbreviations when she's losing interest in a conversation.

"Avery!" Dad says in a low voice, his teeth gritted like he's trying to yell at me without anyone else noticing. "Didn't you hear me? I said, put the phone away. Stop texting. Participate in the conversation we're having in real life."

I could say, *Texting is real life.* I could say, *Oh, yeah? I'd be happy to if you'd have let me bring a* real *friend with me.* I could say, *I'm not having a conversation with Kayla. You are.* But I take one look at Dad's face and say, "I'm just telling them good-bye. It's rude not to do that."

Quickly, I type, Gtg. Boarding. Next time I text I'll be in Spain!

It's not a bad thing to make them feel a little jealous. Remind them that even if I have to put up with Kayla, I get to do it in a cool place.

Dad still has that look on his face like he's about to explode. I'm saved from whatever he was going to say next because his phone pings. He looks at it and groans.

"Now it's a forty-five-minute delay," he says. "We're really going to have to run to catch our next flight."

"Run?" Kayla repeats, like that's something else she's never heard of.

"During the layover," I say. I want Dad to see that I'm trying with Kayla. Or to think that I am. "We're flying from here to Washington, DC, where we'll change planes, and then the new plane will take us on to Madrid. That plane will be at a different gate, maybe even in a different terminal. How fast we run could be the difference between making the flight and missing it. Dad, remember that time we had to run to make that flight home from Aruba? Because customs took so long?"

Kayla bites her lip.

"I know we have a layover," she says in a tight voice, like I've offended her. "I read the schedule your dad sent."

Maybe I really did sound like, *How stupid are you, not to know this?* instead of *Here. I'll be kind and explain everything.*

"And I said we'd eat at the DC airport, didn't I?" Dad chimes in. "Looks like there won't be time for that now. We should get sandwiches here. Avery, come help me carry things. Kayla, you can stay here and hold our seats. What do you want us to get you?"

Dad's in boss mode. This is how he sounds on the phone, talking to people at work. But I have a bad feeling about the way he divided us up.

Sure enough, as soon as we're in the Wolfgang Puck to-go line, he says in his hardest, coldest voice, "You will *stop* making fun of Kayla to your friends. And you will erase that entire conversation from your phone. The one about Kayla being from Nowheresville."

I gulp.

"Dad, that was *private*!" I protest. "Nobody else was supposed to see it! Why were you reading over my shoulder?"

"Because you were so clearly tilting *away* from Kayla, trying not to let her see," he tells me.

"Well, *I* never said Kayla was from Nowheresville," I defend myself. "That was Shannon. I can't help what my friends say."

Dad's lips are pressed into a thin, disapproving line.

No, I'm reading his face wrong. It's more like . . . he's in pain.

"Avery, thirty years ago, I was the one from Nowheresville," he says. "You know I wasn't on an airplane until I flew to that first job interview in New York."

"Yeah, yeah, I know that story," I say. "You panicked because you thought you'd have to pay for the Coke they gave you on the plane, and you barely had enough cash with you for the cab to the interview, and this was before you had a credit card, and you were imagining yourself as a homeless person in New York City the rest of your life."

Sometimes, when Dad tells that story he turns it into some big comedy, making his every mistake and misperception sound ridiculous. Usually, when Mom's around, she'll add something like, *No, David, you would have found a nickel on the sidewalk and invested it, and you would have been a millionaire inside of three months.* Or *No, you would have put all the other homeless people to work for you and built the biggest company in town.*

I decide since Mom's not here, I need to finish the story.

"But, Dad, you knew you were going to be a success regardless," I say. "Even if you didn't have enough money for the cab, you would have thought of something. You always do."

I give him my best adoring-daughter grin. But it's like he can't see that either. He seems to be looking straight through me. Back toward Kayla.

"Still," he says. "I was nobody from nowhere. I could have stayed a nobody. It's not, it's not—"

"Dad, you're not even making sense," I say. I try to laugh, but it comes out wrong.

"I didn't get to fly to Aruba when I was five," he says. "Most people don't. It doesn't make you any better than Kayla, that you've grown up flying all over the place and she hasn't. It just means you got lucky."

"Because of you," I say, grinning again. Trying to make it up to him. But he's not listening.

The line moves, so now we're by the sandwiches and drinks. I grab a turkey pesto and a bottle of water. Dad gets his and Kayla's orders, and we put everything on the counter. Dad hands the woman at the cash register his credit card. She swipes it and shakes her head.

"That card does not work," she says. I'm trying to decide from her accent if she's Pakistani, like my friend Rima, or Indian like my friend Sruti. Then it registers what she said.

"Try swiping it again," I suggest.

But Dad's already pulling a different credit card from his billfold.

"Never mind," he says. "Try this one instead."

*Why doesn't he even sound surprised?*

## Kayla, Not Keeping Up

**"Run!" Mr. Armisted cries behind** me as we're getting off the plane in Washington, DC. "As fast as you can!"

My foot falters against the little gap between the plane's doorway and the ramp pressed alongside it. There's nothing to trip over, but I stumble anyway, bashing one shoulder against Avery's backpack ahead of me.

Mr. Armisted grabs my arm, steadying me. I look back to thank him, but apparently he's serious about the running thing. He's got his head down and his shoulders bent forward, like he'd already be sprinting full-out if I weren't in his way.

I face forward again, and Avery has somehow sped halfway up the exit ramp. I take three large steps, and then stop behind people crowded around a little door.

"No—keep going!" Mr. Armisted calls behind me. "They're waiting on gate-checked bags! We didn't gate-check anything! Our bags are going straight to Madrid! Without us, if we don't make this plane!"

I'm not sure what he's talking about—*"Gate-check"? What's that even mean?*—but I don't want him to think I'm stupid.

"I *know* we've got to hurry," I answer. "I'm just trying not to . . ."

Before I can finish, *run anybody over*, Mr. Armisted is shoving his way through the crowd, tugging me along. He says, "Excuse me, excuse me," again and again, but people step aside for him even before they hear him, in a way they didn't for me. He looks rich and powerful—and handsome. Of course they step aside.

*Did they step aside for Avery, or did she just shove them out of her way?* I wonder.

It's strange how much I want to know the answer to that.

It's also strange how, the whole time we were on the plane from Columbus, I wanted to tell Avery or Mr. Armisted, *This isn't the first time I've been on a plane, you know.*

I'd even half stammered, "Th-this—" just as we were taking off, but Avery had patted my arm and said, "It's really cool, isn't it? Things look so small down on the ground when you fly. Just wait till we get up in the clouds." And then she'd glanced over at her dad, in his single seat across the aisle, as if she were really saying that for him, not me. Like she didn't really want to be nice to me; she just wanted him to *think* she was.

But I made myself agree with her, anyway, and pretended to admire the view out my window. There was no room for me to say, *I flew once before, when I was two. We were in California when my dad got hurt, and my mom needed to be with him at the hospital. One of her friends, Sonia Lopez, flew me home to Grandma and Grandpa, so they could take care of me while Mom couldn't. All their friends on the base chipped in so there'd be enough money for the flight.*

It felt like I could remember seeing clouds on that airplane ride; it felt like I could remember Grandma and Grandpa meeting us at the airport, and hugging me and hugging me. But I was only two. Maybe I just think I remember because Grandma and Grandpa and Mom have told me the story so much. Grandpa's version always includes a line about how he'd looked right past Sonia and me when we first stepped through security, because "nobody told me it'd be some *Mexican* girl bringing us our granddaughter." And then, if Mom is around, she scolds him, "I told you her name was Sonia *Lopez*. Wasn't that enough of a clue? Anyhow, Sonia was Mexican *American*, not Mexican." And then afterward, out of my grandparents' earshot, Mom usually reminds me that Grandma and Grandpa don't really mean to sound prejudiced; they just grew up in a different time period, and . . .

And Mr. Armisted and I are falling way behind Avery as we run up the ramp toward the main part of the airport. I've lost sight of her blue shirt and her swinging dark blond ponytail. No, wait—there she is, stepping off the ramp into the terminal.

"Avery! Wait up!" Mr. Armisted calls.

"You said to run as fast as we can!" Avery calls back over her shoulder. "That's what I'm doing!"

She's not even panting. My mind flashes back to one of those nature shows Mr. Lang at the nursing home likes so much. Avery is like a gazelle or maybe a cheetah: incredibly, effortlessly fast. A woman in front of her totters on high heels, and I half expect Avery to spring at the woman and bring her down, like a cheetah attacking an antelope.

Maybe I've spent too much of my life watching nature shows with Mr. Lang.

"Kayla and I aren't soccer players," Mr. Armisted calls to Avery. "Just stay with us. You can't get on that plane . . . without us."

I kind of like it that he has to stop and gulp for air. It's not just me slowing the Armisteds down.

"Told you you should exercise more!" Avery calls playfully over her shoulder. She turns around and runs backward, and I swear she's still faster than I could ever be. "I mean that for you, Dad. An old man like you, you really need your exercise. Use it or lose it!"

Is she trying to make it so that taunt *isn't* aimed at me?

Somehow that makes me mad, anyway.

*Yeah, I know I should exercise more too*, I want to spit back at her. *Skinny people always think fat people should exercise more. But ever heard of genetics? Ever seen my dad? I take after the big-boned side of the family. That's all.*

Being mad helps me run faster for a few moments, but then I slow down again. I'm *really* not a runner. In phys ed, when Mr. Dunham makes us run laps, I'm always in the group that clumps at the back and ends up doing half as much as everyone else, because most of the class can circle the gym twice in the time it takes me to circle it once. Even when I cheat and run as far inside the corners as I dare.

I think Mr. Dunham knows, but he's a heavyset guy himself. He never says anything.

"We want Gate D4," Mr. Armisted pants beside me, as Avery dances ahead. "We'll have to take the shuttle up ahead—"

"It's there right now!" Avery calls back to us. "The sign says it's leaving in one minute! No—fifty-nine seconds. Fifty-eight seconds. Fifty-seven . . . Oh wait, I'll do it in Spanish. Uh, *cincuenta y cuatro, cincuenta y tres . . .*"

What if she's this annoying the whole time we're in Spain?

Avery reaches the doorway out to the shuttle, and turns around to urge us on: "Come on, come on—hurry!"

I put on a burst of speed (which is a lot like saying a turtle puts on a burst of speed). Mr. Armisted grabs my arm and pulls me along. Avery reaches out and yanks him forward too. For a second it feels like we're a team, linked together. All three of us stumble through the doorway, and a split second later, the door swishes shut behind me, shoving a gasp of hot air at me.

"You almost missed it!" Avery scolds. She's looking at her dad, not me, but I know who she's really accusing. Just like that, any link we had is broken.

She's not even sweating.

Mr. Armisted bends forward, his hands on his knees. *He's* sweating, the droplets beading along his hairline. He gulps in air like someone who's just run a marathon.

"Yeah, well"—he pauses to gulp in another breath—"I could run fast too, when I was fourteen. Just wait until you're fifty-four."

He doesn't look at me either, but he might as well have said, *I could run fast when I was* sixteen, *too.* Any *teenager should be a good runner. I have an excuse, being so old.*

I want to yell, *I'm sorry! I didn't mean to hold you back! Go ahead and say it: I'm fat and out of shape! Isn't that what you're thinking?*

But speaking those words would be too much like that time in third grade when our teacher, Miss Nolan, who was straight out of college, had us write about "what our mommies and daddies do." I wrote, *My daddy lies in a bed. He can't talk. Sometimes he grunts. My mommy says that's how he says, "I love you." But his brain doesn't work right anymore. If he doesn't know how to say easy words like "I" and "love" and "you," how does he even know what love is? How does he even know who I am? I don't think he knows anything.*

And then there were conferences between Mom and Miss Nolan and the school psychologist, and then between me and a school psychologist. And Grandma and Grandpa kept asking me, "Why didn't you just write about your daddy being a marine? How he went through training to hunt down terrorists and keep Americans safe? How he joined up because he was such a patriot? You should be proud of your daddy!"

And I said, "Miss Nolan didn't say to write about what our mommies and daddies *did*. We were supposed to write about what they *do*." I was a little too proud of knowing the difference between past and present tense.

I was a dumb third grader. I didn't know yet that sometimes the last thing people want to hear is the truth.

"Is this shuttle ever going to leave?" Avery asks, peering toward the front, where there's a man in a little cab—the driver, I guess. "We've only got ten minutes. What if we waste it all standing around on this shuttle?"

It's almost as if the driver hears her, because just then, the shuttle eases away from the terminal behind us.

"Catch your breath, and then let's get as close as we can to the door on the other side," Mr. Armisted says. He's not panting so hard anymore. "This is going to be really close."

Avery starts shoving her way through the crowd immediately. Mr. Armisted follows her, and I trail behind.

I can see out the shuttle windows, to airplanes lined up along the runways, and to other shuttles coming toward us. The shuttles have long rows of wheels beneath them; they look like ungainly, oversize bugs compared with the sleek, graceful planes. Or maybe they look like military transports—like the amphibious vehicles I've seen in the World War II movies Mr. Lang switches to when he gets tired of nature shows. The shuttles look like they could have landed on Omaha Beach on D-day.

Maybe if my father hadn't been injured, he would have stayed in the marines for good. Maybe I would have grown up *playing* on vehicles like this, able to recite details about them the way Grandpa can with tractors built between the 1930s and the 1980s. Maybe my father would have been stationed all over the world, and I would be as used to traveling the globe as Avery is.

I bet I'd be good at running through airports then.

The shuttle docks at the opposite terminal with a *thud*. The door opens, and Avery jumps out, first in line.

"Okay, you run ahead of Kayla and me," Mr. Armisted tells her, as he glances at his watch. "Tell the gate agent we're right behind you. Got it? *Right behind you*."

"Got it," Avery says, and dashes off.

I need to go to the bathroom. I'm kind of hungry, too. My muscles ache from running through the last terminal, and my sweaty jeans chafe against my legs. They *hurt*. But I force myself to run alongside Mr. Armisted, dodging strollers and rolling suitcases and people who seem to be talking to themselves—no, they're talking into phones linked to headsets. It all goes by in a blur.

"I don't like running either," Mr. Armisted gasps. "But—"

"I know! I know!" I snap. "I'm trying to go fast!"

I don't feel hungry anymore. I feel more like throwing up. Can running do that—make someone throw up?

That would be really embarrassing.

I try to leap over someone's leg, stuck out from the seat he's sprawled in, but I misjudge the distance and kick the guy instead. He's kind of cute, college-aged maybe, with a beard.

"I'm sorry! I'm sorry!" I gasp, and keep struggling to run.

I don't belong here. I'm not suited for this. Maybe I would have been, if my dad hadn't been injured and I'd grown up differently, but that didn't happen. I'm suited for nothing more extravagant than going to McDonald's with Grandma and Grandpa. I'm suited for sitting around watching nature shows with Mr. Lang and soap operas with Mrs. Lang. I'm suited for putting up with the cabbage smell of the nursing home.

I'm suited for Crawfordsville. Poor, run-down, beat-up Crawfordsville. And I want to go back.

I keep running anyway, through this glitzy airport, where—I just saw this on a sign—even a bottle of plain water costs four dollars.

"Almost there," Mr. Armisted pants beside me. "Three more gates . . . Can you see? Is the door at gate D4 open or shut?"

"Shut?" I say. I keep running, because I'm not sure I'm looking at the right door.

"But so many people are still standing around," Mr. Armisted murmurs. He keeps running too, even as he wipes sweat from his forehead.

Avery appears before us.

"You can stop running," she says flatly, as if she's mad.

"Because it's too late?" Mr. Armisted asks. "Or because . . . they're holding the plane for us?"

"No," Avery says disgustedly. "Because they just canceled our flight."

## Avery, Annoyed

**"These things happen," Dad says,** sneaking a glance at Kayla. It's like he's more worried that she's going to be upset over the canceled flight, than that I am.

Kayla looks like the Sweat Queen of the Universe. Her face is red, and she gulps in air like there's not enough of it around. She tugs at her jeans, as if that's going to make them cooler. Didn't anybody tell her it's crazy to wear such tight jeans for a long flight?

*Oh, guess not*, I think, almost guiltily. Because Dad wouldn't have known. About the most dressed-down he ever gets is khakis. Anyway, male clothes are always looser. Guys don't ever have to deal with feeling like their legs are surrounded by concrete. Or sausage casings.

"They'll put us on another flight, right?" I ask Dad.

He's already on his phone, calling his company's travel agent. He tilts the phone to the side, and says, "They're checking. It'll probably be tomorrow."

"Tomorrow!" I explode.

Dad's eyes dart from me to Kayla.

"Why don't you two sit down while I work this out?" Dad asks.

She does kind of look like she might fall over. But it's not going to make us friends, to have us sit together.

"Kayla can sit," I say. "I'm going to go buy another water bottle. Either of you want one?"

"Um, no, thanks," Kayla says, in a small voice. Or a voice that's trying to be small. It's like she's an ant cowering because she doesn't want to be stepped on. "Isn't there a drinking fountain somewhere?"

"Get water bottles for all three of us," Dad commands me. Then he moves the phone back toward his mouth and says into it, "Well, if that's the only choice . . ."

Maybe it's the bad airport lighting, but the lines in his forehead seem deeper than usual. A few gray hairs curl over his ears and at his temples. I don't remember how long ago Dad started dyeing his hair to cover the gray—maybe it's been my whole life. Mom and Dad both were kind of old when I was born. But they still try to look young. Mom says professional people have to do that. So usually, Dad—or maybe Mom—is religious about scheduling his hair appointments, so no gray ever shows.

*These things happen. . . . That's the only choice. . . .*

Has my real dad been taken away and replaced by some pod-person wimpy pathetic guy?

Normally, my dad can conjure up solutions out of nowhere. That time we had to run through the airport on the Aruba trip? He also managed to sweet-talk the gate agent into letting us on after the door was closed. So, yeah. That's how he operates. Mr. Charm and his golden smile can accomplish anything. I was kind of expecting him to say, *Okay, now we have a private jet taking us to Madrid. Don't worry about water bottles; forget those awful sandwiches we bought back in Columbus. We'll have Perrier and gourmet meals on this plane.*

I walk over to a little Au Bon Pain food stand for the water.

*These things happen. . . .*

Dad used those exact same words back at the Columbus airport when I asked why his credit card wouldn't work. But then he tried way too hard to make me understand how credit card companies sometimes overreact with security measures—which, duh, I already knew, because Lauren's mom works for Chase, and Lauren always acts like she herself is the expert on identity theft.

And then he walked over to the opposite side of the hallway to call the credit card company and complain. And I could see how his shoulders slumped before he even put the phone to his ear.

Something is going on. Something I really don't understand.

## Kayla, Excited

**I don't just get to** see Spain. I get to see Washington, DC!

If I were, say, Stephanie Purley, I'd jump up and down and do splits in the air and squeal, *Yes! Yes! Yes!* And then maybe I'd make that spinning motion cheerleaders do with their arms, and cry, *Bonus! Bonus!*

But—me, cheerleading? That would be as ridiculous as a *pig* cheerleading. As ridiculous as, uh, me running.

And Avery acts like she wants to ruin Washington, DC, for me.

When her dad gets off the phone and says we can't go to Madrid until tomorrow night, he announces, "So we have almost twenty-four hours. I'll have to do some work, but that shouldn't hold you two back. I can arrange some sort of tour for you. What would you like to see?"

Avery kind of whines, "Dad! We're not going to do some stupid *organized* sightseeing tour. And remember? I was just here for the eighth-grade DC trip. I just saw everything!" She turned toward me. "You probably did too, on your eighth-grade trip, right, Kayla?"

"Uh . . . what eighth-grade trip?" I repeat, like an idiot.

"Not all schools have them, Avery," Mr. Armisted says gently.

"Oh," Avery says.

My face, which was just starting to cool down, gets hot again.

"And, anyhow, it's not possible to see everything in Washington,

DC," Mr. Armisted says. "This is probably where I should quote some famous line about how cities are ever-changing, and you never see the same thing twice, but . . . I was a business major, so I don't happen to have anything like that memorized."

"That's okay," Avery says. "*Mom* would know the quotes like that, so that would make it like she was here too. And you know she hates flight delays. So let's not think about it."

I'm not really listening. I'm biting my tongue to keep from saying something really stupid, like, *Wait, are you talking about, like, a* field trip *to Washington, DC? Your eighth-grade class took a field trip to an entirely other city? Hours and hours away? I thought that kind of thing only happened in movies and on TV!*

Then I almost said something even stupider: *Well, we had* some *field trips. Back in, oh, I don't know—first grade, maybe?—we got to walk over to the Crawfordsville Fire Station.*

The Crawfordsville Fire Station only has one fire truck. And all the firefighters are volunteers who also work other jobs, so no one was there that day. Our elementary school principal was married to the fire chief, so she was the one who told us everything. And she just kept saying how safe we all were, having a fire station nearby.

I'd sound like a fool saying any of that. Maybe on this trip, I should just keep my mouth shut the whole time.

When I tune back in, Avery and her dad sound like they're really arguing. About . . . the Holocaust Museum?

"That is the one thing we didn't get to see," Avery says. "You know how the teachers said it was just because of a mix-up with the tickets, but everybody knows—"

"Avery, it's not an everybody-knows situation," Mr. Armisted says. "If the teachers told you there was a mix-up, that's what happened. The school wouldn't have let a handful of over-protective parents prevent everyone from going."

"Except that they *did*," Avery says. "You know Tristan and Alexandria's mom runs the PTO, and Serena's parents donate a lot of money to the school. And they probably said it wasn't fair to treat their kids differently, to single them out. So going to the Holocaust Museum was canceled for everybody." She flips her ponytail over her shoulder. "Kayla, see, what happened was, some parents of kids in my class thought their precious little babies were too *sensitive* to have to deal with going to the Holocaust Museum, and so—"

"Avery, regardless of what happened back in April, I just don't think . . ."

Avery smiles sweetly at her father, then at me.

"Kayla, you don't have a problem with going to the Holocaust Museum, do you?" she asks.

*What? I'm supposed to have an opinion? I'm supposed to solve their argument?*

"Um . . ." I swallow hard. "I've never been in Washington, DC, before. So anything's fine."

"See?" Avery says triumphantly. She puts her hands on her hips, challenging her dad. "Kayla doesn't mind."

I don't know much about dads—I mean, dads who walk and talk and are capable of telling their kids, *Yes, you can do that* or, *No, you're not allowed.* But I think I see a glint of anger or irritation or maybe just sorrow in Mr. Armisted's dark eyes—which, now that I think about it, are the exact same color as

Avery's, with the exact same flecks of gray circling the iris.

"Fine," Mr. Armisted says, turning his palms up in resignation. "We'll tour the monuments tonight, all of us together. Then the two of you can see the Holocaust Museum tomorrow morning while I work at whatever Starbucks is the closest. And then, if there's time—and we'll make sure there is—*Kayla* can pick whichever of the Smithsonians *she* wants to see. Air and Space? Natural History? The National Gallery?"

"Don't go trying to tell Kayla what she should choose," Avery says.

"Don't you, either," Mr. Armisted retorts.

I don't know much of anything about dads and daughters. Grandpa and Mom don't count, because, well, Grandpa's old and Mom's a saint.

But something is really wrong with the way Mr. Armisted and Avery talk to each other.

## Avery Gets Her Way (Until She Doesn't)

**There would have been jokes.**

I know it's awful, but if I had gone to the Holocaust Museum with the rest of my class on the DC trip back in April, some kids—okay, let's be honest, some *guys*—would have started cracking jokes the minute we walked in the door. They wouldn't have let the teachers or parent chaperones hear, but they would have purposely whispered stupid, immature things behind certain girls' backs, just to get us to whirl around and hiss, "Stop it! Can't you ever be serious? Don't you know how many people *died* in the Holocaust?"

Tristan Chambers, Alexandria's twin, would have been one of the worst. Yeah, Mr. Mommy's Boy isn't too sensitive to make fun of people dying. We read *Night* and *The Book Thief* in language arts class leading up to the DC trip—when we still thought we were going to the Holocaust Museum—and once Tristan figured out Death was the narrator in *The Book Thief*, he was always saying, "I'd be on Team Death. I'd love helping that dude!"

Mrs. Chambers *should* worry about Tristan, but not because he's too sensitive. I think he just likes to shock people; it's not like he really wants to kill anyone. But isn't *talking* about wanting to kill people bad enough?

The thing is—and this is awful too—it kind of would have helped to have the guys making jokes, so we girls could squeal and tell them how stupid and immature they were. It would have helped to have Lauren and Shannon and my other friends around me, almost psyching each other up: *I hear it's really hard seeing the room with all the shoes left behind. . . . My sister said on her DC trip two years ago, all the girls came out crying. And, since everyone was crying, it was like a bonding experience or something. Like, it made them really care about each other, not just about the people in the Holocaust. . . .*

Is that what I wanted—some bonding experience with Kayla? Is that why I wouldn't back down when Dad tried to talk me out of going to the Holocaust Museum?

I don't think so. Kayla and I are like apples and oranges, oil and vinegar, uh . . . Wonder Bread and quinoa. We'll never bond. It's just, Dad was trying so hard to get me to back down; that's what made me refuse.

And I did want to see the Holocaust Museum. I wanted to see if I could handle it.

I'm sure I could have, if we'd come on the eighth-grade trip, with its jokes and bonding.

Kayla and I are quiet as we stand in line in the lobby.

"This entire museum is about the Holocaust?" she asks.

"Yes," I say.

Her shoulders sag, as if walking here from the Metro stop already defeated her. Dad walked with us, and then he went on to a Starbucks ten minutes away. The walk was *nothing*, but Kayla's hair is plastered to her face with sweat, and she's even panting a little.

So was Dad.

*Just because he insisted on wearing business clothes, instead of shorts and a T-shirt*, I think. *That's stupid when it's eighty-five degrees out.*

He says he didn't pack shorts and a T-shirt, because once we get to Spain, I'll see: Nobody there considers that appropriate attire for an adult male.

At least *I* made sure Kayla had something to wear besides those stupid jeans.

Dad forgot to tell her that you should always pack a change of clothes in your carry-on, and because so many flights were canceled it would have taken hours to get our checked luggage before we went to the hotel. We didn't want to wait. So we stopped at Target, and Dad was too embarrassed about telling Kayla to buy spare underwear, so he left me to take care of her, and I said, "Here, let's get you a sundress or shorts and a tank top or something like that too, because it's going to be too hot for jeans tomorrow. And I don't know about you, but I'm not sleeping in the same clothes I wore all day, so let's get some T-shirts and jogging shorts too. . . ." And then at the checkout counter, Kayla was just standing there in a daze, and when Dad asked her what was wrong, she said in that small, pathetic *I'm an ant, so don't step on me* voice she has, "You're really going to spend more than a hundred dollars for stuff we wouldn't have needed if we'd just waited a few more hours at the airport? Really, it's okay. I can make do." But—this was me being a hero—I would *not* let her put anything back.

Nobody should have to sleep in the same clothes they wore all day. Or walk around in hot jeans in eighty-five-degree heat. And that sundress I found for her was really cute. Even if it was just from Target.

And . . . now I'm feeling a little guilty even thinking about jogging shorts and sundresses when we're standing in line at the Holocaust Museum.

Maybe I'm thinking about jogging shorts and sundresses because I'm a little scared about going in here. Maybe *I* am too sensitive for this place.

We move up, and it looks like maybe we'll make it onto the next elevator. Kayla picks up some kind of brochure—no, it's one of those deals where you assume the identity of someone who experienced a historical event, so it's more real to you.

Kayla keeps her head down, reading silently. She flips the papers over.

"This girl died," she whispers. "She was only sixteen. The same age as me."

"You're not supposed to read the final outcome until you've gone through the whole museum," I say, because I'm paying attention now. "You're supposed to wait."

"Oh," Kayla says. "Sorry."

She starts to put her identity card back, then tucks it into her purse instead.

Even though I've just told Kayla it's cheating to look ahead, I kind of want to check out everyone's fates before I pick a card. Because it seems like it could be a bad omen if I get someone who died too. I'm pretty sure I would have found a way to survive, if I'd lived in Europe during World War II.

*I'm not Jewish*, I think. *Not gay*. I can't remember the other types of people the Nazis killed. But I know none of them had labels that apply to me. I *would have survived, regardless*.

Still . . . would I have been brave enough to help other

people? If I'd known Anne Frank, would I have hidden her?

I don't pick any of the cards. The elevator door opens. Kayla and I manage to squeeze in.

When it opens again, we spill out into a big, dark, crowded room. It's hard to see the displays because so many other people are gathered around them. I try to stay by Kayla, because Dad would be mad if either of us got lost. And it would be even scarier to be here alone. But Kayla navigates this room like some big dumb ox. She waits and waits and waits behind people until they move away from each display, and then it seems like she is trying to read every single word written on the walls.

Every single depressing, awful, unbearable word.

We are going to be here forever.

And I already feel like I can't quite breathe.

"Was there anybody Hitler didn't hate?" Kayla whispers. "I thought the Holocaust was just about Jewish people. Not, like, Gypsies. I didn't even know Gypsies were real. I thought they were just in stories."

"Shh," I say, because I think "Gypsies" is one of those words you're not supposed to say. Kind of like how you're supposed to call Native Americans "Native Americans," not "Indians."

Who knows who could be standing near us, overhearing?

I'm having this weird reaction to the darkness and the crowds and the pictures from eighty years ago. I'm okay as long as I just look at the people around me—real, live people, not dead people in pictures. But if I glance up at one of those pictures, oh, those eyes . . .

In the first section, the eyes are awful because they're so normal. Ignore the old-fashioned hairstyles and clothes and just look at faces, and these pictures could be of anybody, anytime. The kids in the pictures could be my friends.

They could be me.

Then, in the next section, the eyes are awful because they stare out of terrified faces, skeletal faces, helpless faces. Accusing faces. Faces that still ask, even after all these years, *Why won't anyone help me? Why doesn't anyone stop this?*

I grab Kayla's arm.

"We're taking too long," I say. "It's a big museum. We have to move on so we'll be done in time to meet Dad for lunch."

"Oh. Okay," Kayla says, startling. See what I mean? Big, dumb ox.

We rush past the next several displays without looking, and I can almost breathe right again.

Then we get stuck behind a woman in a wheelchair.

She's maybe in her twenties—an adult, anyway, but still young enough that she could almost pass for a teenager. She's pretty. She's got long dark hair, pulled back in a ponytail that bounces against the back of her chair. She's also got friends walking on either side of the wheelchair, like wingmen, and it's really the *three* of them who are blocking us.

I see that the next display is an exhibit about how the Nazis hated people with disabilities. How the Nazis went to hospitals and mental institutions and killed the patients there.

Instinctively—because I *am* a nice person—I step forward and angle my body between the display and the woman in the wheelchair. She shouldn't have to see that display. But she's rolling right toward it.

"Ex*cuse* me," she says, as if I'm being rude.

I take a step back. What else can I do? The woman rolls up to the display and turns her chair around.

"Take my picture," she tells her friends.

And then she smiles.

I can't help it: I grab Kayla's arm again.

"Did you see that?" I mutter to Kayla, because she's the only one I have to talk to here. It's not like I'm going to text Shannon and Lauren about this. They wouldn't believe me. "Why would she want that picture? Why would she want to remember that display? Why would she even want to look at it?"

Kayla turns, and even in the dim light of the museum, her eyes are fierce. Just like the eyes of the woman in the wheelchair.

"Because she can," she says. "Because the Nazis lost. Because she's here, and the Nazis aren't."

Too late, I remember that Kayla's dad is in a wheelchair too. He might be, anyway. He was a soldier who got injured really bad. He's some kind of hero, I guess. Maybe he can't even sit up very well. Maybe he's one of those disabled people who has to stay in bed all the time.

"Oh, sorry," I say quickly. "Sorry. I forgot about your dad."

Kayla's face goes hard.

"If you want, I could take a picture of you with this display," I say. "So you could show it to your dad."

"That's okay," Kayla says. "Never mind."

She clips off her words the same way the woman in the wheelchair did, saying, *Excuse me*. As if they think I'm some stupid little kid who would never understand anything.

As if I'm the big, dumb ox.

## Kayla, About to Fly Far, Far Away

**We are finally on the** airplane that's going to take us to Europe, and it doesn't feel like an airplane.

It feels like a boat. It's that big. There are *eleven* seats in every row; there are so many rows we have to board from the middle of the plane.

Even Avery is looking around in awe.

Except for our visit to the Holocaust Museum, the whole time we were touring Washington, DC, Avery was all like, "Yeah, yeah, I saw this before. My friends and I already did this back in April, when I was here on the eighth-grade trip. . . ."

We had to go to the same pizza restaurant she'd gone to then. Of *course* she—and her friends—already saw the Washington Monument, the Lincoln Memorial, the Jefferson Memorial, the Martin Luther King Memorial, the Air and Space Museum . . .

And of course the pizza tasted better in April, the stars shining over the Jefferson Memorial were brighter in April, the weather wasn't as hot and humid, the Air and Space Museum wasn't as crowded . . . (And I'm sure back in April she never once said anything like, *Dad, it's not fair you made Kayla pick this museum. I bet she really wanted to go somewhere else.*)

I didn't know enough about any museum to pick anything. That's why I asked Mr. Armisted, "What's your favorite?"

I guess I should have asked Avery if she had a favorite too.

But then Mr. Armisted would have complained, *Avery, you need to let Kayla make up her own mind. It's not fair if you make her choose what you want.*

I don't think either Mr. Armisted or Avery are happy people. How can they not be happy when they have so much money? Enough money to spend a hundred dollars at Target like it's just a dollar or two?

Enough money to go to Spain? Enough money to take a stranger to Spain with them?

Because that's what I am: a stranger. I don't know anything about these people. I don't understand them. I'm not like them.

Because of how Avery and I used to play together, all those years ago, I thought we were connected. I always felt so special when Mom consulted me about the best Christmas presents for Avery. Then when we drove back to Crawfordsville after exchanging gifts, I always wanted to stop at the nursing home to show everyone what I got: one of those fancy American Girl dolls one year, a toy laptop with educational games another year . . . Back then, I don't think I even understood that those were expensive gifts, or that Avery's family was rich. I was just proud to be able to say, "Avery gave this to me. Avery's my friend from far away."

Even when I was in third grade, I can remember telling Miss Nolan at the beginning of the year, "If I ever had a little sister, my mom would name her Avery." That was before Miss Nolan knew anything about my family, when Miss Nolan was so new to Crawfordsville she sometimes got lost driving to school. And then even Miss Nolan found out about my family; even she started giving me those overly sympathetic looks all the other adults in Crawfordsville always gave me. Even she knew I would never have a little sister or brother.

But I guess I used to think of Avery as the closest thing to a little sister I'd ever have. I kind of thought, there for a while, I was like the closest thing to a big sister Avery would ever have.

I guess I wasn't ever anything to Avery.

Most of the time now she just looks right through me.

There was one moment back at the Holocaust Museum when she really looked at me, when she acted like she wanted to know what I thought, and it didn't have anything to do with arguing with her dad. It was when she asked me about the woman in the wheelchair who posed for a picture beside the one Holocaust Museum display.

That woman in the wheelchair was beautiful. No, not *just* beautiful—strong. Dignified. Amazing. Confident.

Defiant.

Like if Hitler was standing right in front of her, she would punch him in the nose. Even if it was Hitler and thousands of his Nazi soldiers. She wouldn't care.

I wish I had a picture of that woman to put up in my locker at school. It would help me get through any day.

I wish I had a picture of that woman to help me get through the next eight weeks.

I guess I do have one in my head.

Avery kind of looked like she was listening to me when we talked about the woman in the wheelchair. But then later, we got to this display where they had pictures of everyone who had been killed from one little village in . . . I don't know . . . Lithuania? Latvia? Poland? I'd never heard of any of those countries before, except Poland. Still, the people in the pictures seemed like people I might know. Those pictures circled the walls all the way up this column over our heads, like a smokestack. (I guess it looked like a smokestack on purpose. They had smokestacks at the concentration camps.) But the pictures were of people doing happy things: getting married, smelling flowers . . . They looked so *alive*. But the Nazis killed them all.

"It's like if all of Crawfordsville just vanished," I whispered to Avery, because it felt like my heart would burst if I didn't say *something*.

She didn't even bother answering me.

"You two can take turns sitting by the window," Mr. Armisted says behind me, and I kind of jump, because I'm thinking so much about Avery and the Holocaust Museum I've almost forgotten he's there. "Who wants the last view of the United States for the next eight weeks, and who wants the first view of Spain?"

"I don't care," Avery says in a stiff, unnatural voice.

We're awkward when we reach our row of seats. I take a step backward. Avery steps too far ahead. Mr. Armisted makes an annoyed noise deep in his throat.

"Kayla, you're closer," Mr. Armisted says. "Why don't you go in first?"

We sit down. Avery and I arrange our backpacks under the seats in front of us, and Mr. Armisted does the same with his briefcase.

"When do the movies start?" Avery asks, staring at the little screen in the seat in front of her.

"After takeoff," Mr. Armisted says. "But don't just watch movies the whole night. Try to sleep as much as you can. That will help you avoid having such bad jet lag."

"I *know*, Dad," Avery grumbles, rolling her eyes. "But I can't sleep when I'm not sleepy."

I look out the window. Workers toss suitcases onto a conveyer belt, to load onto the plane. I don't remember any airport before yesterday's, but already this scene looks familiar to me. We're still in America. It's an American sky overhead. All the signs I see are in English.

I shiver, thinking of the chilling words I saw at the Holocaust Museum this morning: ARBEIT MACHT FREI, scrolled onto the gates of concentration camps.

*That was German and Germany, not Spanish and Spain*, I tell myself. *You're going to Spain. Same continent, but totally different places. And anyhow, World War II was a long time ago.*

Not so long ago that people from then aren't still alive.

I remember the maps from back at the Holocaust Museum, showing how Germany took over most of Europe before and during World War II. Was Spain colored in along with France and Austria and Hungary and Poland and all the other countries Germany attacked? Why hadn't I paid attention to that?

If I meet any old people in Spain, what if they're people who did terrible things to other people back when they were young, during their war?

## Avery, in Her Last Moments of American Cell Service

**"Avery, as hard as it** is, you *have* to shut off your phone," Dad says as the flight attendants shut the overhead luggage compartments, getting ready for takeoff. "Stop texting Shannon and Lauren. Say good-bye and put your phone away."

"Just a minute, just a minute . . . ," I mutter.

I'm not texting Shannon and Lauren. I'm looking up what happened in Spain during World War II.

I've never been to Europe before. I whined about coming with Dad—because, duh, with a total stranger like Kayla? To spend eight weeks away from my real friends? But I always thought I would go to Europe someday: maybe studying in England or France or Italy when I'm in college; maybe backpacking around the whole continent after I graduate. Dad took Mom to Paris when I was ten, but they left me home with a babysitter, and I was so mad not to get to see the Eiffel Tower and Disneyland Paris.

But the Holocaust Museum made Europe seem like a totally different place. A horrifying place with an awful history lurking just beneath the surface. How can anyone want to go there?

By the last parts of the Holocaust Museum, I couldn't even speak. Stepping out into the sunshine afterward only helped a little. The rest of the day, I made myself chatter, chatter, chatter, *happy memory, happy memory, happy memory—don't think about the Holocaust!*

But now I'm on a plane to Europe.

*Please make it so Spain wasn't even a part of World War II. They're off on a whole other peninsula; please make it so they were too far away from Germany, and it was too much trouble to invade them. Please make it so they were more like their own little island. . . .*

It's almost like I'm praying.

"Avery," Dad says again, warningly.

I've mistyped "Spain" as "Sapin," so I erase and start again. The little circle spins and spins. Blindly, I click on the first site that comes up.

Dad reaches for my phone, and I have to jerk it to the side, closer to Kayla, to keep it out of his hands.

"I said, just a minute! I'm doing it!" I protest. I get a quick glimpse of the screen. I press in the power button, and show Dad the screen blacking out. "See?"

"All right," Dad huffs, as if he has to get the last word. "I just didn't think you'd like having the flight attendant confiscate it."

I ignore him. I saw what I wanted to find out: Germany didn't invade Spain during World War II. Spain had some war of its own right before World War II started, but I'd never heard of the Spanish Civil War before, so how bad could it have been?

Dad's mad at me now, and I'm a little mad at him, and anyhow, he didn't even care enough to go to the Holocaust Museum with us today. So it's not like I'm going to tell him what I read, or even why I wanted to know. But it's weird: I kind of want to tap Kayla on the shoulder and whisper, *Spain wasn't part of World War II. We've got nothing to worry about there.* ¿Comprende? She's not my friend, but we were at the Holocaust Museum together. We survived it together. She knows what I saw.

But Kayla's looking out the window, turned completely to the side so she's got her back to me. What can be so interesting about watching baggage handlers and fuel trucks?

It's almost like she's pretending I don't exist.

## Kayla in España! (Or Ka-ee-la)

**We're landing. Or, as the** captain puts it in his announcement, "starting our final descent." He makes the announcement in Spanish, too, but I can't make out a single word.

*Never mind. It's just because you're not awake. . . .*

I came out of a deep, deep sleep when they suddenly flicked all the lights on. I'm still blinking. Mr. Armisted whispers that Avery and I missed the breakfast service—he actually calls it "breakfast service"—but he got food for both of us. He hands over a banana and a little juice container and something wrapped in red foil. I can barely get my fingers to bend, to hold on. Avery doesn't even try: She moans and kind of bats the food away and squeezes her eyes even more tightly shut.

Mr. Armisted laughs.

"She always was hard to wake up in the mornings," he says. "And this probably feels like one a.m. to you both. Oh, well. She can have the food later. I'll warn you—she gets really grumpy when she hasn't had enough sleep. So we'll let her sleep as long as possible."

I don't trust myself to put words together to answer. Is this jet lag? It's like my brain is broken.

"You should keep the window seat, since it'd be wasted on Avery right now," Mr. Armisted says. He points past me. "Look. That's Madrid, off in the distance."

I'm grateful to turn to the window—it's easier to look than to talk.

The landscape below us seems dry and dusty, like a desert. It reminds me of the scenery in the John Wayne westerns Grandpa likes to watch. Then swirls of green show up—maybe they're groves of orange or olive trees. Even though I'm barely awake, I can hear Grandpa's voice in my head: *Why didn't they plant in straight lines, not curves? What kind of farmer does that?* Grandpa's never been to Spain, of course, but I know him so well, it's like I'm always carrying him around in my head. He hasn't been a farmer in more than thirty years, but he would have noticed the perfect squares and rectangles of farmland I saw from the plane, leaving Ohio, and he would notice the curlicues of farmland here.

We go lower, and now I see why the trees are planted that way: The farmers were working around hills and mountains. The land isn't flat here like it is back home; that's why there aren't straight lines.

The plane turns, and now I see a small patch of skyscrapers: Madrid. The big city. Except maybe not so big. I've seen pictures of New York and Chicago, and Madrid isn't like that. It has only four supertall buildings, which look a little silly sticking up all by themselves. The rest of the city spreads out far beyond the four skyscrapers, a diorama of red-tiled roofs and narrow, windy streets, glowing in the early rays of sunrise.

*Spain! I'm landing in Spain! My first foreign country ever!*

I wish I had texting on my phone, like Avery does. I'd snap a picture and send it to show-offy Stephanie Purley: *You didn't believe me, but look where I am now!*

I'd send it to my sort-of-former best friend Harley Seitz too, with the line, *See? And you said you'd die of boredom if you had to be me and didn't even have a boyfriend. THIS isn't boring!*

But mostly, it's Mom and Grandma and Grandpa and all my friends in the nursing home I want to show. I blink, because I am still so tired, and my family and friends suddenly feel so, so far away, because I can't show them what I'm seeing.

I remember I do have a camera with me, a little one Mom bought for my birthday.

"So you can take pictures of everything on your trip," she said. "So you can remember it forever . . ."

I reach down into my backpack and struggle to unzip the compartment where I stowed the camera. But by the time I untangle it from my earbud cord, the plane has turned, and my window faces straight out into the rising sun, nothing but glare on glass. The scene I wanted to capture is already gone.

*That doesn't matter*, I tell myself. *I'll never forget, anyway.*

And I can tell Mom and Grandma and Grandpa and my nursing home friends, even if I can't show them.

We're on the ground before I know it, and Mr. Armisted starts trying to shake Avery awake, even as she groans and pushes him away.

"You're going to be embarrassed if I have to carry you through the airport like a little baby," he jokes, and that finally makes her open her eyes. A little.

"I hate you," she mutters, her eyes still barely slits.

"Good morning to you, too, sunshine." Mr. Armisted laughs.

I hold back a gasp. If my father hadn't been injured, if I could talk to him and he could answer back, I would never,

ever ever tell him I hated him. I wouldn't be able to speak that word.

And it's the very first thing Avery says to her dad when we're in a new place and it's a new day and everything is golden and exciting before us?

It seems to take forever for everyone to file off the plane. I'm wobbly setting off down the aisle, trailing Avery and Mr. Armisted. We get into the jetway, and then into the first section of the airport, and Spanish is *everywhere*: It's all *salida* and *recogida de equipajes* and *control de pasaportes* . . . I squint—I guess some of the signs have English, too, but it's always smaller and harder to see.

"*Baño*," Avery mutters. "*¿Donde baño?*"

Oh, no—what if they decide that they won't speak anything but Spanish either? I'm going to be totally lost. Maybe I won't be able to communicate with *anyone* for the next eight weeks.

"It's '*¿Donde está el baño?*'" Mr. Armisted corrects. "That's how you say, 'Where is the bathroom?' What you said was like caveman-speak: 'Where bathroom?'"

"You understood me," Avery grumbles. "No grammar lessons today. I've got jet lag."

We keep walking—it's like we're gerbils in a Habitrail. Eventually, we come to a bathroom and stop to use it. Eventually we reach *control de pasaportes*—where the officials check passports. Mr. Armisted takes his and mine and Avery's from his briefcase as we get in line. Mine looks too shiny and new, proving I've never been anywhere. His is battered and worn. Avery pulls her own passport out of his grasp and starts leafing through it.

"I hope they don't stamp over any of my old stamps, like the customs people in Barbados did on that one cruise," she says. "Can I tell them which page to use?"

"No," Mr. Armisted says. "In fact, it's better not to say anything unless you're directly asked. Here, why don't you just give the passport back, before you lose it?"

"Dad! I am not going to lose my passport just standing here in line looking through it!" Avery protests. "Quit treating me like a three-year-old!"

Mr. Armisted gently tugs it out of her hand anyway.

Avery elbows me.

"Wouldn't it be funny if Kayla told the passport officials you were kidnapping her?" she asks, her voice rising.

"Avery, stop," Mr. Armisted says. "That's not something to joke about."

"She *could* do that, you know," Avery says. "And then what could you do, Dad? What would happen? Would they put you in prison? How do they know you're not kidnapping her, anyway?"

Mr. Armisted gives a quick, darting glance around, like he's worried someone in the crowd around us might hear. I just hope no one understands English.

It's weird that that's what I'm hoping for.

"You know I've got a letter from Kayla's mother that says I have her permission to take Kayla on this trip," Mr. Armisted tells Avery in a low, hissing voice.

"It could be forged," Avery teases.

"Avery!" Mr. Armisted thunders. "I said stop it!"

He's yelling at her, not me, but tears spring to my eyes. I'm not much of a crier, but not having enough sleep always brings the tears more easily. I tell myself that's the only reason my eyes flood so suddenly.

I don't want to believe the whole summer is going to be like this, Avery and Mr. Armisted constantly fighting, me caught in the middle.

"I'm not going to say I'm being kidnapped," I say quickly, because if I wait any longer to speak, the tears might choke out my words.

"*Thank* you, Kayla," Mr. Armisted says. "I'm glad *someone's* capable of being mature here."

Avery shoots me a look of such pure hatred it makes my knees tremble.

"I'm sorry," Mr. Armisted says. "We're all tired. Jet lag does this. We'll all feel better after a nap. So let's just . . . try to be as nice as we can for now, okay?"

Neither Avery nor I say anything. But when Mr. Armisted puts his arm around Avery's shoulders, she doesn't shake it away.

I concentrate on making the tears go away. Or, at least, keeping them from multiplying.

*Spain. Fun. Excitement.*

I decide that's too much to think about right now, and I focus on a smaller goal.

*A nap. Soon. All I have to do is get through this airport and get to the apartment we're staying in this summer. Just follow Mr. Armisted. Then it's naptime. Mmm. Sleep . . .*

I think maybe I'm already half-asleep, standing in line. But finally we reach the front. We step up to a little booth where a man in a crisp blue uniform reaches for our passports.

*"Buenos dias,"* he says, and Mr. Armisted answers, *"Buenos dias,"* as he hands everything over. And—*I understood.* Okay, it was just *Buenos dias*, which kids sometimes say jokingly back at Crawfordsville High School, especially on the way to or from Spanish class. But this is *Spain*, and I just understood *Spanish*. It's like I'm . . . international.

Mr. Armisted and the man keep speaking back and forth, whole sentences in Spanish, and I don't understand any of that, but it's okay. I already understood some Spanish, spoken by a real Spaniard.

"*¿Y esta es la chica?*" the man in the uniform says, pointing to me. I don't quite follow that, either, but he's looking down at the picture on my passport. "*Ka-ee-la* Boots?"

It's funny that he thinks the *y* should be pronounced separately in my first name. And funny that he doesn't have any idea how to say my last name. But Mr. Armisted doesn't correct him. He just says, "*Sí.*"

The man hands back our passports and waves us through.

"Well, Ka-ee-la Boots and Avery Armisted, welcome to Spain," Mr. Armisted says, grinning as we walk toward the baggage claim beyond. "Thank you for *not* creating any international incidents."

He pronounces Avery's name only slightly differently—more as if he's faking an accent than anything else. But it jars loose some ancient memory from Spanish class in my jet-lagged brain.

"Wait—would my last name really be 'Boots,' saying it in Spanish?" I ask.

"Yes," Mr. Armisted says. "Their *U* sound is always an *ooo*, not an *uhh*."

I'd rather be "Kayla" than "Ka-ee-la," but to be called "Boots" not "Butts" . . . It's like that man in the uniform just blessed me. It's like he handed me a get-out-of-jail-free card. It's like he gave me permission to be anybody I want to be, here in Spain.

Stephanie Purley was so, so wrong.

I am *not* still "Butt-girl" in Spain.

## Avery, So, So Tired

**You know those posters some** teachers keep in their classrooms when they want to pretend they understand kids? The ones that say, I DON'T DO MORNINGS, usually with a picture of a grumpy-looking cat or some other stupid thing everyone's seen a thousand times as a meme?

I never really understood I DON'T DO MORNINGS before now.

*This* is a morning I really, really, really cannot face.

I didn't fall asleep until, like, five minutes before we were landing. Dad says this should feel like one a.m. to us, but I've stayed up later than that at sleepovers plenty of times, and I've never felt this fuzzy-brained. It's just wrong that sunlight was streaming in the windows as we walked toward passport control—that sunlight totally confuses me.

Now we're at baggage claim, which doesn't have windows, but it's still too brightly lit, with yellowish-orange pillars everywhere. (Here's something Mom and I would agree on: This place needs a better interior designer.) And it's apparently going to take a hundred years for our suitcases to show up.

"Avery, you're asleep on your feet." Dad laughs. "You're *swaying*. Should I be ready to catch you if you fall over?"

"I won't fall," I snap. "I'm awake. I'm . . . just going to text everyone that we're here. You haven't told Mom yet, have you?"

I pull out my phone. I'm really planning to text Shannon and Lauren, to brag, *Hola from España! I made it! Everything is bonita! Hermosa!*

They don't need to know that I've only seen the airport so far, and it definitely isn't beautiful. Eventually, maybe I'll get around to also telling Mom we've arrived.

But Dad puts his hand on my arm.

"There's no Wi-Fi here," he says. "I already checked."

"Dad, I don't need Wi-Fi to text!" I start to laugh.

Then it hits me, one of the many ridiculous things about this Spain trip I was trying to forget: Dad refused to pay to unlock my phone for international cellular use. He says it's too expensive, and it makes more sense on this trip for me and Kayla to carry around little burner phones, which he'll pick up for us later today.

So right now, without Wi-Fi, my phone is worthless. I'm like some poor kid who doesn't even own a phone. I can't connect to anyone.

Somehow, being away from Mom makes me think more like her. She complains that even though Dad's Mr. Financial Hotshot, he acts sometimes like he's still that poor farm kid who arrived in New York City without a spare nickel to his name. I can hear her voice in my head, *You want to economize* now? *About this? Remind me again—what's your net worth?*

She mostly says that when she wants to redecorate, and he balks at the cost of the just-right flooring or window treatments, instead of cheaper alternatives. When she says our house has to look up-to-date and perfect all the time, so other people will hire her to decorate for them.

My stomach churns, and it's not just because I couldn't face that dried-up breakfast sandwich or the half-rotten banana Dad wanted me to eat. I think about his credit card not working at the Columbus airport. I think about the defeated slump of his shoulders when he was on the phone with the credit card company.

*Credit card companies mess things up all the time*, I remind myself. *That was just a mistake. He was just annoyed. And this phone thing? It's just Dad being stupid.*

As soon as my brain's working again, when I'm not jet-lagged anymore, I'll figure out how to talk Dad into unlocking my phone. I can't be stuck with just a burner phone any time I'm away from Wi-Fi. I can't live without texting.

"I'll text your mother, if you're really that concerned," Dad says. "But, you know, she doesn't worry when I fly. She's used to it. It's one—no, two a.m. at home now. I'm sure she's already asleep."

"It's not just you flying this time—it's her precious daughter, too," I tell him, rolling my eyes. "*Yo tambien.*"

I'm not sure I'm using the right grammar. Isn't that how you say *Me too* in Spanish?

Really, I shouldn't have to remind him of stuff like that.

Dad shrugs.

"Would you let my mom know too?" Kayla says hesitantly. "She was going to wait up and keep checking the airline website until it said we'd landed."

Dad's eyes soften when he looks at Kayla.

"Of course," he says. "I fly so much, I forgot what it'd be like for your family." He holds out his phone to her. "Do you want to call and talk to her directly?"

Kayla stares at the phone like she's never seen such a thing before. Or like it's never occurred to her that someone could stand in an airport in Madrid, Spain, and call back to Ohio.

*How stupid is she?* I wonder. Some kinder voice in my head counters, *Or . . . how jet-lagged?*

Kayla literally backs away from the phone.

"No, thank you." She's using her tiny voice again, as if she thinks that could make her disappear. "It'd freak Mom out, to have the phone ring now. She'd think that meant the plane crashed."

An alarm goes off just then, but it's only the signal that the conveyer belt for the baggage is starting up.

"Finally!" I mutter as Dad hunches over his phone sending the message to Kayla's mom.

Kayla stares off into the distance, and I think of the insult Mom throws at Dad when she really wants to hurt him: *Quit acting like some slack-jawed yokel who's never been off the farm.* I never really knew what "slack-jawed yokel" meant, but it's like Kayla's posing for the Wikipedia definition picture. Do I really have to spend the next eight weeks with her—while I can't text with all my real friends?

It would be so easy to start crying right now.

"Dad, can I see my passport again?" I ask, because I need something else to focus on. "I want to see the new stamp."

"Can't you wait?" Dad mutters, not looking up from his phone. "In a minute, we'll have our luggage, we'll be in a cab on the way to the apartment—when we get there, you can study your passport for hours if you want. I'll be taking a nap." His phone pings, and he sighs. "Correction, you two can nap, and I'll need to head to the office right away. . . ."

"That was a big plane—what if our bags are the last ones off?" I say. "This'll just take a minute."

I unzip the side of his briefcase where he tucked all three passports. Dad sighs again, but he doesn't stop me.

I ease out the little blue book and flip it open. There's my passport photo—hideous, of course. It's from two years ago, when I still had braces, and I look like a goofy little kid. My grin's too big, so it must have been before Shannon took that modeling class and taught the rest of us the dangers of wide-smiling. How many hours did we spend practicing in front of a mirror, so we could look perfect even in pictures that weren't selfies?

I turn the pages, leafing through the foreign-country stamps. Aruba. Barbados. Jamaica. Mom really likes Caribbean vacations. There's this cheesy old song called "Kokomo" that Dad always sings to Mom where he lists tropical destinations, and we've been to almost all of them. I think he customizes it to add in places we've been. I wince, remembering how the two of them started fighting over that song on our spring break trip, and Dad snapped at Mom, "What? Are the Beach Boys too *declassé* for you now?"

I think *declassé* is French, not Spanish. I had to look it up. And by then, they'd gone from sniping at each other to giving each other the silent treatment, and talking extra-nice to me.

Parents.

On the bright side, I got a really expensive new bikini out of that, because they wanted to prove they hadn't ruined our family vacation. But, I don't know, every time I look at that bikini, it makes me feel a little sick to my stomach.

It's the most expensive swimsuit I've ever had, but I didn't even bring it on this trip.

I think Mom and Dad being apart for most of this summer will make them nicer to each other. I think it already has. I haven't heard them fighting since . . . since that night they worked out the plans for me to come to Spain.

The conveyor belt in front of me gives a little screech—it's stopped.

"Seriously?" I mutter. "Is there some Spanish union rule that lets baggage handlers take a break in the middle of unloading? Can't they finish the job first?"

"Avery," Dad says warningly. "Don't be rude. You're making assumptions." This is code for, *Even when everyone around you is speaking a different language, you can't assume they don't understand English. And when you're in another country, you always represent America.* . . . There's a whole lecture attached to it about respecting other people's cultures.

Which is ridiculous, because the whole reason Dad's here this summer is that he's trying to get the people working for his company in Spain to behave more like American employees. Which . . . mostly means not taking so many breaks. Being willing to work 24/7, if that's what it takes.

"Did they forget our suitcases?" Kayla whispers. "Look. We're about the last people left."

She's right. There's one other cluster that might be some

sports team—basketball, maybe? They're all tall. (And cute. Hello . . . ) I can make out UNIVERSITY OF on one of their shirts. College men! The tallest guy, who's on crutches, even seems to be looking at me. No . . . He's looking past me, toward a group of very tall girls in University of South Florida athletic gear coming back from the bathroom. So . . . in college, do men's and women's teams travel together?

One of the females laughs walking past me, and it makes me feel as young as my passport photo. It makes me wonder if my hair is sticking up, or if I've got sleep crud crusted in my eyelashes.

It makes me wonder if she thinks I'm as pathetic as Kayla.

*Oh, yeah? Well, I have soccer teammates to hang out with,* I want to tell her. *They're just . . . not here right now. And is the guy on crutches your boyfriend? What kind of basketball player is he if he's already broken his leg, and it's just the start of the trip?*

The female basketball players rejoin the male basketball players. They all pick up duffel bags from the floor and start heading toward the door.

They're obnoxious *and* they already have their luggage.

Dad calls over a worker, who's maybe a janitor. They both reel off a string of Spanish I can't begin to follow, and the janitor gestures toward a desk at the other end of the room.

"He says that's probably everything for our flight," Dad reports to Kayla and me. "We have to go to customer service to report our lost luggage."

"Lost?" Kayla repeats. "All my clothes, everything I brought—it's just . . . gone?"

"Not permanently," Dad says. "I mean, I hope not. Odds are, it just didn't make it onto our plane, because of the switched flights. We'll fill out paperwork, and they'll probably deliver it tomorrow." He's gazing sympathetically at Kayla again. "Not exactly a great first flying experience for you, huh? I'd like to tell you this is really unusual, to be delayed twenty-four hours *and* lose your luggage too. But . . . sometimes that's just how things go."

"This isn't my first flight," Kayla says softly. "I've flown before."

She thinks we're going to believe a lie like that?

*Oh, I guess she means the flight from Columbus to DC*, I realize. Someday, somebody should tell her layover flights don't count separately, but I'm not bothering now. I'm too annoyed that Dad's all about making things easier for Kayla. I decide I need to razz him.

"What this means is, Dad's going to have to pay for another shopping trip," I say. "Only bigger and better this time. European fashions, here we come!"

Dad gives me a chilling look.

"There's a washer in the apartment," he says. "All we have to do is wash our clothes from yesterday. Yes, young lady, you can do your own laundry."

This is something else Mom and Dad fight over. Our cleaning lady always does our laundry at home. But Dad says I'm old enough to do mine myself.

"You want to prepare your daughter to be a maid when she grows up?" Mom sneers.

"No—to be independent," Dad says.

Can this summer get any worse?

We walk over to the customer service counter, and there's a long line—I guess other people figured out way before we did that their luggage was missing. Time slows down. Maybe it stops entirely.

*I will spend the rest of my life in this customer service line,* I think. *I will never see anything else of Spain. I will never see my friends again. I will never play soccer again. I will never start high school. I will never . . .*

Just to have something to do, I go to the bathroom again. This one is out of toilet paper, so I have to use Kleenex from my backpack. I shake my hair out and pull it back into a neater ponytail. I still look too young, so I put on mascara—just a little, not the raccoon-eye approach Kayla uses.

"There," I say out loud. "Perfect."

But my face is too pale, and the mirror reflects an ugly, messy bathroom behind me, with every trash can overflowing.

I go back to Dad and Kayla, and they're still three people away from the front of the line.

After approximately a hundred years, it's finally Dad's turn. I can't follow the conversation, but the woman at the desk doesn't seem to believe anything Dad says. He shows the baggage claim tickets. He shows the airline tickets on his phone. He and the woman use their Spanish like swords, back and forth and back and forth, their voices rising and falling, rising and falling . . .

I put my head down on the counter, right by Dad's elbow.

A moment later—or maybe an eon—Dad shakes me awake.

"Avery, where's your passport?" he asks.

"I—" I begin.

I remember leafing through it while we were waiting on the luggage. Is it still in my hand? Did I put it down and pick it back up when I went to the bathroom?

I'm so sleepy, I have to look to be sure: Both my hands are empty.

Is it on the counter, where I had my head? Or in my backpack? Did I put it in my pocket?

No and no. And no—I don't even *have* pockets because I'm wearing yoga pants.

Did I slip it back into Dad's briefcase?

I can't tease out any memory of doing that. And Dad's got everything out of every compartment of his briefcase. Clearly he looked there before he woke me up.

"Did you put it down back where the bags came out?" Kayla asks in that annoyingly helpful voice people use when what they really mean is, *How could you be so stupid?*

"Of course not!" I snap. "I wouldn't have done that!"

"Avery," Dad says.

"Perhaps you should step out of line and go to look for it," the woman behind the counter suggests.

She knew English all along. I hate her.

Dad, Kayla, and I retrace our steps, all of us staring at the floor as if my passport's going to magically appear. Kayla and I both look in the bathroom, but the sink counter is empty; the stall I used is empty. Kayla starts to look in the trash cans, but the overflowing paper towels are gone; the bathroom's been cleaned since I was here before. Even if I accidentally dropped my passport in the trash, it's gone now. We go back to Dad, and all three of us walk around the baggage claim conveyer belt again and again, in case my passport just fell from my hand and nobody noticed. We walk around the other conveyer belts and the line of locked baggage carts, in case someone accidentally kicked my passport to the side and it wedged under some random metal strip or cart.

But I already know, because I can feel it in the pit of my stomach: My passport's gone. I lost it.

Just like Dad said I would.

## Kayla, Struggling to Stay Awake

**"It's okay, honey," Mr. Armisted** is still telling Avery as we get into a cab to leave the airport. "These things happen. We'll just have to work with the American Embassy to get a new passport."

"Somebody had to have seen it," she says stubbornly. "I bet it was stolen. Maybe even right out of my hand while I was sleeping. I bet someone's using my identity right now. Applying for fake credit cards. Stealing back into the United States."

I wait for Mr. Armisted to say, *Don't be ridiculous. You lost it. It wasn't stolen. Or if it was, it's your own fault.* But he pats Avery's shoulder and murmurs soothingly, "Don't worry. Everything will be fine."

I'm squeezed against the door on the other side of Avery.

"Don't new passports cost a lot?" I ask. Because how can Mr. Armisted not mention that?

"They're cheaper than plane tickets to London or Paris," Mr. Armisted says grimly.

"Daddy!" Avery protests. Her elbow swings out and digs into my side. "Now you're just being mean! That's how you're going to punish me?"

"London, Paris . . . What are you even talking about?" I ask. Did I fall asleep between words and miss some explanation?

Avery whirls toward me.

"It was supposed to be a surprise," she says. "Dad said if

he can get things at work under control, maybe we can take some three-day weekend trips this summer to other countries nearby, like France or England or Portugal." She jerks her head back toward her dad and glares. "You can't take that away from me! From us, I mean—what if it's Kayla's only chance to see the Eiffel Tower or London Bridge?"

"I'm not taking anything away," Mr. Armisted says in an even tone. "This is just a natural consequence of you not having a passport for a while. And I never *promised*. Those other trips were just possibilities." He goes back to patting her shoulder. "They're still possible. I'll try to get the American Embassy to expedite the process."

We've barely even left the airport here in Madrid, and already Spain isn't enough for Avery and Mr. Armisted? They want to start planning trips to other foreign countries too?

I am suddenly really, really tired.

Meanwhile, Avery's gotten a new burst of energy. She's tugging Mr. Armisted's phone from his hand and muttering, "I'll look up how fast they can replace a passport."

"The holdup's going to be getting a copy of your birth certificate," Mr. Armisted says, gently pulling the phone back.

"So we tell Mom to send it by overnight mail," Avery says.

Mr. Armisted gazes out the window. There's nothing to see but highway and billboards in Spanish.

"Let's not bother her with this," he says. "We can just order it directly from the state."

"So you're not going to narc on me to Mom?" Avery says. "Thanks, Dad."

She sounds sincerely grateful.

*Are they both afraid of Mrs. Armisted?* I wonder.

It's too much to figure out when my brain's half-asleep.

"Count yourself lucky," Mr. Armisted tells Avery. "The great state of California is going to save us both from a lecture."

*California?* I think drowsily. *Does he mean Avery's birth certificate would come from California?*

It's on the tip of my tongue to say, *Were you born in California too, Avery? How come I never knew that? That's where I was born! Because my dad was stationed there. So it's not like I've never been anywhere before now. I just don't remember. . . .*

It's too hard to make my mouth form words. I let my eyes slide shut instead, and I'm asleep before we even get off the highway.

## Avery, Actually Alert

**The sound of running water** wakes me, and my first instinct is to call, *Mom? Dad? Who's using my shower?*

Then I open my eyes, and I'm not in my spacious, Mom-decorated room at home, but in a tiny bare cubicle, my arms and legs hanging off a narrow single bed, my backpack spilling open between me and the door.

*Oh right, Spain,* I think. *I'm in the apartment in Spain and . . . I'm* starving.

I pick up my phone—my *real* phone, the American one—and squint at it: one forty-five. Is that Ohio time or Spain time? Vaguely I remember setting my phone to the apartment Wi-Fi when Dad, Kayla, and I arrived. That was about the only thing I bothered doing before falling into bed. All that effort, and nobody had even texted me.

Anyhow. It's afternoon, and I haven't eaten anything since . . . since awful plane food at the beginning of the flight last night. No wonder I'm starving.

I stumble to my feet and hop over my backpack. Out in the hallway, I find that Kayla's left the bathroom door open. *Ugh.* Is that what this whole summer is going to be like? I glance again, and see she's not actually using the bathroom or the shower. Instead, she's bent over the tiny sink.

She turns around.

"Oh, um, hi!" she says awkwardly. She pulls her hand out of

sudsy water. "I'm washing my clothes from yesterday. I can do yours, too, if you want."

"No need. There's a washer," I say flatly.

Kayla's face flushes. Suds drip from her hands.

"Yeah, but I looked at it and everything was in Spanish, so I didn't know how to run it," she says. "And then I started hitting things at random, and nothing happened, and . . . maybe it's broken?"

She looks guilty, like I'm going to accuse her of breaking it.

It's a washer. Who cares?

I glance toward the shower, because I feel sweaty and gross, and maybe that's worse than being hungry. Or a higher priority, anyway.

Kayla follows my gaze.

"Also," she mumbles, as if she's ashamed, "I'm not sure the water heater works. All I can get is cold water. I looked at it, too—it's in a closet in the living room—but it doesn't make sense to me either. Do you want to look and see if . . . ?"

I try to think if I even know what a water heater looks like.

"Dad can figure it out when he gets back," I say. I am not taking a cold shower. It's good to have my priorities clarified. "I just want food."

Kayla's face lights up.

"Oh, me too!" she says. "There's, like, a ton of stuff in the kitchen—fruit and yogurt and eggs and bread . . . but I wasn't sure if I was allowed to eat it, or if it was, you know, for some special purpose or . . ."

*Seriously?*

"There's food, you're hungry, you eat," I say.

She looks at me like she's just found out she isn't Cinderella facing a summer with her evil stepfamily. Something twists inside me, and I don't think it's just because I'm hungry.

I head toward the kitchen and Kayla trails after me.

Mom would critique the kitchen as being too IKEA—she really hates cheap Scandinavian décor—but I'm more interested in what's *in* the refrigerator than what's around it.

"We could do fried or scrambled eggs, and maybe pancakes or French toast, too," Kayla says. "I *think* we could figure out the stovetop. Oh, and there's potatoes, so we could fry up some of them, too. . . ."

*Ugh. Fried food.*

"I'm too hungry to cook," I tell Kayla, even as I grab a handful of grapes. I hold the bag out to Kayla, too. "Dad left money, didn't he?"

"Um, over there." Kayla takes a few grapes and points toward the tiny living room. I see a flash of blue and red at the top of a bookshelf by the front door.

*Oh right, euros are lots of different colors. Not just green, like dollar bills. . . .*

I walk over to the bookshelf and pocket sixty euros.

"Come on," I say. "We're going out!"

Five minutes later—I mean, I do pause to comb my hair and wipe smeared mascara off my face—I'm sprinting down the spiral staircase at the center of our apartment building.

"Wait . . . wait . . . ," Kayla calls behind me.

My feet start to shoot out from beneath me and I grab the iron railing. These stairs are *slick.* They're made of slippery polished wood, and they're worn down in the middle where probably thousands of people have walked on them over the past decades. I'm wearing TOMS without much tread on the bottom, and the combination is dangerous. I could break my leg on these stairs. I could slip and fall all the way to the bottom and be killed.

This would never be allowed in the United States. People would sue.

"I'm waiting," I call back to Kayla. "Be careful. I don't know why Dad didn't pick a building with an elevator."

"He said he wanted a place with three bedrooms, so we'd all have our privacy," Kayla mumbles, catching up. "Maybe that was hard to find."

She sounds like everything is her fault all over again. And . . . she's panting again. After only two flights of stairs.

We make it down the next two flights without either of us falling—a major miracle. I've got half a mind to tell Dad we have to switch apartments. It's bad enough I have to miss most of soccer camp—I really can't afford a broken leg right now. Not if I'm going to make the varsity team my freshman year like I want to.

Then I think about maybe having to share a bedroom with Kayla. Maybe I can treat these stairs like conditioning. They'll make me more graceful and agile.

The apartment lobby is dark and a little dingy, so it's a jolt when I push the door open and we're out on the street. Sunshine!

Our apartment building faces an alleyway, and if I weren't so hungry maybe I would think the cobblestones and the wrought-iron balconies and the overflowing flower boxes were adorable. Mom would. I turn toward the nearest major street. There's a restaurant on the corner with tables out on the sidewalk, and people are eating pizza and pasta and maybe paella, too—that's that special Spanish rice dish, right?

But I don't know if you go into the restaurant to ask to be seated on the sidewalk, or if you just sit down, or what. And whenever we go to Mexico, Dad always translates the Spanish for me. What if I can't even read the menu here?

And . . . okay, I probably shouldn't have left the apartment wearing the T-shirt and running shorts I slept in. I remember Dad saying Spanish people don't consider shorts and a T-shirt proper attire for a grown man, but I thought it'd be okay for someone my age.

Kayla and I are the only people in sight wearing such short shorts.

*Well, whatever*, I think. *I've got good legs.*

Kayla comes up behind me.

"You think that looks too expensive?" she asks, pointing toward the restaurant.

"No, but the food doesn't look very good," I say.

We keep walking. My stomach growls. Kayla grabs my arm.

"Look—that sign's in English!" she squeals. "Sort of. 'Dunkin' Coffee'—is that just a coffee shop, or—"

"Oh, Dad told me about that," I say. "It's what they call Dunkin' Donuts here. It's the kind of thing Dad thinks is really funny. *I* don't know why."

"Donuts," Kayla echoes wistfully.

Could we just buy a bunch of donuts and eat them? Would that be enough?

I think about soccer conditioning and want to puke.

We keep walking, past restaurant after restaurant. And I am so hungry, but you know Kayla isn't going to be able to handle a Spanish menu if I don't help her. And I really don't want to do or say anything embarrassing, not when I'm already wearing these stupid shorts. . . .

"Oh, look," Kayla says, pointing again. "That place has pictures on the wall, like at McDonald's. We could just point. Or say, '*Numero uno*,' when we order, instead of, I don't know, '*sandwich con pollo . . .*'"

She says "sandwich" the same way you do in English, and I swear, she actually pronounces the double *ls* in "*pollo*" like an *l*, not a *y*. As in "polo pony." Somehow she even manages to make "con" sound wrong, too. Like it's part of the term "con man," or "pros and cons." Like it's an English word, not Spanish.

And the restaurant she's pointing to—Pans & Company—*is* like a McDonald's. They even use the same nauseatedly bright yellow décor.

"It's fast food," I say, wrinkling my nose.

"So?" she says. "Don't we want it fast?"

She has a point.

"Okay, if that's where you want to go," I say, as though I'm being generous.

We walk in, and within minutes we both have trays full of sandwiches and fries and Coca-Cola Light. My middle school soccer coach would faint to see me eating this garbage—Coach Landon was all about healthy choices. But I'm ravenous. And the only salad on the menu looked disgusting.

We gobble down the food so quickly we don't even talk. I can practically feel the calories and caffeine hitting my system.

"I think I actually feel human again," I mutter when there's nothing left on our trays but crumpled wrappers and empty paper cups.

Kayla giggles as if I've said something funny.

"I feel . . . international," she says. "We just ate Spanish food!"

"I'm pretty sure *papas fritas* are just French fries with a different name," I tell her. But I smile anyway. I'm too full and content not to.

"Can we walk over there next?" Kayla asks, gesturing toward the front window.

She's pointing at a huge open plaza with a fountain and a statue and crowds of people. I actually recognize it from the guidebook Dad made me read, and from maps he showed me.

"Oh—that's Puerta del Sol," I say. "It's a big tourist attraction. Sure. Why not?"

We throw away our trash and walk out. We're instantly engulfed into a crowd in the street, and I remember to make sure my purse strap crosses my body, instead of dangling from my shoulder, where someone could easily grab it. Dad told me Puerta del Sol has a lot of pickpockets. But all I have in my purse is money and the apartment key, which would be easier to replace than a passport.

Funny how I can feel so relaxed about that now—now that I've had sleep and food. Dad will fix everything. Why was I so worried?

The people around us smile and laugh and point and take selfies. We move out into the plaza, and it's like a festival or a carnival. Or Disneyland or Times Square. Kayla and I stop and watch an Asian couple with two little kids in a stroller pose beside people dressed up as Mickey and Minnie Mouse. Kids in maroon shirts that say People to People walk past in pairs. Four guys with man buns and backpacks—and cute Australian accents—joke about climbing up to pose beside the man-on-a-horse statue in the center of the plaza. At least, I think they're just joking. I decide it might be fun to sit down and see if they actually do it.

"What's Tio Pepe?" Kayla asks as we find a place in the shade, at the edge of a fountain.

"Tio—? Oh, you mean the sign?" I ask, following her gaze. At the other end of the plaza, there's a huge neon sign that lights up at night. "It's a name. It means Uncle Pepe. I don't know, I think it's a brand of beer or something."

"Oh," Kayla says. She stares around like she's never before seen life-size Disney characters, neon signs, fountains, statues, or cute college guys with man buns. Maybe she hasn't.

"Is the whole summer going to be like this?" she marvels. "Eating out, hanging out in fun places together . . ."

Just the way she says "together" sours my mood.

"You're forgetting Dad wants us both to go home with perfect Spanish," I say and groan. "You do know he signed us up for immersion classes starting Monday, right? Because he doesn't want us just hanging out and having fun?"

Even that doesn't wipe the look of wonder off Kayla's face.

"Classes like that are expensive," she says. "I can see why he'd want you to have that, but—why would he pay for that for me?"

For a minute I can almost see things through Kayla's eyes. Was she thinking I would go to class while she stayed in the apartment like some scullery maid? Doing my laundry for me? Not even allowed to eat the food in the fridge without permission?

"Dad's just generous like that," I mutter.

But I almost want to ask Kayla her opinion. Maybe she knows something I don't. Why *did* Dad insist on bringing her instead of some friend whose parents could have paid for the Spanish classes themselves? His excuse about her being older and more mature is crazy. If age mattered that much, he could have hired some junior or senior from Deskins High School. Someone like that might have been really helpful. We could have really been friends. A girl like that would have known how to take me to a sit-down restaurant. And once school started, she could have watched out for me in the school hallways; she could have given me tips about parties and boys and classes. It could have been Lauren's older sister, or maybe Shannon's neighbor, Catrice Simone, whose parents gave her a BMW when she turned sixteen.

Seriously, how does Dad think Kayla is going to be useful this summer, when she doesn't even know how to pronounce "*pollo*," and she thinks fast food is a huge treat, and she doesn't know anything except, I guess, how to wash clothes in a sink?

Something hits me for the first time.

*Oh no, oh no—what if that* is *what Dad wants Kayla to teach me?* I wonder. Not the part about mispronouncing Spanish, but the part about being excited about stupid little things like greasy food, and the part about washing out underwear in a sink.

I think about Dad wanting me to do my own laundry; I think about him arguing when Mom calls him a slack-jawed yokel.

*What if Dad made me bring Kayla along on this trip because . . . because he wants me to be like her?*

## Kayla: Monday Morning

**I wake up to sunshine.** I always wake up to sunshine in Spain.

And I almost giggle at that thought, that there's an "always" about me being in Spain—that there's anything that's normal or typical or usual about me being here. I *am* getting used to waking up every morning in my cute little Spanish room, to having breakfast on our apartment's cute little balcony, to looking out over tile roofs.

But today we stop "just relaxing" and start that Spanish class Mr. Armisted wants us to take.

My stomach has a first-day-of-school feeling—*Nervous? Check. Worried? Check. Certain that I'm going to humiliate myself? Check.*

But this is not a first day of school at Crawfordsville Elementary, Middle or High School. This is a class in *Spain*, taught entirely in *Spanish*, where probably everyone else is a rich kid like Avery whose parents, duh, can pay for them to go to Spain. I won't even know anybody except Avery.

And Avery . . .

*Is this going to be a day she likes me or a day she hates me? A day she acts like we're friends or a day she ignores me?*

I cannot figure Avery out. Every night we go to a park so Avery can run—she calls it "soccer conditioning"—and the first night while she ran, Mr. Armisted had a long talk with me about Avery's moods.

"I don't know if you remember what it was like being fourteen, but Avery's mother tells me that's a difficult age for girls," he said. He stared down at the ground, and I couldn't tell who was more embarrassed, him or me. "A time of strong emotions. If she says or does anything unkind . . . well, she knows that is *not* allowed. You let me know, and I'll make sure it stops."

I wanted to say, *Oh, you mean like this afternoon, when it felt like we were friends again in that soul place—Puerta del Sol?—and then suddenly she stopped talking to me and acted like I didn't exist?*

Of course, I didn't say that. I didn't say, *Don't worry. She started pretending to be nice again when you got home.*

I didn't say, *Hello? Don't you think I'm used to kids being mean to me? Don't you think I can take it?*

But today Avery will be the only other person I know in the Spanish class. In Crawfordsville, I always know *everyone*. I know who will be out-and-out mean and who just doesn't bother talking to me. I know who's as desperate as I am, and doesn't mind serving as a biology lab partner or language arts critique buddy, if we have to pair off. I've known almost every single kid in every single one of my classes since I was in kindergarten.

Before I came to Spain, I don't think I understood how many strangers there are in the world. I walk around just looking at people, and they are *all* strangers.

*Avery probably feels the same way*, I tell myself. *Probably, she'll be glad to have me around in the Spanish class.*

*Yeah, right.*

I slide out of bed and start getting ready. Our luggage came from the airport Saturday afternoon, so I have choices of what to wear. But I still pull on the sundress Avery picked out for me at Target. It's probably the nicest thing I own.

"Girls? You both up?" Mr. Armisted calls from the hallway.

"Yes," I call back.

"Avery?" Mr. Armisted asks.

"Dad! Stop treating me like such a baby! I said I'd set an alarm and I did!"

After that, I hear hushed, murmuring voices coming from Avery's room—probably Mr. Armisted scolding Avery for being grumpy. Or promising her the sun, the moon, and the stars if she'll cheer up; that's more the kind of thing he does.

*Yeah, it's going to be a* bueno *day with Avery*, I tell myself.

I step out into the hall and head toward the bathroom just as Mr. Armisted is coming out of Avery's room. Mr. Armisted says something in Spanish I can't understand, and when I look at him blankly, he adds, "That's 'Learn a lot! Have fun!'"

"Oh," I say. "Okay."

"And make sure you and Avery leave in plenty of time to catch the Metro," he adds. "You remember how to get there and how to use it, right?"

He gave us a very detailed Metro-riding lesson over the weekend. Avery rolled her eyes the whole time.

"Sure," I say.

"Watch out for Avery," he says. "She's . . ." He shrugs, as if I'm supposed to understand.

"I will," I promise.

"I appreciate that," he says. He doesn't quite meet my eyes. He walks on down the hall and out of the apartment.

Twenty minutes later, I'm ready, but Avery still hasn't emerged from her room.

I linger over rinsing my juice glass and plate—my *vaso de jugo y* . . . I have no idea what the Spanish word for "plate" is, and anyway, what if I'm wasting all this time trying not to bother Avery, and she went back to sleep? Wouldn't she want me to wake her back up?

I make myself go over and knock at her door. I knock a little too hard—or the latch doesn't work right—and the door creaks open.

Avery is still lying in bed, hanging over the side, watching something on her iPad.

"Avery! We need to leave in five minutes!"

She cocks her head, as if listening.

"Did Dad already leave?" she whispers.

"Yes, but—"

"Good," she says. She flops over in the bed and pulls the covers up to her chin. "I'm not going today. I'm sick."

"Sick! Why didn't you tell your dad? He wouldn't make you go if he knew you were sick!" I automatically step toward her and hold out my hand, ready to feel her forehead. "Do you have a fever? Is your stomach upset?"

Avery shoves my hand away.

"Not *that* kind of sick," she says. "It's . . . you know. Cramps. I'm not telling my dad about *that*."

"Oh," I say. For about the millionth time of my life, I try to imagine being a normal girl with a normal dad who's not in a nursing home. I guess if I were Avery, I wouldn't want to tell Mr. Armisted about having my period either.

"That's why I can't go today," Avery finishes.

"Oh," I say again. I slump against the door frame, my own resolve draining out of me. "Then . . . I guess I should stay home too, and make sure you're okay. Do you want me to fix a hot water bottle for your back?"

I blush, because I sound like Grandma. Even Mom kind of makes fun of Grandma offering a hot water bottle for everything. And it's not like I've seen anything resembling Grandma's blue-glass hot water bottle anywhere in this apartment.

I swallow a lump in my throat that I refuse to believe is homesickness. I am not going to be homesick for a hot water bottle.

"*No*," Avery says. "You have to go to that Spanish class and cover for me. So Dad doesn't know I stayed home. So I don't have to explain to him about the cramps."

She blinks. And in that moment, I can see her as a three- or four-year-old again. She may be a decade older, but she has the same wide, worried greenish-gray eyes, the same sun-streaked hair, the same anguished expression she did back when we were friends. I remember, when she was three or four and I was five or six, she used to cry sometimes when Avery's nanny and my mom said playtime was over and I had to leave. This is just the same, just like that.

Well, the same except that today she's upset because I'm offering to stay, not because I'm leaving.

"You have to help me," Avery says. "You go to that Spanish class and tell me how it goes, and tonight *we'll* report to Dad what we learned."

She blinks again, all innocent-like. She's playing me. I know that. I mean, even in the nursing home there are manipulators—Mrs. Cooper wheedles for butterscotch pudding even though she's got diabetes; Mr. Bantoff tells every female who will listen what a good husband he was and how his dying wife's last wish was that he marry again. (Personally, I think her dying wish was that she wouldn't die. Unless it was to get away from him.)

Still. I weigh in my head the two ways this day could go: I could be trapped in this apartment with a cranky, moody Avery, who doesn't even want me here, or I could go to a Spanish class on the other side of Madrid with absolute strangers. Maybe it's the sunshine calling to me from outside the window. Maybe it's the thought that, after I go home from Spain, I will probably never leave Ohio again. Maybe I just don't want to fight with Avery.

But I straighten up.

"All right," I say. "If you're sure. . . ."

"Oh, I am," Avery says, blinking prettily yet again. "Thank you, Kayla. Thank you *so* much."

I walk out the door before I can tell Avery how full of it she is.

Or before I chicken out.

## Avery, Alone

**I hear the front door** whisper shut. There. Kayla's gone.

I let my whole body relax, from my scalp down to my toes.

This is the remnant of something I learned in an exercise class Mom took me to, back when she was into mother-daughter bonding, but it annoys me to remember that.

I don't have cramps. I'm not even having my period. I just couldn't get up today. I just couldn't spend another day with eager-beaver Kayla, always looking so happy and grateful and helpful and hopeful. I just . . . couldn't.

Not when I keep thinking, *Is* that *what Dad wants me to be like? That weird and awkward and oblivious?*

I feel a twinge of guilt. This isn't like me. If Shannon or Lauren were here, I wouldn't tell this kind of lie. They wouldn't let me, even if I tried—they'd see right through me. They *know* me.

I shove the guilt aside. Kayla didn't know I was lying. I didn't hurt her, one way or another. Anyhow, this is Dad's fault for yanking me out of my normal life this summer, for pulling me out of how my life was supposed to go. Back home, I don't have any problem getting up for school. At soccer camp, I was usually the first one up.

Back home, I wasn't the type of person to lose her passport, either.

Why can't I be the same here as I am at home?

*Because I need my friends. . . .*

I close my eyes. I've been staying up late every night texting and messaging and Snapchatting back and forth with Shannon and Lauren and my other friends. Between the time difference and my iPhone being worthless without Wi-Fi, that's the *only* time I can connect. For my friends, it's six p.m. to midnight—normal times to text. For me it's midnight to two, four, six a.m. This schedule is killing me. Maybe I'm still jet-lagged, too. It would be great to slip back into sleep for another four or five hours. But the sunshine streaming in my window is *so* bright. My eyelids can't seem to block out any of it. I might as well be staring straight at the sun.

*Hasn't Spain ever heard of room-darkening shades?* I grumble to myself.

I get up, head into the kitchen, and grab an orange. Spanish oranges *are* really amazing. I take the orange and an energy bar and a water bottle out onto the teensy-tiny balcony and look down at our alleyway, even though it makes me a little dizzy.

Last night I came out here to text because my prison-cell-size room was starting to feel like a cage. There's a dance club down on the corner, and even though Dad would kill me before he'd let me go to a place like that, I was thinking maybe I could record a little audio and make my friends *think* I was going to places like that. Our apartment's soundproofed or something, but out on the balcony you can hear everything. Maybe I could go back to school as the kid who knows all the hot new European music.

But guess what? The joke's on me, because that club was playing nothing but *eighties* music. You hear eighties music all over the place over here—in restaurants, in stores, in taxicabs . . . I asked Dad why Spaniards love eighties music so much, and he actually managed to keep a straight face when he said, "Because Spain has a long tradition of appreciating great culture."

Right. Boy George, Wham!, Madonna . . . *Ugh.*

Of course the dance club's closed this morning, and the street is quiet. Dad says Spain parties late and sleeps late and goes to work late and then expects a long lunch break. And he won't say it, because he's Mr. Diplomacy, but that could be the reason his company's having so much trouble getting the new subsidiary they bought to show a profit.

It is kind of nice sitting on the balcony eating breakfast in the sunshine, with nowhere to go, nowhere I have to be, no one to bother me. It's like I have the world to myself.

Then I'm done eating, and there's nothing to do. All my friends are asleep right now, and nothing online would have changed much since last night. Something gurgles behind me—something with the air conditioner, I guess. A lot of Spanish buildings don't even have air-conditioning, and Dad says we're lucky we don't have to make do with fans. But the air conditioner isn't the best, and the landlord told us someone has to empty this huge tub of water from it every night or it will break down.

Dad thinks Kayla and I are taking turns doing that, but we never officially set up who was doing which night. I guess she just started taking care of it.

Why couldn't we have rented an apartment where everything worked? Besides the air-conditioning, the washer is still messed up too. And the water heater is annoying—*it* wasn't broken that first day, but you have to switch it on five minutes before you need it, and then it shuts itself off afterward.

Someone's whistling down below. I peek down through the railing, and there's a man with a toolbox headed toward our building.

I remember that Dad talked about having someone come fix the washer someday this week. What if it's this guy?

Mom always freaks out about having workers at our house if I'm home alone. This is something else I've heard Mom and Dad argue about. Dad's side of it was, *Don't be so paranoid. What do you think is going to happen? I'm not so high up in the company that anyone's going to kidnap my daughter and hold her for ransom.*

And Mom's reply was, *Why does everything have to be about you and your money? It's not just kidnapping we have to worry about. What's wrong with you, that you don't want to protect your little girl?*

Dad: *She's not a "little" girl.*

Mom: *Exactly!*

Thinking about their arguments makes my stomach hurt.

The washer repair guy is going to think he's coming into an empty apartment. I could just hide in my bedroom and be quiet until he's gone.

Except that would make my prison-cell-size room seem even more prison-like. What if he's here for hours?

I could also leave before he gets here. I look down at what I'm wearing: running shorts and a T-shirt. Not exactly street attire, but . . .

*It's not weird if I'm on my way to work out*, I tell myself.

It's not like there's a gym nearby, but I could go to the park and get a long run in now, before it gets too hot. If I start running twice a day, I will really be in shape for soccer tryouts when I go home. And—it's something that I like. That I choose.

I slip back into the apartment. I stuff my feet into socks and my running shoes, and I'm out the front door in a flash. When I get down to the street, I see that the man with the toolbox is going into the building next door, where there's some sort of renovation project going on.

I should have figured that out.

But I'm already outside. A breeze tugs at my hair, and it makes me feel like a little kid again, like when I used to talk my nanny into letting me play on the playground for hours. Nobody knows me here. I can do what I want.

I turn toward the park and take off, my feet already propelling me into a jog.

## Kayla, on Her Own

**The Spanish classroom is on** the third floor. Of course it's on the third floor. Whoever designed Spanish streets and buildings likes to make people suffer by having to walk as far as possible. It would have been nice to stand in the entryway of the school for a few moments, and bask in the glow of having found the right building. Of having navigated the subway and reached this school on my own. Victory!

But I have only a minute left to climb two flights of stairs. I'm not victorious yet.

I take a deep breath and start hiking up. Rivers of sweat trickle under my dress. I reach the first landing. The second. As senile old Mrs. Grayson at the nursing home likes to shout out at the oddest times, thank the good Lord almighty, for all his mercies. I don't have to climb up any more stairs.

But as I move down the hall, all I see are dark classrooms labeled with the wrong numbers: twenty-three, twenty-four, twenty-five . . .

Was I so delirious climbing those steps that I counted wrong?

I go back to the stairway and climb halfway up the next flight. Above me I can see the first classroom of the floor above: thirty-one.

I climb the rest of the way up, trying to figure it all out.

*Oh, wait. Is that what Avery and her dad were talking about the other day, how people in Spain don't count floors the same way Americans do? So when they said our apartment was on the fourth floor . . . have we really been climbing up and down* five *flights of stairs every single time we go in or out? And . . . I've just followed along?*

No wonder I feel so exhausted already. Exercise is deadly.

Finally, I see classroom thirty-eight, and I slip inside the door. It's my bad luck that the door opens into the front of the room, and the teacher has already started talking. I couldn't even begin to guess her age—it's somewhere between twenty-five and fifty. She's one of those severe-looking European ladies with her hair pulled back in a tight twist. And while I'm sweating in a sundress, she's got on long sleeves with fitted wrists. She looks like she doesn't even possess sweat glands. She turns my way with one eyebrow raised so high I think maybe it could reach the fifth floor.

"*Buenos dias*," she says, and then a whole bunch of other Spanish words I don't understand.

"Um, I don't really speak Spanish, so could you say that again in English?" I whisper.

She says something else in Spanish. At least, I think it's Spanish. It could be Swahili, for all I understand. No, wait, she's saying the same thing again and again, making the words slower and slower and slower. And then I get it: She's saying, "*En español, por favor.*"

"Um, *no hablo español*?" I say. *I don't speak Spanish. Come on, lady, can't you tell how completely I can't speak Spanish?*

The other eyebrow shoots up, and she releases another stream of Spanish. But she also points to a desk in the back of the room. I can read hand gestures. I trip my way toward that desk like it's the Promised Land and I'm one of the Israelites who's been wandering in the wilderness for forty years.

I melt into the desk and imagine turning myself invisible, just like I'm always invisible back at Crawfordsville High School.

*I'm nothing but a puddle of sweat in this wooden seat—why would anyone want to look at me?*

The teacher's voice flows over and around me. Her dark eyes are still directed at me. Oh, good grief, she's asking me another question. She holds up a piece of paper and points at it.

"Ka-ee-la Boots *o* Avery Armisted?" she repeats.

Oh, she's trying to take attendance. I point to myself.

"Kayla," I say. "Or, I guess, Ka-ee-la. Whichever."

*"En español."* The teacher glowers again.

*"Yo soy Ka-eel-a,"* I say, and even I know that's wrong. You're supposed to introduce yourself with some phrase that sounds like you're talking about a pet llama. The teacher mutters something—correcting me, I think—but I see her put a check mark next to my name.

"And Avery—I mean, *y* Avery—she's sick," I say.

The teacher raises an eyebrow at me again, waiting. She could wait forever for me to translate that into Spanish, because I do not know the Spanish word for "sick." Still, she waits. Maybe she is going to wait forever. I can feel the silence in the room like it's part of the air—the thick, heavy, hot air blanketing us all. There are fifteen or twenty other kids in the class, and they're all turned toward me like they're waiting too. Nobody's whispering or passing notes or typing into their cell phones under their desks. They're just watching me.

If I ever learn the Spanish word for "sick," believe me, I will never forget it.

"You know, *sick*," I say. And then, because I have to do something to stop everyone from staring at me forever, I open my mouth and mime putting my finger down my throat. I mime gagging and vomiting.

The boy next to me, a tall, thin beanpole of a kid, shouts out, "*Enfermos!*"

He jumps from his seat and runs toward the door. No, not toward the door—he grabs the trash can sitting in the corner and runs it back to me.

"*Ella es enfermos!*" he cries, holding the trash can under my chin like he's encouraging me to throw up into it.

The teacher laughs. Laughs! And then she starts to applaud.

"*Ella está enferma*," she says, very precisely, enunciating every syllable. I guess Beanpole Boy's grammar wasn't right either. She goes on, and the only word I can make out in this new stream of Spanish is "*actores*," but it's weird—it's like I really do understand what she means. I think she's praising Beanpole Boy for helping me, and maybe even praising both of us for acting out what we didn't know how to say.

Finally, the teacher looks away from me and starts talking about something else. Beanpole Boy lowers the trash can and shoves it back toward the corner. He sits back down.

"*Gracias*," I whisper to him.

"*De nada*," he says.

Oh my gosh. I just had a conversation in Spanish. With a boy.

## Avery, Still Alone

**Did you see my Instagram?** I type into my phone.

A moment later, **Yeah, yeah** pops up on my screen from Shannon. Lauren must have decided Shannon could speak for both of them, because nothing comes back from her. I wait, but Shannon doesn't write anything else.

I hold myself back from typing what I really want to say, which is, *Oh, come on. My pictures of Retiro Park are* beautiful. *They are the best things any of us have ever posted on Instagram. You're my best friends. Where's the love?*

I remember Shannon telling me once that she has automatic replies set up on her texting program, so she can just hit one key when somebody's sent her something she really doesn't care about, but it'd be rude not to reply at all.

I wonder if *Yeah, yeah* is one of her auto-replies.

I click back to Instagram. I only have twenty likes so far, and four of them are from things like @madridtravel, because of how I tagged my collage. So—only sixteen likes from actual friends.

*My pictures* are *beautiful, aren't they?* I wonder.

Maybe all my real friends are just jealous.

I put down my phone. It's nine o'clock here, which means it's only three o'clock in the afternoon back home. Probably Shannon and Lauren's afternoon break at soccer camp ended a little early. Probably that's all that happened.

What am I supposed to do when everybody who really matters is on a completely different time from me, on a completely different continent?

I stand up and stretch my legs, which are cramping from all the running I did earlier in the day. I may have pushed myself a little too hard on my morning run, but I did a long cool-down. I started just walking around Retiro Park, and then I started taking pictures on my phone. . . . It was strange to be there alone, but also kind of cool. I took, like, fifty pictures of the Neptune sculpture by the little lake in Retiro, and there was no one whining at me, *Come on. Aren't you done yet?* I could wait until the sun was in the perfect spot, until the paddle boats were at the exact right angle away from the dock.

But that was this morning, and except for dinner with Kayla and Dad, I've mostly been alone all day.

When was the last time I spent so much time alone?

Have I ever?

I decide to grace Dad with my presence—unlike Mom, he doesn't call it "bonding" when we spend time together, but I know he likes it. But when I push my door open, I find he's at the kitchen table with his back to me. He's hunched over his laptop with his phone to his ear.

"No," I hear him say. "That would backfire. Morale is already at rock bottom—yes, their unemployment rate is high, but that doesn't make them feel good about having to work for their corporate American overlords. . . . I jest, I jest, but try putting yourself in their shoes. . . ."

Work stuff. It could be hours before he comes up for air.

I start to step back into my room, but then I see that

Kayla's door is kind of half-open. I should probably thank her for covering for me earlier today. Dad came home early—right behind Kayla, actually—so there wasn't time for us to confer and make up any good stories. So at dinner, every time Dad asked a question like, "What did you learn today?" or "What were the other kids like?" I would say something vague like, "Oh, we learned so much!" or "They were fine," and then Kayla filled in details. She said the teacher, Señora Gomez, doesn't speak any English at all, and a lot of the other kids are actually from Bulgaria, of all places, and most of them don't speak any English either, unless you count things they've learned from movies, like, *May the Force be with you*. Which I guess would be kind of funny with a Bulgarian accent.

Dad asked once, "Avery, did you like the Bulgarian kids too?" and I said, "Sure." I thought maybe he would ask something else, and maybe even figure out that I'd skipped the whole class. But he just started reminiscing about how he had so much trouble with Spanish back when he was first learning it.

And then he got a work call, and dinner was over.

This is how desperate I am tonight: I'm actually looking forward to talking to Kayla. I'm seeking her out.

But when I poke my head around the corner, she's not reading or playing on her phone or watching TV like I thought. She's turned away from the door, facing Dad's iPad propped up on her desk. I can't see the screen, but she's apparently Skyping or FaceTiming with someone.

"No, Spanish people don't just look like Mexicans," she's saying. "A lot of them don't even have dark hair. That surprised me. I guess I should have known that, but . . . nobody warned me."

An old man's voice rumbles out from the iPad speaker, "Yeah, Elmer, it's not like someone learns how to speak Spanish and their hair turns dark."

"You two old fools need to stop asking stupid questions," an old lady's querulous voice interrupts. "Kayla, honey, are they feeding you okay? I know those Europeans eat strange things sometimes. . . ."

She says "European" like it's part of the punchline in that stupid old kid's joke: *I can tell where you're from, 'cause you're a'peein'!*

I try not to giggle, and listen for Kayla's reply.

"Yes, Mrs. Lang, I'm getting plenty to eat," Kayla says. "Mr. Armisted had food delivered to our apartment before we even got here. And we've been eating out a lot too. At fancy restaurants."

We have not been eating at fancy restaurants. We've been eating at restaurants that would have made Mom sniff at Dad, *Slumming again, David? If you want to eat like the locals, you should at least try eating like the* rich *locals!*

Kayla is going on and on about the "fancy" restaurants.

"They bring out these little plates of olives and cheese and meat as soon as you sit down," she says. "And those olives—I've never eaten olives like those. I have *dreams* about those olives. But . . . I'm also really craving Doritos. Isn't it weird, I haven't seen any Doritos in Spain? I thought you would be able to get those anywhere!"

"And 'Dorito' sounds so much like a Spanish word!" one of the old people she's talking to marvels.

I can't hold back my giggles over that one, but at least I manage to keep them totally quiet. I can't let Kayla know I'm behind her.

"And everyone's being nice to you, right, honey?" It's the same querulous old-lady voice from before. Mrs. Lang, I guess. "All those foreigners—they better not be mean to you!"

"Don't worry, all the foreigners have been nice," Kayla says.

She pauses, and I wait for her to say, *Avery and Mr. Armisted have been nice too*. But she doesn't.

"At that class today," she says instead, "we had to break into pairs, to practice our conversational Spanish. And two of the Bulgarian boys, Andrei and Dragomir, they kind of argued over who got to team up with me. At least I think that's what they were saying—it was in Bulgarian, so it was hard to tell."

"Of *course* those foreign boys are fighting over you!" Mrs. Lang again. "You're a beautiful girl."

"I *think* it's just because I'm an American," Kayla says. "If I understood him right, Andrei said he'd never met an American before."

"Oh, pish, Americans." Another old lady's voice. "I've never met anything *but* Americans. I never got to have adventures when I was young like you."

"You're American *and* beautiful." It's an old man this time. "I bet those foreign boys weren't fighting over Avery as much as they were fighting over you. Were they?"

"Um, no," Kayla says. She starts to glance back over her shoulder, as if she's looking toward my room or out toward Dad in the living room. I duck behind the door frame. "Avery wasn't in the room then. She was . . . busy somewhere else."

I'm kind of amazed. Kayla's keeping my secret even from a bunch of old people back in Nowheresville, Ohio.

A younger, official-sounding voice says from the iPad, "It's almost time for the residents to get their medications before dinner."

"All right," Kayla says. "Good-bye, everyone."

"You'll do a TV show for us again tomorrow, won't you?" It's another old lady, whose voice sounds so simultaneously sad and hopeful that it sends shivers down my spine.

"It's not a TV show, Mrs. Reeves. It's something called Skype," Kayla explains patiently. "It's like using a phone with video. But yes, of course I'll call again tomorrow."

"Your calls are the most interesting thing that have happened at Autumn Years since I've been here," a man says. "I could listen all night. No matter what that sourpuss nurse Brenda says."

"I heard that!" the nurse retorts.

There's laughter—old-people laughter—but it still makes me feel a little sad and left out. Which is crazy, because it's not like I'm jealous of Kayla talking to a bunch of old people in a nursing home. I'm not.

The laughter shuts off, and I can tell Kayla hit the end call button. I knock softly at her door. Kayla turns around, the soft smile on her face hardening into something that looks a lot more like fear.

Though I've got to be wrong about that. What does she have to be afraid of?

"Oh, were you talking to someone?" I ask, pretending I just walked in.

"Your dad said I could use his iPad anytime," Kayla says, almost as if I've accused her of stealing. "I Skype with my mom and grandparents every night. And with my friends."

"High school friends?" I ask. My voice sounds mean, even to me. I don't know why I had to say that.

"Just friends," Kayla says, her voice tight.

I really do know how to be nice. It's not like I *want* to be mean.

"Thank you for not saying anything to my dad," I tell her. "About . . . you know."

"Sure," Kayla says. "Are you feeling better?"

"Some," I say.

"So you'll go tomorrow, right?"

Does she want me to?

It's weird that I'm even wondering that.

"I heard something you said a little bit ago. I mean, not that I was eavesdropping—the walls are kind of thin," I rush to explain. "Did you really have boys fighting over you in that class today?"

Kayla recoils as if I've punched her.

"I . . . ," she begins. She drops her head, winces, then jerks back up. "The old people at the nursing home where Mom works like to hear happy stories. Their lives are hard enough without me telling them anything sad."

"So there *weren't* boys fighting over you," I say, and I almost sound relieved, like that's how things should be.

"I don't know, Avery," Kayla says, sweeping her arms out in an exasperated gesture. "We weren't speaking the same language. I barely understood anything today. But . . . that's how it *seemed*."

For a moment, I think I see how she must have looked Skyping with all those old people. For just that split second, her eyes are wide and excited, and her broad cheeks don't seem bloated but . . . generous. Joyous.

She *is* pretty. She can be.

She has European guys interested in her.

"I won't go tomorrow," I say. "You can have your choice of the Bulgarian boys."

In my head, the words sound magnanimous, but as soon as they're out, something in Kayla's face shuts down.

*Oh. Because I made it sound like if I'm there, nobody would look at her.*

"I mean, because then you'll still be the only American!" I rush to explain. "You'll still be . . . exotic!"

This only makes things worse. Kayla could never be exotic. She's *chubby*. Her hair's frizzy. She's like a walking ad for Walmart. Or wherever poor people shop.

"Okay," Kayla says, in a voice as rigid as steel.

And it's funny. English is the language I understand. I know what "okay" means. But it really feels like Kayla is saying, *Whatever. It's not like you're my friend, anyway. It's not like you and I could ever be friends.*

I didn't even do anything!

I hear Dad coming down the hall behind me.

"Avery?" he calls. "Your mom's on the phone. She wants to talk to you."

He hands me his phone and I put it to my ear.

"Sure! Everything's fine!" I tell her.

Because that's all she ever wants to hear.

Huh. I guess she's like Kayla's old people.

## Kayla, after Another Day of Spanish Class

**I giggle to myself as** I walk home from the Metro.

Andrei, the Bulgarian kid I thought of as Beanpole Boy the first day, is such a clown. Any time he understands a Spanish word that I'm confused about, he starts acting it out for me. Señora Gomez saw him doing that today when she was giving a lesson about taking the subway, and instead of yelling at him she had both of us go to the front of the class and pretend to work a ticket machine.

I would *never* have willingly acted out anything in front of a whole class back in Crawfordsville. All my teachers would have known not to ask me.

But I don't know anybody here, so it doesn't matter.

And Andrei was so funny, shouting, "*Pongo! Dinero! En la maquina!*" as he pantomimed paying for his ticket.

At one of our breaks, I tried to ask him and the other Bulgarian kids why they wanted to learn Spanish—what good is it to know Spanish in Bulgaria? I *think* he said that they couldn't afford to sign up for any language programs in England, because it's more expensive to live there for the summer than Spain. He spent a long time toying around with his phone after that, and I thought he was embarrassed. But then he played something from a translation app, and it was a robotic voice repeating in English what he just had typed in Bulgarian, because he wanted to make sure I understood:

*It is better to learn something than nothing at all.*

No kid I know back in Crawfordsville would ever say that, in any language.

The kids who are class clowns at Crawfordsville High School act out because they *don't* want to learn anything, not because they're trying to help the teacher.

And it's not like the Bulgarian kids are just nerdy brainiacs, because Dragomir told me he's getting everyone he can to play football every day after class. Well, I guess it's actually *fútbol*—soccer—not American football. But that's cool. He even invited me today, but I said no, because I had to get home.

Not that I'd be any good at playing any sport, anyway.

It's just amazing that Dragomir and Andrei and the others talk to me so much: about *fútbol* and about this restaurant that they're obsessed with called 100 Montaditos, and about all the ways Spain is different from Bulgaria, and what's America like?

I mean, I think that's what they're talking about.

I got off at the Puerta del Sol Metro stop, so most of the people around me are tourists; the stores and restaurants around me are tourist spots. And it's funny how I can tell that now. The neighborhood by the school isn't a place where tourists usually go, so when I'm there it always feels like I'm spying a little bit: *Oh, that's what Spanish people keep on their apartment balconies. That's how they hang their wash out on the line to dry. They really do shop in those little corner fruit markets, like Señora Gomez told us about in class. She wasn't lying. (Well, if I actually understood her right, when she described Spaniards buying fruit.)*

I'll have to remember to tell Avery the lesson was about

food and transportation today, so she's ready to answer her dad's questions at dinner.

My giggles stop. Avery. I can't decide what I'm maddest about: that she's making me lie to her dad, or that she's got a dad who brought her all the way to Spain and is paying for her to go to some special fancy Spanish class—and all she wants to do is lie in bed watching Netflix and texting her friends back home. This is the fourth day in a row she's missed. She's not even pretending anymore that it has to do with cramps.

Maybe I'll walk up the stairs and yell at her, *It is better to learn something than nothing at all, Avery!*

I can't help it. I giggle again, imagining that.

It wouldn't have much of an effect, anyway, with me huffing and puffing from climbing up the stairs. The *five* flights of stairs, even though we're only on the fourth floor, because the Spanish lie when they're counting floors.

I turn off the main street and head up the alley toward our apartment building, with its wrought-iron railings at every balcony, its tidy rows of window boxes spilling over with flowers. On Saturday, I'll see if the nursing home can move my Skyping time earlier in the day, and maybe Mr. Armisted will let me bring the iPad outside, so I can show everyone back in Crawfordsville what this street looks like. Or will the Wi-Fi not work this far away? Grandma and Grandpa don't have Wi-Fi back home, so I always have to go to the library or the nursing home if I want to use a computer. So I'm just figuring these things out.

I'm good at unlocking the front door of the apartment building now, even though I couldn't figure it out at all that first day.

I step into the lobby. There's a strange man in a uniform I don't recognize standing by the row of mailboxes.

"*Disculpe*," I murmur, reaching past him to open the box for our apartment. Picking up the mail is something else that Mr. Armisted wanted Avery and me to take turns being responsible for, but—yeah, you guessed it—Avery never does.

Of course, Mr. Armisted also thinks Avery and I are going back and forth to school every day together. He probably thinks we skip and hold hands, too, like we did when we were little.

*Oh well, Avery's loss*, I think. She can ignore me all summer—I'll make other friends. That's already happening. And then we'll go back home and we won't have anything to do with each other, ever again.

There's nothing in the mailbox, and I flip it shut, pull my key out, and take a deep breath, ready to start on those crazy stairs.

But the man in the uniform suddenly springs to life. He starts practically jumping up and down, and pointing at the mailbox I just opened. He reels off a long string of Spanish, and I'm lost before he even gets to the second syllable.

"I don't speak Spanish," I say. "Sorry."

He points at the 4I label taped on my key. I was so confused at first about why our apartment is "4I," when the only other door on our floor is "4D." Why isn't there a 4A, 4B, 4C, etc.? But Avery actually asked about it, and it's not anything alphabetical; it's fourth floor left side and fourth floor right side—*izquierda* and *derecha*.

Maybe there are apartment buildings in big cities in the United States where it would be 4L and 4R.

The longer I'm here, the more I realize I don't know anything.

"*¿Es esta su piso?*" the man asks—or something like that. I think "*piso*" means "floor," not "apartment," but he had to have seen the *I* part too.

"Yes," I say. "I mean, *sí*."

I don't understand what he says after that, but he sounds really happy. He holds out a stiff, formal-looking envelope addressed to Mr. Armisted. The man also holds out a little machine, like a credit-card machine, and hands me a stylus. He wants me to sign.

"I'm not David Armisted," I say.

The man grabs my hand and presses it toward the machine. The stylus makes a line and two dots on the screen.

"But I'm not—"

The man keeps jabbering away. He points to the stairs.

"*Gracias. Gracias*," he says.

Oh. He's thanking me for signing for the envelope so he didn't have to climb five flights of stairs.

I actually understand!

"*De nada*," I say, as though I've been speaking Spanish my whole life.

I glance down at the envelope—I haven't committed Mr. Armisted to paying thousands of dollars for some unwanted letter, have I? But the return address is the records division of the state of California. It's got to be Avery's birth certificate.

I think Mr. Armisted actually would pay thousands of dollars for that.

"*Gracias*," I tell the delivery man.

I am just speaking Spanish like crazy now.

The man heads for the door out to the street, and I start

climbing the stairs. It's not so bad if I pause on every landing. I can do this if I'm alone or with both Avery and Mr. Armisted, because he likes to pause every now and then too. But any time I'm with Avery, it's like she's a mountain goat, and she gets annoyed that I slow her down.

I guess the only time I climbed up and down these stairs just with her was that first day, when we went to Pans & Company and then sat in Puerta del Sol. And she seemed to get mad at me for no reason, over nothing.

*Well, she's got her birth certificate now, so she can get her passport right away*, I think. *Maybe she'll beg and plead with Mr. Armisted, and she'll get her way, and she can be mad at me in London or Paris or Lisbon, not just in Madrid.*

Being annoyed with Avery gets me up the stairs with only two breaks to catch my breath. I unlock the door to our apartment and call, "Hey, Avery, your birth certificate just arrived."

She dashes out from her room as if she's actually eager to greet me—or to get her birth certificate, anyway.

"Let me see," she demands.

I stifle the impulse to say, *Hello to you, too*. Or I could be really bratty and spout off, *Buenas tardes*, and a bunch of other Spanish words, and make it seem like I've learned tons in the Spanish class she's been skipping.

Nope. I couldn't carry that off.

Avery takes the envelope from my hand and pulls the little tab on the back to open it.

"It's addressed to your dad, not you," I can't resist saying.

"Yeah, but it's *my* birth certificate," she says. "And Dad says government bureaucrats mess things up all the time. If there's any problem, we'll want to know right away, so Dad can call and make them fix their mistake."

It figures she thinks other people are going to make mistakes. When it was her mistake—losing her passport—that meant her dad had to order her birth certificate in the first place.

Avery pulls a sheet of paper out of the envelope. I can't help looking over her shoulder.

"Certificate of live birth," she reads, and giggles. "Okay, good to know I'm alive!"

"Avery Nicole Armisted, female, single—who would expect a baby to be married?" I ask, lulled by her giggle into making a joke of my own. I brace for her to tell me it's a stupid question; that word in that box just means she wasn't a twin or a triplet.

But Avery gasps and moves the certificate farther back, then closer to her eyes.

"What?" she says in a strangled voice. "That's not my mom's name!"

I bring my own head down, peering more closely.

"Stacy Lynn Carter?" I read numbly.

"There *is* a mistake!" Avery complains. "This is wrong! Those stupid bureaucrats just put down some random name, and—"

I grab Avery's arm.

"But Avery," I say. "That's not random. That's *my* mom's name!"

## Avery, Stunned and Outraged

**"Your mom's last name is** Butts," I tell Kayla, like she's the stupidest person alive. "Stacy Butts."

"That's her married name," Kayla says. "Her maiden name was—"

"Don't say it!" I warn. It's like I can stop any of this from being true if I don't let her finish. I blink again at the birth certificate, as if that will make the right name appear. But that just makes me see that "Carter" is listed as a maiden name. There's no space for a married name.

"This is just a coincidence," I snarl at Kayla. "Just a really dumb mistake."

"Your dad and my mom?" Kayla sputters out. "They didn't . . . They wouldn't have . . . ."

"No, of course not," I snap. This, at least, is something Kayla and I can agree on.

I drop the birth certificate and go running for my phone.

Kayla catches the certificate in midair.

"Mom was already married," she says. "I was already born. My dad . . . my dad had just had his accident. . . ."

She's almost whispering, but the words still cut like knives.

"Dad will fix this," I say.

I dash into my room and retrieve my stupid burner phone from the tangle of sheets and blankets on my bed. I hit the call button like *I'm* swinging a knife.

"Honey, this isn't a good time," Dad says, by way of a hello.

"This is an emergency," I tell him. My voice doesn't even sound like my own. "You have to come home."

"Are you okay?" he asks, and I can tell he's snapped into high alert. "Remember, the emergency number in Spain is one-one-two, not nine-one-one, and you should call immediately if . . . Is something wrong with Kayla?"

Just the way he says Kayla's name feels wrong.

*If this birth certificate says my parents are my dad and Kayla's mom, then what does her birth certificate say? Could my dad be . . .*

I don't let myself finish the thought.

"We don't need nine-one-one," I tell Dad. "We need you home. Now."

"What happened?" Dad begs.

"My birth certificate came," I say. "And it's got the wrong name on it. The wrong *mother's* name."

Dad goes silent. And it's a *long* silence. This is all wrong. He's supposed to say, *Avery, what are you talking about? That doesn't make sense. Are you sure you aren't reading the wrong line? Like maybe the doctor's name or something? Look for Celeste Marin Armisted. Or Celeste Marin Sterling, if it's the maiden name listed. You know your mother's name!*

Finally, finally, finally, Dad says, "Oh."

"*That's* all you can say?" I rage. "'Oh'? When you and Mom have evidently been lying to me my whole life? When—"

"It's not what you think," Dad begins. "We didn't—"

But I can't bear to hear whatever he's going to say next. I stab my finger at the phone to end the call. A split second later, the phone starts ringing, but I don't answer it. I will never answer any of Dad's calls again. I will never even speak to him again.

I let myself fall back flat on the bed.

"What did he say?" Kayla hovers just outside the doorway of my room, like she's afraid to step inside.

"Nothing," I mumble.

"Nothing?" Kayla repeats. "He didn't have any—"

"Shut up," I tell her, and I don't care how rude I sound. "I'm thinking."

But my thoughts don't go anywhere except in circles: *This isn't possible. This doesn't make sense. There's no way. This isn't possible. . . .*

"Would your mother . . . ," Kayla begins, and it's a lifeline.

*Mom*, I think.

I know my mother. My parents have been married for a million years. (I do the actual math: It's twenty-three years. They were married for nine years before I was born.) If Dad had an affair and the other woman got pregnant, there is no way in the entire universe that Mom would adopt the other woman's child and raise it (her? me?) as her own. There is no set of circumstances under which that would happen. My mom knows how to watch out for herself. She has rules. Boundaries. No one—and I mean, no one—crosses those boundaries.

If Dad had an affair, she'd divorce him so fast his head would spin.

Not that my dad would ever have an affair.

And I look like my mom. I do.

So there. I've proved it. The mother's name on my birth certificate is just one huge mistake.

*But what about the way my dad said, "Oh"?*

I reach up, grab my pillow, and pull down it over my face.

"Avery?" Kayla calls from the doorway. "Don't hurt yourself. Whatever this means, that's no reason to . . ."

Seriously? She thinks I'm going to suffocate myself over this?

She must, because she steps into and across the room—the floorboards creak beneath her lumbering feet—and she tugs the pillow back from my face.

"I'm not doing anything!" I snarl at her. "Go away!"

I grab the pillow back. I sit up and clutch the pillow against my stomach, as if I'm just daring her to take it away again.

Kayla takes a step back.

"I'm sorry," she whispers.

I hold the pillow tighter. I hunch over like I have to protect it, like it's a . . .

Baby.

My mind's eye jumps, and I can see how I'm sitting; I can see exactly what I look like. Back home, there's a picture that's been hanging in our upstairs hallway for as long as I can remember. It's Mom holding me when I was a tiny baby—a newborn. Mom's wearing a red sweater shot through with threads of gold that almost look like brocade. The gold glints a little, and it's echoed in the gold highlights in Mom's hair and even in the peach fuzz of my own hair, peeking out from my baby blankets. Mom took a lot of art history classes in college; back when Mom and Dad were getting along better, I can remember him joking once that she always wanted to reenact her own *Madonna and Child* portrait. But who could blame her? It's a beautiful picture. *She* looks amazing.

*Can a woman really look that good right after giving birth?* I wonder.

I think about the childbirth video they showed us in eighth-grade health class. They cut away really fast from showing the actual birth, but they had interviews with mothers immediately afterward, and they all looked *awful*. Like, if you knew you were going to be on camera, wouldn't you at least comb your hair?

*But the point of those childbirth videos was to make us girls think we wouldn't want to get pregnant. At least, not until we're thirty, which is practically forever. So maybe they were making those women look terrible on purpose*, I tell myself.

If anyone was going to look beautiful and perfectly made-up after going through childbirth, it'd be my mom.

So there, again.

I'm still not convinced.

"I said, go away!" I repeat to Kayla, and it's almost like I'm just talking to my own brain, my own thoughts. I want to stop analyzing. I want to go back to five minutes ago, when I didn't wonder anything about my parents.

Or about Kayla's mom.

"Fine," Kayla whispers.

She keeps walking backward and rams her thigh into the corner of my desk. I see tears spring into the corners of her eyes, and I *should* say something kind and sympathetic. I should apologize.

I just can't.

Then Kayla's out the door. I don't know where she goes. I don't care. I stay huddled on my bed, because that's all I can do.

I don't know how much time passes before I hear the door of the apartment banging open, and Dad crying breathlessly, "Avery? Avery, honey, where are you?"

Then I find I can use my legs again. I spring up and go running toward him. I forget I was never going speak to him again. I reach him before he's taken three steps past the front door. He wraps his arms around my shoulders and pulls me close.

"Oh, Avery," he breathes into my hair.

I let him hug me. This is my dad—my daddy—who's always been able to make things better.

"I kept trying to call your mom from the cab getting here, but she never picked up," he says. "You really should hear this . . . explanation . . . from both of us."

I shove back against Dad's chest. I pull away from him.

"I am not waiting until you fly Mom over here to talk to me," I say. "Or until we go home."

"No, that wouldn't be fair," he mutters distractedly. He runs his fingers through his hair, and it sticks up in tufts. He doesn't notice. "I was thinking we should bring her in remotely. She could Skype in and—"

He's reaching into his pocket like he wants to pull out his phone and try calling Mom again. I grab his wrist to stop him.

"I just found out my mother isn't my real mother, and you want to set up a conference call?" I ask incredulously.

"Right, right," he murmurs.

"Wait—am I right that Mom isn't my mom?" I wail.

"No! I mean, she *is* your mom, but . . . Where's Kayla? Did she see your birth certificate too?" Dad asks, glancing around. "If she did, then—"

"Oh, *Kayla*," I erupt, because how could he worry about her right now?

*Unless she really is his daughter too? Who knows who anyone's parents are now?*

A floorboard in the hallway squeaks, and I see Kayla creeping out, her face tearstained, her hair tangled. But she doesn't say anything. She is such a mouse. Such a timid, ugly, colorless little mouse.

Dad actually goes to her and pats her shoulder.

"I know this must seem very confusing to you," he says. "We could have *your* mom talk to you by Skype. Or . . . you could just call her right now and let her explain her side of things . . . I'd let you use my phone. You could talk as long as you want."

"Mom's at work right now, and she's never allowed to get personal calls unless someone's died," Kayla says in the tiniest voice ever. "Besides. I don't want to talk to my mom right now."

Dad grimaces.

"Oh," he says. "Then . . ."

He squares his shoulders, and I can practically see him shifting into business executive mode. One time I overheard him on the phone with somebody he'd just had to fire. He's got that same tone in his voice now, the tone that says, *This is going to be a really unpleasant conversation, but I am the most patient man alive. No matter what you say, I will stay calm and reasonable. You will not even be able to tell that I have feelings.*

"Both of you, sit down," Dad says, steering Kayla and me toward the couch. He sits down in the chair across from us.

This apartment living room is tiny, but it feels like the narrow coffee table between the couch and the chair has grown.

Dad might as well be on the other side of the Grand Canyon. Or like Mom: on the other side of the entire Atlantic Ocean.

I want to ask, *Why are you putting me with Kayla? Why isn't it you and me on the couch and Kayla alone in the chair?*

But my throat seems to have grown shut. Or my vocal cords have stopped working. I can't say anything.

Dad looks down at his hands, looks back at me and Kayla.

"Avery, you are absolutely my daughter *and* your mother's daughter," he says. "We never lied about that. You have her genes and mine. Period. That birth certificate is wrong. A nurse in the hospital filled out the original paperwork wrong, but we *thought* we'd cleared up the confusion. The birth certificate we have for you back home has the right parents' names on it—Celeste Sterling and David Armisted. But it sounds like the state of California kept some electronic version of that original, incorrect birth certificate, and that's what they sent by mistake."

"So it was just random that my mom's name is on that birth certificate," Kayla squeaks. And there's something weird in her tone, almost as if she expects Dad to lie to her. Or as if she's picking holes in his story.

"No." Dad winces. "It wasn't random." He shifts his gaze back to me. "Genetically, Avery, you belong one hundred percent to your mother and me. Legally, you belong one hundred percent to us. But . . . has your mother ever told you how much trouble she had getting and staying pregnant?"

It takes a moment to realize he expects an answer.

"No," I whisper.

Mom would never talk to me about anything like that. She

would never talk about anything she failed at.

Dad presses his lips together like he's not surprised.

"We tried for six years to have a baby," he says. "That was an awful time. We both wanted a baby so badly. We wanted *you*. You have to know that, to understand . . ."

"Yeah, yeah, how much you love me," I burst out. I didn't know about the six years of trying for a baby, but it almost feels like I *did*. I'm an only child; everyone expects only children to have overprotective parents. But Mom carried that to extremes. She used to treat me like I was made of glass. Like I was some fragile ornament to be kept on a shelf.

When did that stop?

"Of course we love you," Dad says, and I see that that wasn't what he'd planned to say next. He seems to be visibly shifting gears. "For many, many, many reasons. But back before you were born . . . we came to believe that your mother and I could never have a child together. She would never be able to give birth. Doctors told us that."

"Well, obviously *that* was wrong," I say. I'd been hugging my arms, holding myself together. But now I wave my hands in the air, waving away the silly opinions of those stupid doctors. I try to make myself forget that mistaken birth certificate. "Because here I am. Obviously, Mom gave birth to *me*."

"No," Dad says. His gaze is so steady on my face, I have to look away. I hope that will make him stop talking, but it doesn't.

"No," he repeats. "Your mother never was able to give birth. After six years, we hired a surrogate mother. So you are genetically ours. But . . . Kayla's mom was the one who gave birth to you."

## Kayla, Too Stunned to Speak

***Surrogate mother.***

I don't even know what that means.

Even when Avery's dad adds the explanation, *Kayla's mom was the one who gave birth to you*, my brain is still flailing about. How could Avery have her mother and father's genes but come out of my mother's body?

"So, I was, like, a test tube baby?" Avery wails. "Put in a *stranger's* body?"

*My mother is not a stranger!* I want to yell at her. *You know her! She gives you Christmas presents every year!*

But it's like I don't even have a voice anymore. Nothing comes out.

And now my own thoughts haunt me: *She gives you Christmas presents. . . .*

It's something I never questioned. Avery Armisted was just on Mom's Christmas list every year. And Avery's family kept giving us gifts too, even though they became less personal, like gift cards and fruit baskets. Why didn't I think that was weird, when it was Avery's nanny that Mom had been friends with, and we never saw Angelica again after she stopped taking care of Avery?

*Was Mom actually ever friends with Angelica, or was that just an excuse for why we kept going to visit Avery? When Avery was really Mom's . . . Mom's . . .*

I can't come up with the right word to describe Avery's relationship to Mom.

It's not "daughter." It can't be.

"We made sure Kayla's mom was someone we could trust—and that she could trust us—before we signed any paperwork," Avery's dad is saying. "It was an immensely generous gift she gave us, allowing us to have you, to have a family."

"But if she was a surrogate mother . . . you paid her, right?" Avery asks. "So was it really a gift? Or a business transaction? It's like you *bought* me!"

I flush, as if Avery is insulting me. Even staring at Avery's birth certificate, I never really believed that Mom could have had an affair with Mr. Armisted. Not my mom. But it still feels like Avery thinks Mom did something dirty and disgusting. And I'm dirty and disgusting too, because I'm her daughter.

Her real daughter.

*But Mom's a saint*, I think, automatically. *Everyone knows I'm the daughter of a saint. A saint and a hero.*

It's like I can't wrap my brain around anything Avery and her dad are saying. I think about the talk Mom gave me back in sixth grade when I had my first period, the talk that was a mix of *You're a woman now and it's amazing what your body can do* and *You're a woman now, and that means you can get pregnant. But it's not good to get pregnant until after you're married and you and your husband know you're ready to have a baby.*

There was nothing in that talk about having a baby for some other family.

For strangers. On purpose.

Who does that?

*Cows*, I think. *Sheep. Pigs. Livestock.*

It's Grandpa's fault I think of that. Sometimes, when he gets talking about his old days of farming, he forgets who he's talking to. How many times have I heard him tell the story of how, right toward the end of his years as a farmer, one of his neighbors talked him into trying "that newfangled artificial insemination" on his small herd of cows?

To hear Grandpa tell it, it didn't work very well.

But to the Armisteds, my mom was just like a cow. Good only for getting pregnant.

My face flames.

I've missed some of what Avery and Mr. Armisted are saying. They're still sitting across from each other, but it's like they're moving in opposite directions: Mr. Armisted's voice keeps getting softer and softer, calmer and calmer; Avery's keeps getting louder and angrier.

"So you're trying to make me believe I'm *lucky* to have one dad but two moms who made me? That is so weird, Dad," she practically screeches. "This whole thing is just *bizarre*. And you've been lying to me about it my whole life?"

"We never *lied*," Mr. Armisted says. He's gripping the arm of his chair so tightly his knuckles are white. So maybe he's having a hard time staying calm too. Or thinking. "We just didn't . . . tell you every single detail about your birth. Your mother felt . . . I mean, we both agreed that not telling you was for the best. It seemed . . . logical. We were just in California for those few years, and then when we moved back to Ohio, you were so little, and nobody there knew, so . . ." He shoots me a quick glance. "I mean, nobody in Deskins knew . . ."

*Of course* Mom *knew,* I think. *And she moved back to Ohio, too. But she wouldn't tell either, because, because . . .*

I can't follow that thought.

"Anyhow," Mr. Armisted says, focusing on Avery again, "do you think any kid knows every detail about his or her birth?"

"This is a pretty big detail not to tell me!" Avery fumes. She whips one hand toward me, pointing my way, and for an instant I actually think that she might yell that this is all really awful and bizarre for me, too.

But there's no sympathy in the gesture. It's more like she's accusing me of some crime too.

"And then you had to go and make me bring Kayla on this trip?" she snarls. Her face goes a little white. She looks like she might throw up. "Oh, no. Oh, no. Were you trying to make us feel like sisters? *Are* we sisters? Is Kayla Butts my sister?"

She makes it sound like this would be the worst part of finding out what her parents and my mother did. Worse than her mother not giving birth to her. Worse than my mother being paid. Worse than anyone lying to her.

She makes it sound like being my sister would be the worst thing in the world.

I can't think. I don't plan anything, but I find myself shoving back against the couch, shoving myself to my feet.

"I don't want to be your sister either!" I scream at Avery.

"Kayla—" Mr. Armisted begins in that maddeningly calm, patient voice.

I can't stand another minute of this. I fling myself toward the door. I can feel the pathetic awkwardness of my running—my fat belly swaying, my feet half tripping over the corner of the rug. I can feel Avery staring at me in disgust. But then I reach the door. I yank it open, dash through, and slam it behind me.

And then I am running down the stairs.

## Avery, Jealous

**Dad jumps up and runs** after Kayla. He reaches the door just as she slams it in his face.

It takes him two tries to grasp the doorknob—his hands are shaking that bad. He whips the door open and steps out on the landing.

"Kayla?" he calls, leaning out over the railing.

Kayla is nowhere in sight. I can't tell if I'm hearing the clattering of her feet on the stairs or just the creaky banging of the air-conditioning.

Dad gulps in air like he's just run two miles. He whirls back toward me.

"You'll have to go after her," he says. "You're faster."

"What if I decide to run away too?" I snarl back at him.

He sags against the door and starts to pull it closed, as if now he's decided he needs to trap me here.

"I have to keep both of you safe," he huffs. "I promised both of your mothers—"

"You promised both our moms Madrid is a very safe city," I remind him. "Kayla will be fine."

I sound callous. I *am* callous. How can I care about Kayla when my whole world just turned upside down—and she's part of that?

*If my parents have been lying about this my whole life, what else have they lied about?*

Dad glances back and forth between me and the half-closed door. He looks caught.

"I'll call her," he says. "I'll let her know we understand that she needs a little time to herself, but I'm here for her any time she wants to call back. . . ."

He sounds like a Hallmark card. Numbly, I watch him pull out his phone.

From down the apartment hallway—from Kayla's room—I hear the ascending and descending chords that Kayla, for some stupid reason, chose as her ringtone on the stupid burner phone Dad gave her.

"She didn't take her phone," I tell Dad, as if he can't figure that out for himself.

Dad yanks the door back open and starts rushing down the stairs.

"Dad, you're going to fall and break something, running like that," I say. But I don't say it very loudly. Do I think Dad deserves to fall and break something? Does he deserve to be punished?

I go out onto the landing and look down the dizzying spiral of the staircase. I see his hand on the railing one flight below. Two flights below. Three. Even from up here, I can hear his raspy panting, his breathing becoming more and more like gasping for air. I hear the *click* and *thud* that must mean he's flung open the door out to the street.

And then—nothing. No *click* or *bang* of the door closing again, no footsteps of him coming back up the stairs to me. Has Dad left me behind to go in search of Kayla or not?

I start tiptoeing down the tricky stairs myself. I'm in

slippery-soled TOMS again, and the steps seem slicker than ever; the worn-down grooves in the middle seem especially deceptive and diabolical. They're optical illusions: The spots that look most inviting are actually the most dangerous.

*My whole life is an illusion*, I think. *Ever since I was born. The most basic fact I thought I knew—who are my mommy and daddy?—that was always wrong.*

I keep creeping down the tricky, twisty stairs. I keep listening for Dad.

Nothing. Unless—did he just whimper, "No . . ."?

Dad wouldn't whimper. And he's so far below me I can't be sure he said anything. My ears aren't working right. I'm probably just hearing the echo of my own footsteps.

Finally, I reach the last curve, the first moment when I can see the front door.

Dad is still standing in the open doorway, right on the threshold. It's like he's torn between running after Kayla and guarding me. He's got one arm bent and pressed against the door, his forehead pressed against that arm, his phone clutched in his other hand, tight against his ear. While I watch, his hand and the phone slide down, down, down. . . . Did someone just call him? I don't think even he would answer a work call right now. So was it Mom? Or Kayla?

*Kayla doesn't have her phone*, I remind myself, as if my brain can't hold on to even basic facts right now.

Dad's shoulders tremble. They heave up and down.

He might be sobbing.

"There's something else you're not telling me," I say, because it feels like this has to be true. It feels like Dad—my strong, capable, fix-everything Dad—would not sob over a secret he's known for fourteen years. "Something about Kayla?"

Dad keeps his face pressed against his arm and the door, but he shakes his head.

"You can't—," he begins, but I'm not interested in *can'ts*.

"Then it's . . . something about the credit card being denied, back at the Columbus airport," I say. "Or maybe something about Mom getting so upset when we left home . . . Did she just call you back? What's *she* got to say about lying to me all these years?"

Then Dad turns his face to me. His eyes are red and watery; tears stream down his cheeks. But it's like he doesn't even know they're there.

I have never seen my father cry before.

"We're getting divorced," he says. "Your mother and I are getting divorced."

## Kayla, Seeking Comfort Where There Is None

**I'm lost.**

I've been running blindly for what feels like an eternity—turning corners at random, finding something new on every block that I have to get away from: Happy tourists. Ice cream shops. Stores labeled in Spanish.

I run away from all of it.

And now I am out of air and I stumble to a stop, but I don't have the slightest idea where I am. There is not a single thing around me that looks familiar, a single indication that I have ever stood on this street before. Spain feels more foreign than ever, more incomprehensible. I can't understand a single word I hear or see around me. People's faces leer up toward me and pass by me, and they're all distorted, unreal. It's like when I was five and Grandpa took me into the fun house at the county fair, and it wasn't fun at all. It was just scary, everything reflected back at me the wrong shape and the wrong size. I couldn't recognize my own face in those fun-house mirrors. I couldn't recognize my own grandfather.

I can't recognize my own family now.

*Do Grandma and Grandpa know what Mom did?* I wonder. *Were they keeping secrets too? Were they too ashamed to talk about it?*

I think about how Grandma and Grandpa's faces light up whenever someone says to them, *Oh, I just admire your daughter so much! She's so steadfast. The way she dealt with her husband's accident, the way she works with those old people at the nursing home, the way she raised her little girl on her own. . . . Oh, there you are, Kayla. Aren't you proud of your mommy?*

I think about how Grandma and Grandpa have always bragged about Mom to me, always urged me to see her as a role model. *She's so loyal and faithful and true—you'll understand this better when you're a grown woman, when you have a husband of your own. But not every woman would stand by her husband like your mom did with your dad, after an accident like his. . . .*

Grandma and Grandpa can't have ever known what Mom did for the Armisteds. They couldn't know and talk about her that way. They're old-fashioned; they don't like newfangled things or ideas. When they thought they could never have children, they accepted it as God's will. Until God surprised them with their very own miracle: Mom.

*Did surrogate mothers even exist way back when Grandma and Grandpa were trying to have children?* I wonder. *If artificial insemination existed for farm animals, then . . .*

It makes me squeamish to think about things like that in connection with my own grandparents, my own mother.

But I force myself to turn dates over in my head. I can barely even add and subtract right now, but eventually I manage to count back from the date on Avery's birth certificate. Avery was born in October, fourteen and a half years ago. Nine months before that was January. So Avery was . . . conceived . . . right after the last Christmas Mom and Dad and I had together when

Dad was healthy. I wasn't even two yet, so I don't remember it, but I've heard about that Christmas: We stayed in California, because Dad didn't have much time off, and anyhow, Mom and Dad couldn't afford airplane tickets or gas for a cross-country trip. Mom and I were supposed to go home to Ohio for Easter that year, after Dad was deployed, but his accident changed everything. Instead, it was Mom's friend Sonia Lopez who flew with me to Grandma and Grandpa's, while Mom stayed with Dad at the hospital.

Avery was born during the year of my family's life when everything changed—a year I've heard about in excruciating detail for as long as I can remember.

How could Mom have been pregnant with Avery then? How could I have never heard about *that* detail?

I can put it all together. I can kind of see how it might have worked: between that January and the October when Avery was born, Grandma and Grandpa never saw Mom in person. I don't think Skype existed then—and even if it did, Mom and Grandma and Grandpa wouldn't have known how to use it. So they never would have seen Mom pregnant.

She must have been so ashamed, if she kept everything secret.

She must have been ashamed, since she never told me. Not even when I was coming to Spain with the Armisteds. She left me . . .

*Defenseless.*

I was starting to catch my breath, but this thought makes me gasp for air again. My breathing is so ragged that people give me strange looks—maybe that's part of the reason their faces seem so distorted.

What if I look like such a crazy person now that someone calls the police?

What do Spanish police do with crazy people?

I try to move back, away from the throngs of people on the sidewalks. I'm looking for a shadow to hide in, but the sunlight is too bright—there's no shadow big enough. Nothing can be hidden here. *I* can't be hidden.

The crowd presses against me—oh, a traffic light has changed, and people are trying to cross the street. I let the crowd carry me along because it's easier than resisting.

No matter what side of the street I'm on, I can't unsee Avery's birth certificate. I can't unhear Mr. Armisted explaining that my mother gave birth to Avery. I can't unsee Avery's face or unhear her voice as she gasped in horror, *Is Kayla Butts my sister?*

I trip over the curb on the other side and keep blindly walking forward. I bump into something big and hard and gray: a building. No, a sculpture.

It's a sculpture of a baby's head that's almost twice as tall as I am.

I turn, and there's a second huge baby head across the plaza, on the other side of a row of motor scooters. The one I'm standing next to has its blank eyes open; the other has its eyes closed.

Babies. Two babies.

*Is Kayla Butts my sister?*

My face twists, and a moan escapes me. I am not a crier, but I am about to lose all control. In a moment, I'm going to be wailing and weeping in a way that I've only heard about in the

Bible readings at church, when the prophets wore sackcloth and ashes and tore at their clothes and gnashed their teeth and beat their fists on the ground and were thrown into the outer darkness.

I don't know anyone around me—they're all strangers. I'm in a city of strangers, in a country of strangers, on a continent of strangers. But surely even strangers would react if I threw myself to the ground and started weeping and wailing in front of this baby head sculpture.

I have to find a place to hide.

I rush into the nearest building, and it's some kind of train station.

Train stations have bathrooms. Bathrooms have stalls. Stalls have privacy.

I am on a mission.

I try to follow the signs pointing to the nearest *baño*, the nearest WC, but my eyes are already swimming with tears, and I can't see very well; I can't think very well. I get turned around and have to retrace my steps. Finally, I find a line of people by a bathroom door.

The woman in front of me reaches into her pocket and pulls out two coins.

I see the sign on the bathroom door, in English and Spanish: Going to the bathroom costs fifty cents, fifty Euro cents, and I don't have so much as a Euro penny. I left the Armisteds' apartment with nothing.

I'm too poor to go to the bathroom.

A wail starts deep in my chest. I hold it back so nothing

comes out but a whimper, but even that is too loud, and the woman in front of me starts to turn around.

I run away again.

I careen blindly, retracing my steps—or maybe not. I can't tell where I am in this maze of people and luggage carts and stairs and escalators and signs I don't know how to read. There's a door off to the side and I jerk it open, because I'm making a scene; I have to get out of sight. I have to hide.

Nobody stops me.

Another door looms ahead of me, and I jerk it open too. I scramble through.

And then I'm alone.

The door settles closed behind me, and it feels like I'm being sealed off from the rest of the world, like no new air or sorrow or hope or fear can escape or penetrate this space, from any direction. I step forward into a dim, empty room and reach a long, low black bench. The bench stretches in front of a window that looks out on the ordinary bustle of the train station. But this can't be just an ordinary train station waiting room: It's too empty, too eerie, too . . . grim. The window before me is made of some thick, distorting glass that keeps me from hearing any sounds from the other side; even though I can see out, it feels like nobody out in the train station can see in.

*Is this what it feels like to be dead?* I wonder. *To be a ghost? Or . . . to be my dad?*

Over the years, the doctors have told us he can see and hear; he just can't communicate. He can't control much of anything about his body. They're not really sure how much he can think or understand.

Did he know Mom was pregnant with Avery before his accident?

Did that maybe even . . . somehow . . . contribute to his accident?

I don't have a phone with me to call and ask Mom, even if she were available to answer.

I don't really want to ask Mom, anyway. I couldn't say a single word to her right now.

Everything in me recoils from that.

But I don't start weeping and wailing like I longed to back when I was surrounded by other people in the train station or out in the plaza with the giant baby heads. Something about the deep blue peacefulness of this strange room has calmed me down.

I step back from the window, back to the only other source of light in the room, coming from a break in the ceiling. Only when I'm standing directly under that break do I see that it's not just a skylight. It's actually a funnel of words flowing up toward the sky: words written on some sort of translucent material that lets the sunlight through. The words are in lots of different languages, I think, not just Spanish and English. I see "Memoriam" and "people that suffer their lost" and "Peace and freedom in the world" and "*todos las familias* . . ." That means "all the families."

This is some kind of memorial.

I press myself back against the blue, blue wall, like someone's going to catch me—like someone's going to quiz me about who this memorial is for, and then they're going to throw me out when they find out I don't even know.

I don't belong here. This isn't my city, isn't my country, isn't my continent. Whatever dead people I'm supposed to be honoring here had nothing to do with me.

But whoever set up this memorial wanted people to have peace and freedom. I think they wanted people to find peace and freedom in this room.

Maybe I do belong here.

## Avery, Weeping

**I lie facedown on my** bed. I don't remember climbing the stairs, coming back up to our apartment. Maybe Daddy carried me.

"Shh, shh," he says, hovering above me. He's patting my back, rubbing my shoulders. "I'm sorry. Oh honey, I'm so sorry. I didn't want it to be like this. . . ."

I turn my face to the side. I still can't put together what I saw, what I heard: Dad's phone against his ear, then sliding down; that word, "divorce."

Mom did call him back.

"Is it because I saw that messed-up birth certificate?" I moan. "Because now I know . . . Would Mom really divorce you over *that*?"

I can't say what I truly mean: *Is she divorcing you—or disowning me? Because I'm not her real kid?*

"This isn't your fault," Dad says, and there's steel in his voice, something solid to hold on to. "Never think that. Your mother . . . she . . . It bothered her so much that she couldn't give birth to you herself. That's her problem, not yours. But the divorce . . ." Just like that, the steel's gone. Dad's as lost as I am. He whispers, "We were already on this path."

"Then why didn't you tell me before?" I wail. "When I was still home, when my friends . . ."

*When my friends could have helped me*, I want to say.

Lauren's parents have been divorced since she was two; if we were together right now, she'd be saying to me, *Oh, who cares? It's not like parents even* matter.

Except Lauren's the one who sometimes used to whisper to me at sleepovers after everyone else was asleep, *My parents got into a fight again today about who gets my sister and me for Christmas. They've been divorced for almost my whole life, and they're* still *fighting. I wish my family were like yours or Shannon's.*

I can't tell Lauren this news while I'm still in Spain and she's back home.

Maybe I won't ever be able to tell her.

I can't tell Shannon, either. Her parents are still married.

And they don't even fight.

And Shannon and Lauren weren't born from surrogate mothers. I can't ever tell them about *that*.

Dad keeps patting my back.

"We weren't sure," he says. "I . . ." He gulps, an ugly, rude, desperate sound that no one should ever hear from another person. Especially no kid should ever hear from a parent. "We agreed to wait to see how the summer went, to see . . . to see how much we missed each other. . . ."

He goes silent. I close my eyes because I can't look at him right now.

But I don't have to look at him—or hear him—to know that his face is contorted, and he's shaking with sobs.

Because Mom probably doesn't miss him. She probably doesn't miss me, either. The day I left, she couldn't even lie and pretend that she would.

*The way she cried—was that even about me? Or was she just thinking about getting divorced?*

Isn't it a good sign, that that made her cry?

"We planned to sit down with you together and explain all of this," Dad chokes out. "Once we were home from Spain. After this trial separation. She— Your mother planned that. I thought there was still hope, still a chance. . . ."

It's unbearable to hear the remnants of hope still in his voice.

*Dead hope*, I think. *Ashes of hope.*

"She wouldn't even talk to me, when she called just now?" I ask forlornly. "Wouldn't you let her?"

It's like I want to be mad at my father, to blame him for being the one who told me everything.

For being the one who's been with me all week, and who didn't tell me until now.

For being with me my entire life and never telling me I had a surrogate mother.

Why am I madder at him right now than I am at my mom? She didn't even give birth to me!

I open my eyes a crack. My father has his face buried in his hands. Then he lifts his head. I can practically see how hard he's trying to regain control.

"Your mother is . . . struggling," he says. "This is very hard for her. You wouldn't understand. She was already having problems, and . . ."

He's making excuses for her? Seriously?

He starts patting my back again, and it's too much pressure. It hurts to be touched. I jerk away.

"Go away, Dad," I snarl. I turn my face away from him again. The pillowcase fills my mouth like a gag. I already felt like I was choking and couldn't breathe. Now I have a *reason* to feel like I'm choking and can't breathe.

"But—will you be okay?" Dad asks.

*No. Of course I won't be okay. I won't be okay again ever in my entire life.*

I don't say anything to Dad.

Because he should know this already. He should know everything. He should have protected me from all of this.

Isn't that what parents are for?

## Kayla in the Blue Room

**I sit down on the floor.**

For a while, that is enough, just to be here, just to be. It's like sitting at my father's bedside: There's quiet and there's peace, and it doesn't matter what I tell him. But when I'm visiting my father at the VA nursing home, the moment always comes when my mother says, "It's time to go," and she leads me out, her arm around my shoulder.

I always thought it was talking to my father that made me feel better, but what if it was really my mother leading me away afterward, and the feel of her arm around me?

There is no one to lead me away from here. There is no one to hug me.

My mother is on the other side of the ocean. And, anyhow, she is the last person I want to see right now.

What am I going to do?

I think about how Grandma and Grandpa and probably three-fourths of the Autumn Years nursing home residents would tell me to pray—half of them say prayer is the answer to *everything*.

Maybe I am already praying. Maybe that's what I've been doing ever since I stepped into this room.

The see-through funnel of words above me quivers—it's a harbinger, a sign that the air pressure in this room is changing because someone is opening the door. I scrunch back tighter against the wall as if that can make me invisible. But the young woman who steps through the door and toward the light seems to be looking just for me.

"*Es la hora de cierre*," she says. "*Tienes que salir.*"

"What?" I say. "I'm sorry. I don't speak Spanish."

"We are closing," she says, in such accented English that it still sounds like she's speaking Spanish. "You leave."

"Oh," I say. I scramble up. My left foot has gone to sleep, so I limp toward the door.

"*Espera, por favor*," she says, putting her hand on my arm as I pass through the first doorway. She waits until that door closes behind us before she opens the second door, letting us both out.

I blink in the sudden bright light of the train station. The woman says something that could be "Thank you" or "good-bye" or some expression I've never heard before.

What am I going to do now?

Where else can I go to hide?

I don't even have enough money with me to go to a train station bathroom. Where do I think I can go? How many choices do I have?

## Avery, Still Facedown

**From my bedroom, I hear** the front door rattle, the lock click.

"Avery!" Dad calls from the living room. "Kayla's back! She came home!"

I don't even turn my head. I keep my face buried in my pillow.

"This isn't home," I mutter.

## Kayla's Return

**I went to the only** place I could: back to the Armisteds' apartment. I thought maybe I would get lucky and the door would still be unlocked; maybe I could sneak in and grab my purse and my passport and all my money, and I could leave again. I'm thinking wild thoughts: There are things called youth hostels somewhere in Madrid. The train station might be open all night. Maybe the American Embassy would help. . . .

Mr. Armisted is standing on the landing waiting for me when I round the last corner of the spiral stairs.

"You came back," he murmurs dazedly. "You came back."

I have nothing to say to him.

In spite of myself, I am a little proud I found my way back. I was calmer after the blue room. I found an information booth at the train station and asked how to get to Puerta del Sol.

I know how to get from Puerta del Sol to the Armisteds' apartment. But it was a lot of walking, and on the stairway up I was starting to think that maybe I would just crawl into bed at the Armisteds'; maybe I would just hide there.

I stumble my way up to the landing. Mr. Armisted throws his arms around me. I jerk back a little in surprise.

"I was giving myself until nine o'clock," he says. "And then I was going to call your mom. And maybe the police, too. But I thought you were too sensible and practical to . . . to do anything wrong. I didn't want to worry your family. I was sure you'd be back in time to Skype."

*To Skype? What?*

I remember I've been talking with the nursing home residents—and Grandma and Grandpa and Mom—every night at nine p.m. Nine o'clock for me; three in the afternoon for them.

I hadn't even thought about it until now.

The girl who babbled on to the entire nursing home about mangling Spanish verbs and taking the subway and eating Spanish olives was somebody else. Somebody who had nothing to hide.

"I'm not Skyping tonight," I tell Mr. Armisted. "I'm never Skyping again."

His face sags the same way it does when he looks at Avery, when she's been rude. But he reaches into his pocket and pulls out his phone.

"Here," he says. "Just call your mom. She deserves to know . . . I mean, you deserve . . . You should hear her side of the story."

I step around him and his phone like it's a trap.

"No," I say. "I don't think so."

I step on in to the apartment and go to my room. I shut the door and sit down on the bed. I don't pick up my purse because I remember that Mr. Armisted still has my passport—after Avery lost hers, he put mine and his somewhere safe, and I don't know where that is.

Without my passport, I couldn't go to the American Embassy. I'm not even sure I could go to a youth hostel—during Spanish class, we talked about checking into hotels, and I know Señora Gomez said something about handing the *recepcionista* our *pasaportes*.

Mr. Armisted might as well be holding my passport hostage.

He might as well be holding me hostage.

Without my passport, I am trapped in this room.

This makes me think about the Autumn Years nursing home, the way some people see their rooms as cages. Sometimes new people get depressed there. Was I seven or eight when Mom sent me in to say hello to Mrs. Kelly, thinking I could cheer her up? And the old lady snapped, *Don't you go smiling at me, you little brat. Surely even you know there isn't anything here to smile about. My family sent me to this prison to die. They* want *me to die! They might as well have shot me in the heart and been done with it. More honest that way.*

And then she did die, a week later. I remember hearing the nurses and aides whispering about how there was nothing really that wrong with her, except that she'd given up.

I am not Mrs. Kelly. I don't want to die. I don't want to give up. I don't want . . .

Someone taps at my door.

"I have a question for you," Mr. Armisted says from the hall. "Can you . . . can you come out to hear it?"

I walk over and open the door. I stand there with my arms crossed.

"I think I have to call and tell your mother what happened," he says. "What you and Avery saw on the birth certificate. I don't know . . . I can't entirely predict, but . . . she might want you to just go home. It doesn't seem fair to you to . . . I mean, I can buy you a plane ticket. You could leave tomorrow morning."

"You want to get rid of me," I say, the words as flat as Ohio farmland.

Mr. Armisted winces. His face quivers like he's one of the old men in the nursing home with palsy.

"No!" he says quickly. "I want you to stay. I think Avery needs you now more than ever. I think if you leave, I would have to send her home too, and—well, it's complicated. But I can work that out if I have to. If you want to leave. What *do* you want?"

*To never have met you and Avery*, I think. *To unwind fourteen years of time and make it so that Mom was never that weird thing, a surrogate. And Dad never had his accident. And . . .*

And why stop there? Why not go back even further, and make it so Grandpa never lost his farm? Or why not help the whole world and make it so the Holocaust never happened?

The old people in the nursing home who survive, the ones who aren't like Mrs. Kelly, they're always telling me, *You can't change the past.* They say things like, *Any day you wake up and you're still alive, it's a good day. A blessing to praise God for. No matter what happens.*

I am suddenly so homesick for Mr. and Mrs. Lang, for Mrs. Shrivers and Mrs. Delaney and Mrs. Reeves and everyone else at the nursing home. For Grandma and Grandpa. Even for my dad in his VA bed.

But how can I go back to all of them, knowing what I know now? When Mom was too ashamed to tell anyone herself? I can't even Skype with the Autumn Years residents without fearing I'd blurt out the words *My mom had another baby she never told any of you about. She was a surrogate mother. It's like she's been lying to you all these years, pretending she doesn't have secrets. . . .*

And if Mom kept such an important thing as a baby secret, who knows what else I don't know about her?

I can't even talk to my mother on the phone right now. If I went home, I'd have to talk to her. I'd have to look her in the eye.

"I don't want to go home," I tell Mr. Armisted.

His face smooths out. I realize he's been holding his breath.

"Thank you," he whispers.

I slip back inside my room and shut the door. I sag against the wall.

*That was a trick question*, I think. *He only offered one choice.*

I don't want to go home, but I don't want to stay here with Avery and Mr. Armisted, either. The list of what I don't want is really, really long: I don't want to be the Butt-girl of Crawfordsville High School. I don't want to be Avery's nanny or "paid companion" or . . . or sister. (*Take that, Avery! I don't want to be your sister either. So there!*) I don't want to be the girl whose mom was a surrogate mother and was so ashamed she kept it secret. Or whose dad has been in a nursing home almost her entire life.

I thought I would be someone else, coming to Europe. And I am—or I was starting to be.

But the past can always come back and bite you.

What I know about myself now is even worse than what I thought about myself before.

My phone rings inside my purse. I walk over and look at the number on the unfamiliar burner-phone screen: It's Mom.

I hit ignore.

There's a moment of silence, then the phone starts ringing again.

I know my mother. If she has to, she will call and call and call. She won't stop. She never gives up.

I scoop up the phone and scream into it, "I don't want to talk to you, Mom! Stop calling me!"

And then I hang up and turn the phone off.

I don't want to talk to anybody.

## Avery, Who Hasn't Moved

**I hear Dad and Kayla** talking in the hallway; I hear Dad offering her a plane ticket home.

*What about me?* I want to scream out to Dad. *Let* me *go home too, if you're throwing around airplane flights! Let me go back to soccer camp, and let's pretend none of this ever happened!*

But it would take too much energy to open my mouth, to say anything.

I imagine going back to Ohio, back to our house, so perfectly decorated and silent and empty, except for memories. Memories of fights I'd witnessed between Mom and Dad; memories of moments when I'd walked past Dad sitting in his office, and he was just staring off into space, or I caught Mom dropping soggy Kleenexes into the kitchen trash can and turning her face away, as if that would keep me from seeing that she'd been crying . . .

*I'm so stupid*, I think. *A five-year-old could have seen those two were headed for divorce. When was the last time I heard either of them say something nice to the other?*

I'd been away a lot at my friends' houses, so how would I have heard? Or at school or soccer practice. Or at soccer camp. I was supposed to be away at soccer camp this whole summer. That was what I'd wanted.

It was like I'd known without knowing.

*But they always argued and disagreed. For as long as I remember. Even when they were saying nice things to each other in between. Dad always said that's just what happens when two dominant personalities marry each other. Two only children.*

When they were arguing about me, Mom usually got her way.

*Mom had to have been the one who didn't want me to know how I was born*, I think, putting together everything Dad had and hadn't said.

It is a stretch to let myself think that—"how I was born." I don't want to go any further than that, to think about the birth certificate out in the living room that has the wrong name on it. To think that some woman I barely remember from my childhood is actually . . .

*My mom?*

No, Kayla's mother isn't my mom.

But is my mom really my mother anymore? Was she ever?

It's like I'm playing word games. It's like finding out that I actually had two mothers means I really don't even have one.

*I'm fourteen years old. It's not like I need a mommy and daddy anymore, anyhow. I'm going to get up and demand that Dad just send me back to soccer camp, first thing in the morning, and . . .*

I don't get up. I can't. I picture myself at soccer camp, lying facedown like this, and Shannon and Lauren hovering over me, *Oh, Avery, what's wrong? What happened? Are you sick? Do you want us to go get the camp nurse?*

Or worse—not hovering over me. Not even caring. Or just being disgusted that I won't tell them what's wrong, that I don't want them gossiping about me or my family . . .

I can imagine them telling the other girls in the soccer camp bathroom while everyone brushes their teeth at night. *Did you hear about Avery? Did you hear what she found out about her parents? What they weren't ever going to tell her until she found out by accident?*

My iPhone buzzes. I think it's been buzzing for a while, but I've been ignoring it.

I summon the energy to flip it over, and I see a row of texts on the screen from Lauren and Shannon: **Are you there? . . . Aren't you going to answer? . . .**

I can't make sense of the other words. It's like I've forgotten how to read. Or like they're not even using English. Or Spanish. Or anything else I'd recognize.

I stab my fingers at the screen, typing like a toddler.

**Phone battery dying. Can't talk now.**

That's not enough. I can just see Lauren and Shannon hunched over their phones together, wrinkling up their noses together, racing to tell me, **Duh. Then use your iPad.**

Should I tell them the Wi-Fi isn't working right?

No, they'd say to go to the nearest Starbucks. Or Dunkin' Coffee. Whatever.

I steady my shaking hands.

**Dad's taking away my phone/Internet privileges. Because I snuck out last night and went to a dance club. And he caught me.**

There. That should do it.

Ooo, I want to hear all about that! pops up almost instantly on the screen from Lauren. When do you get privileges back?

I don't answer. Let them think Dad confiscated my phone. Let them think I'm never getting it back.

That's better than anyone knowing the truth.

## Kayla, Still at a Loss

**I could sit for hours,** back at the nursing home, watching nature shows with Mr. Lang. Or *The Price Is Right*, or *The Andy Griffith Show*, or John Wayne movies, or anything else the old people wanted to watch. I probably spent half my childhood watching TV with old people.

I might as well have been the nursing home's pet cat.

But I can't sit here in my room now. I can't sit still when there's a loop of thoughts going in my brain: *Mom lied to me. Okay, she didn't really lie, but she didn't tell me the truth. Almost the same thing. What if I can't ever go home again? Mom lied to me. . . .*

I look around for Mr. Armisted's iPad—maybe I could distract myself watching YouTube videos or something. But I've been so careful every night to return the iPad after I'm finished Skyping. Once or twice, Mr. Armisted told me, *You know, I've got a laptop to use, myself. You could just keep the iPad in your room, if you want.* But I never felt right about doing that. Keeping it in my room would have felt like I was stealing it, trying to make it seem like I was rich enough to own something like that.

Or dishonest enough to steal it.

A saint's daughter wouldn't steal things.

*My mother isn't a saint. She never was. Because she was ashamed, she kept secrets. . . .*

The air-conditioning clicks on, but it sounds gurgly, like a car engine just barely managing to start. I know why: I didn't empty the water container out on the balcony like I've been doing every afternoon after Spanish class. And, even though Avery and I are supposed to take turns, I know *she* wouldn't have done it. The water container's probably about to overflow. That means the air conditioner will just start blowing hot air. That's what the landlord said would happen if we forgot.

*So what?* I tell myself. *Who cares if Avery and Mr. Armisted don't have someone else taking care of them for once? Let them feel what it's like to be normal people. Let them suffer. The Armisteds are so rich, they paid Mom to get pregnant for them! I bet the problem wasn't that Mrs. Armisted couldn't have babies—I bet she just didn't want to get fat for nine months!*

*Whoa. Where did that come from?*

I'm not normally the type of person who gets mad easily, but suddenly I am boiling.

Now I really can't sit still.

I propel myself off my bed. I open the door and peek out into the dark hallway. Both Avery's and Mr. Armisted's bedroom doors are shut. I tiptoe down the hallway and through the living room and out the sliding glass door to the balcony. Right now it's a toss-up whether I'm planning to dump the air conditioner water into the kitchen sink like I'm supposed to, or if I'm going to stalk into Avery's room and pour it over her head, soaking her entire bed.

*That's what she deserves, the way she treats me, the way she acts, the way she is. . . .*

But when I reach for the plastic water container on the dark side of the balcony, it's empty. It rattles in my hand.

"I took care of it."

I whirl around. Mr. Armisted is sitting at the table on the far side of the balcony, the part that's half in shadow, half bathed in light from the dance club across the street.

"I—I didn't see you," I stammer. I've still got the plastic water container in my hand, and I realize what's wrong: It's *too* empty. The air conditioner is a jimmied-together system; you have to take it apart and put it back together every time.

"You didn't do it right," I tell Mr. Armisted, and there's still enough anger in me—enough of the wanting to pour water on Avery—that the words come out sounding mean. "You have to put the cut-off garden hose back in the bottom of the tub after you empty it, or it will leak everywhere. See?"

I hold up the two detached pieces, the water container and the end of the dripping hose.

"Of course," Mr. Armisted says apologetically, as I put everything back together. He clears his throat. "Believe it or not, I used to be good at things like that. And that's when my wife says I was just a dumb farm boy. My . . . well, I guess I'm going to have to get used to calling her my ex-wife. My soon-to-be ex-wife . . ."

"What?" I say.

"Sit down," Mr. Armisted tells me. "Please."

I step across the patio and slide into one of the chairs. Mr. Armisted leans back, like he's giving me space. Or trying to stay in the shadows. But someone must have opened the door of the dance club, because the music gets louder for a moment, and a slice of red light shoots up at us and then vanishes again. In the one flash of light across his face, it looks like his expression has crumpled, like he's about to fall apart completely.

But I must be wrong about that, because when he speaks again, he's got the same measured, calm tone I've heard him using on the phone every night when I come out of my room to return his iPad. It's an *I'm in charge* tone, an *I know what I'm doing* tone. It's his usual voice—he only sounds different when Avery's annoying him.

"This wasn't entirely unexpected," he says, quite formally. "But my wife informed me this evening that she wants a divorce."

"Just because Avery found out . . . ?" I begin.

Mr. Armisted waves that question away.

"I believe that's part of the reason for the timing," he says. "But we were headed in that direction anyhow. I was just hoping that we could hold off until the fall. Or . . . that I could talk her out of it." His voice wavers. But then he immediately snaps it back into control. "I'm very sorry. I never intended to drag you into our family's . . . mess. That wasn't why we invited you to come to Spain with Avery."

"Why did you invite me to come to Spain with Avery?" I blurt. "*She* doesn't want me here."

And there it is, the thing that's been hanging over us since the Columbus airport. Who knew it could be so easy to ask? I just needed to be mad about other things that were harder to talk about.

Mr. Armisted freezes.

"Avery's fourteen," he says, and I see he's going to give me the same lame excuse he's been making all along.

"Yeah?" I say sarcastically. "So? When I was fourteen, my mom hurt her back lifting one of the nursing home residents, and she was out on disability for a month. Disability's reduced pay, you know? The nursing home owner was really nice—she paid me to clean her house so we'd have enough money to pay the electric bill that month. So it wouldn't be turned off. You could just let Avery clean other people's filthy toilets. That'd cure her of any problems she's having, being fourteen."

I hear a tinkling sound, like something's breaking. But it's only Mr. Armisted swirling ice in a glass I just now notice he's got in his hand. He takes a gulp.

"You think Avery's spoiled," he says. I start to protest, but he holds up his hand like he's telling me to wait. "That's what I would have thought too, if I'd met her when I was sixteen. But it looks different from this side of the table. It was just always easier to give her things, than to . . . And her mother always said . . ." He stops. Shrugs. "You know a lot better than Avery does, how to deal with hard things. Because she's never had to. And she's going to have to, with this divorce. I thought, I thought if she had you, if she had one friend who was resilient, who didn't act like a broken fingernail was the tragedy of a lifetime like all her other friends do, then . . ."

I clutch the table and pull myself half out of the chair.

"Then what?" I demand. "Then everything's okay for *Avery*?" I say her name like it's poison in my mouth, like I hate every syllable.

I say her name like she's been saying my name this entire trip. That makes me even madder.

"Well, guess what?" My voice shoots higher. I'm almost yelling. "I don't exist just to make everything okay for Avery. My *family* doesn't exist just to make your family's life better. We haven't had our problems just to make Avery's problems go away!"

"That's not what I'm saying!" Mr. Armisted protests. "I wanted you to have this experience, too. I was a lot like you when I was a teenager, okay? A lot. My dad lost his farm in the eighties, just like your granddad did. If I'd had a chance to have a trip like this when I was a teenager, then—"

"Then you would have wanted to know what you were getting into," I say. "You would have wanted to know if your own mother had some weird connection to the family you were traveling with. You would have wanted to know that people were getting divorced!"

I want to yell more, maybe, *You would have wanted to know ahead of time that the kid you'd be traveling with hates you and skips class and lies to her dad!* But Mr. Armisted clenches his jaw on the word "divorced," and that makes me falter.

"I *wasn't* like you," I say instead. "I was perfectly happy staying in Crawfordsville."

Now *I'm* lying to Avery's dad. But I don't care.

"I'm not saying anything's wrong with Crawfordsville," Mr. Armisted says in a perfectly even tone. "I still miss the town where I grew up. But it's good to be a citizen of the world, too, to know what's outside your cozy little town. To be able to belong in more than just one place."

*I don't belong anywhere now*, I think. And that's it—that's what I'm angriest about. I never fit in at Crawfordsville High School (or at the middle school or elementary school, years ago). I had no hope of fitting in with Avery or Mr. Armisted or Spain. But I belonged in my family, with Mom and Grandma and Grandpa and even Dad, in his nursing home. I belonged at Autumn Years, running up and down the hallways I practically grew up in, knowing I could knock on just about any door and have a resident break out grinning just at the sight of me. I had that.

And that's what Mr. Armisted stole from me, telling me my mother's secret, the one she was too ashamed to tell me herself. I won't be able to look *anyone* in Crawfordsville in the eye anymore. I won't be able to talk to any of the people who love me anymore.

I can't even talk on the phone with my own mother.

"You know my father was never a hero, don't you?" I ask Mr. Armisted, because somehow it's important to show him I don't have anything left.

"Your father?" Mr. Armisted repeats. "But he—"

"Did Mom tell you the story?" I interrupt. Suddenly, I'm not sure if Mr. Armisted really knows or not. But I want him to. "My father's unit was going to be deployed to Afghanistan. It was the night before they were supposed to leave, and a bunch of them went out partying. One last time. And one of Dad's buddies was driving, and he'd had too much to drink, and—"

"I know what happened," Mr. Armisted says. There's steel in his voice now. "We knew your parents then. Your mother was already pregnant, carrying Avery."

It's that word, "carrying," that gets me. It makes my mother sound like a pack mule.

"Oh right, you were already *using* my mother," I say. I have never been so bold before in my life.

I have never been so angry before in my life.

Mr. Armisted bolts upright. He slams his glass down against the patio table.

"Don't," he says, and the word is like granite. He leans forward, his angled jaw dividing the shadow and the light.

"You can hate me," he says, in a quiet voice that's somehow even meaner and angrier than shouting. "You can hate my wife. You can even hate Avery, when she's not being nice. As a family, you . . . you've not seen us at our best." He gulps. "But you do *not* dishonor what your mother did. What she did—and it was *her* choice; she wanted to help us—that was the most kind, loving, generous thing I've ever seen anyone do in my life. And she did it for *strangers*. She picked our profile out of the agency listing, and she told us she wanted our family to have the same joy in having a child that she and your dad had, with you. . . ."

His jaw trembles. Or maybe it's just that my eyes have gone blurry.

Over at the dance club, there's a song blaring about someone turning around, someone falling apart.

"Your parents are *both* heroes," Mr. Armisted says. "Your father was *willing* to die for his country. He knew that was a possibility, signing up. That's a lot more than I was ever willing to do. The only thing I ever risked was money. And your mother . . . Do you know sometimes women die in pregnancy or childbirth? It wasn't *likely*, but . . . she was willing to risk that for us. For Avery to exist. For my wife and me to be happy . . ."

Across the street at the dance club, a new song has come on, someone asking again and again "Don't you want me, baby?"

Mr. Armisted turns his head like he's noticing the music too. He lets out a wail and buries his face in his hands.

I sit frozen, watching Mr. Armisted weep.

"I'm sorry, I'm sorry," he moans, attempting to wipe his eyes. "That was an important song to my wife and me. Years ago. But this is probably quite upsetting to you. You're probably not used to seeing a grown man cry."

I am, actually. At the nursing home, it happens a lot. Men come in wearing John Deere caps or Harley-Davidson jackets, and they look so tough and strong. And then you see them a little while later crouched in the hallway outside their mother's or grandmother's rooms, and they've got tears streaming down their faces. You can tell they aren't really used to crying; they don't know how to handle it.

When I was little, sometimes I'd go up to those men to silently offer them boxes of Kleenex. I heard one man swear there was an angel of mercy roaming the Autumn Years, and it turned out he was talking about me. But I'm pretty sure he was drunk or high or both, so who knows what he thought he saw.

When I got to be a teenager, Mom pulled me aside and told me she was glad I was trying to help, but I really should stay away from strange men crying in the nursing home hallways. Because they might want different things from teenagers.

But those men were always crying about death, or

approaching death. I know all about that. I know about men in Harley jackets who aren't as tough as they look.

I don't know anything about rich men like Mr. Armisted, crying over music.

"Sometimes it helps to cry," I finally tell Mr. Armisted.

He doesn't answer. I'm not sure he heard me. I'm not sure he even remembers I'm there.

After a few moments, I get up and slip back into the apartment.

## Avery, in a Nightmare

**I fall asleep. I can** still feel the tears on my face; I can still hear slivers of music when someone opens or closes the door out to the balcony. And I think it's that music from the dance club across the street that wraps itself into my dreams.

*Don't, don't you want me . . .*

In my dream, I see Mom and Dad dancing. They're young. And somehow I know that they're still in college, and they've just met, and though there are lights flashing around them and people with Mohawks and safety pins in their noses, Mom and Dad are only looking at each other.

And then they're their real selves—middle-aged—and they're yelling at each other, Dad screaming, "Supportive? Come on—I've underwritten your little hobby business for years!" And Mom sneering, "You'd be nowhere without me! You wouldn't even know which fork to use—when I met you, you didn't even know there *were* different forks!"

*Don't, don't you want me . . .*

And then they're fighting over a doll wrapped in a blanket, each of them pulling the arms in opposite directions. No, it's not a doll. It's a baby.

Me.

And then another woman walks into the room, and she takes the baby away from both of them—they *let* her take the baby away. They both give up. They step back and fade away, and then it's just the woman and the baby. It's like the woman is standing on a stage, in front of everyone I know.

"You know this baby was mine all along," the woman says. "And now I get to keep her. Now I have two. Avery and Kayla."

I wake up gasping. And even though I know the air conditioner isn't working very well, it's like I feel a huge wave of cool air flow over me. No, it's not air—it's *relief*.

*That was only a dream*, I realize. *Nothing bad* really *happened. I just had a nightmare.*

That relief lasts a millisecond before I remember what's real.

Mom and Dad are getting divorced.

Kayla's mom gave birth to me.

Mom and Dad have been lying to me my entire life.

*They were probably lying about ever loving each other, ever loving me*, I think. Now I'm just wallowing.

But I can see where my dream came from. It's so obvious.

Mom and Dad did meet in college, when they were both out dancing, each with their own set of friends. It was the 1980s, and Dad laughs about how there were a few people trying to bring a punk-rock vibe to Ohio State University.

"I was straight off the farm," he always says, when he tells the story. "I'd never seen anyone use safety pins as jewelry before. I was trying so hard not to stare. Then I saw your mother, and I forgot everything else."

When Mom's in a good mood, when Dad's telling that story, she always says, "But *I* had to go ask *you* to dance!"

Their first dance was to this song called "Don't You Want Me," by a group called the Human League. Sometimes when

I was younger and he was being silly, Dad would make up different words to the tune and sing them to Mom: *I was working as a fry cook at a Ma-ac-Donald's/Then I saw you!* Or *I was working on the li-ine/At the chee-eese curd plant/And I stunk to highest heaven/Before I met you . . .*

It's kind of all true, I guess. Dad had to work a lot of crappy jobs to pay for college.

One time last year when Mom and Dad were fighting, I heard Mom say, "Do you realize that first song we danced to was actually a breakup song? And we didn't even notice? I looked up the lyrics online. We were doomed from the very beginning!"

Now that I think about it, I haven't heard Dad sing "Don't You Want Me" to Mom even once since she said that.

Tears stream back into my eyes. I missed so many clues that Mom and Dad were going to get divorced. I should have paid more attention. I should have known—so I could brace myself.

So I could just hate both of them from the very start.

So I wouldn't care.

How many clues did I miss that they aren't even my real parents?

Lying down is making my head feel like it's filling up with tears and snot. I sit up, but that just means that all the tears and snot roll down my face, and that's even worse. I wipe it all away.

I've got to get ahold of myself. I, Avery Nicole Armisted, just wiped my nose on my bedsheets—the same bedsheets I'm going to have to sleep in tonight, because we don't even have a maid here.

And the washer doesn't work, anyhow.

"Facts," I tell myself firmly. "Facts, not emotions."

I'm like a drowning person clutching at one of those rings lifeguards throw. "Facts, not emotions" is what my eighth-grade science teacher always said we should be guided by. Lots of people said Mr. Dandridge was really mean—because he was a hard grader, and he took points off for the tiniest mistakes. But when I was going through a spell last winter where Lauren and Shannon were kind of fighting with each other, and I was caught in the middle (and Mom and Dad were fighting at home), it was always a relief to sit in Mr. Dandridge's class and know that all I had to think about for that hour was facts.

I reach for my iPad and open Safari and type, "Babies born from surrogate mothers."

Mr. Dandridge would be so proud of me. Really, so would all my teachers, and Mrs. Chiu, the Deskins Woods Middle School librarian. I skip past Wikipedia. I skip past the entries marked "Ad"—though, how could there be so many people searching for surrogate mothers? Or for families who want to use surrogate mothers?

I'm looking for the driest, most boring link I can find. I want this explained the way my eighth-grade health teacher, Mrs. Stubbins, taught all year—she made talking about sex mind-numbingly dull. Egg. Sperm. Embryo. Done.

I remember some of the boys snickering anyway and muttering about things they'd seen online.

Mrs. Stubbins would fix them with a cold stare and lecture, "You cannot believe everything you see online. This is how all of you came into being. Show some respect."

Something hits me: Mrs. Stubbins was wrong. We did not all come into being the way she told us.

*I* didn't come into being like that.

The tears start up again, and I tap randomly on a site I can barely see.

"Surrogate Mother Sues to Keep Baby. . . ."

I tap back out of that one so fast I almost drop the iPad. I sit there panting for a moment.

*If Kayla's mom were going to try to keep me, she would have done it when I was born*, I tell myself. *It's not like she's going to do anything now.*

But it's too much like my dream, too much like what I imagined.

*Dad and Mom are rich*, I remind myself. *Kayla's family's poor. They can't do anything.*

I blink away the tears and tap on a different link, one that looks like the WebMD of the United Kingdom. I've noticed that being in Spain means we see different websites, too. More from England. Not so many from the United States.

This UK site *is* as dry as Mrs. Stubbins's health class.

I find out that there are really two different types of surrogate mothers. With a host surrogate mother, she's not genetically related to the baby she carries at all; the baby comes from somebody else's egg. She's just a gestational carrier.

With a gestational surrogate mother, it is her egg. The baby is genetically hers.

*Daddy says I am genetically his and Mom's*, I remind myself. *Completely. He says I'm not related to Kayla's mom at all. She was only the host. She's got nothing to do with me.*

I know this is a lie. She gave birth to me. That's something.

I make myself keep reading, and it helps calm me down. I read about contracts, agreements, rights, birth plans. And it feels like none of this actually does have anything to do with me.

Then I come to the line, "It is illegal to pay for a surrogate mother arrangement in the UK."

*What?*

I start new searches, looking for lists. Surrogacy is illegal in lots of places. Some places consider it baby buying if any money changes hands. Some places just think it's immoral: rich people taking advantage of poor women; children created like lab rats.

Spain is one of the places where people like me aren't supposed to exist.

*I'm an outlaw*, I think. *A science experiment. A total freak.*

This can't be *me*. I'm Avery Armisted. I'm rich. I'm pretty. I'm good at school, good at soccer, good at managing my friends. Everyone always wants me on their team.

*No. Not anymore. Not if they really knew. . . .*

I throw the iPad on the floor and bury my face back in the sheets.

Maybe I was made wrong. Because I am nothing now but snot and tears.

# Kayla, on Her Own

**In the morning, the apartment** is dead quiet. I don't hear Mr. Armisted tiptoeing down the hall or talking on the phone or starting coffee in the kitchen. I don't hear Avery rustling around her room, pretending for her dad's sake that she's getting ready to go to Spanish class with me. I've been in Spain for barely a week—I didn't realize how much I'd gotten used to those sounds every morning. I don't know what to do without them. For a while, I just lay in bed watching the numerals click forward on the digital clock. Seven forty-five. Seven forty-six. Seven forty-seven.

When the clock gets to eight fifteen, I know it's too late even for me to go to Spanish class.

Did I want to?

*Nobody there knows my family or Avery, anyhow. I could have gone and sat there for hours not thinking about anything but Spanish. And maybe thinking about some Bulgarian kids too. . . .*

I blink. With everything else that's happened, am I really going to get upset about not learning Spanish? Or about not hanging out with kids who don't even speak the same language I do?

At eight thirty, I give up on waiting for Mr. Armisted or Avery. I get up and tiptoe to the kitchen. There's nothing but fruit left for breakfast—Mr. Armisted said something a few days ago about making another food order, and he asked Avery and me what we wanted.

But I guess he hasn't actually ordered anything yet. Or it hasn't been delivered.

I remember Avery saying I could eat whatever I wanted, and I get mad all over again.

*Well, yeah, after my own mother gave birth to you . . .*

I grab a handful of grapes and an apple and slip out to the balcony.

Mr. Armisted is still sitting at the table. Or he's sitting there *again*. He has a cup of coffee in front of him, but it's got that dead-looking sheen that coffee gets when it's been sitting out for hours.

"Oh, um, sorry," I say.

Mr. Armisted turns his head, and it seems like it takes a full minute for his eyes to focus on me.

I turn around, like I might be able to squeeze back inside before it really registers with Mr. Armisted that I'm there.

"No, no, there's room," Mr. Armisted says, drawing his coffee cup closer to his side of the table.

Hesitantly, I put my plate of grapes down on the table. Mr. Armisted rubs his hand against his jaw and winces. He's got stubble.

"I'm not going in to work today," he says. "I couldn't sleep. I've been out here since three a.m."

"I missed going to Spanish class too," I say, like I'm apologizing. "I mean, Avery and I missed it."

Mr. Armisted stares past my ear.

"One of my employees used to call this 'taking a mental

health day,'" he says vaguely. "I ended up having to fire her."

I don't like this new drifty, vague version of Mr. Armisted. He's almost making me feel sorry for him, and I don't want to.

I'd rather stay mad.

He shakes his head like he's trying to wake himself up.

"Did you read your mother's e-mail?" he asks. "She was going to send you an e-mail. Explaining."

"No," I say. "I did not read my mother's e-mail. I'm not going to. And you can't make me."

It's like I'm channeling Avery. *I* don't say things like that.

I half expect Mr. Armisted to snap, *That's it! I'm sending you home!*

But he just tilts his head and says sadly, "No, I can't. I can't make anyone do anything."

## Avery, Immobile

**It's morning. I keep expecting** Dad to come into my room, to tell me what to do. He'll have a plan. He'll make me get up, make me take a shower, make me get moving. He won't let me lie around in snotty, tear-soaked sheets all day.

Or . . . maybe he will. He doesn't knock on my door. Nobody comes for me.

*That's a fact too,* I want to snarl. *Sometimes facts are the enemy. Sometimes it's facts that make you cry. Did you ever think of that, Mr. Dandridge?*

## Kayla, at Loose Ends

**It looks like Mr. Armisted** is going to sit out on the balcony all day, not drinking his cold coffee.

It looks like Avery is going to lie in bed all day.

*So what? Let them*, I think.

I do not like how much I sound like Avery today.

But it looks like I'm going to spend the whole day thinking, *Maybe I should read Mom's e-mail. I wouldn't have to answer it. I wouldn't even have to read the whole thing. If it bothers me, I could stop any time I wanted. Maybe* . . . And then instantly my next thought is, *No! I am not going to read that! Mom kept everything secret my entire life! I don't owe her anything!*

I have a harder time not reading Mom's e-mail when I don't have anything else to do. And when Mr. Armisted's iPad is sitting right there on the kitchen table. Tempting me.

Avoiding Mom's e-mail means I can't even let myself pick up the iPad to watch YouTube.

I make myself find things to do. I brush my teeth and take a shower and rinse out yesterday's clothes in the sink, because the repairman *still* hasn't come to fix the washer. My Crawfordsville High School T-shirt has that stiff, crusty feeling that clothes get when they haven't been rinsed right. I let the water run over the shirt again and again and again, even though I know it won't really do any good.

And that doesn't stop the nagging voice in my head, *Maybe I should read Mom's e-mail. All I have to do is pick up the iPad, and . . .*

I have to get out of this apartment.

I hang up my wet clothes and go stand in the living room. I should walk out onto the balcony again and let Mr. Armisted know where I'm going, so he doesn't worry. But I can see through the glass that he's got his face buried in his hands again; his shoulders shake with sobs.

*Not my problem*, I tell myself, steeling my heart. *My mother gave him and his wife a baby, and they still couldn't be happy. They raised Avery to be a spoiled brat, and they wouldn't even tell her what my mom did for them. I'm not helping Mr. Armisted. I'm not a little kid anymore, taking Kleenex around the nursing home to crying men. I don't have to do anything.*

Thinking this way makes me feel guilty. But I don't slide open the glass door and step out onto the balcony. I leave a note on the kitchen table: *I decided to go on to Spanish class late. I think Avery is still sleeping, so I didn't bother her. I'll be back this afternoon the usual time.*

Will Avery or Mr. Armisted even miss me? Will they notice my note? Or read it?

*Like I'm not reading Mom's e-mail . . .*

I make myself hurry down the stairs, so I can't focus on anything but trying not to fall.

I don't realize until I'm at the very bottom, but I've managed to speed down the entire staircase without taking a single break.

And I'm not even panting.

*Because you went down*, I remind myself. *Down is always easier than up.*

Out on the street, I hesitate. I can't really see going to Spanish class this late. Everyone would stare.

I test myself: *What? Do you think they could take one look at you and know you found out last night that your mother was . . . what she was? Or that the Armisteds, the people you once thought of as the perfect family, are getting divorced?*

Of course no one in the Spanish class could figure that out just by looking at me.

*But Andrei would be able to tell that something was wrong*, I think. *He'd notice. He'd ask. Maybe Dragomir would too. And then what would I want to tell them?*

I don't want to tell anyone anything. It doesn't even matter that I don't know enough Spanish to describe my problems, anyway—probably having people ask would be enough to make me cry. I'd make a fool of myself in front of everyone.

I walk to Puerta del Sol and go down into the Metro, but I take the subway to the Atocha train station, not to Spanish class.

I'm going back to the blue room.

Even knowing it's there, I still have to wander for a while through the train station to find it. I'm starting to wonder if it was just a mirage last night—or like that old musical Grandma and Grandpa like, "Brigadoon," where a whole town shows up only one day every hundred years.

Maybe it only shows up for people who need it.

Maybe I don't actually need it today.

Just when I'm about to give up, I see the window of thick,

wavery glass. I see the door and the solemn attendant beside it.

"Can I go in?" I ask her.

"Oh, yes," she says, in English. I have to strain to understand even those basic words. "Here, take a brochure."

She escorts me through the double sets of doors, making sure the one closes behind us before she opens the next. Is she afraid birds will fly out or in? Or bugs?

We finally get to the blue room, and she leaves me alone with the emptiness and the silence. And the brochure in my hand.

It's in Spanish.

"*Monumento en recuerdo de las victimas del 11-M,*" it says on the front.

I don't know what "*recuerdo*" means. I've never heard of the victims of 11-M.

I open the brochure and it seems to be more about the building of the monument than the *victimas del 11-M*. It's like whoever wrote the brochures thought everyone would already know about 11-M. Finally I see a paragraph that includes the words *sufridos en Madrid el 11 de marzo de 2004*.

Something happened on March 11, 2004.

Does "*sufridos*" mean "suffered"?

I can't figure out much else on that page. Knowing that "*entre*" means "between," doesn't help when that's practically the only word I understand in an entire sentence. My eyes glide over the beginning of the next paragraph, but I can actually puzzle out the words at the end.

. . . *al mismo tiempo, con todos los que han sufrido la violencia terrorista.*

What happened on March 11, 2004, must have been a terrorist attack. And the *con todos* part means that this memorial connects to everyone who suffered from terrorism.

I feel even more like I belong here.

I wasn't even born yet when September 11, 2001, happened, but it changed my life.

Before that, my father was taking community college classes, planning to become a firefighter. Maybe a paramedic, too.

But after September 11, he thought it was his duty as an American to join the military, to go off and fight the people who wanted to attack us.

That's how Mom and Grandma and Grandpa always explained it. That's what my other grandparents say too, though they moved to Florida after Dad's accident and we don't see them very often.

If Dad hadn't joined the marines, he wouldn't have been in his buddy's car the night of the accident. He wouldn't have even known the man.

He wouldn't have been stuck in a VA nursing home for fourteen years, unable even to say my name. He'd be a paramedic or firefighter in Crawfordsville, saving other people's lives.

If Dad hadn't joined the marines, Mom wouldn't have been in California at the same time as the Armisteds. She wouldn't have been there to give birth to Avery. Would Mom have become a surrogate mother if she'd stayed in Ohio?

Would Avery even exist?

Everything feels balanced in this room, where the air isn't allowed to go in or out, and consoling and sorrowful words swirl together above my head.

Mom says when bad things happen, you can always find good things in the results, if you look hard enough. She says it's like a balance sheet, and the good things are what you have to focus on. But I've never seen a counterbalance before for Dad's accident. If he'd been hurt in battle, it would have been *He was injured defending his country. He sacrificed for us all.* But his accident was just a mistake. It was bad, and it ruined his life. It kind of ruined Mom's and mine too.

*Mom was already pregnant with Avery when Dad had his accident*, I tell myself. *One thing didn't cause the other.*

Am I trying to say it would have been okay for Dad to be hurt so badly—so badly he almost died—if it happened in exchange for Avery getting to live? To exist at all?

*Because of course* Avery's *life would be worth more than my dad's? Is that what I'm working toward?*

I'm mad again. But it's like this room with its blue walls and its funnel of words can absorb my anger.

I sit there until it starts to get too hot. It's like being in a greenhouse—the light from overhead is too focused.

And I'm hungry. Grapes and an apple aren't much of a breakfast.

It kind of feels good to be able to think of something that simple. I'm hungry; I should eat.

I stuff the "Victims of 11-M" brochure in my pocket and walk out of the blue room. I don't want to go back to the apartment—and anyhow, there's barely any food there. I decide to go to Pans, the place Avery and I ate our first day. I could order by pointing, if I have to. But as I'm walking in that direction,

I pass a sign that says 100 MONTADITOS, and something clicks in my brain.

"100 *montaditos*" means something like "a hundred sandwiches." This is the restaurant chain that Dragomir and Andrei talk about constantly, where you check off what you want on a piece of paper, and you don't even have to ask out loud for what you want.

"*Muy bien para mi*," Dragomir said, and pantomimed how he could gobble down all sorts of food at a 100 Montaditos, but he starves at a restaurant where the waiters have to understand him. His pantomime even showed the waiters in regular restaurants bringing him weird things—shoes, an umbrella, an old belt—rather than actual food. And then he'd pretend to try to eat it.

At least, I think I understood Dragomir's pantomimes. He was probably mostly joking, because if he really wanted to, he could always use the translation app on his phone.

I go into the 100 Montaditos. I'm still not really sure what I'm ordering, but I end up with a lot of little sandwiches and a pile of French fries and a Coke.

*See? I did this by myself. I don't need you, Avery. I don't need you, Mr. Armisted.*

The food makes me happy.

After lunch, I walk around. And it's crazy, because it's really hot and I'm still avoiding reading my mother's e-mail, and who knows what I'm going to face when I go back to the apartment. But I am still happy. As long as I keep walking, I don't have to think about much of anything.

I see a Hard Rock Cafe on the Gran Via.

I see fancy stores, and women walking out of those fancy stores who look like they just bought everything straight off the mannequins.

I see the Plaza Mayor, this huge open square that doesn't even look real. It looks like something out of a movie.

I see the royal palace.

I see an Egyptian temple that came straight from Egypt and was rebuilt here. I don't know why there would be an Egyptian temple in Madrid, but there is.

When my feet get tired—beyond tired—I sit down in a park where there's a statue of a man on a horse and another man beside him on a donkey or a mule. A tour bus pulls up behind me and a bunch of old people hobble off. I think they're all Japanese, and they're obviously not nursing home residents if they're traveling the world. But watching them makes me think of everyone back at Autumn Years. They hold on to one another's elbows; they give one another a hand down from the last step of the bus.

*They're not here alone*, I think. And suddenly the huge pile of 100 Montaditos food doesn't feel so good in my stomach.

"Listen up! Listen up!" a young, non-Japanese woman with a bullhorn calls to them in English. "This is the Plaza de España. The man depicted seated in the chair on that pillar over there is Miquel de Cervantes, commonly regarded as the best writer in Spanish literature. And in front of him are his most beloved creations, Don Quixote and his trusty sidekick, Sancho Panza. In his travels, Don Quixote thought he was on a noble quest, but most of his efforts were misguided. He is known for tilting at windmills . . ."

The Japanese tourists take picture after picture.

I think about my mother.

*Mr. Armisted wants me to think that she did something great, being a surrogate mother. Like she was on some noble quest.*

I decide I like the word "misguided."

*If she thought she was doing something noble, why else would she keep everything secret for the past fourteen years?*

One of the Japanese men lowers his camera.

"What means, 'tilting at windmills'?" he asked.

The guide seems rattled, as if she's so used to saying the same words every time, she's forgotten they have any meaning.

"He—*¿como se dice?*—he saw windmills, and he thought they were fearsome beasts he had to slay," she says. "So he tried to fight the windmills. He thought he was heroic, but he was *loco*, a crazy man trying to fight a windmill."

The Japanese man still looks confused—I mean, the guide's accent makes her English hard for even *me* to understand. But the statue guy on the horse does look foolish.

It'd be embarrassing to be his sidekick.

*It's embarrassing to be my mother's daughter. . . .*

I don't want to think about my mother anymore. But when I stand up, my legs ache. I have a blister starting on each of my big toes where my flip-flops rub. I decide I can go back to the apartment. I can hole up in my room, just like Avery's doing, and I can watch YouTube videos without opening Mom's e-mail.

I can be that strong.

It seems to take forever to get back to the apartment building. When I step into the lobby, I see that the mailman is just leaving.

Checking the mail gives me an excuse to put off climbing the stairs. But as soon as I unlock and open the box, I realize I've made a mistake.

There's a letter from Grandma.

## Avery, Stuck

**I sleep. I wake up.** I cry. I go back to sleep.

I'm not even sure what day it is anymore. Friday? Saturday? Sunday?

Isn't anybody ever going to come for me?

## Kayla, Confounded

**Grandma knew all along,** I think. *And now she's writing me too, to persuade me that . . .*

What? What would Grandma want me to think about Mom being a surrogate mother?

I can't help myself. I slide my finger under the flap of the envelope and rip it open. I pull out a thick sheaf of pages.

As soon as I see the date at the top of the first page, I realize my mistake. It's from last week, from the day after I arrived in Madrid. It's a *letter*. It took days to get here. It's not going to tell me what Grandma wants me to know now, only what she wanted to tell me last week.

I see Grandpa's goofily tilted writing in the middle of the page too.

*This isn't going to say anything about surrogate mothers or Mom giving birth to Avery*, I tell myself. *It's perfectly safe to read this.*

Except for the fact that just seeing Grandma's firm, precise script and Grandpa's helter-skelter scrawling brings tears to my eyes.

I start reading the letter anyway.

*Dear Kayla,*

*I hope getting this letter doesn't make you homesick. I remember sometimes when I was about your age and I'd go spend the night with my cousins, I'd get a little homesick. And that was still in Ohio (you remember, my cousins lived in Cleveland. The big-city part of the family.), and I was with people I'd known all my life.*

*But your grandfather and I were talking, and we miss you, and we thought maybe we could help you with something you're having a problem with. And then it would be like you weren't so far away.*

*I know you said the washing machine where you're living isn't working right, and maybe by the time you get this, that Mr. Armisted will have figured out a way to fix it. But your mom says he's some big businessman, and you know how your Grandpa's always saying that the more money someone has, sometimes that means he has less sense. Your Grandpa has always been good at fixing anything with a motor—you know, he had to do that all the time on the farm. He basically kept the whole place running with baling wire and WD-40. So, anyhow, we thought he could tell you all the things to look for. And maybe if you can fix that washing machine yourself, you won't have to worry if Mr. Armisted is a little absentminded. It's always good to know how to take care of things yourself.*

I sink down and sit on the bottom step of the stairs. Grandma writes exactly the same way she talks. And this is crazy. If Grandpa really wanted to tell me how to fix the washing machine—er, washer—he could have done it any one of the days we'd Skyped. But I flip through the pages, and he has diagrams and drawings of exact sizes of belts and bolts. . . .

*Maybe he couldn't have done this in a Skype,* I think.

Unlike Grandma's words, Grandpa's are all technical. If my eyes weren't so blurry with tears, I could study his drawings and know everything there is to know about washers.

At least, what they were like in about 1970.

The front door of the apartment building rattles, like someone's put a key in the lock. I haven't actually met any of our neighbors yet, and I don't want to try having a conversation in Spanish when I can't even see straight. I grip Grandma and Grandpa's letter and start rushing up the stairs.

By the time I get up to our floor, I'm gasping for air. But I stand on the landing for a few minutes catching my breath before I unlock the apartment door. I tiptoe in.

The coast is clear. Mr. Armisted must still be out on the balcony. Avery must still be in her room.

I'm hot and sweaty, but I just splash water on my face in the bathroom, rather than taking a full shower. The washer is actually in the bathroom. I don't have any confidence that I could fix it, even with a million diagrams from Grandpa, but I feel like I ought to at least make an effort.

His first direction is *Scoot the washer out from the wall so you can see*, and I'm pretty sure I can do that much.

I grab the washer on each side and tug it forward. There's a *clunk*ing sound in the back.

*Seriously? I already made things worse?*

I peek over the back edge of the washer. Oh. The cord just fell to the floor. It must not have been plugged in all the way.

*Not plugged in all the way?*

I realize what this means. I stuff the plug in the outlet, making sure to line up the holes and the weird round metal tips, which look so different from the prongs on American plugs. The plug goes in securely. I hit one of the buttons on the front panel, and it lights up.

The washer was never broken. It just wasn't plugged in all the way. We could have been using it all along. I wouldn't have had to wash anything in the sink.

I laugh giddily. I've been perfectly fine being alone all day, but I want to share this news with *somebody*.

If I told Avery, she'd just snarl, like she did the first day, *Who cares? It's just a washer.*

She probably owns so many clothes, she doesn't even need to wash anything.

If I told Mr. Armisted, he'd probably just look sadder, and say what he said out on the balcony: *Believe it or not, I used to be good at things like that.*

I leave the washer flashing numbers and possible commands, and I go out and grab the iPad from the kitchen table. I type a message to Mom:

I haven't read your e-mail. I'm not going to. But tell Grandma and Grandpa I figured out what was wrong with the washer here, thanks to them. Tell them I said thank you for the letter.

It's ten o'clock in the morning back home, and Mom's

probably at work, making beds or moving old people around. Or—maybe not. Almost instantly, there's a ping, meaning I got a message back.

Let me call you. Please.

She must be sitting beside the computer at work. Maybe she's not even working. Maybe she's just waiting to hear from me.

*No,* I write back. But I don't hit send yet. *I'm not ready to talk*, I add. I think about Mom running behind me when I was learning to ride a bike without training wheels. I think about her straining to make happy chatter in the car while we're driving to see Dad at the VA, and then in the car on the way home. I think about how she said she'd fix the flat tire herself, when she was driving me to the airport.

*But I'll send you a message every day, so you know I'm okay,* I type. And then I send the message.

I feel powerful, for once in my life. Like I'm taking control.

Or have I just proved I'm not quite as cruel as Avery—just almost?

## Avery, Outraged Again

***Is Kayla right outside my*** *room actually* laughing? *Is she really that heartless? When I'm in so much pain?*

I want to slap her.

But more than that, I don't want to get up.

I burrow deeper into my bedding and cry harder.

## Kayla, on Day Three of the Longest Weekend Ever

**"What *is* that?" Mr. Armisted** asks behind me.

I turn around, knocking against the skillet handle in front of me.

"Um, a grilled cheese sandwich?" I say, and instantly hate myself for making my answer sound like a question. I mean, I know what I'm making here. And Mr. Armisted should be able to see for himself.

Friday and Saturday, I ate at restaurants—100 Montaditos again, and Pans, and I even found a McDonald's. But that was getting really expensive, and I was getting tired of being the only person sitting alone, while the tables around me overflowed with happy families and boisterous groups of friends. So I had the brilliant idea this morning to stop at a grocery store I found on Calle de Atocha, the street that leads up from the train station. I found out they have bread just like the bread at home, except it's labeled BIMBO, with an image of a cuddly teddy bear on the wrapper. (I guess "bimbo" means something different in Spanish than in English.) I looked around for American cheese—I would have even paid extra for Kraft singles, instead of the Supervalu store brand Grandma and Mom always buy. But I couldn't find any cheese that was orange, so I got this stuff called manchego instead. I know this grilled cheese sandwich won't taste like the ones at home, but I told myself back at the grocery store that at least no one would stare at me while I ate it.

I hadn't expected Mr. Armisted to come off his balcony. I hadn't expected Avery to come out of her room. At least, not to talk to *me*.

The past two days, it's been like all three of us are ghosts haunting this apartment. We pass through. We don't speak. We don't even look each other in the eye.

But now Mr. Armisted's looking at me and my grilled cheese sandwich.

"Um, it's okay if I use the stove, right?" I ask.

"Of course, of course," Mr. Armisted says, waving away my question. "It's just . . . that smells good. I . . . I couldn't figure out what it was."

He sags against the half wall that separates the kitchen from the living room. I wonder when the last time was that he ate anything. It's only been three days since Avery saw her messed-up birth certificate, but Mr. Armisted kind of looks like he's aged thirty years. He's got hollows in his cheeks. His eyes are red and puffy. His shoulders slump like he's lost the ability to hold them up.

He doesn't look rich and handsome and powerful anymore. He just looks sad.

I slide a spatula under my grilled cheese sandwich and transfer it to a plate.

"You want this one?" I ask. "I've got more bread and cheese. I bought a lot."

Mr. Armisted's eyes flood with tears.

"Thank you," he says. "Thank you. I . . ."

He looks down at the sandwich almost as if he's forgotten how eating works. Then he walks down the hallway toward the bedrooms, still carrying the plate and the sandwich with him.

"Avery!" he calls. I hear him knocking at her door. "Come on out. Kayla's making grilled cheese sandwiches for everyone."

*Um, no?* I think. That wasn't the plan. But I do have plenty. I butter four slices of bread; I assemble two complete sandwiches and slide them into the skillet.

While the butter and cheese are melting, I set the table and fill three glasses with water and dump carrots into a bowl. I really wanted to buy potato chips or the Doritos I've been craving to go along with my grilled cheese, but the grocery store didn't have any.

What kind of grocery store doesn't have potato chips?

The sandwiches are ready by the time Mr. Armisted returns to the kitchen. He's clutching Avery's arm like he thinks he needs to hold her up. Her hair hangs down over her face like a curtain; she's swaying slightly.

*Geez*, I think. *When was the last time either of them ate?*

"It's all ready," I say brightly, like I'm Suzy Sunshine and I've totally forgotten that Avery wouldn't want me for a sister.

I sound like my mother. My mother at the nursing home, when some resident is shouting obscenities at her, and Mom keeps smiling and explaining in her most patient voice, "Yes, I know it hurts to move into the wheelchair, but bedsores would hurt even worse."

Mr. Armisted and Avery sit down, and I take the third chair. Avery pushes her hair back and picks up a carrot. She winces as she bites into it. It's like she's not sure her teeth work anymore.

Mr. Armisted chews, swallows, chews some more. He takes a long drink of water. He puts his glass down.

"This is good," he says. "It's okay that we took a couple days to . . . adjust. I think we all needed that. But we can't stay . . . stuck like this. Tomorrow I'll go back to work. You two will go back to your Spanish class, like usual. We'll have a normal life again. Thanks to Kayla, we're easing back into it. Eating grilled cheese sandwiches is normal."

It feels like he's just dropped something onto the table in front of us. I don't know what to do or say. Now would not be a good time to mention that Avery has *never* gone to the Spanish class her dad is paying for.

But . . . I kind of want to. I want to punish Avery for what she said about me.

Avery lifts her head.

"This is not my normal life," Avery says, and each word is like a knife thrust.

Mr. Armisted flinches, and his emotions are so naked and close to the surface, his face is like a war zone. I watch in fascination: Will he cry? Will he yell? Will he run back to the balcony?

Would he jump if he got out to the balcony?

It scares me that I think of that.

"I wasn't even born in a normal way!" Avery says. "My parents aren't normal! And now you're getting divorced!"

Mr. Armisted clenches his teeth. He's facing Avery; maybe to her he looks like this stern, totally sure-of-himself authority figure.

But I'm off to the side. I can see a muscle twitching at his jawline.

"Maybe 'normal' wasn't the right word," he says quietly. "I

meant . . . good. Your life can still be good. Like . . . this grilled cheese sandwich is good."

Avery looks down at the sandwich on her plate.

"She used white bread," Avery says. "Who buys awful squishy white bread like this? Especially in Spain, where they have all sorts of good food?"

The muscle on Mr. Armisted's jaw goes crazy. But he turns his head slowly toward me.

"Kayla," he says in an unnaturally loud voice, "I apologize for my daughter's rudeness." He faces Avery again. "Avery, you and I are going out on the balcony to have a little talk."

"Fine," Avery says, getting up so fast she knocks her chair over. "I didn't want this food, anyway."

They leave. For a moment, I just sit there, staring down at my sandwich. I haven't even taken a bite, but I'm not hungry anymore.

I pick up my sandwich and throw it in the trash.

I throw everybody's food in the trash.

## Avery, on the Balcony

**I don't put my hands** over my ears, but I might as well. I block out every single word my father speaks. I don't want to listen to him ever again.

But my ears betray me. I hear the word "mother."

"She finally called again?" I ask, too eagerly. "Has she . . . has she been trying to call me, too?"

I hate myself. It's like I'm a puppy, jumping up and wagging its tail because Mom *might* be trying to get in touch with me.

Dad's face sags. His shoulders droop.

"I'm sorry, honey," he says. "No. At least, I don't think so. She . . . she needs time."

"But you said . . . ," I begin, trying to replay in my mind the words that surrounded "mother." The words I'd tuned out.

"I said *Kayla's* mother has been frantic," Dad corrects me. "Kayla refused to talk to her, so Mrs. Butts sent a long e-mail explaining everything. But Kayla's refusing to read it."

It's weird: I kind of want to cheer for Kayla: *You go, girl! Let's unite against our awful, lying, secret-keeping parents! We'll show them!*

But I don't *really* want to unite with Kayla.

And we've got nothing in common. *She* wasn't born from a surrogate mother. *Her* parents aren't getting divorced.

*Her* mother isn't ignoring her.

## Kayla, Wandering Again

**Are there rules for crying** in public in Spain?

That should have been in the tourist information Mr. Armisted sent me ahead of time, instead of the brochures about the Alhambra and the Aqueduct of Segovia and the Prado. It's like he lured me here with promises that Spain would be so, so different from Crawfordsville.

I forgot "different" could mean "worse."

I had to get out of the apartment again. But now I'm wishing I'd just gone to my room and slammed the door. Because now I'm stumbling through Puerta del Sol with all its happy tourists and sunshine, and tears are streaming down my face.

*I managed to hold back the tears Thursday night until I was alone in the blue room*, I tell myself. *And that was after I found out that my mother was a surrogate mother and Avery said, 'Does that mean Kayla's my sister?' in that awful, awful way. Why can't I stop crying now? Just because Avery didn't like her grilled cheese sandwich? Who cares?*

I do. I thought I was being so nice, making those sandwiches.

I thought I was doing better. I'd taken care of myself all weekend. I'd walked all over Madrid without getting lost. I'd "fixed" the washer. I'd gone grocery shopping.

I thought I was so much better off than Avery or Mr. Armisted. *I* was helping *them*!

But I guess it's a crime to like white bread.

A wail comes out of my mouth, and I can't stop it.

A woman pushing a stroller says something to me, but I can't even tell what language she's speaking. I shake my head and push past her. I dart down a side street, but it's crowded with happy people too, shopping or sitting at sidewalk cafés eating or drinking or smoking.

What is wrong with the people in Spain, that they're all so happy all the time?

I am pathetic. Even after Avery was so mean to me, I *still* made her that sandwich. I set myself up.

I cry harder.

I'm walking with my head down now, looking at the sidewalk. The manhole covers I pass all say BOMBEROS, and I don't know what that means. Should I be worried about bombs, on top of everything else? I keep bumping into people, and I think they curse at me, but what do I know? I don't understand Spanish. I don't understand anything.

I have to get out of this crowd.

I glance around, and there's a church up ahead. I remember how Mr. Armisted said a lot of the churches and cathedrals in Spain are tourist attractions, so they're open pretty much all the time.

This church is a lot smaller and plainer than others I've walked past, so probably there aren't that many tourists who want to see it.

Maybe I could sit at the back and nobody would bother me, because they'd think I was praying. Maybe I *could* pray.

*Yeah, lot of good that's done me*, I think, as if I'm talking back to Grandma and Grandpa and the Autumn Years residents who are always urging me to pray.

It doesn't matter. The church is a place to hide, and that's what I need right now. I walk across an open courtyard and up the stairs. I pull back a heavy door.

The sanctuary is huge. There are statues and pillars and a dome and practically floor-to-ceiling paintings. And the ceiling is the equivalent of three or four stories off the ground.

I'm so stunned that it takes me a moment to realize that there's a priest chanting at the front, and people lined up in the pews, repeating after him.

It's Sunday. I've walked in on a church service.

Guilt twists in my stomach, because Grandma and Grandpa and several of my favorite Autumn Years residents told me to be sure to find a "church home" in Madrid, because that would make everything better. They just assumed that I would want to go to church every Sunday. And I hadn't even thought about it until now.

I sit down in an empty pew.

But the service is in Spanish, of course, and I can't understand a single word anyone is saying. Anyhow, I'm pretty sure this is a Catholic church, and I'm not Catholic.

My mind wanders. I think about this woman who died a few years ago at Autumn Years: Bethel Smith. She'd tell her story to anyone who'd listen. Back in the days before smoke detectors, her house caught fire in the middle of the night. Her husband shoved her out the window to safety right before he ran deeper into the flames to try to save their three little kids. And just then, the roof collapsed. She lost her entire family.

"Prayer was the only thing that got me through that," Mrs. Smith always said. "I've been clinging to the hand of God ever since."

The thing is, Bethel Smith was one of the most cheerful people I've ever known.

For that matter, though she doesn't talk about it all the time like Bethel Smith did, I know my mom prayed a lot after my dad's accident. And she still does. I see her lips moving silently sometimes when we're walking into the VA.

*Well, yeah, my mother's a saint. Of course she prays.*

My mother isn't a saint. She just has secret shame. I keep forgetting.

The priest at the front of this church is droning along as if he's just saying words—as if even he's stopped paying attention to what's coming out of his mouth.

*He's probably saying, "Turn the other cheek." And "The meek shall inherit the earth." And "If someone sins against you, forgive them seven times seventy times."*

This makes me so mad I want to run up the aisle and start shoving things off the altar: candles, flowers, statues . . . .

*Wait a minute. Didn't Jesus do something like that once?*

The story comes back to me—Jesus was mad at the money changers in the temple. So he threw their tables over.

*If it was okay for Jesus to get mad, can't I be mad too?*

What is wrong with me that I'm thinking things like that in a church?

Everyone in front of me bows their heads and starts saying the same words altogether: *"Padre nuestro que estás en los cielos . . ."* I don't recognize all the words, but I recognize the cadence. It's the Lord's Prayer: "Our Father who art in heaven . . ."

*Yeah, well, that father image never really worked for me. I never saw* my *dad as strong and powerful.*

My mom, maybe, but not my dad.

*Do I think my mother was weak because she got pregnant? Because she* wanted *to get pregnant for the Armisteds?*

I stand up and walk out while the congregation and the priest still have their heads bowed, before they get to the "Amen." I'm pretty sure that's rude and disrespectful in any church, any culture.

But at least I'm not crying anymore.

I walk back to the Puerta del Sol and I sit down near a statue I didn't notice before. It's a bear standing up against some kind of tree, like he's trying to eat its berries. The tree seems too small or the bear seems too big; things are out of proportion.

I sit there and I watch the people walking by. I was wrong before. It's not like *everybody's* happy. That couple over there by the fountain—I think they're mad at each other. The girl's got her back turned; the boy's looking away. The guy in the Winnie the Pooh costume—he's got to be sweating himself half to death. He keeps shoving the head to the side like that's the only way to get air. That group of teenage boys over there—I just saw one of them punch the guy next to him on the arm. But maybe it was just in a joking way. It's hard to tell with boys.

*And that group of teenage boys . . . oh, crap.*

It's the Bulgarians from my Spanish class.

Quickly, before any of them see me, I slip past the bear statue and scurry out of the plaza.

If I had a different life, if I were somebody else—Stephanie Purley, maybe—I would have rushed *toward* them. I would have flirted: *Oh hey, funny seeing you here!*

Not that I know how to say that in Spanish.

And anyhow, I'm sure my eyes are still red from crying, and I've got tear tracks streaked down my face. And it's not like I bothered combing my hair before I stumbled out of the apartment.

I'm mad again, because I don't have a different life. I'm not somebody else. I stomp back toward the apartment, back up the stairs, back through the door.

Mr. Armisted is in the kitchen, putting a box in the refrigerator.

"Oh good, there you are," he says. "Avery and I went out and got pizza. We brought some back for you."

Avery made fun of my grilled cheese, and he rewarded her by getting pizza instead? Really?

"I'm not hungry," I mumble.

"Well, it's here if you want it later," he says. "And I'm having food delivered tomorrow. I promise, the rest of the summer won't be like this weekend. We'll . . . pull ourselves back together."

"Okay," I say. I resist the urge to add, *Whatever.*

I start to head down the hallway, then turn back.

"I figured out what was wrong with the washer," I say. "We don't need a repairman."

"You did?" Mr. Armisted says. "You're amazing!"

Now I can't tell him it just needed to be plugged in.

"Thank you," Mr. Armisted says. "Thank you for agreeing to

stay the rest of the summer, and thank you for trying with the grilled cheese sandwiches earlier, and . . . thank you for being the stable one."

Stable? *Stable?* Can't he see that I'm not stable either?

I speed down the hallway before I start yelling at him.

But I don't make it all the way to my room. I pass Avery's door—closed tight—and somehow just the sight of it makes me madder than ever. Before I can stop myself, I knock.

There's a long silence, and then a grumpy, "Go away."

"No," I say.

I turn the knob and shove my way in. Avery is sprawled facedown on her bed.

I'm not going to feel sorry for her.

I go over and crouch close to her ear.

"Tomorrow," I say, "when your dad thinks we're both going to Spanish class together . . . I'm not going to cover for you anymore. If you don't go, I'm not going to pretend that you did. Do you understand?"

I hate myself for adding that last part. *Do you understand?* is what the principal of Crawfordsville High School, Mr. Ockston, always says at assemblies when kids get rowdy. Everyone ignores him. Even the teachers think he's an idiot.

"No—you know what?" I tell Avery. "I don't even care if you understand or not. That's how it's going to be."

I stand up. I haven't yelled at her. I haven't slapped her. I haven't even used swear words.

But I feel self-righteous and vindicated and strong.

I'm not even mad about the grilled cheese anymore.

## Avery at Midnight

**I tiptoe out of my** room. I've been planning this for hours. I peer down the hall at the other bedroom doors, and both of them are shut tight, surrounded by darkness. Both Dad and Kayla have got to be asleep by now.

Silently, I creep toward the living room and kitchen. I don't turn on a light, but grope along the couches and tables. There. Dad's iPad is on the coffee table, right where Kayla always leaves it after she's done with it every night.

*So . . . is Kayla as stupid as I think she is?* I wonder. *Dumb enough to leave herself logged in on someone else's device?*

I flip open the iPad cover and sit down on the couch. The screen glows at me. A twinge of guilt hits me.

*Think about how mean Kayla was, threatening to tattle if I don't go to Spanish class tomorrow,* I tell myself. *Think about how unfair everything is.*

Think about how she won't talk to her mother, when my mother won't talk to me.

I go to Gmail, and, yes, Kayla *is* stupid. A whole string of e-mail pops up. The sender of each one is listed as Stacy Butts. Kayla's mom.

*You don't have anyone else who wants to talk to you, huh, Kayla?* I think, as if she's around to taunt. *Do you have* any *friends?*

This is silly, because how many teenagers communicate with their friends by e-mail?

It does seem possible that someone like Kayla might.

I click on the top e-mail, the newest one. It opens up:

Oh, Kayla, I was so glad to hear from you today, and so glad you say you're doing fine. But what did you do all day? Where did you go? Please please please let me call you . . .

The woman's pathetic. My mother would never beg like that.

My mother won't even call. . . .

I click out of the e-mail because it's not the one I want. I scroll back to one that's date-stamped Thursday night.

Kayla, my sweet, sweet Kayla, this was never the way I wanted you to find this out. I never imagined things could happen this way. It feels like you're a million miles away. No matter what time of day or night you're reading this, CALL ME! I'd rather talk about all of this. You know writing's not my thing.

I never thought the Armisteds would breathe a word about this. They were the ones who wanted to keep this secret, not me. I was proud of being a surrogate mother. The plan in the beginning was that I would tell you, I would tell Grandma and Grandpa . . . Even Avery was supposed to know, her whole life.

I frown. *Is this true? What changed?*

I keep reading.

You know some of the things that were different fourteen, fifteen years ago. But it's hard even for me to remember. . . . What was it? The hope? The optimism? The faith that I had?

The blindness?

You only know your daddy the way he is now. And from the stories your grandparents and I have told you, I guess. But he was a force of nature. When he said he was going off to Afghanistan to kick some Osama bin Laden butt, I believed him. I thought your daddy could single-handedly finish off Al-Qaeda.

But . . . that meant killing people, you know? I couldn't quite get my head around that. Sure, he'd be killing bad people, the enemy. But innocent civilians were dying in the war too. Women and children.

Like me and you.

Your daddy would leave for training and I'd be standing there changing your diaper and you'd coo up at me, and all I could think about was the Afghan women on the other side of the world who were probably changing their kids' diapers too. They probably loved their children the same way I loved you. And THEY hadn't done anything, but they were going to be killed. By good American soldiers and marines like your daddy.

I have to look away for a minute. War—people die in war. Everybody knows that.

What I can't help wondering is, *Did my mother actually ever change one of my diapers when I was a baby? Or did she always make the nanny do it?*

Would Celeste Sterling Armisted even touch a baby's diaper?

Did Kayla's mom ever wonder about that too?

The unkind way to look at what I decided is that I was trying to bargain with God. That's what some of my friends said, the ones who tried to talk me out of being a surrogate mother. I would bring new life into the world as a gift for some other family; God would keep your daddy safe in the war, and even make it so he didn't have to kill anyone but bad guys. But I didn't think of it as bargaining. It was more like . . . trying for some balance. I wasn't looking for any guarantees or promises. I knew that wasn't possible. There was terrible, terrible evil in the world that meant your daddy was going to have to go off to war and kill people. I accepted that. But I didn't want to sit home doing nothing while he was away. I wanted to do something good, something BIG and good. As big as war and killing, except on the opposite side. Giving someone life, not death.

You know your grandma and grandpa had trouble having children. The whole time I was growing up, I heard about how sad they were, all the years before I was born. Grandma told me once it almost drove them to divorce—and you know how much they don't like divorce. You know how much they belong together.

I grip the iPad so tightly I accidentally hit the X at the top of the screen and the e-mail disappears. Why do some couples belong together and others don't?

Why do my parents have to be the unlucky ones, a bad couple, people who can do nothing but fight?

If having a kid was what kept Kayla's grandparents together, why didn't that work for my parents?

I can't answer any of those questions, and I don't like thinking about them. I bring the e-mail back, but I skim down a ways.

I found out when I was pregnant with you, Kayla, that I'm one of those lucky women who don't have any problems with it. I was never sick with either you or Avery. I never made a big deal about this with you—because it's not really something to emphasize with a teenager—but I LOVED being pregnant. I don't know that I looked like I glowed, like people always say, but I felt that way. Your dad and I wanted more kids after you, but we knew we'd have to wait until he was back from the war, until we had a little bit more money saved. So I thought, why not get pregnant for someone else in between?

Just to be clear: Even though we didn't have much money, I DIDN'T become a surrogate mother because of the payment. There are rules about that. And, really, if I was only looking at making money, I could have started babysitting and practically made the same. This is not complaining about what the Armisteds paid me—I wouldn't have wanted the money to be my reason. They were just paying for my medical care and my time and . . . the risk. That was fair. Don't let anyone tell you different.

I want to talk back to Kayla's mom.

*Oh, so if you just say it wasn't like my parents bought me, does that keep it from being baby buying?*

Didn't she read any of the websites I read the other day, about why so many countries make it illegal to pay surrogate mothers?

I guess she wouldn't have read them before she got pregnant. Because they wouldn't have existed fourteen years ago.

Didn't she know about Baby M or any of the other babies that came from surrogate mothers, who became legal hot potatoes, when surrogate mothers or the parents who'd paid surrogate mothers changed their minds about keeping or giving away or even wanting the babies?

Was she crazy, that she just did this thing—having a baby that wasn't hers—without seeing all the ways it could go wrong?

The agency I worked with gave me a lot of profiles to look at. Picking the right family seemed like a sacred duty. The Armisteds stood out because they were from Ohio originally, just like I was, and I was a little homesick. And they planned to move back to Ohio eventually, just like your dad and I did. And Mr. Armisted had a farm connection, just like we did. And they seemed . . . golden. They were both so smart and so talented, and they wanted a baby so badly. . . . I knew they would take good care of any child they had. And that child would have so many advantages; surely she'd grow up to do great things for the whole world. . . .

*Well. You see how idealistic I was.*

What does that mean? Doesn't Kayla's mom still think I could do great things for the world?

The timing worked out that I got pregnant—with the very first implantation, which I thought was a good sign—just as your dad was preparing to deploy. He thought the surrogacy was a good thing too, because it would give me something happy to focus on while he was away.

Of course, you know that he never deployed, because of the accident.

Wait—what? Does "deploy" not mean what I think it means? Didn't Kayla's dad go off to war, and wasn't that where he got hurt?

I try to remember why I thought that, what I'd ever heard about Kayla's dad. But even when Kayla and I were pretty much besties, back when we were little, I'd never really paid attention to anything I heard about either of her parents. They were adults—who cared?

Probably, Angelica was the one who told me Kayla's dad was a war hero. She always was good with the fanciful stories.

She also assured me every single day that my parents loved me.

Blinking hard, I go back to the e-mail.

But I've never told you the whole story of the night of the accident. Your dad and I went to a good-bye party. My friend Sonia said you could spend the night with her—her husband wasn't being deployed. I've never wanted you to be mad at Lester, the friend who was driving the car that night. I think now that the whole unit was terrified of going off to war, but they were too tough to let it show. I think that's what their problem was. But I also don't want you to be mad at your dad when I tell you how things happened. We were at this party, and I was pregnant, so I had to be careful about everything. And I was at the stage of pregnancy where it's like my body was saying, Sleep . . . All I want to do is sleep. . . . So I kept yawning. And that upset your dad. He said something like, "I'm leaving tomorrow and you can't even stay awake?" I said we should both just go home, and he said no, and that made me mad. I understand now—I know if we'd gone home, we would have talked about how scared I was for him, and maybe even how scared he was. And he didn't want to talk about any of that. But that night I was nothing but mad, and I said, "Fine, I'll take a cab." And he said, "Go ahead."

If I'd known that was going to be the last conversation your dad and I would ever have where it was both of us talking, of course I'd have turned around. If he'd called out, Wait! I would have turned around anyhow. But we were both just twenty-one, and I don't think you can understand how impossibly young that is. I regretted everything the minute I was in the cab, but it felt like that was already too late.

The thing is, if I hadn't been pregnant, if we hadn't had that fight, we would have stuck with the original plan, which was for Lester to drive both of us home. That would have happened no matter how much he'd had to drink. You could never tell by looking at Lester how drunk he was. I saw pictures of his smashed-up car; I know where I would have been sitting. And you may think I'm making too much of this, but I know this as well as I know anything else about that year: If I hadn't been pregnant with Avery, I would have died that night. You would have lost me and, for all practical purposes, your father, all at once.

Being a surrogate mother saved my life.

It saved me later on too, because it was so hard those first few months after your dad's accident. The only reason I bothered to eat was because Avery had to stay healthy. You were with Grandma and Grandpa by then; I knew you were in good hands. But just then, I was the only one who could take care of Avery. So I had to take care of myself, too.

I sink deeper into the couch cushions. So there—I did something great before I was even born. I saved Kayla's mother's life.

I'm not sure I buy her spin. She could also argue that if she hadn't been pregnant, she would have been there with Kayla's dad when it was time to go home. She could have stopped that drunk guy from driving. She could have saved everyone.

Or maybe not. It seems like marines would take orders only from other marines.

I like thinking I saved somebody's life.

I went into labor with Avery the same day the doctors told me your dad was never going to get any better. This lady—a social worker, I guess—was saying, "You know the VA will always take care of his medical expenses," and I said, "You think THAT'S what I'm concerned about?" and that was when I felt the first contraction. Maybe it was the shock that sent me into labor. When I got pregnant with Avery, I never dreamed she would be the last baby I'd ever give birth to. But that day, when I went from standing beside your father's hospital bed to lying in one of my own . . . I don't want you to feel sorry for me. But I never knew how hard everything was going to be. For me, it felt like an end, not a beginning. It was an end.

Mr. and Mrs. Armisted were really kind. I wasn't one of those surrogate mothers who had second thoughts. Not quite. I never wanted to keep Avery. At that point, I wasn't even able to take care of YOU. But Mrs. Armisted and I both changed our minds about one part of what we'd agreed to in the beginning. She held Avery in her arms for the first time and said, "We can't ever let her know she's anything but one hundred percent OURS." And I looked at Avery in her parents' arms and thought, This can't be the last time I ever see that child. I didn't want to raise her—I COULDN'T raise her. But I had to know that she would be all right, from more than pictures and letters and e-mails that could say anything.

I think Mr. Armisted would have agreed to anything, just to keep everyone happy. Because he loved that little baby so much.

When you hold a newborn baby, it's really hard to throw your imagination ten, fifteen, twenty years into the future. It feels like a miracle that the child even exists, let alone that she's going to grow up someday, that she's going to have thoughts and feelings and rights of her own. The agency advised us not to change anything in our agreement; they said we'd change our minds again. They warned us. But after Avery was born, we did change things. We agreed to keep the surrogacy secret from everyone who didn't already know, and in exchange I would get to see Avery every now and then, as long as I never told. I was just relieved that everything worked out.

It was only later that I thought how much I was like someone in a fairy tale, not seeing how a wish could backfire.

I've wanted to tell you for years, but it didn't seem fair to tell you and not have Avery know. And I'd promised. And I had no right to tell Avery. Only her parents have that right. So I was stuck keeping a secret I wanted desperately to tell. Stuck having to act like I'm ashamed of having been a surrogate mother. When, really, it was one of the two best things I ever did.

Of course, having you was the very best.

Would my mother have ever said that about me? That I was the best thing that happened to her?

*No? Yes? Once upon a time, but not now?*

I feel like I understand Kayla's mother right now better than I understand my own. And that's not right.

I click out of the e-mail and shove the iPad away. It slides across the couch cushions.

I shouldn't have read this. It doesn't belong to me.

I can never let Kayla know what I did.

## Kayla, Headed Back to Spanish Class

**In the morning, I'm not** sure what's going to happen. Will Avery actually go to Spanish class with me? And if she doesn't, will I actually have the nerve to tell Mr. Armisted?

Or will I chicken out?

Who's more likely to back down, Avery or me?

*Me*, I think, still lying in bed. *Definitely me.*

Angrily, I throw the covers off. I rush through the bathroom, yanking my comb through my tangled hair so roughly it makes my eyes water.

I tell myself it's only because of the snagged hair that I have tears in my eyes.

I go out to the kitchen, and Mr. Armisted and Avery are both sitting at the table eating breakfast. At least, they have rolls and yogurt and fruit on the plates in front of them. Neither of them actually lift food to their mouths.

"Good morning! *Buenos dias!*" Mr. Armisted says. He seems to be trying to smile, but the corners of his mouth tremble. He and Avery both look pale and washed-out, as if the weekend bleached away everything vivid about them.

Avery doesn't say anything, and neither do I.

Mr. Armisted's phone buzzes beside him, and he glances at the screen.

"It's official—there are now a hundred fires I have to put

out before noon today, when everyone starts waking up back in America," he says. "Better be off."

He kisses Avery's forehead and awkwardly pats my hair. Then he's out the door.

I expect Avery to groan and roll her eyes and race back to her room and slam the door, but she doesn't. She keeps picking at the roll on her plate. She drops the crumbs one by one.

"Is the Metro crowded with rush-hour traffic?" she asks. "I'm not riding it if it's crowded. That's when you have to worry about pickpockets."

"It's not that crowded," I say, as if I've been riding subways all my life. When, really, all I have to compare it to is Crawfordsville's empty streets, where it's a big deal if five cars pass by in an hour. I open the refrigerator and pour myself a glass of orange juice. "Remember, your dad said people go to work late here. Our classes start early, by Spain standards."

I think I'm quoting her father exactly, which is a little embarrassing.

"You know, fruit juice isn't really that good for you," Avery blurts as I take my first sip. "You'd think it would be, but it's mostly empty calories. It's almost as bad as drinking soda. It's kind of the same thing with white bread. I wasn't criticizing you last night, just pointing out—"

"Avery," I say, "shut up."

Her eyes widen.

"I'm just trying to help!"

"No," I say. I tilt my glass back and drink the rest of the juice. "You aren't. You're trying to make me feel fat and stupid.

And I'm not going to let you do that to me. Not anymore. I don't care what you think about me."

The juice feels like it's already curdling in my stomach, but Avery doesn't have to know that. I grab an apple and a granola bar. I'll eat them later. I'm not eating in front of Avery right now.

Her jaw drops and she stares at me as I dart out of the kitchen.

*That's it*, I think. *I just made sure that she won't go to Spanish class.*

But when I head for the door twenty minutes later, she's waiting beside it. I don't say anything. She trails after me out the door and down the stairs like a whipped puppy.

*I'm not going to feel sorry for her*, I tell myself. *I'm not.*

We're out on the street, headed toward the Sol Metro station, when she says, "The other kids are nice, right? In the class, I mean."

"As far as I can tell," I say. "I mostly don't have any idea what anyone's saying."

She takes this in. When I look back again, she's biting her lip.

*Oh, for crying out loud*, I think, one of Grandma's favorite expressions. I fight against letting this make me homesick.

"I've really just hung out with the Bulgarian kids, and they're nice," I say. "And funny."

"Those are the guys who were fighting over you, right?" she says, starting in on a teasing grin.

How is she so good at knowing the exact right thing to say to make me feel miserable?

I turn to face her.

"I never told *you* that," I say. "You were eavesdropping when you heard that, and it's not right to eavesdrop, so I'm not even going to talk about this with you."

For some reason, Avery's face turns a bright, painful red, as if I've really embarrassed her.

## Avery, in Class

***I will not think about*** *my parents getting divorced.*

*I will not think about how I was born.*

*I will not think about how my dad's falling apart.*

*I will not think about how my mom won't even text me.*

*I will not think about how I read Kayla's e-mail.*

I thought it would be easier to avoid thinking about any of those things if I went to Spanish class. But it's like just walking down the street is an obstacle course, with pitfalls everywhere. There's a little girl holding her mother's hand, and I think, *Oh, Mom used to hold my hand like that. Was she thinking even way back then,* This isn't really my daughter*?*

There's a young couple kissing in a doorway—maybe just because one of them's leaving for work?—and it's way more passionate than you'd ever see in public in the United States. It's almost embarrassing to watch, but you can't not watch. And I think, *Can you kiss someone like that and still fall out of love? Are those people married? Will they ever get divorced? Would they get divorced if their daughter found out a secret she wasn't supposed to know and ruined everything?*

More than once, Kayla has to take my arm and pull me forward, to get me to move at all.

Maybe I'm getting sick, for real this time. With something worse than cramps. If that's true, I shouldn't be going to Spanish class. I should be tucked into bed, with someone feeling my forehead for a fever, someone bringing me chicken noodle soup.

But who's going to do that? Dad's at work. Mom's on the other side of the ocean. Angelica stopped being my nanny years ago.

And Kayla . . .

*How could I have ever thought she was mousy? If she had a bowl of chicken noodle soup right now, she'd throw it in my face.* After *she made sure it was boiling hot. What changed?*

I know what changed. She found out her mother gave birth to me.

But shouldn't that make her nicer to me? As if we're connected?

*Like finding out we're connected made* me *nicer to* her*?*

I tell myself it's not a fair comparison. Kayla only found out one little detail about something her mom did fourteen years ago. What her mother did, being a surrogate mother, that really doesn't have anything to do with Kayla.

I found out my parents have been lying to me my entire life, and now they're getting divorced because I found out. That has everything do to with me.

Kayla *should* be nice to me. It really is like I'm sick. Or injured.

"This is the school," Kayla says, jerking my arm back because I'm about to walk past the door. "*La escuela.* Remember, the teacher will yell at you if you don't speak Spanish."

"Does she correct pronunciation too?" I ask. "'School' is 'la es-squay—'"

Kayla lets go of my arm so suddenly I almost fall over.

"You know what?" she says. "I don't care what happens to you. I'm done trying to help. Find the classroom by yourself."

Kayla whips open the door and darts up the stairs much faster than I would have thought possible.

I stand there blinking back tears. I want to go back to the apartment and crawl back into bed, but I don't remember how to get back to the subway. And I can't even look it up, because I never got Dad to unlock my iPhone to use in Spain. I just have the stupid burner phone. Could I call Dad and tell him I got sick, and get him to come in a cab to pick me up? And then . . .

"*Disculpe*," someone says, brushing past me.

It's a guy who's maybe just a little older than me. He's flanked by two other guys and a girl who's reaching for the door handle. Guy #1 flashes me an apologetic smile. He's got straight white teeth and an even tan, and just the way he walks makes me think his family is really rich. He probably owns his own polo pony. Maybe he's even related to royalty.

"*Va* . . . I mean, *¿Vas a la clase de español?*" I ask. Which I hope means, *Are you going to the Spanish class?*

"*Sí*," Guy #1 says.

I totally drop my plans to call Dad.

"Okay, *gracias*," I say. "*Bien.*"

*So there, Kayla*, I think. *I don't need your help. And I wouldn't want to be seen hanging out with you right now, anyway. You'd ruin my image for sure!*

I follow Mr. Amazing and his friends through the school door. I want to explain, *I missed last week because I was sick, and then I got lost, and this mean girl I was hanging out with abandoned me. So you're my hero!* But maybe these are the

Bulgarian kids, and it sounds like they actually like Kayla. And anyway, it would take me ten minutes to figure out how to say any of that in Spanish. So I just trail after Mr. Amazing and the Amazing-ettes as they head for the stairs.

We go up so many flights I lose count. Mr. Amazing doesn't look back at me again, but I rehearse things I could say if he does. Maybe *¿Cómo se llama?* Do I want to know his name, or do I want to keep thinking of him as Mr. Amazing?

We reach the final landing, and the Amazings turn down the hall and into a classroom. I am a little relieved to see Kayla sitting at one of the desks. So I am in the right place. But I turn my head and pretend I don't even notice her.

"Avery?" This comes from a woman standing at the front of the classroom. She's got her dark hair pulled back into one of those French twists, and it hurts a little to see that. I can remember Mom and Dad going to a party once, and Mom had her hair fixed that way. It was a special-occasion hairstyle for her, and she and Dad looked so happy. So beautiful. So handsome. But this woman wears her hair in a twist on an ordinary day, just to teach Spanish to teenagers, and Mom and Dad are getting divorced, and . . .

"Avery?" the woman says again.

"Oh—yes," I say. "I mean, *sí*." Now, why didn't I look up and memorize my explanation for the teacher? "Uh, *la semana*, uh . . ."

"*¿La semana pasada?*" the teacher asks.

Yes, that would be how you say "last week" in Spanish.

"*La semana pasada, yo es*, uh . . . ," I try again.

"*Enferma. Ella está enferma*," a male voice says from

somewhere out in the classroom. I want to believe it's Mr. Amazing helping me, but the voice came from the wrong side of the room.

The teacher corrects whoever it was—I think he forgot to use past tense. But I'm relieved that the teacher points me to a seat. Unfortunately, it's next to Kayla, not the Amazings.

A guy with a faceful of acne leans toward me. Don't they have Clearasil in Europe?

"*Hola, Avery*," he says. "*Me llamo Dragomir.*"

A guy who's so skinny he could double as a scarecrow tries to shake my hand.

"*Me llamo Andrei*," he says.

Oh, no. Are these Kayla's Bulgarian friends?

I shoot a glance toward the Amazings, because I want to give them one of those looks that say, *You can tell these aren't the type of people I would normally hang out with, right? I'm just being nice.*

But the Amazings are in a tight circle, talking to one another. They're not even looking my way.

The teacher calls up kids to prepare for some presentation—something neither Kayla nor I are part of, because we weren't here on Friday. We're left alone in a sea of empty desks. Maybe I've jumped to the wrong conclusions. I lean toward Kayla and whisper, "Where are the hot guys who were fighting over you?"

Kayla shoots me an annoyed look and whispers back, "I didn't say anyone was hot. I said they were *nice*."

"Can't they be both?" I ask, almost as if I'm joking around with Shannon and Lauren.

Two angry red spots appear on Kayla's cheeks.

"No, Avery, from what I've seen, people aren't like that," she snarls. "People who think they look good are usually mean. Like, you're really pretty, and . . ."

My face flames.

*No, no, no, no . . .*

"You're prejudiced against good-looking people!" I snap.

"I've *learned,*" she snaps back.

The teacher comes and stands behind us. I don't have to understand a single word she says to know she wants us to shut up.

Dragomir and Andrei and a few other kids start a skit where they shout and laugh a lot, but I can't really follow any of it. Then the Amazings do a skit that's more dignified, but just as incomprehensible.

I thought I knew a lot of Spanish. I got all As in my eighth-grade class.

*You're just . . . thrown off this morning*, I tell myself. *Distracted. It's not like there are going to be tests or grades here. This doesn't even matter. You don't care about learning Spanish.*

I let the Spanish flow past me. I'm just floating in a river of bungled verb tenses and messily trilled *R*s. I'm not thinking about anything.

Then it's lunchtime.

We go down to a cafeteria that could be a cafeteria practically anywhere in the world. I slide a tray along the railing and I end up with a plateful of overcooked pasta and bread and a salad that's mostly iceberg lettuce. Spanish people eat their main meal at lunchtime—a really late lunchtime—so it's a lot of food.

It looks disgusting.

Kayla's ahead of me, and she goes to sit with Dragon-Face Dragomir and Skeletor Andrei and the other kids who were in their skit.

I see there's an empty seat at the opposite side of the room, at the same table with Mr. Amazing.

I lift my head high and walk toward Mr. Amazing's table.

"*¿Puedo?*" I say, pointing with my tray at the empty space in front of that empty chair. I hope "*puedo*" really does mean *Can I?* or *May I?* or something like that.

Mr. Amazing says something I can't understand but he moves his tray over to make more room for me.

I sit down. I smile at Mr. Amazing.

It takes me a minute to assemble the words I want to say, so everyone's already gone back to talking when I attempt, "*¿De donde son?*" I want to know where they're from.

Mr. Amazing says, "Inglaterra," and the guy across from him says, "Londres," and maybe someone chimes in, "Gran Bretaña." I put it all together.

"You're all from England? London, even?" I ask. "So we could all be speaking English right now? That is so great! So much easier!"

The girl says something that includes the word "*español*" three times. When I look at her blankly, she tucks her chin-length blond hair behind her ears and sits up straight, as if she's spoiling for a fight. Then she switches to one of those posh, prissy British accents, "Except *we* want to learn Spanish. So we *shan't* be speaking English."

I think it's the "*shan't*" that does it. My bottom lip starts trembling and my eyes flood.

This is not like me. I do not cry over nothing. Even if something's really wrong, I would never cry in public.

But I can't hold back these tears.

"Excuse me," I mutter. "*Disculpe.* I have something in my eye. *Mi ojo.*"

I abandon my tray and all but run out of the lunchroom. I make it to a bathroom—and then into one of the bathroom stalls—before wails start coming out of me. This is ugly crying at its worst. I sound like a siren, and I can't make it stop. Tears flow out of my eyes and snot floods out of my nose. And I've locked the door and there isn't any toilet paper and . . .

The main door to the bathroom squeaks open. I hear footsteps.

"Avery? Are you in there?"

Somebody came for me.

But it's only Kayla.

## Kayla, Resigned

**"I thought . . .** I thought you were done helping me," Avery wails at me from inside the bathroom stall.

I sink to the floor beside her metal door.

"I thought so too," I admit.

"But you came looking for me. . . ."

I lean my head back against the block wall. It's the same color of Grandma's refrigerator back home: harvest gold. I think she's had that same refrigerator since the 1970s.

I'm in Spain, and I'm homesick for an old refrigerator.

And I'm crouched on a bathroom floor talking to a girl I don't even like.

"You . . . you still cared enough to . . . ," Avery moans. "You saw me run out of the cafeteria, and—"

"*I* wasn't watching you," I say quickly. This is a lie. I saw Avery go over and sit with the group of kids who seem to know so much Spanish, who always seem to have the right answers. Who—okay, let's admit it—are all hot guys and pretty girls.

As far as I could tell, they were the Ryan Deckers and Stephanie Purleys of our Spanish class.

Seeing Avery sit with them, I thought, *It figures.* And then I turned back to the Bulgarian kids, and thanks to Avery, I saw Andrei as Beanpole Boy again, and I noticed that Dragomir had developed a really bad crop of zits over the weekend. And their clothes were all wrong. Thanks to Avery, I saw how Spanish class is divided into winners and losers, just like Crawfordsville High School always was.

And of course I was sitting with the losers.

Then, two minutes later, the cutest of the hot guys had his hand on my shoulder and was saying in one of those incredible British accents you hear only in movies, "Excuse me? I'm a bit concerned about your friend. . . ."

I sigh.

"Hugh asked me to look for you," I tell Avery.

"Hugh?"

"The cute guy you were sitting next to?"

"So he is hot *and* nice," Avery marvels.

"I guess it's possible," I admit grudgingly. "He said you remind him of his little sister."

Avery's silent. I'm pretty sure that isn't how she wanted him to see her.

"Maybe you just didn't understand his Spanish," she says. "Do you even know the word for 'sister'?"

I don't, but I'm not going to admit it.

"He was speaking English," I said. "He probably didn't think I'd understand otherwise."

For some reason, this makes Avery start wailing again.

"Avery? Maybe you should open the door and let me, uh . . ."

I am not crawling under the stall door to get to her. I'm not.

"Do you have a Kleenex?" Avery cries. "My nose is running and my face is covered with snot, and stupid Spain doesn't even have toilet paper in its bathrooms. . . ."

She wants me to be like the little girl handing out Kleenex in the nursing home again. But I left my purse back in the cafeteria. (I guess I *was* worried that I wouldn't find her if I didn't hurry.) I sigh and stand up. At least there's a roll of towels in the dispenser by the sink. I unfurl some of the stiff brown paper, tear it off, and hand it under Avery's stall door.

"Here," I say. "But if you complain that it's hard and scratchy and you can only use, I don't know, those special Kleenex for sensitive skin, so help me, I'm walking out of here right now."

I hear Avery blow her nose. She makes a noise that's halfway between a hiccup and a final sob.

And then she opens the stall door a crack. Her nose is still snotty and her cheeks are red where she must have wiped her tears away with the scratchy towel.

She probably does have sensitive skin.

"Why is everything going wrong?" she asks. Tears tremble in her eyelashes. "From the minute we got to the airport in Columbus . . . and then I lost my passport. . . . if I hadn't lost my passport, my parents wouldn't be getting divorced! It's all my fault!"

I squint at her, trying to figure out this logic.

"I don't think that's why your parents are getting divorced," I say. I think of what Mr. Armisted told me on the balcony, how his wife made fun of him for being a poor, dumb farm boy. How could anyone live with that?

I can't summon up a single memory of seeing Mrs. Armisted in person. I only know her from the Christmas card pictures. I don't think she was ever around when Mom and I went to visit; Avery was always just with Mr. Armisted or, a long time ago, the nanny.

Mrs. Armisted wasn't even at the airport a week and a half ago saying good-bye.

*Was that maybe because I was there?* I wonder. *How did she feel about my mom giving birth to Avery? Did she ever even say thank you?*

Hot shame hits me in the gut, followed by a wave of anger, and I almost miss what Avery says next.

"If I hadn't lost my passport, I never would have known . . . *anything*," she says. "Everything would still be normal. I bet my parents are going to make up and decide to stay together, after all. They have to. But even if that happens, I'm still . . . still . . ."

"You're still Avery Armisted?" I fill in. I'm not sure if I'm trying to be sarcastic or helpful. I just don't want to hear her say anything about my mother.

"*No*, you've got it backward," she wails. "It's like I'm *not* me anymore. There's, like, this gigantic hole inside me where everything about me is missing."

I almost say, *That's how I feel.* But Avery doesn't want to hear about my mother the misguided saint or my friends at Autumn Years or Grandma and Grandpa. She doesn't want to hear about what she took away from *me*.

"You still *look* the same," I say instead, because with the tears and the runny nose, Avery is throwing me into some flashback from when we were best friends, back when we were little. "You still look like when you were four or five, and you could just raise an eyebrow and say, 'But *I* want to play dolls,' and I'd do it. I bet you could do that with all your friends."

Avery sniffs, the way you do when you're trying to keep snot from running down your face. I'm almost happy to see her do something so gross.

"If I still look like I'm five, no wonder Mr. Amazing thinks of me as his little sister," she grumbles.

She was thinking of that Hugh guy as "Mr. Amazing"? Seriously?

I guess she is only fourteen. I guess there is a big difference between fourteen and sixteen.

"Avery, this Spanish class is for high school and college students," I remind her. "Fourteen is the youngest anyone *could* be in the class. So yeah, everyone else is going to be older than you. I just meant . . . You're still pretty. You're still rich. You still get people to watch you. You've always been that way, as long as I've known you."

"But who would I be if I lost all that, too?" she asks. "If I can lose my parents being my parents, and my parents being married, I could lose anything. What if I'm never really me, ever again?"

I could say, *That's what I want to know.* I could say one of the things the Autumn Years people say when a tragedy happens: *Well, you know, we're all in God's hands. So that's a comfort. That's all we need to know.* But I don't think Avery wants to hear that right now.

"You know I'm not the type of girl who runs away and cries in the bathroom," she says. "*You* know that. How am I ever going to show my face in Spanish class again? How am I ever going to look that Hugh guy in the eye?"

*What if you just never had anything to cry about before?* I want to ask her. *Don't you know everybody gets that eventually?* I think about rich, powerful Mr. Armisted, crying on the balcony back at the apartment. I think about the men in John

Deere caps or Harley-Davidson jackets crying at the nursing home. I think about Mom taking me to see Dad at the VA every weekend.

I think that maybe one of my problems back in Crawfordsville was that I got so good at *not* crying.

I feel about a million years older than Avery.

"Spanish class is over for the day, anyway," I say. "How would you feel about working up to looking Hugh in the eye again . . . while you're playing soccer?"

## Avery, on the Field

**I should have cleats on.** I should have shin guards. I can hear my middle school soccer coach in my head saying, *You play without proper equipment, you're just asking to get injured!*

But it feels amazing to run on green grass, a soccer ball zooming ahead of me.

Finding out that everyone plays soccer after class is the first *pleasant* surprise I've gotten in Spain.

"*How* could you have waited until now to tell me?" I griped to Kayla in the school bathroom.

"You haven't exactly been easy to talk to," she muttered.

"Whatever. I forgive you," I said.

She looked outraged, and I switched to, "Kidding! I mean, I'm sorry. Thank you. Let's go play!"

I dried my tears and scrubbed my face at the bathroom sink. It's amazing—it was possible to stop crying. And now, running a few warm-up plays, I can almost forgive Kayla for everything mean she said to me today. Forgiving my parents, well . . .

*At least soccer's a better distraction than Spanish class.*

"*Tú eres rapido.* Er—*rapida?*" Dragomir calls to me, complimenting my speed.

Then he steals the ball.

"Hey!" I cry out. "That's not fair!"

"*Solo en español!*" the British girl, Susan, yells at me from the goal, where she's batting away other kids' shots.

When we choose teams, I really hope she's on the other side. I'll show her.

We're in a park that's far from the tourist areas; it's built over a highway. It has a wacky twisted pedestrian bridge that just kind of stops in the middle—I don't get that. But it also has a real soccer field with real regulation-size goals. I didn't think I'd get to play on a real field again until I was back in the US. Or, really, to play at all.

It's the Bulgarians, the Brits, and me warming up. Kayla insists she can't do anything but stand on the sideline watching.

"*No puedo jugar*," she says, again and again. "I can't play."

Embarrassing.

Some more guys show up—from the easy way they talk, I'm guessing they're actual Spanish kids. They kind of look like juvenile delinquents, but I don't care. Everyone starts lining up, shaking hands, and I figure out the teams: It's foreigners against Spaniards. There's some discussion, and Dragomir goes and stands with the Spaniards, evening up the teams.

We foreigners get to kick off first. I hear shouts back and forth as we hustle the ball down the field, and though it's all in Spanish, and my mind doesn't work fast enough in Spanish, I enter this Zen phase where I don't hear the actual words, but I think I know what my teammates mean: "Good pass!" "Watch out behind you!" "I'm open!"

I get my foot on the ball, and I'm flying down the field. Dragomir's the right defender, and I zip past him. Then suddenly, I've lost the ball and it's speeding in the opposite direction, toward the other goal. Dragomir grins at me.

I didn't even see his feet move.

"How'd you do that?" I demand. "*Cómo*, uh, *cómo . . .*"

"*Secreto de Bulgaria!*" He pounds his chest like any American guy I've ever known, showing off.

"Wait till next time!" I warn him. "Um, *el tiempo próximo . . .*"

I look around, hoping Mr. Amazing didn't see me lose the ball. But he's playing defense for our team, and he's already sending the ball up the other side.

We score three in a row. The third time, I even get an assist.

My team lines up for the next kickoff, but the Spaniards start shouting angrily. I'm not sure any of us foreigners understand until the biggest guy starts pointing at the chests of his teammates and counting off: "*Uno, dos, tres . . .*"

Oh, yeah. We still have one more player than they do.

Andrei touches a finger to his temple and holds it up in the air as if he's just gotten a brilliant idea. He points at Kayla standing on the sideline.

Kayla backs away.

"*No, no puedo. . . .* I can't run."

"*Ella no puede correr*," Susan, the most annoying girl ever, translates.

"*Ella puede ser tu segunda portera*," Andrei says, pointing toward the goal. "*Una portera que no corre.*"

Does he mean Kayla could just stand in the goal behind the Spaniards' regular goalie, without ever having to run? He thinks that's going to make them happy?

Surprisingly, the Spaniards shrug and wave Kayla toward the goal.

Kayla's still saying no. Andrei runs over and gets down on one knee.

"*¿Por favor?*" he says. "*¿Para mi?*"

He puts his hands together under his chin like he's praying to her. Then he pantomimes that all she has to do is stand there, and maybe raise her hand once or twice to swat away a ball.

Kayla actually laughs and goes trotting off toward the goal.

We get back to playing, and it's glorious again. This is what countries should do instead of having wars: play soccer. I guess that's the idea behind the Olympics and the World Cup.

Even though Kayla insisted she can't run—and I saw her trying at the DC airport, so I know she wasn't lying about that—the rest of my team acts like having her in the goal is an extra obstacle. They're more cautious, waiting for the right shot.

Then Andrei kicks the ball to me, and *I'm* not cautious. I wish I had cleats to dig into the turf, but I still get my toe under the ball; I send it sailing toward the goal. The Spanish goalie leaps a second too late. He's too far out, and the ball flies above his fingertips.

Then the ball arcs down—and slams into Kayla's face before dribbling off to the side, out of bounds.

The Spanish kids roar and surge toward the goal. They slap Kayla on the back so hard she pitches forward. Then they pile on top of her. Is this some kind of Spanish goalie initiation rite? Is the whole team going to end up on top of Kayla?

I catch a glimpse of Kayla's face: There's a red circle on her cheek where the ball hit, and her eyes are wide with shock and maybe even panic. But Spanish guys keep slamming against her.

"Hey, hey—careful! You're hurting her!" I cry. I remember how I had to scare off a guy at a party who was being too friendly with Shannon. I remember how I did that with just a look. But even screaming isn't working now.

*Oh wait, en español. . . .*

"*¡Cuidado!*" I try again. "*¡Mi amiga es . . . frágil!*"

Still nothing.

I wade into the crowd, pulling back on shoulders, shoving Spanish boys away from Kayla. I dig my fingernails into one arm after another.

"Leave her alone!" I scream. "*¡Basta!*"

Now the Spanish guys move out of my way. They laugh and mutter about how crazy I am. One points and calls me something like *El Fuego*, which I think means "fire."

I get down to Kayla, and she's got grass stains on her shorts. Her hair's sticking up all over the place.

And she's glaring at me.

"You're just mad because I stopped your goal," she says.

## Kayla, Confused

**For the rest of the** game, I stand in the goal doing nothing. Once or twice I move out of the way of the Spanish goalie.

I think my team loses, but I'm not really paying attention. I'm not sure I'm really on the team anymore. I was for about five minutes, and then I wasn't.

Because of Avery.

The game breaks up, and everyone from the Spanish class heads toward the Metro stop. I guess the Spanish guys live nearby. People call out, "*Adios*," but I'm not really part of that until Dragomir grabs my arm.

"*¿Hasta mañana?*" he asks.

"*Mañana*," I echo. I'm not sure if I'm just agreeing to see him in Spanish class tomorrow, or if I've committed to standing around on a soccer field again, feeling awkward and stupid.

Nobody else lives near the Sol station—if I understood right, Avery and I are the only ones who aren't in dorms near some university. We're both silent riding the Metro, but once we get off and start walking home, into our deserted alley, Avery says suddenly, "It wasn't about the goal."

"Liar," I spit out. I'm shocked at myself, but she's the one who brought it up. I think about the way she looked at me, down on the ground.

"No, really," Avery says, like she's pleading. "I've been

playing soccer since I was five. If I miss a goal, I shake it off. I wasn't—"

"You were jealous," I say. "Because someone who's never played before could make you look bad."

Of course, it's not like I was really trying to stop her ball. It was just dumb luck. Or—bad luck. My face still hurts. I'm going to have a bruise.

"I was worried about *you*," Avery says. "We don't know any of those guys, and they were all on top of you, and—"

"And you looked at me like I was about to have sex with an entire Spanish soccer team. Like I wanted to. Like I was a slut."

I didn't know I was going to say that until the words are out of my mouth. But there it is. That *is* how Avery was looking at me.

I'm glad nobody's near me now.

Nobody but Avery.

"No!" Avery cries. "I was afraid *they* might do something to *you*. Something you *didn't* want. Hasn't your mom ever had the talk with you about—"

I whirl toward her, my hands balled into fists.

"This is about my mom, isn't it?" I ask. "You think what she did, having you, was . . . was dirty, like she was a prostitute or something, and so I'm like that too, and—"

"Kayla, nobody had to have sex to have me," Avery says quietly. "Nothing about that process was *dirty*. Just . . . weird." She puts up her hands like a shield. "What your mom did, to become a surrogate mother—that was a medical procedure. An *implantation*."

I don't put my fists down. But I don't swing them either.

"I looked it all up online," Avery continues. "I got the facts. Some people would say it's not even right to call your mom a surrogate mother. They prefer the term 'gestational carrier.'"

I step back, scraping my heel on the side of the building. I don't really like hearing the words "medical procedure" or "implantation" either, connected to my mom. Or "gestational carrier." I think about what Avery's dad said, out on the balcony that first night, about how Mom giving birth to Avery was the most generous gift ever. It seems like it would be a kindness to Avery to tell her what he said.

But I'm still too mad.

"Of course *you* were smart enough to look up everything online," I say. "Because *you* have your own iPad, and you don't have to borrow anyone else's. Because you're rich. And you're this amazing soccer player, and you can tell the difference between a team hugging someone and being about to rape someone. . . . I just thought I was part of a team for once, and then you had to go and make it seem like something awful!"

"I'm not used to playing soccer with guys," Avery says, in a way that makes me remember she was crying on a bathroom floor just a few hours ago. "It's always with other girls, and there are coaches and refs, and . . . you know. Adult supervision. I'm sorry. I guess I wasn't sure what I was seeing."

And for a minute, there's an opening. It feels like I could say, *Yeah, it was kind of confusing for me, too.* Because it's not like you could say a bunch of sweaty soccer players were respectful, exactly, throwing their arms around me. So maybe *I* was wrong, thinking they were just glad I was on their team, just grateful I'd stopped the ball. Maybe things could have turned dangerous. Maybe Avery did save me.

I would have wanted her to save me, if I'd been in danger.

It almost feels like I could say, *I don't have experience with any of that. I read the regency romances the old ladies at the nursing home give me, and it seems like a totally different thing from what kids at school talk about, when they talk about having boyfriends and girlfriends. And that's nothing like what we hear in health class. . . .*

Maybe it even feels like I could say, *It* is *weird, what my mom did for your parents. I can't make sense of that either.*

But Avery is still talking.

"What your mom did—I'm not mad at *her*," she says. "Have you read her e-mail yet, explaining everything?"

I freeze.

"How do you know she wrote me an e-mail?"

"Dad told me."

But Avery turns her head, not meeting my gaze. She's what Grandpa would call "shifty-eyed."

*I've always looked at my e-mail on Mr. Armisted's iPad. I put it back in the living room every single night. Anyone could glance at it, out in the living room.*

I feel like she's seen me naked. I feel like she's seen my mom naked. Which . . . is something even I haven't ever done.

"Avery! Did you read my mom's e-mail?" I demand.

She waits too long before saying, "N-no."

I shove her against the wall.

"I'm never speaking to you again," I hiss in her ear.

She jerks her chin up, almost hitting me.

"I'll tell Daddy to send you home. I'll tell him he has to!"

I look her in the eye. Our eyelashes are practically touching. And—is this power?—she's scared, and I'm not.

"I don't care," I say. "I don't care at all."

## Avery, Confused

**We both stomp up the** stairs, and it's hard to say who's madder, Kayla or me. But I can run faster. I burst into the apartment ahead of her, and there's a key and a little pile of Euro coins on top of the bookcase by the door, so I know Dad's home.

"Dad! Dad!" I shout.

Kayla steps up behind me, but then she stops. Silently, she points at the couch.

Dad's sitting right there, but he's got his head in his hands, his fingers twisted in his dark hair. The scariest thing is, he doesn't move.

"Dad!" I yell again. I go over and shake him and finally he looks up.

His eyes focus slowly on my face.

"Oh, sorry, I must have dozed off," he says distantly. "I didn't hear you come in. Are you done with class already?"

We're home late, and he's early. And nobody could sleep through the noise I was making.

"Dad, are you okay?" I ask cautiously.

Dad slumps back against the couch.

"There should be a law," he says. "That only one part of your life can fall apart at a time."

I'd go along with that.

"Did something happen at work?" I ask.

Dad's spine practically curves in on itself. All he'd have to do to roll into a fetal position is pull his knees up to his chest. He waves a hand vaguely.

"This always happens when we acquire a company that doesn't want us telling them what to do," he says. "Even if they're on the verge of going out of business. Even if they would have all lost their jobs if we hadn't intervened. I'm still the bad guy. They still hate me. And, of course, your mom already . . ." He kind of shakes himself. "Sorry. Work's no different from usual. It just feels worse because . . ."

"Because of the divorce," I say. The word sticks in my throat. "Has Mom . . . ?"

Dad shakes his head so slowly it hurts to watch.

"I can't talk about your mom right now," he says. "If you can't say something nice about somebody, don't say anything at all. Did I ever tell you how your grandmother had that cross-stitched on a pillow when I was a kid? And I always thought it was funny, because neither of my parents said much anyway, good or bad. They were strong, silent types. Stoic. When he lost the farm, the only thing my dad said was, 'Well, that's that.'"

Dad's not even looking at me now. He's just staring at the wall.

"Well, that's that," he repeats.

He's scaring me. All my grandparents died before I was born: Dad's parents from a heart attack and cancer; Mom's from diseases I can never remember, because of course she'd almost never talk about death. That's even worse than talking about divorce.

I guess Dad's not so great about talking about problems

either. Usually, the only thing he says about his parents is how hard they worked.

"Okay, but, Dad—" I begin. I want to say, *Stop it! Go back to being yourself! You need to help* me!

Kayla creeps up behind me.

"Why don't you let us fix you dinner?" she says gently, as if Dad's an invalid. "Eat, and you'll feel better."

Dad shrugs, as if he's barely heard her.

I turn around to stare at Kayla because, wasn't she furious with me a few minutes ago? Weren't we yelling at each other? But she's looking past me, squinting anxiously at Dad.

She's worried about him too.

"I can make the salad," I hear myself say. "Because you know I can't cook. If I try anything more complicated than that, I'd probably poison us all. Or I could run out to that—what's it called?—the Museo del Jamon? The place with the Spanish ham you like so much?"

"Why don't you do that," Kayla says. "I'll take care of everything else."

Her eyes meet mine, and it's like we're agreeing on a truce. Nothing's fixed; nothing's solved; she hasn't forgiven me. We might yell at each other again tomorrow. Or later tonight.

But maybe we are capable of hiding all that from Dad.

Maybe we need to.

## Kayla, Tempted

**I hold the iPad with** both hands, my fingers curving around the hard edges. I hear Mr. Armisted's voice in my head: *Did you read your mother's e-mail?* I hear Avery's: *What your mom did—I'm not mad at* her. *Have you read her e-mail yet, explaining everything?*

I go to Gmail and click that I want to write an e-mail. I type in:

Hi, Mom,

We played soccer after school today. I was the backup goalie, which meant I didn't have to run. I stopped a goal, but it was just by mistake.

Then Avery and I made dinner together for Mr. Armisted. We fixed

I move the cursor back and erase everything about Avery and me making dinner, all the way back to "mistake." I don't want Mom reading that and thinking Avery and I were all buddy-buddy, just a couple of girls working happily together, like . . .

*Like sisters*, I think.

Before I can type in, You want to know the truth? You want to know how Avery really treats me? You want to know what's really going on? Well, let me tell you. . . . I quickly add after "mistake":

That's all for today.
Love,
Kayla

I hit send.

I lean back against my bed's pillow. What would I even say if I told Mom the whole truth?

Avery and I did make dinner together. I made macaroni and cheese—the truly homemade kind like Grandma's, not the kind that comes in a box with orange powder. I used the last of the Manchego cheese, so it didn't really taste the way Grandma's does. (Grandma uses Velveeta, and I don't think they have that here.) Avery came back from shopping with both Spanish ham and cans of Campbell's tomato soup and Oreos. She said she got a little lost coming back to the apartment, and she found a store that sells American food to homesick Americans. She said those were two of her father's favorite foods, so she thought that might cheer him up.

It probably would have been a good idea, except that then he started talking about Avery's mom making fun of him for liking canned soup and Oreos.

So that's where Avery gets it.

The funny thing is, I almost felt like I belonged, sitting there with Avery and Mr. Armisted at the little apartment table. Because I was the one who made that meal happen. Avery would have never thought to offer, *Hey, Dad? How about if I cook you dinner?* if she were here alone. She would probably still be staring at him, wondering what to do.

*Because I'm used to serving people, taking care of them, and not even thinking about what* I *want*, I think, flushing. *I'm like Mom, so eager to help the Armisteds that she was like,* Oh sure, use my body for nine months! No problem! I don't have anything better to do!

I grip the iPad tighter, feeling the anger and shame surge through me again. How could Mom have done that? How could she have let people like the Armisteds take advantage of her?

And how could I have let a bunch of Spanish soccer players grab me and hug me and not think about what that looked like to Avery? Or to Dragomir or Andrei or the kids from London?

*But nothing actually happened except that they hugged me*, I remind myself. *I didn't do anything wrong. The Spaniards didn't do anything wrong.*

It's weird how that one moment could look so different to me and to Avery.

I can see that one moment in the living room when I offered to fix dinner in different ways too.

It could seem like I was being all meek and mousy again: *Yeah, yeah, I'm really upset, and Avery and I are in the middle of a fight—but never mind! If Mr. Armisted's upset, of course that's more important.*

Only, I didn't feel meek and mousy. I felt . . . powerful. Just as powerful as I'd felt yelling at Avery. She didn't know what to do to fix anything, but I did. I was stronger than her.

I kind of do want to tell Mom that. But I don't start a second message to her. I don't go and ask Mr. Armisted for his phone so I can call her.

*Did you read your mother's e-mail?*

That's what stopping me. I can't *really* talk to my mother until I've read her e-mail explaining why she gave birth to Avery, why she wanted to be a surrogate mother (or a "gestational carrier"), why she kept that secret from me the past fourteen years. Why she wouldn't even tell me the truth when she sent me off to Spain with the Armisteds.

What if there are other secrets she tells in that e-mail that I've never known?

*None of it's secret now*, I tell myself. *Avery knows.*

I take a deep breath and click on the e-mail at the very bottom of my inbox.

Kayla, my sweet, sweet Kayla . . .

And that's as far as I get before I snap the cover back over the iPad screen. I'm picturing Avery reading this, and I can't go on. It's like I'm ashamed of Mom calling me sweet, ashamed of Mom loving me. Ashamed of anyone thinking I'm special or beloved.

I let the iPad slip from my hands. I get up and dash into the bathroom and throw up into the toilet. Of course it clogs when I try to flush it, and I have to use the plunger to get it to work. Then I splash water on my face again and again and again.

When I go back to my room, the door is slightly ajar. I push my way in, and there's something on my bed: a big bag of nacho-cheese-flavored Doritos.

And there's a note:

*They had this at the store for homesick Americans too.*

## Avery, Going on as If Everything's Fine

**"Thank you for the Doritos,"** Kayla says the next morning as we're headed toward school.

Her voice is stiff and unnatural. I give her a sidelong glance.

"I was afraid you were still mad, because you didn't come and thank me right away," I say. "Because I knew about you liking Doritos only because I was eavesdropping. . . ."

"I already knew you'd eavesdropped," Kayla says impatiently.

She's got her eyes trained directly ahead of her, as if all she cares about is seeing the Sol Metro sign in the distance.

"So you are going to go back to talking to me?" I ask.

"As long as you don't say anything about my mother," she says. "Ever again." She waits another three steps before she adds, "So you're not going to tell your father to send me home?"

"No," I say. "Not . . ." It's my turn to bargain, but I can't think what I want. Or—I want too much. *Not if you promise to help me take care of my dad when he's acting weird. Not if you come find me if I have to run crying to the restroom again. Not if you make sure I'm not alone.* I settle for parroting, "I won't say anything to my dad about sending you home."

Another pause. Then Kayla says, so softly I almost miss hearing her, "I was lying about not caring."

I tilt my head and gaze sideways at her.

"Do you actually *like* Spain?" I ask.

She shrugs. "I can't go home right now. I can't. And I don't have money to go anywhere else."

I think about how last night, when Kayla hadn't thanked me, I picked up my phone to text Shannon or Lauren. I was even ready to text one of them, Want to talk? If it was Lauren who answered first, I could have even told her about my parents getting divorced. She could have given me advice.

But Lauren's mother didn't refuse to talk to her when Lauren's parents were getting divorced.

And Lauren wasn't born from a gestational carrier.

The only thing I texted to Lauren and Shannon was, Still grounded. No end in sight.

## Kayla, Adjusting

***Me llamo Kayla* is not** the same as saying, "My name is Kayla." Not exactly. It's almost as if Spanish leaves you room to lie. Or hide: *I'll tell you what I call myself, but who's to say if that's my real name or not?*

Avery giving me Doritos and me thanking her and then us walking into Spanish class together is not the same as us being friends. But that's probably how it looks to everyone else. Dragomir invites both her and me to work on a skit with him and the other Bulgarian kids. Avery casts a glance over to the British kids—who aren't looking her way—and says okay.

She's a better actress than I am, of course.

After class, Andrei invites both of us to join in the soccer game again, and when I say I need to go straight home instead, he gets down on his knees and begs, "*Necesitamos!*" He forgets the pronoun. I think he just means that they need Avery, but Dragomir joins in the begging, and I give in.

When we get to the soccer field, the girl from England, who's named Susan, announces that I'm on her team; she wants me to stand in the goal behind her.

She's never said a single word to me before. But when everyone else runs far down the field, away from us, chasing the ball, she turns to me and actually speaks in English: "Some of the Spanish blokes playing today have roving hands. Be careful."

I flush red.

"You think I did something wrong yesterday," I say. "You think—"

"I think females get blamed for a lot of things that aren't their fault," she says. "I didn't see anything yesterday, except that you were upset when you walked off the field. And I think we girls have to watch out for each other."

I watch Avery flying toward the opposite goal. Her feet don't seem to touch the ground.

"Did you tell Avery?" I ask. "Should we warn her now?"

Susan's eyes follow Avery's progress. Avery gives the ball a hard kick, and the ball soars toward the opposite goal.

"I think that one can handle herself on the soccer field," Susan says. "Off the field—that's a different story."

Avery's jumping up and down, celebrating her goal.

"Avery and me, we're not really friends," I tell Susan.

"I'm not her friend either," Susan says. "But I still told Hugh what I'd do to him if he goes after such a little girl."

Now, at the other end of the field, Avery's teaching Dragomir how to do a high five. Or maybe he already knows, and he's pretending not to so she'll hang out with him longer.

"Avery *is* really pretty," I say. Then it slips out: "A lot prettier than me."

Susan looks me up and down.

"I think you should wait until you've both grown into yourselves before you make that determination," Susan says. "Determination" is an amazing word when it's spoken with a British accent.

"You mean . . . ," I begin.

"Are you truly going to fish for compliments for your future self?" Susan asks, rolling her eyes in a way that makes me think she sees me as a little girl too.

"How old are you?" I blurt.

*"Diecinueve,"* she says. *"Basta con los ingles! Tú sabes los numeros en español!"*

It takes me forever to work it out: She's nineteen. And she's done talking to me in English.

I stick with English for my next question anyway.

"Why are you so stubborn about speaking Spanish?" I ask. "Why is it so important to you?"

She sighs. Down the field, there's a kickoff, but our team steals the ball right away and drives it in the opposite direction.

"Because this is how I really talk," Susan says, switching back to English again. She still has an accent, but it's different now. The vowels aren't so crisp.

"I don't understand," I say. "How is that . . ."

"Are you Americans really that dense?" she asks, and now she sounds exactly like all the other British kids. "I'm from a part of London no one wants to live in. Anyone in England can hear the minute I open my mouth that I'm faking my accent. So I need something else, some other language. Something that doesn't give me away."

*Is she saying she's poor, like me?* I wonder.

I have a million questions I want to ask, but she adds, "I'm not talking about this anymore. And I'm not speaking English the rest of the summer."

The rest of the time we're in the goal together, any time I say anything in English, she only says, "*¿Que? ¿Que?*" as if it's not even a language she's heard before.

Is *everyone* here carrying around secrets?

Is everyone in the world?

## Avery, in Darkness

**Kayla and I tolerate each** other. Spanish class is bearable, as long as there's soccer afterward. But Dad keeps acting messed up.

One night I can't sleep, and when I go get a drink of water in the kitchen, I see him sitting on the balcony, staring at nothing. It's so late that even the dance club across the alley has closed down. So he's sitting in the dark, in silence.

I open the sliding door.

"Dad, you should go to bed," I tell him.

He jumps, as if he's forgotten I exist.

"Not worth it," he says. "It's almost time to get up. The way farmers tell time, anyway."

"You're not a farmer," I say.

"But shouldn't I be?" he asks, as if this is a serious question. "Isn't that what I was meant for? Isn't that how I still think? A lot of guys I grew up with, they waited out the bad economy and then borrowed money to buy land and equipment again as soon as they could. Bret Stelzer, he's got a thousand acres now. He's probably worth more than I am. Maybe I would have done that too, if I hadn't met your mom."

Why does him saying "your mom" make me feel like it's my fault somehow?

She still hasn't called or texted me.

"Dad, if you were a farmer again, you'd be covered in dirt

and manure all the time," I say. "You'd stink. You'd have blisters on your hands. Remember all the stories you've told me?"

"Maybe I'd be happier," he says. "Maybe that's who I really am. Standing on my own, working for myself, not kissing up to people I don't like . . ."

This has to stop.

"If you hadn't met Mom, you wouldn't have me," I say.

Even in the near-total dark, I can tell that his face softens in just the right way.

"You're right," he says. "That makes everything else worthwhile."

"And you and Mom can . . ." I want to say, *work things out*. Or *go back to normal*. But there's still that whole thing about Kayla's mom giving birth to me. That's still between us, between me and ever feeling normal again.

"Sweetheart, your mother's not talking to me either right now," Dad says. "There's a lot she blames me for."

"I could quit soccer," I say, and even I'm not sure where this comes from. "I could take dance lessons again, the way she always wanted."

"*No*," Dad says, and for a minute it's like my real father is back, the forceful, decisive one. But then he seems to be blinking back tears. "That is exactly the type of thing I *don't* want to have happen. I don't want the problems your mom and I are having to ruin your life. . . . You love soccer."

I do. And I always hated dance. I took tap, jazz, ballet. . . . Mom finally let me quit last year, when my soccer schedule got too intense. The only reason I'd let her force me to stick with dance classes that long was because Dad said it'd help with my soccer footwork.

And, okay, because Mom really wanted me to grow up to be a ballerina. When I was younger, I did try to make her happy, even when it wasn't what I wanted.

Why did I do that? When did I stop?

Was it always because of Dad? And . . . because I saw Dad stop trying to keep her happy too?

I step out onto the balcony and sit down beside Dad.

"We used to be a happy family, didn't we?" I ask, as if I really don't know. I don't trust my own memory anymore. "Didn't it used to be, when you and Mom talked about her teaching you which fork to use, it was like the two of you were a team, like you were proud of each other, proud of how you were together, proud . . ."

*Proud of me*, I want to say. But there's no way I can push those words out.

Dad stares over at the darkened dance club without answering. But I've unleashed a torrent of images in my own head, like a video of my entire childhood: Mom and Dad taking turns reading me bedtime stories, all three of us snuggled together until the very last page; Mom and Dad and me on happy Caribbean vacations, where all we did was play on the beach, all week long; Mom and Dad in the audience for every one of my school plays and dance recitals and soccer games, both of them applauding as if I was the biggest star, no matter how I actually performed; Mom and me going for manicures and pedicures together when I was only five or six, and coming home to show

Dad as if we were grand society ladies; Dad taking me out into the countryside to show me where he grew up, and to make sure I learned the difference between corn and soybeans and wheat—and Mom just laughing when I came home covered in mud. . . .

For most of my life, I never doubted that my parents loved me, or that they loved each other. Not until, until . . .

"What changed?" I whisper. "*When* did everything change?"

Dad's gaze darts back to me, and even in the dark I can feel the misery in it.

"Whose version do you want?" he asks with a harsh laugh. "Maybe I got sick of hearing your mother take credit for my success. As if knowing which fork to use mattered the most! Or maybe I started feeling I wasn't being true to myself, being her puppet. Trusting her opinion on everything that wasn't business. Or maybe *I* was too cruel, too quick to make fun of things she cared about. Art. Music. Culture. Beauty. Maybe I was too cheap, and she was too quick to indulge in retail therapy, shopping to heal her every wound. . . ."

Something falls into place in my mind.

"That problem with the credit card, back in Columbus," I say. "It *wasn't* the company's fault. Mom had just maxed it out, right? To deal with . . . to deal with . . ."

"The pain of watching you and me leave," Dad finishes for me, and it's like those words are being carved out of his heart. He's silent for a moment, then he adds, "In her defense, we hadn't been communicating well for months. She says she'd told me she was putting some extra orders for her decorating business on that card, and I just forgot."

It strikes me what a decent guy my dad is, that he's telling her side of things. That he didn't tell me it was her fault from the very beginning.

Or maybe it just means he still believed back then that they could stay together. Maybe it means he *still* believes that.

*If only* . . .

My heart sinks, as I realize what he's *not* saying. What he's still hiding.

"None of that has anything to do with me finding out Kayla's mom gave birth to me," I say. "And that's what had just happened that night when . . . when . . ."

*That night Mom told you she wanted a divorce. The night she stopped talking to me.*

Dad's quiet so long I don't think he's going to answer.

"Your mother says . . . ," he begins. He swallows hard, and tries again. "She says I could never understand how much it hurt her, not being able to get pregnant or give birth. I said, 'Hey, I can't get pregnant or give birth either!' She never appreciated . . . me joking about it. She said, being a man, I couldn't understand. Do *you* understand?"

His question sounds desperate. Maybe I'm too much like my dad. I want to answer with a joke too: *Eighth-grade health class didn't make pregnancy or childbirth look like much fun! Who* wouldn't *want to outsource that?*

But then I think about Kayla's mother's e-mail, the one I wasn't supposed to read. She loved being pregnant. It made her feel like she was glowing.

It made her feel connected to me, even though . . . even though . . .

I can't answer Dad. After a moment, he goes on.

"Starting, I don't know—maybe a year ago?—your mother and I talked about going to marriage counseling," he says. "We needed it. But every time we got close to making an appointment, she backed out. She'd heard you had to tell *everything*; she thought she'd have to talk about her feelings about being infertile and needing another woman to give birth to you. And . . . she thought the counselor would say we had to tell *you*."

A small nuclear explosion takes place inside me. I'm so mad I can't even speak. But I wish Mom were here right now so I could yell at her.

*You thought it was more important to keep me in the dark than to stay married? You were so ashamed of me you wouldn't even go to a marriage counselor? I hate you! You ruined my life!*

Dad is still talking.

"But . . . maybe I'm just like your mom," he says.

"What?" The word jerks out of me.

Dad bows his head as if he can't even look at me.

"I haven't been much of a father to you this summer," he says. "I'm holding it together at work, but . . . just barely. I've thought about going to a counselor or a therapist or . . . something. Here. On my own. But if I did, I would have to tell—"

"You're that ashamed of me too?" I explode. "Oh, because we're in Spain, and they think paying a woman to have a baby is, is—"

I start to scrape my chair back from the table—I want to flee. But Dad puts his hand on my arm, to hold me in place.

"*No*," he says. "That is *not* the reason. You have to believe me. If it had been up to me, I would have shouted it from the rooftops from the very beginning, how everything worked out. We thought we weren't going to be able to have children, but look—now we have Avery! It's a miracle! We're so lucky! But . . . I also thought we should have done more for Stacy. We owed it to her. Especially after her husband's accident."

*Kayla's mom*, I think. Just the way he says her name sends my thoughts veering in wild directions. *Did he and Kayla's mom end up having an affair, after all? I am not sitting here listening to Dad confess that. No way. Not—*

Dad's grip on my arm tightens. Now I'm trapped.

"Just listen," he says. He raises his head for only a moment. "Stacy gave birth to you. I thought that made it like she was family, and family helps family when they're going through tough times. She was most concerned about Kayla, and I thought you and Kayla should grow up like, I don't know, *cousins*—sure, fine, you wouldn't know your real connection if it bothered your mother so much, but it would be good for both of you to spend time together. You would see that not every kid gets—or needs—thousand-dollar birthday parties, and Kayla would see more of the world outside her little town. All the things I wished I'd seen as a kid."

"Yeah, yeah, so that's why you wanted Kayla to come to Spain with us," I say. It's infuriating, but I almost understand—if I try to think like Dad. But I don't understand why he's acting so ashamed.

Is this just going to lead to another lecture about how I should be nicer to Kayla?

I kind of want to yell at him, *Are you blind? Can't you see how much Kayla hates* me? *How we have* nothing *in common except who gave birth to us—and the fact that we've been stuck together all summer?*

But it's hard to yell at someone who's already so slumped over.

"*Was* that my reason?" Dad asks. He sounds dazed. "I always wanted you and Kayla to have more contact, but I never fought for it until your mom and I were already . . . alienated. And I had to bargain so hard with your mom to get her to agree for this summer. In the end, I just kind of . . . made the arrangements. Even though I knew it'd make her go ballistic. Would a therapist tell me I had—what's it called?—subliminal reasons? A purpose even I didn't understand? Underneath it all, was I just desperate to get the secret out, and did I think forcing you and Kayla together would reveal everything? Did I want to force your mother to choose between me and keeping her secret?"

I stare at him.

"You didn't know I'd lose my passport," I finally mutter. "And, what, are you trying to tell me *you* forged that messed-up birth certificate?"

"No, of course not," Dad says. "But . . . was it all just a power play on my part? Am I that much of a jerk?"

Were both my parents just thinking about themselves, not me? I've seen how it works for other kids, how they just become pawns in their parents' divorce. Is that what's waiting for me?

*Will I end up like Lauren—a rag doll caught in a constant tug-of-war?*

I'm too sad now even to get angry again. Dad's watching me like he'll accept whatever I tell him. I can't take this. I'm *fourteen.* I'm not even sure I can handle high school, and Dad wants me to act like a marriage counselor for him and Mom.

Who won't even talk to me.

"Of course you're not a jerk," I say, but it comes out sounding too dutiful, too rote. "I don't think you need a therapist. Maybe . . . maybe you just need to get away. We both do." For the moment, I let myself forget that Kayla would be involved too. "Maybe this should be the weekend we go to Paris. . . ."

As soon as I say "Paris," I know I've made a mistake. Dad's whole body goes stiff.

Paris is where my parents went on their honeymoon. It's where they took their last trip without me.

Their last *romantic* trip.

Is there anything I can say that *isn't* poison?

"Or London or Lisbon," I say quickly. "Or Barcelona or Seville or Granada . . ."

But he's stopped listening to me. And I can tell: None of those trips are going to happen.

I don't even want them to.

## Kayla, the Spanish Inquisition, and Dying Saints

**Just when I get to** the point where I can understand about half of what Señora Gomez says in Spanish class, the class part ends, and we have a bunch of field trips instead. We traipse around Madrid in the crazy heat, following a guide who tells us in too-rapid Spanish what happened on this or that spot hundreds of years ago.

Plaza Mayor, the square I thought looked straight out of a movie, is where people were executed during the Spanish Inquisition.

In my history classes back in Crawfordsville, King Ferdinand and Queen Isabella sounded like good guys, the people smart enough to give Christopher Columbus money to sail to America.

But I guess mostly what they did was try to kill all the Jewish people. And the Muslims, too.

While the guide talks, I sidle over to Avery.

"It's like they thought of the Holocaust five hundred years before the Nazis," I whisper.

"Yeah . . . ," Avery says, and I realize she wasn't even listening.

"But Ferdinand and Isabella helped Christopher Columbus!" I say.

"Columbus? He was a murderer too," Avery says, like I was supposed to know that.

When it gets too hot for any living thing outdoors, Señora Gomez takes us to art museums. We begin with the Prado, which is full of paintings of Jesus being crucified and Saint Sebastian being shot to death by arrows. Oh, and St. Agnes having her head chopped off.

"Why did people want pictures of such awful things?" I ask Avery, because I'm too overwhelmed to try to put that thought into Spanish and say it to Dragomir or Andrei, who would probably just make a joke.

But Avery is standing in front of the worst painting yet: a naked old man with wild eyes and wild hair holding a headless, bloody corpse. I glance at the English label for the painting: *Saturn Devouring His Son*.

"This," Avery says. "This is exactly what this whole summer feels like."

I guess that's her answer.

## Avery, Guernica, and Churros

**Señora Gomez tells us about** the Spanish Civil War the same day she takes us to see *Guernica*. From what I understand, the Spanish Civil War was like a preview of World War II, but all fought on Spanish soil, even though people came from other countries to take sides too. It went on and on and on in the 1930s, and something like a half million people died.

It was a big deal, a really, really awful thing. Even though I'd never heard of it before this summer.

"But it ended before World War II started, right?" I ask Señora Gomez. I even translate my question into Spanish quickly enough that she doesn't scold me.

"The civil war ended," she says, in Spanish that's so weighted down and deliberate that no one asks her to repeat it. "But Franco's side won. He stayed as dictator until 1975. My country was not free. It was like we were all in prison for forty years."

My parents were alive in 1975.

Señora Gomez was probably already alive in 1975.

Probably half the people we pass on the street, walking around Madrid, were alive while Franco was in power. When Spain was a prison.

Then we go see *Guernica*, a Picasso painting of a Spanish town being bombed during the war. We stand there in a group, the whole class, and everyone's silent.

The painting is kind of what you would expect from

Picasso—blobby bodies and heads, and a thing hovering at the top that looks like an eye until you look at it closely, and then it's a lightbulb, or maybe a bomb falling through the air. You feel like people are running and screaming, but they can't escape. There's a horse and a bull, and both of them look miserable, too.

How did Picasso do that—capture misery with just blobs and shapes, and black and white and gray paint?

*If Mom were here, she would say to look at the beautiful paintings instead*, I think. *Whenever she's redecorating a house, she always asks, "Why would anyone want to live with ugly things?"*

I don't think Picasso was thinking about harmonious home décor.

I also can't stop looking at *Guernica*.

Afterward, everyone files out of the art museum and seems to wilt in the afternoon heat. Still, I reach over to tap Dragomir's shoulder.

"*¿Fútbol? ¿Ahora?*" I ask, hoping for a soccer game right *now*, because I really, really want to kick something. It's Friday afternoon, and I'm not sure how I can face two days straight of hanging out with no one but Kayla and my dad. And no soccer.

I don't know how it happened, but it's like Dragomir is the one who organizes all the soccer games.

But even Dragomir makes a face.

"*Damasiado caliente*," he says. *Too hot.*

"*Pero yo necesito . . .* ," I begin. *But I need. . . .*

"*Churros*," Andrei finishes for me. "*Todos nosotros necesitamos churros.*"

Why would we all need churros? Churros are these really gross, tasteless things they sell at Taco Bell.

"*No quiero churros*," I say, making a face. Which is kind of funny, because I only remember the word "*quiero*" because of old Taco Bell commercials.

"*A todo el mundo le encantan los churros en España*," Dragomir insists. *Everyone loves churros in Spain.* "*Churros con chocolate.*"

And then everybody else is agreeing, even Kayla.

I don't want to go back to the apartment where Dad might be acting strange. And where I would know that to talk to Shannon and Lauren, all I'd have to do is pick up my iPhone.

And where I would find out once again that Mom hasn't called or texted.

"*Lo que sea*," I mutter, which is "whatever" in Spanish, even though I don't think they use it the same way.

Maybe I'll start a trend of teenagers saying that here. Maybe that will be *something* good that comes out of this summer.

Dragomir and Andrei lead us all to a *churros con chocolate* shop that's not far from Puerta del Sol. Kayla kind of jumps when we pass a church about a block away, and I say, "Do you know that place? Was it someplace else in Madrid where thousands of people died?"

"No," Kayla mutters. "Never mind."

Whatever.

We take a bunch of tables at the churro shop, and Dragomir goes in and orders for us all, and then the food arrives and—it is nothing like Taco Bell. The churros are like the best doughnuts ever, and they come with huge cups of thick, pudding-like chocolate.

Andrei pretends to conduct an orchestra with one of the thickest of the churros—they're called *fartons*, which I think the Bulgarians would really laugh at if they knew what word that sounds like in English. Dragomir actually licks the chocolate out of his cup, which has got to be terrible for his acne.

"This must have a million calories," I moan to Kayla, who's sitting beside me.

She spins on me.

"Why do you do that?" she demands. "Can't you ever eat food that tastes good, and just enjoy it?"

I stare at her.

"No," I say. "No, because . . . my mother never did. And . . . she never let me."

"Oh," Kayla says. She looks down into her little pot of chocolate as if I've ruined it for her now too.

Andrei reaches across the table to pat her hand.

"*Sonrie*," he says, telling her to smile. "*Tenemos churros con chocolate!*"

But he accidentally hits one of the pots, and before anyone can catch it, it tips and sends chocolate oozing across the table.

Everyone jumps back except Kayla, who begins attacking the mess with napkins.

"*Qué desastre!*" Dragomir cries.

Suddenly, his joking around really annoys me.

"How can you say that when we've spent this whole week learning about real disasters, real tragedies?" I ask him. "When there's real pain in the world, and it's like all of Spanish history was terrible?"

I translate that into Spanish, and I'm mad enough that I do it quickly.

"*La historia es siempre triste*," Dragomir says with a shrug. *History is always sad.* He finishes with something that I think means, "That's why we should be happy now."

"*La historia de los* Estados Unidos *no es siempre triste*," I said.

"*Pero nosotros somos de* Bulgaria," Andrei argues. "*Nuestra historia es muy, muy triste.*"

What can I say to that? I don't know anything about Bulgaria.

"*Basta con los tristeza!*" Enough with the sadness! "*Nosotros tenemos una sopresa*," Dragomir announces.

A surprise?

He and Andrei lean their heads together and half sing, half chant, "Joost seet rot bok und yule hir a tail . . ."

It takes me a moment to realize that's supposed to be English.

Kayla claps and joins in: "'A tale of a fateful trip . . .' It's the *Gilligan's Island* theme song!"

"We learn English," Dragomir says solemnly. In actual, real English. "From TV." He glances at me, then seems to be trying to peer deeply into Kayla's eyes. "For you."

Kayla blushes.

"That's . . . really sweet," she says.

"Really sweet," Andrei echos, though it's clear he has no idea what the words mean.

*Gilligan's Island* is this really, really ancient—and really stupid—TV show that dates back to when my parents were kids. Dad made my friends and me watch it with him once when we were at a soccer tournament in the middle of nowhere, and all our games were rained out, so we were trapped in the hotel. And there wasn't even a pool.

The show's about a bunch of different people who just happen to take a short boat trip together—for three hours, I think—but there's a storm and they get shipwrecked and they're stranded on an desert island. I felt really sorry for the movie star, stuck with a bunch of weirdos like that, for years.

"Couldn't you have watched any modern TV shows in English?" I ask. Then I translate it into Spanish. "That would help you more. Nobody says things like, 'Golly gee, Gilligan,' anymore."

Dragomir shrugs and says something that includes the words, "*solo negro y blanco*," so I guess the only English-language shows he's seen so far are in black and white. They're the only ones he's found with Spanish subtitles.

He's learning English from *Gilligan's Island* and what little he knows of Spanish? That's ridiculous.

"Which *Gilligan's Island* episodes have you watched?" Kayla asks excitedly in Spanish. "Have you seen the one where the Howells mess up the professor's plans for getting off the island?"

Dragomir and Andrei answer just as excitedly. They seem to be trying to throw in English phrases, but they know more Spanish, so pretty soon we're back to just speaking that. And then Susan and Hugh chime in, discussing how they would get off a desert island if they were stranded. Hugh has to ask Susan the Spanish words for "wind turbine" and "solar panels." But, surprisingly, Kayla answers before Susan does. And then everybody's discussing whether "solar panels" would be masculine or feminine.

*Oh.*

*Oh, oh, oh.*

This summer, it's like I'm the one trapped on Gilligan's Island with a bunch of weirdos. It's like Spain is still a prison.

Except, as I sit there rolling my eyes while everyone else laughs, I start feeling like maybe I'm not the movie star. Maybe I'm more like the rich people—the Howells?—who think they're so much better than everyone else.

Except they're not.

## Kayla, Enchanted

**When my old friend from** Crawfordsville, Harley Seitz, was first falling in love with her boyfriend, Gunnar Graves, I was at her house one Friday night when he sent her a text demanding she sneak out and meet him. He didn't ask if she was busy; he just wrote, **Get out here now**. And I watched through the window as she tiptoed into the alley. It was raining pretty hard, but Gunnar didn't even open the car door for her.

I said something to her the next day about that, and she sneered, "You're just jealous because you don't have a boyfriend! You hang out with old people too much. It's not the 1950s anymore, where guys did that kind of stuff. I'm not some helpless girl, going, 'Ooo, I'm too weak to open my own car door.'"

The thing is, unless you count not being able to keep his hands or lips off her (and sometimes I did see her try to push his hands away), I can't think of anything nice Gunnar ever did for Harley.

The hands-and-lips part always seemed more for his benefit than hers.

Did she *really* want him squeezing her breast in the middle of math class? In front of everyone?

Or was she just pretending to, because that's what he wanted?

Andrei and Dragomir binge-watched hours and hours of

fifty-year-old TV shows in a language they don't even understand, just to be able to talk to me better. It turns out that they have been watching *Gilligan's Island*, *Green Acres*, *Petticoat Junction*, and *Beverly Hillbillies*. As a way to try to understand English, America, and Americans, this is crazy.

But as a way to understand *me* . . .

*Somebody besides my family and the Autumn Years residents actually* wants *to understand me? Somebody cares what I think, figuring out which of the professor's ideas for getting off Gilligan's Island was the best?*

As we're getting up to leave the churro place, I catch the English girl, Susan, watching me.

I check to make sure Avery and all the other British kids are out of earshot—they are—and I half whisper to Susan, "What do you know about Bulgarian guys? Do they have roving hands?"

Susan raises an eyebrow. She answers in Spanish, but I totally understand: "Do you want them to? And which of those guys do you want? I think it's your choice." Then she grins at me.

I get a choice?

Back in Crawfordsville, I couldn't have imagined even one guy being interested in me.

*Whatever I do, I won't hurt Andrei or Dragomir. I won't be like that.*

But I have possibilities. Choices. Opportunity.

I love Spain.

We pass the church where I stumbled in to find a place to hide when I couldn't stop crying. It feels like that was an eternity ago, a different lifetime. I want to send a shout-out to

God, maybe: *Oh hey, I'm not so mad anymore. Thanks. Sorry I haven't, um, visited lately.*

I feel a twinge of guilt, because God would probably also want me to call my mother, to start Skyping again with my Autumn Years friends.

Maybe I will.

Eventually.

For now, I just want to think about the next time I'll see Andrei or Dragomir. I'm even looking forward to seeing Susan and Hugh next week. I haven't opened the bag of Doritos Avery gave me yet—maybe on Monday I'll take it in to Spanish class, and share with everyone during break. Maybe I'll buy some Oreos this weekend too—I bet the Bulgarians, at least, have never had Oreos before. I don't know about the Brits. And maybe I'll ask them to bring in Bulgarian or British foods, if there's a store anywhere in Madrid for homesick Bulgarians or Brits. Maybe there's even a Bulgarian or British restaurant somewhere in Madrid, and the whole class can go together. . . .

*Possibilities*, I think. *Choices. Opportunity.*

## Avery, Sour

**Our apartment stinks.**

"Do you know what that smell is?" I ask Kayla, who's sitting on the couch beside me gazing at Dad's iPad. I tilt my head—she's looking up Bulgaria. Once I might have teased her about that, but now I just wait for her to sniff and wrinkle her forehead.

She better appreciate my restraint.

"I think it's only the wet clothes," she says. "You should hang them outside. They'll dry faster that way, anyhow."

It's Saturday morning, and the only thing on my schedule for the entire day is washing my clothes. Which I've already done. And now Kayla is pretty much telling me I did it wrong.

"Why didn't Dad rent an apartment with a washer *and* a dryer?" I gripe.

"I don't think many Spanish apartments have dryers," Kayla says absently, turning back to the iPad. "Haven't you seen how many buildings have clotheslines outside?"

I wait for Kayla to offer to help me move my wet clothes to the little clothes rack out on our patio. But she doesn't.

"You could just open a window, but it's about ten billion degrees outside, so I don't think you want to do that," Kayla says mildly.

This is annoying—I can't even annoy her today.

I transfer my clothes outside. Standing on the balcony for

five minutes makes me sweat like I've been playing soccer for an hour.

I go and knock on my father's bedroom door.

"Dad!" I call through the door. "We have to get out of this heat pit. I don't think the air-conditioning's working right again. Didn't you say there were great beaches in Spain? Near Valencia, maybe? Let's go!"

Silence.

"Dad?"

The door creaks open, and Dad stands there, swaying slightly. He's got a crease on the side of his face, as if his pillow was wrinkled and he lay on it too long in one position. His hair stands up in weird patches that make me see that it's thinner than it used to be. It's gone even grayer, too, and it's about a week past the time when he usually gets it cut.

Even his skin looks a little gray.

"Oh, sorry," I say. "I thought you were already awake."

"I was but . . . then I went back to bed," he says, as if it's a struggle just to speak those simple words. He blinks. "I . . . I did kind of promise you a great summer in Spain, didn't I?"

*No*, I think. *You promised me a summer in Spain with Kayla. Without telling me anything about anything. That is* not *my definition of a great summer.*

He glances at his watch.

"It's too late in the day to head to the coast now," he says, wincing. "Sorry."

"Then let's go to Toledo," I say. "Or Segovia. One of those day trips that aren't so far away."

"Avery, those are places where it'd be really hot today too,"

Kayla says behind me. She holds up Dad's iPad. "I was just looking at possibilities nearby, because Dragomir asked about doing something with him and Andrei and some of the others. . . ." She blushed. "I mean, he was asking if both of us were available. . . ."

But she was the one he contacted.

In our Spanish class, she's more popular than I am.

How did that happen?

Kayla's gaze takes in Dad's rumpled, haggard appearance.

"Dragomir said it's so hot, maybe we'd want to just go swimming," she says. "Then, um, you wouldn't have to worry about us, Mr. Armisted, and you could go back to sleep."

She wants to get away from my dad. My rumpled, sad, rejected dad.

That makes me so mad I almost say, *Do you really want Dragomir and Andrei—or Hugh!—to see you in a swimsuit, Kayla?*

But that is so mean, and I can already see in my head how disappointed my father would look if I said that.

He might even cry. He already looks like he's on the verge of tears.

And—I look Kayla up and down—and she doesn't actually look so lumpy and ugly anymore. I don't know if it's because she's been eating healthier food and getting more exercise, or just because she's standing up straighter.

Really, she looks almost . . . pretty. Her cheeks are flushed in an *I have an exciting life* kind of way, not an *I've been running through the airport and I can't catch my breath* way. She's got her dark hair pulled back in a ponytail, and the strands that have escaped the elastic are curling around her face and neck as if she styled it that way.

*If Mom were here, she would tell Kayla she needs a swimsuit that hides her flaws. And . . . it would come out sounding like she just wanted Kayla to know how many flaws she has.*

Was Mom always so mean?

I actually don't think so.

*But she still hasn't called or texted me. Or Dad.*

"We can swim anytime," I tell Kayla. Too late, I remember that there might not be a swimming pool in her little town back home in the United States. Or she might not have a membership. I forge ahead. "Anyhow, we do things with the kids from Spanish class all week long. We should do something with Dad today, while he has time off."

It's weird for me to be arguing for doing something with my dad rather than friends. But, I don't know. It doesn't seem right to leave him alone when he's like this.

"Okay," Kayla says. "I'll tell Dragomir we're not available."

I can hear the disappointment in her voice. I could say, *You do something with the other kids, and I'll have special time with my dad.*

But . . . I kind of want her help with Dad. How do you take care of someone who's this sad?

"Isn't there someplace in the mountains you were talking about, back when you were telling me everything about Spain, to try to get me excited for this trip?" I ask Dad. "Somewhere that's really close to Madrid?"

Dad looks at me blankly.

"Valley something?" I add.

"Oh, Valle de los Caidos," Dad says. "Valley of the Fallen. The memorial for the victims of the Spanish Civil War. And the basilica where Franco's buried."

*Right, because it's a great idea to take someone who's sad and depressed to a war memorial and an awful dictator's tomb*, I think. Maybe Dad had mentioned the Valley of the Fallen having something to do with Franco and war, but it hadn't meant anything to me then.

But Dad's face looks a little brighter.

"It is pretty up there," he says. "Out in nature, away from the city . . ."

"Let's go," I say.

Because our apartment still stinks, even without the wet clothes.

## Kayla, Making a Choice

***It's Saturday. Don't I ever** get a day off work?*

I'm surprised to think that. It's been a long time since I thought of my time in Spain as a job, exactly. And we never really discussed time off. Back when we were planning everything—or when my mom and Mr. Armisted were planning everything—I guess it never occurred to anyone that I might not want to spend every moment possible with the Armisteds.

Back then, I was in awe that *they* might want to spend time with *me*. In Europe. On a trip Mr. Armisted was paying for. With Spanish classes Mr. Armisted would pay for. And with spending money provided, and deposits made to my bank account back home every week.

I thought I was the luckiest girl alive.

But now I really want to go to the pool with Dragomir and Andrei and the others. I just want to be an ordinary teenager having fun. I want to splash water in the boys' faces and shriek when they splash me back.

I want to see Dragomir and Andrei—and, okay, *Hugh*—in their swimsuits. I don't want them to see me in my swimsuit, but . . .

Well, maybe I don't actually care.

I know that even if they don't think I look that great, they won't say anything mean. They aren't like that.

They like me.

But I hear the way Avery's voice cracks when she says, *We should do something with Dad today, while he has time off*. I see the pleading in her eyes, as if she's really saying, *Help me. I don't know what to do*. She and her father stand so awkwardly together—do they have any clue how broken they both look?

How different they are from the rich, glamorous jet-setters I saw them as, that first day at the airport?

Being poor isn't the only way to be in need.

I lift the iPad I'm still carrying.

"Want me to look up the best way to get to Valle de los Caidos?" I ask. "Does the Metro go out there, or do we have to take a train? Or a bus?"

"I think there's a tourist shuttle, but it probably already left for the day," Mr. Armisted says. His voice sounds like he's a million miles away. "Getting a rental car may be the only option left, but even that . . . I don't know . . ."

I wave the iPad like it's a magic wand.

"I'll find out what's available," I say.

I have never rented a car in my life. I don't even have my driver's license yet.

But I sound like I know exactly what I'm doing.

*Ohhhhh . . .*

I sound exactly like my mother.

## Avery, in the Mountains, Where You Can See Everything If You Dare to Look

**"You'd think a place named** 'Valley of the Fallen' would actually be in, you know, a valley," I say as the car climbs higher and higher around hairpin curves.

Dad kind of grunts, "Uh-huh," as he shifts gears. Kayla's in the backseat looking out the window at the pine trees around us, and she doesn't seem to hear.

And suddenly I miss Mom. Mom's the one who would get outraged along with me at things being misnamed. I can hear her in my head ranting, *Words deceive. And they* shouldn't. *Language should be precise and clear.*

"*Claro*," I mutter to myself. In Spain, people say "*claro*" all the time—I think Señora Gomez is addicted to the term. But I've figured out people use it more like *Sure, sure, uh-huh, okay, go on*, than *Clearly*.

Dad should have grunted, *Claro*, at me. I would have understood.

*And Mom should have called me by now. And Mom and Dad shouldn't be getting a divorce. And they shouldn't have hired Kayla's mom to have me. . . .*

I guess I can't really argue that last point. If they hadn't hired *some* other woman to give birth to me—either Kayla's mom, or somebody else—I wouldn't even exist.

I gasp. How is it that that never really occurred to me before now?

Neither Dad nor Kayla look over at me to ask why I gasped. Dad's still fighting with the gearshift. Kayla's still staring out the window like she's just a passenger on a bus with strangers.

*But words do deceive, Mom.* I've got no idea which direction is west, because it's almost noon and the sun is directly overhead. But I'm directing my thoughts across the Atlantic Ocean like they're arrows I'm shooting at Mom. *Take the word "mother." Even if you forget how I was born, can someone still be considered an actual mother when you haven't even bothered to try to contact your daughter in weeks? When your daughter is dealing with devastating news? News that's pretty much all your fault?*

I'm kind of not even sure if I mean the whole surrogate-mother mess or the divorce.

Mom asked for the divorce. But Dad argued with her just as much as she argued with him.

And the surrogate-mother mess . . .

*Am I actually blaming Mom because she couldn't have a baby without help?*

Dad grunts again, but it's just because the gearshift won't slide into place right. The car bucks a little.

"Sorry," he mutters. "It's been a while since I've driven a stick. Especially in the mountains."

Before we left Madrid, Dad took a shower and combed his hair and put on a nice polo shirt and khakis. He switched back into his usual Mr. Workaholic mode so much that he put his laptop in the trunk, just in case something came up that needed his attention. I was even glad to see that, to see him acting normal.

But his face still looks a little gray; his eyes still look puffy. Everything about him still looks . . .

"Unloved" is the word that jumps into my mind.

Words deceive. I love him. Mom must still love him too. She has to. *Claro que si.*

That means "of course."

But if Dad looks this bad, I wonder what Mom looks like right now. What's she been doing, all this time she hasn't called or texted me?

Dad pulls into a parking lot near the top of the mountain. He inches our car around one that's abandoned between two rows of parked cars.

"That's not a parking space, is it, Dad?" I ask.

He squints.

"I'd say they forgot to put their parking brake on," he says. "And so it's been sliding downhill inch by inch. . . ."

It sounds like he's really talking about something else.

"Shouldn't we tell someone?" I ask. I remember how Kayla said sometimes I look like I did when I was five. Now I *sound* like a little kid.

Back when I was five, I really did believe my parents could fix anything, between the two of them.

"Uh, sure," Dad says.

After we park—and Dad presses down hard on *our* parking brake—he goes off to talk to a guy in a security uniform. The guy only shrugs.

"There's a funicular up to the cross at the top of the mountain," Dad says when he comes back. "We should do that first, and then—"

"Didn't you see the signs on the way up?" Kayla asks. "The funicular's *cerrado*. For repairs."

It's like she doesn't even realize she's mixed Spanish with her English. I don't care that much about funiculars. I've been on ones in Quebec and California and—maybe Pittsburgh? They go sooo slow.

But I still burst out, "Is *everything* broken in Spain?"

"Well, you know, the economy . . . ," Dad begins. But even he seems to lose interest in explaining all the things Spain can't afford to fix.

We climb stairs to the enormous plaza that lies in front of a lineup of pillars. The plaza's so broad you could play soccer here—it's probably bigger than a regulation field.

But if you kicked the ball too hard to the right, it'd go flying off the side of the mountain, into the pine trees below.

It feels like we're really high up. Even the air is different here—a lot cooler and clearer, somehow. Purer.

"This view is amazing," Kayla says grudgingly. As if she didn't want to have to admire it.

As if she wanted it to be a mediocre view, so she could tell herself, *See? I really should have gone swimming.*

I feel a little guilty, and I don't even know why.

"You want to go over there to get pictures?" Dad asks, pointing toward the low wall at the edge of the plaza, with the blue sky and the evergreen trees and the whole valley spread out below. "Selfies, or whatever they're called?"

"Okay," Kayla says.

I try to remember the last time I posted anything to Instagram.

When we get over to the wall, Kayla pulls out a prehistoric camera, the kind people used before there were smartphones.

"I'm not very good at selfies," she says. "Could you . . . ?"

She holds out the camera to me.

"Sure," I say.

I take a picture of her, but she's not really smiling. Then she takes one of me and one of me and Dad together.

"Have you had that camera all along?" I ask her.

"Yes," she says. "I just keep forgetting to use it. Too many other things to think about, I guess."

I realize I've totally forgotten to bring a phone. I tug on Dad's arm.

"Dad, can I use your phone, then send the pictures to myself when we get back to Madrid?" I ask.

"You can do that?" he asks, raising his eyebrows and making his eyes widen in fake astonishment. "Kidding, kidding! I'm not that out of it."

I feel a little better. I take a few selfies, then we hand the phone around getting all the same combinations that Kayla already got.

*But I have better plans for my pictures . . .*, I think.

Just as Kayla's taking the last picture, a man calls to us in an American accent, "Want me to take a picture for you of the whole family? You and both your girls?"

I freeze. I can feel Dad's arm go stiff against my shoulder. But he says, "That would be very nice."

Kayla crowds in, and Dad kind of fakes putting his arm around her the same way he has his other arm around me.

"It *is* just the three of you, right?" the man says.

Is there any way he could make this worse?

"Yes," Dad says, and even the most clueless person in the world should be able to tell that Dad's gritting his teeth. But the too-friendly man hangs around to ask questions about where we're from and why we're in Spain. He tell us he was born in Chicago but lives in Atlanta now, and he sells computer software, and . . .

"I'm sorry, but we really should go into the basilica now, if we're going to make it to El Escorial this afternoon," Kayla interrupts.

"Oh, you haven't even been over to that Escorial place yet?" the man says. "There are a lot of rooms in that palace. . . . Go! Go!"

"Thank you," Dad mutters to Kayla as we walk away.

When did Dad become so helpless? He should have been able to get away from that man all by himself.

We pass through the pillars and step into the basilica, which looks like a hollowed-out cave. It takes my eyes a moment to adjust, but then I see a row of angels on columns. Except they look more like demons than angels, leering down from their pedestals. They're terrifying.

"I'll warn you," Dad says. "This is the creepiest church I've ever been in. We don't have to stay long."

"It's controversial, too, right?" Kayla asks, in a near whisper. "Because of how it was built?"

"Huh?" I say.

"Some of the workers were political prisoners, and critics say that was like using slave labor," Dad whispers back. "They say it's the same as Nazis using workers from concentration camps."

I feel sick to my stomach.

And Dad's right—this *is* a creepy church. It's too dark, and I feel like the demon angels are watching me.

"Why build a church on a mountain with a great view, if you're just going to hide the whole thing underground, without windows?" I ask. "You know what Mom would say. 'Natural light! Make use of the natural light! Fake it if you have to!'"

And then I freeze, because Dad stops walking in front of me.

I shouldn't have said that around Dad.

But Mom *would* want to fix this place, and suddenly I miss her so much I want to sob like a little baby. I miss her acting like better lighting and the right flower arrangement can work miracles, and a perfectly decorated room could change your life. I miss her always trying so, so hard to make everything look good. Even if it's rotten underneath.

I miss her acting like problems are things other people have.

*Not us*, I think. *Never us.*

"Franco's tomb is up by the altar," Kayla says, as if yammering on like a tour guide is going to make any difference. "It's supposed to be really plain and understated. But he's the only one buried within the monument grounds who didn't die in the Spanish Civil War. There's one other leader buried here in the church, and something like forty thousand people buried out in the valley."

I bet she just got that from Wikipedia. Unless those details were in one of the Spanish lessons I didn't listen to last week.

We start creeping forward again. Now there's eerie music coming from speakers I can't even see. We're almost to the stone on the ground that says FRANCISCO FRANCO, when an old woman in front of us plants her feet before it and lifts her arm straight out from her body—exactly as if she's saluting Hitler.

"Dad—" I gasp.

"Let's get out of here," he says.

We speed away from the altar as if we're race-walkers. We burst out into the sunshine again, and now it feels too hot and too bright.

"I thought Franco was a dictator," I say. "I thought people were glad when he lost power. . . ."

"I always heard that some of the older people were still loyal," Dad murmurs, looking around as if he's afraid of who might hear him. But the plaza is deserted now. "I'd just never met any of them."

"But if Franco had political prisoners and, and concentration camps . . . ," I say. "Why did you bring us here?"

"To Valle de los Caidos?" Dad asks.

"To *Spain*."

"Franco and the concentration camps and even this monument—they're Spain's history," Dad says gently. "Not Spain now."

"But that old woman—" Kayla interrupts.

"She may not believe the stories about the concentration camps were ever true," Dad says. "Or maybe she thought the prisoners deserved it. She may have felt like she had a pretty good life under Franco. To her, it was the good old days. When she was young. There are two sides to every story. Or . . . two hundred."

"I don't want to be here anymore," I say.

"Right," Dad says. But he just stands there, looking helpless and lost.

"Lunch?" I remind him. Even on a Spanish meal schedule, it's getting late for that.

Dad kind of jerks back to attention, and we head back to the car.

"Dad, can I have your phone again?" I ask.

"Service is spotty out here," Dad says. "I couldn't even get e-mail when I looked a little while ago."

"I want to check my pictures," I say.

Dad hands over his phone.

"Don't run the battery down," he says. "I forgot to charge it last night. And then I forgot to bring my charger."

As Dad backs out of our parking space, I click straight to the photos of Dad and me together at the edge of the mountain. My plan is to find the best one and edit it to perfection.

Then tonight, when we're back in Madrid, I'll send it to Mom. It will be like a secret message: *Look how happy we are without you! Look how beautiful everything is here! We don't miss you at all! We don't NEED you!*

But my hair's blowing into my face in one of the photos, and Dad's got his eyes shut in another. Our expressions aren't right in the others.

I switch to evaluating the pictures where Kayla's with us, because wouldn't that be even more of an annoyance to Mom, that someone like Kayla is taking her place as the third person in our family?

But there's something wrong with these pictures too. We all look really sad.

That's the problem with all the pictures: They tell the truth.

## Kayla, Descending

**Up in the front of** the car, Avery and Mr. Armisted are talking about how far it is to the nearest town, and whether the restaurant where Mr. Armisted ate a delicious bull tail twenty years ago is still there.

"Dad, the words 'delicious' and 'bull tail' do not belong in the same sentence!" Avery protests, and she sounds so much like her usual self that I'm relieved. It's safe to tune her out.

What I can't get out of my head is that old woman saluting Franco, back at the basilica.

She could have been Grandma. She could have been Mrs. Lang or Mrs. Harrison or any of the other old women back at Autumn Years. She had the same rounded belly that a lot of older women get, and she wore the same kind of sensible shoes, and she had the same wispy, old-lady white hair.

And she had a soft, kindly old face like theirs. Except that her face stiffened with pride when her arm went up.

*So what?* I tell myself. *She* wasn't *Grandma or any of your Autumn Years friends. She probably lived her whole life in Spain. Only the first part of it was under Franco. Grandma and your friends lived their whole lives in the United States. With democracy, and winning World War II, and winning the Cold War . . .*

And, okay, even Americans didn't do very well with the Korean War or the Vietnam War. Or 9/11 or the Afghanistan

War or Iraq. Or the Great Depression or the situation with farmers like Grandpa losing their farms in the eighties . . .

Either way, it's all history, and it's over. And who cares?

*And Mom giving birth to Avery . . . Isn't that just history too?*

I'm not sure what I'm getting at. I think about Mr. Armisted saying, *To her, it was probably the good old days. When she was young.* I think about how Mom makes excuses for Grandpa referring to her friend Sonia Lopez as "Mexican" instead of "Mexican American" because he grew up in a different time period. I think about how Avery told me way back at the Holocaust Museum that you're not supposed to say the word "Gypsy." She said it was like how you're supposed to use the term "Native Americans," not "Indians."

I didn't know that.

Before I came to Spain, I didn't know that any other country besides the United States had had a civil war. I didn't know that the term "civil war" meant a country fighting itself. I didn't know much of anything.

Except that I did.

I knew that Mrs. Lang lost a baby the very day it was born, and for the past fifty-nine years she's wondered if that child's blue eyes would have stayed so blue and innocent if he'd lived, or if they would have turned an ordinary, muddy brown like everyone else's in her family by the time of his first birthday.

I knew that Grandpa still thinks about what he could have done differently to hold on to his farm back in the 1980s—if only he'd known that the spring and summer of 1982 was going to be so rainy all the way through, he wouldn't have bothered going further into debt to buy more seed and replant the fields that flooded. Or maybe he shouldn't have ever tried to buy more land; maybe he should have planted more soybeans and less corn that year the corn blight was so bad... If only, if only, if only.

I knew that Grandma had a pair of red patent leather shoes when she was six, and that made her feel like the most special child in her entire Sunday school class. Even though she knew it was prideful and wrong to be looking around at the other girls' shoes when she should have been learning about Jesus.

I knew that one of the things that made my mother fall in love with my father was the way he could run down the football field, shaking off opponents like they were nothing but thistledown. The way he made it seem like nobody and nothing could stop him.

Mom never told me that story—Grandma did. Grandma Butts, that is—the one who moved to Florida because she couldn't take seeing her beautiful running son trapped in a bed the rest of his life, barely able to move.

*There are two sides to every story*, Mr. Armisted said. *Or . . . two hundred.*

And I see now how much all the old people's stories I know are just that—stories. It's like they're reshaping how they see their lives every time they retell their pasts: *those innocent blue eyes . . . more soybeans, less corn . . . red patent leather shoes . . . he ran like the wind . . .*

Probably, the woman who saluted Franco more than forty years after his death does that too.

I understand old people so well.

Can I really understand anyone else? Even my mother?

Even myself?

I think about how the old people are always telling me to pray. But their prayers are always about acceptance: *Oh Lord, let me accept my arthritis/broken hip/lost children/husband's death.*

I think, back in Crawfordsville, I accepted way too much.

Because that's what my mother taught me to do.

*And she never even told me everything I had to accept. Everything* she'd *done in the past, that affects me now . . .*

Except she has tried to tell me now. The last time I looked at my e-mail account, there were twenty messages from her I never opened.

I look up, because I *could* ask to read Mom's e-mail on Mr. Armisted's phone right now. I kind of feel . . . ready. But Avery's holding the phone in her hand, complaining, "Dad, I'm trying to look up the directions, but Google Maps isn't coming up *at all.*"

"Never mind," Mr. Armisted says. "It's such a small town, I'm sure we can find the restaurant just by parking near the main square and walking around a little."

We're not even to the town yet. We're curving through a roundabout where the spokes point to a hospital in one direction and El Escorial in another.

"Is it just one kilometer to El Escorial the town, or El Escorial the palace?" Avery asks.

"The palace is in the middle of the town, if I remember right, so it doesn't really matter," Mr. Armisted says, shifting gears to pull back out onto the straight road.

The gears grind a little, and I think about Grandpa being upset that my driver's ed class back in Crawfordsville only included training in an automatic car. He borrowed a friend's pickup truck and took me out in the country to practice how to coordinate easing up on the clutch at the same time I pushed down on the gas. I wasn't very good at it.

"If Edsel Sparks finds out how much I've let you strip his gears, he'll never speak to me again," Grandpa said.

I never told Grandpa *my* problem with driver's ed was thinking about my father lying in his nursing home bed, and three other people dead, because of how one person drove.

Maybe even if Mom had had the money to insure me as a driver, I would have been too freaked out to pass the test. Maybe that will be true even after I go home.

Is that something I'm going to fret over when I'm an old lady lying in a nursing home?

Maybe Mr. Armisted isn't that great with manual cars either, because as he shifts again, one of the front tires veers slightly off the road, bumping down onto the berm.

"Dad!" Avery shrieks. "What are you doing?"

Mr. Armisted slumps to the side.

The car keeps going, shooting toward the ditch.

## Avery, Anguished

**"Grab the wheel!" Kayla screams** from the backseat.

"What?" I say. "Dad?" His head lolls toward my shoulder. "Dad, wake up!"

Suddenly, Kayla is in my face—what was she thinking, ripping her seat belt off when the car's gone crazy?

"Get his foot off the gas!" Kayla yells.

I don't do a thing, and she reaches past me, knocking at Dad's knee. The car shudders violently and comes to a halt, half on and half off the road. I shove at Dad's arm.

"Dad, this isn't funny," I complain, because maybe he's just joking around. *Oh please, let him just be joking around. . . .*

"Daddy, stop it!" I yell.

Kayla grabs his shoulders from behind and shakes.

"Mr. Armisted! Mr. Armisted!"

Dad's body flops around like he doesn't have a spine. His eyelids don't even flutter.

Kayla puts two fingers against his neck.

"CPR," she says. "Call nine-one-one."

My brain translates as if she's speaking Spanish. She's saying she'll do CPR; I'm supposed to call 911. I can tell because she's already opening her door and Dad's, already reaching for Dad's chest. I look at the phone in my hand like I've never seen it before. My hand shakes so much I need two tries to hit the right icon. And then I can't get the number keyboard to come up. . . . Finally, I manage to hit a nine and two ones. And then I remember that Spain has a different emergency number.

I just can't remember what it is.

"Is Spain one-one-nine?" I scream at Kayla. "Or . . ."

I drop the phone and have to swipe at the car floor to pick it back up.

Kayla's reaching in through Dad's car door. She's pressing on his chest with one hand, and reaching for something on the side of his seat with the other. Oh, the seat release. His seat plunges backward, so he's almost lying down.

A *ding*ing noise keeps coming out of the car dashboard. Kayla ignores it and keeps pressing down on Dad's chest, again and again and again. His arms flail out like he's waking up—

No, that's just from Kayla giving him CPR.

His face is blank.

"Call!" Kayla screams at me.

"I don't remember the number!" I scream back at her. But then I do: 112. I hit those numbers and put the phone to my ear.

Nothing. There's only the slightest buzz at the other end of the line. No ringing.

"There's no service!" I shout, my voice squeaking with panic.

"Please, God, please, God, please, God," Kayla moans. Then she shouts at me, "Get out of the car! Flag someone down!"

I drop the phone and jerk on the door handle. I fall to the ground because my legs are shaking too much to stand up. But then I do stand up, and I dash out to the middle of the road. I don't care if someone hits me—they'll have to stop, then.

There's not a single other car in sight.

I run back to our car. Dad's head bumps up and down with

the force of Kayla shoving on his chest. But his face stays empty. Empty of life. Empty of *him*. It's like he's somebody else now.

Or some*thing* else.

"Does he . . . does he have a pulse?"

"Get somebody! Get help!" Kayla screams. Then she goes back to, "Please, God, please, God, please, God . . ."

Sweat drips from her face down onto Dad's shirt. Her face is so red it looks like she's going to have a heart attack.

Heart attack. Did Dad have a heart attack?

Is he going to die?

Is he already dead?

"Nobody's coming!" I scream at Kayla. "Do something!"

"Please, God, please, God, please, God . . ."

What if she gives up?

It feels like she's been doing CPR on Dad for a million years.

I jerk my head around, scanning the horizon, just *willing* another car to appear. Or a nearby house I overlooked before. I gaze up and down, too, as if the horizon is tilting, as if I think a car or a house might fall from the sky.

I twist my neck farther—and the sign pointing to the hospital comes into sight.

"*You* drive him to the hospital!" I yell at Kayla. "You're sixteen! You know how to drive!"

I don't actually know this—it's not like I ever asked. But again, I'm trying to will something into being true.

*And Daddy's not dying. He's not dead. He's not going to die. Daddy, Daddy, Daddy* . . .

Now I'm crying so hard I couldn't see a car coming even if it ran over top of me. The *ding*ing sound coming out of the car's dashboard blends with Kayla's "Please, God, please, God, please, God . . ."

Kayla lets out a horrific wail.

"Don't stop!" I scream at her.

"You," she says, gasping for air.

And my brain translates again:

It's my turn to do CPR.

## Kayla, Frantic

**"I don't know how!" Avery** screams at me.

"Try!" I scream back at her. There's so much else I don't have enough air in my lungs to say: *I can't drive a stick shift and give CPR at the same time! I'm not sure I can drive a stick shift, anyhow! But we have to work together! Or else your father's going to die!*

I feel like I'm going to faint. I remember what my health teacher said when he taught us all CPR: "Basically, if the person you're trying to help needs CPR, he's already dead. His heart has stopped, and that's the definition of death. So you can't hurt them. You're bringing them back to life."

I'm just Kayla Butts from Crawfordsville, Ohio. I'm not good at anything, let alone bringing someone back to life. I don't even feel like I can breathe myself, right now.

*Please, God, please, God, please, God . . .*

I give Mr. Armisted's chest an extra hard push, and then I reach over and yank Avery back into the car. She's almost as rag-doll limp as her father.

"Shut the door," I order her.

Avery's crying so hard, I'm not sure she can see the door, but she grabs the handle and tugs it closed. She sprawls sideways in the passenger's seat, and I grab her by the wrists and put her hands on her father's chest.

"Up down up down," I coach.

"I don't know . . . how many times per minute," Avery whimpers.

"Please, God, please, God . . . ," I say robotically. "Please—down. God—up."

Finally, she pushes hard enough that she doesn't need my hands on her wrists. I shove Mr. Armisted's legs to the side and perch on the very edge of the driver's seat. My forehead is practically touching the windshield, but I slam the door against my own hip.

"Keys," I whisper to myself.

I reach to turn them in the ignition, but there aren't any keys.

"Push button," Avery says behind me. "Push—down—the button. Up."

The car is too new to have keys. I've never driven a car like this.

Avery reaches past me and crams a finger against a button on the dashboard. Maybe it says START or POWER or something like that—I don't even take the time to read it.

The engine turns over and dies.

"What happened?" I scream. "What?"

But it's like I can summon up Grandpa's voice in my head: "You don't turn the keys in the ignition until you've got the brake and the clutch mashed clear to the floor."

Hitting that button is like turning keys in the ignition.

The car died because I didn't push in the clutch at the same time.

I hear Avery behind me chanting, "Please . . . God . . . Please . . . God . . ."

I don't even know if she believes in God. We've never discussed it. I don't know if she feels more like she's praying or cursing.

But the words help me.

I put my feet on the brake and the clutch, and I push the ignition button, and this time when the engine roars to life, it stays alive. I put the car into first and move my brake foot to the gas and the engine roars like an angry tiger.

It's Grandpa's voice I hear again: "Get your foot off the ding-dong clutch!"

I take my foot off the clutch and the car lurches forward. I swing the steering wheel back toward the direction of the road again. I should have checked for traffic first, but if there weren't any cars coming when we needed them, why would there be a car coming now?

*Because this is the summer of everything breaking, everything falling apart, everything going wrong . . .*

I can still hear Avery behind me: "Please, God, please, God . . ."

By some miracle, I manage to swing the car in a wide loop, and settle into a wobbly path back toward the roundabout. I really thought I'd have to stop and back up and do a three-point turn just to keep from going into the opposite ditch—and who knows how many times I would have killed the engine then?

Too late, I realize I'm going the wrong direction through the roundabout—clockwise, not counterclockwise—but that gets me to the spoke that leads toward the hospital sooner.

I hit the gas coming out of the roundabout because it looks

like an uphill climb. The engine roars again, but the car only inches forward.

I have to shift gears.

*Please, please, please, please . . .*

I stab my foot against the clutch and . . .

We're in second gear.

Nobody in the history of the universe has ever been so grateful to shift gears without killing the engine.

I hit the gas again, and I barely have time to be happy before it's time to shift to third. And then fourth.

And then Avery screams, "Is that the hospital? Is that the emergency room over there?"

She points past me, and I yell, "Keep doing CPR! We're not there yet!"

I roar through a parking lot—is there a fifth gear I really should be shifting to? Who cares? Either the parking lot is designed like an obstacle course or I have no understanding of curbs, because we jerk and bump toward the entrance Avery pointed out. I slam on the brake when we reach the door and the car bucks to a halt.

Oops. Forgot to downshift.

"Run!" Avery screams at me.

I look into her eyes and it's like we're connected, both of us thinking it's faster for me to go in than for us to switch off and let her go beg for help.

I shove the car door open and almost crash face-first into the hospital's doors before they part silently before me.

I don't even look to see if there's a receptionist behind the doors. I just start screaming, "*¡Ayúdame! ¡Ayúdame!*"

A woman wearing scrubs runs up to me like I'm the one in pain, I'm the one having the emergency. I point out the door and scream in her ear, "*¡El padre! ¡Su corazón!*"

I don't know the word for "attack" in Spanish, only "heart." So I pantomime it. I clutch my chest and make my body quiver. Then I flail my arms out and go limp.

"*Sí, sí,*" the woman says.

What seems like an entire herd of paramedics stampedes out the door.

And then my body really does go limp. I practically fall to the floor.

Because there's nothing else I can do for Mr. Armisted.

And I don't know if he's dead or alive.

## Avery, Hoping, Fearing, Hoping . . .

**Medical personnel flood out of** the hospital doors, and for a moment I think it's just a mirage. But then they're swarming the car and pushing me back—and pulling Daddy away.

"*Vaya, vaya,*" someone says, opening my car door and pointing me toward the hospital doors.

"But is he going to be okay?" I ask. They have Dad on a stretcher now. "Let me see—"

Someone pulls me out of the car and actually shoves me toward the hospital doors. Something's wrong with my ears—I think someone says, "This is the best way for you to help him now" in Spanish, but I can barely make out the words. Even though I can see the woman's mouth move, just three inches away.

I stumble into the hospital—and practically trip over Kayla. And then I'm hugging her and sobbing, "You helped me. You helped me. Even though you hate me."

"I don't *hate* you," Kayla says. "Is he—is he—"

Then there's someone leading us into a private room, and I start to get frantic all over again.

"Is this where you give people bad news?" I cry.

But Kayla is holding on to me. She pats my arm and says something to the woman leading us, and the woman points to a computer and says what must be the Spanish word for "paperwork."

At first I answer the questions: "David Armisted." "105

Hanover Court, Deskins, Ohio. *En los* Estados Unidos." "Fifty-four. He'll be fifty-five on September twenty-fourth." I try not to think about how far it is to September twenty-fourth, how many heartbeats away that is. And then the questions get harder, and I blank out. Maybe Kayla answers a few on her own; maybe she's explaining to the woman why nobody should expect me to answer anything right now.

Not while I don't know. Not while I'm waiting to find out.

It feels like anything could happen now, and that's why I can't let myself think or feel.

Kayla shakes me.

"Next of kin," she says. "They need to know an emergency contact."

"Me," I say. "I'm all he has now." The tears stream back into my eyes. "He's all I have too."

"No, he's not," Kayla says irritably.

"My mother doesn't count," I blubber.

"Who just drove you here?" she asks. "Whose arm are you crying on *right now*? You've got me, too, you *idiota*."

And then I start laughing, because of all the words to use Spanish for, why does Kayla go for the one calling me an idiot? Why does she make that the thing the woman taking our paperwork answers is actually going to understand?

And then I can't stop laughing, and the woman says something that is probably the Spanish for asking if I need a sedative.

"No!" I say, because what if something happens? What if my dad comes back to consciousness and wants to talk to me, and *I'm* knocked out?

"She'll be all right," Kayla tells the woman in Spanish.

Kayla even sounds like she knows what she's talking about, and that makes me calm down.

I wish she'd tell me that my dad's okay.

Kayla starts asking if Dad has any brothers or sisters, which he doesn't. Dad's an only child and Mom's an only child—no wonder they both always wanted to get their way. (Will Dad ever get his own way, ever again?) Kayla tries a different question: *Is there anybody from Dad's work that the hospital should call?*

"No!" I say, and then I can't explain how Dad always says it's better not to show any weakness in a business setting.

A shadow falls across the woman's desk. A man stands in the doorway.

"Is he—" I cry.

"*Vuestra cosas*," the man says. He's just talking about our things. He's brought us our purses and Dad's phone from the car. He says he moved our car for us.

"*¡Pero mi padre!*" I scream. "*Cómo—*"

"This is just someone helping out," Kayla whispers to me. "He doesn't know any more than we do."

She takes the purses and the phone. And then the parking lot guy hands her the key fob to the car.

"He took that out of Dad's pocket! What happened? Where's Daddy now?"

The parking lot guy holds up his hands like I've accused him of stealing and rattles off a lot of Spanish I could probably understand better if I weren't hysterical.

Kayla goes back to patting my arm.

"Calm down," she says. "I think he's saying the key fob was on the floor of the car. It must have fallen out of your Dad's pocket."

But I'm lost. I can't stop crying. I don't have anything to hold on to at all.

Except Kayla.

## Kayla, Trying to Hold It Together

**I have Mr. Armisted's phone** in my hand. I'm gripping it so tightly it cuts ridges into my skin.

All I want to do is call my mother.

My mommy.

But it's not really fair to do that in front of Avery, and anyhow, I already know what my mom would tell me to do right now: Take care of Avery, while the poor girl doesn't even know if her father is alive or dead.

That's like what my mother has done for the past sixteen years: taken care of me, while my father hangs in his weird limbo between life and death. I can see it; I can feel it, everything my mother did that was for me, not for herself: moving back to Crawfordsville, where Grandma and Grandpa could take care of me while she worked. Taking a job at the nursing home, where a lot of the time they'd let her bring me to work with her.

Not divorcing my dad, not leaving him behind the same way his own parents did.

The same way Avery's mother wants to leave Avery's dad. She wanted to leave him even *before* he was a body on a stretcher.

"Avery," I say gently. "I think I have to give them your mom's name and phone number. Because they *are* still married."

Avery's holding on to my arm even tighter than I'm holding

on to the phone. She buries her wet face against my shoulder.

"You should probably call your mom first," I say. "To warn her. Let her know *you're* all right."

A sob wracks Avery's body so hard that I shake too.

"You," she wails. "You call. I can't."

I gulp. I pull up the right number and put the phone to my ear. I want Avery's mom to answer and say, *Okay, then. Thank you for calling, Kayla. I'll take care of everything from here.* I wouldn't even care if she said it rudely. Like, *You're dismissed now, servant.*

But I get her voice mail, a brisk, professional explanation of how the renowned interior decorator Celeste Armisted is unavailable at this time, but she will respond to messages in a timely fashion.

It's almost a jolt to hear English from someone besides Avery. I don't think anybody at this hospital knows anything but Spanish. But of course Avery's mom is in a different country from us, on a different continent, even in a different time. It's still Saturday morning for her, and we're caught in the longest afternoon of my life.

The beep startles me, and I begin my message badly. "Um . . . ." But then I recover. "Mrs. Armisted, this is Kayla Butts. I'm at the hospital with Avery. Avery's fine, but I think your husband had a heart attack. Avery and I did CPR, but . . . now we're waiting. The hospital might call you. But call Avery back. Please. On this phone. And, oh, it's the hospital in El Es—"

A second beep cuts me off, and I hang up. She can call back if she wants to know more.

"Told you," Avery whimpers. "Told you she wouldn't care."

"She was probably just away from her phone," I say, and now I sound as brisk and heartless as Mrs. Armisted's answering machine. "She'll call back."

The phone doesn't ring.

Should I call Mr. Armisted's office, even though Avery told me not to? Should I text or call Dragomir or Andrei? Susan? Hugh? Señora Gomez?

Before I can decide, Avery straightens up and peers at the paperwork lady. She keeps her death grip on my arm, but there's a fierceness in her face that wasn't there before.

"Nobody else is going to come," she hisses at the paperwork lady in Spanish. She even gets the verb tenses right. "My dad doesn't have anyone but me. And Kayla. So you have to tell us what's happening. How my dad is. We have to know."

*Oh, Avery, no,* I think. *Didn't you see how long we did CPR on him, and he didn't come back? Don't you know you're asking for bad news here? Don't you see how they're waiting for someone official to show up—some adult who can take responsibility?*

But Avery's right. There isn't anyone coming. There isn't anybody to summon. Señora Gomez is not the comforting type. She's never given any sign that she's anything but a Spanish-speaking robot. And I like the other kids from our class—Susan could be particularly helpful, with her obsession with speaking perfect Spanish. But the kids I like annoy Avery.

And she really hates Susan.

Doubt crosses the paperwork lady's face. And . . . maybe sympathy.

"*Uno momento*," she says, holding up one finger.

She slips out from behind her desk and walks out the door.

We wait, clutching each other's arms.

I try to think how I'm going to console Avery when the bad news comes. I know all the things you murmur when old people die: *He's in a better place. He had a good life. Everyone could see how much he loved you. I'm sorry for your loss. May God comfort you. May your memories comfort you.*

A lot of the dead people I knew also had do-not-resuscitate orders. They didn't *want* to be brought back if their hearts stopped. They were ready to be done with life.

Mr. Armisted wasn't that old.

He isn't.

A man in scrubs appears in the doorway. His face is grim, and Avery begins to sob just at the sight of him.

"He's dead, right?" she wails, and manages to switch to Spanish: "*¿Muerto? ¿Muerto?*"

The man—a doctor?—rushes over to pat her shoulder.

"*No, no, no!*" he cries. He lets out a burst of Spanish that includes the same word again and again: *cirugía*. But neither of us knows what that means. Finally, I hold out Mr. Armisted's phone.

"Type it," I say, and I don't know if I've said that in Spanish or if the doctor understands my English, or if he just figures out what I mean because I'm shoving the phone into his hands. But he types in the word, and I hit the translate key, and the English word appears.

"Surgery!" I scream. "He's in surgery!"

"He's still alive!" Avery cries. But then her face falls. "What kind of surgery? How serious is it?"

"*Cirugía de bypass*," the doctor says, and I don't need help understanding that.

Avery's face quivers, as if she's struggling to hold back more sobs, struggling to keep from falling apart again.

"Can we . . . ," she begins, and gulps. "Is there anything we . . ."

"*Rezad*," the paperwork lady says. It's another word I don't know, but I don't need to look it up.

She's telling us to pray.

Or maybe she's saying she'll pray for us herself—it all kind of feels like the same thing.

The doctor leaves and the paperwork lady leads us out into an open waiting room, and then Avery surprises me by saying, "You should call your mom."

"What? Why—?"

Has Avery read my mind?

Does she think she can boss me around? Even now?

But this is entirely different from when she told me to read my mother's e-mail.

"We've got one functioning parent between the two of us right now," Avery says. "Call."

And it's funny—it's like she's allowed to say things like that to me now. It's okay that she's kind of putting her mother and my father in the same category.

Because we don't know what category her father's going into next.

In a daze, I click on my mother's contact information and lift the phone. I hear my mother's phone ringing. All the way across the ocean, all the way back in Crawfordsville, Ohio, I know her her phone is sending out a Taylor Swift song. I downloaded it for her myself. That was one of my birthday gifts to her.

*She might be working*, I think. *She might have picked up somebody else's Saturday shift. . . .*

But she answers: "Hello?"

I hear the hesitation in her voice, because this is Mr. Armisted's phone. This isn't how she would answer if she knew it was me.

"Mom?" I say. "Mommy? I love you. I miss you so much. . . ."

And that's when the phone goes dead.

## Avery, Who Can Actually Be a Nice Person

**"Does anybody have a phone** charger?" I shriek as Kayla sits there staring at the blank screen on Dad's phone. I remember Dad saying he forgot to charge it overnight; he forgot to bring a charger. That seemed a lifetime ago.

*A lifetime* . . .

Around the waiting room, Spanish faces stare blankly at me.

"*¿Un telefono?*" I try again. "Uh . . ." I don't know the Spanish word for "charger." I mime shoving a plug into the wall behind me.

A haggard-faced woman hesitantly brings over a cord, but it's not the right type. There are only seven or eight other people in the waiting room, and they all either offer up choices that don't work or apologetically shake their heads.

"It's okay," Kayla whispers. "I said what I wanted to. She'll know . . ."

I dig into Kayla's purse and pull out her burner phone. I press it into her hands.

"Call her back!"

"But—your dad said not to use this one for international calls. He said it costs, like, a dollar a minute. . . ."

"*I'll* pay," I say. "Talk as long as you like. Because you *can*. Because *your* mother wants to talk to you."

Kayla's eyes flood with tears, and she hugs me. She keeps her arm around my shoulder even as she dials the phone. And

I'm not trying to eavesdrop, but she is talking right in my ear. She sounds more and more like a hick from the country, the longer she talks to her mom. It's as if she's picking up an old accent, one I hadn't even noticed her losing.

But I like it. It's what makes Kayla Kayla. And . . . it's kind of how my dad sounds sometimes, when he starts talking about his life back when he was a kid.

"Tell Mr. Wilkins when you see him at church that I wouldn't have known how to do CPR if he hadn't drilled us again and again in health class," Kayla says. "All those signs he told us to look for . . . I remembered them all. I didn't remember until afterward that I was supposed to use the rhythm of that song 'Stayin' Alive,' but . . . I did my best. And tell Grandpa I shifted gears three—no, four!—times without killing the engine. I wouldn't have known how to do that without him."

Is she going to end up thanking everybody in Crawfordsville?

Maybe she wants to thank everybody in Crawfordsville.

Kayla finishes the story of where we are now, what's happening with my dad. And suddenly they're talking about Kayla's mom giving birth to me.

"Mom, it's okay," Kayla says. "I understand. None of that matters now."

She sounds like she means it. Is it that easy to let go?

"Can I talk to your mom?" I whisper to Kayla. "When you're done, I mean."

"Um, sure," Kayla says.

She hands me the phone immediately.

"Mrs. Butts?" I say. "I just . . . Whatever happens, I need to thank you. Thank you for helping my parents the way you did. And me. I wouldn't be here without you."

It's the most basic thing in the world, a statement of the obvious. But I hear her gasp as if I've given her some huge gift.

Maybe it's not such a basic thing. Doctors said my mother couldn't give birth, which meant that someone with my combination of genes would probably never exist. But I do. I'm here. I'm alive. Thanks to Mrs. Butts. My hands throb—hands with DNA from both my parents, hands that just worked so hard trying to save my father's life.

I can't take anything about life for granted right now. Mine or Dad's or anybody's.

"Oh, Avery, honey—can I do anything for you *now*?" Mrs. Butts says. "Is there anyone I can call for you from here, anything I can—?"

"No," I say. "Kayla's taking care of me."

And it strikes me how true this is. I'd probably still be sitting in the car by the roundabout, sobbing my eyes out, if it weren't for Kayla. Even if it had occurred to me to do CPR, I couldn't have driven the car to the hospital. Who knows how long it would have taken for someone to come along and help?

Daddy would have died if I'd been alone.

*It doesn't matter*, I tell myself. *I wasn't alone.*

Then Kayla leans over and says into the phone, "You can pray."

"Oh, honey, I will," Mrs. Butts says, and her voice is so soothing it's like a balm flowing over me. "I'll call up the church and get them to add Avery's dad to the prayer chain as soon as I hang up. And I'll call the prayer chain at the nursing home, and probably some of those ladies will call *their* churches. . . . You'll have the whole town of Crawfordsville praying for the three of you!"

After we hang up, Kayla says in an embarrassed voice, "You probably think that's foolish, getting people you don't even know to pray for you."

"No," I say. "I don't." I hesitate. "What you kept saying in the car—'Please, God, please, God'—that was a prayer, wasn't it?"

"Sure felt like it," Kayla says. She looks down at her hands. "It felt like those were the words giving me power. That wouldn't let me give up. I—I've never felt like that before, praying."

"Dad always wanted me to go to Sunday school and church when I was little," I say. "But Mom didn't."

"Huh," Kayla says. "I don't think I ever had the right attitude either."

We're silent for a minute, leaning against each other.

"How long do you think we gave Dad CPR?" I ask. "When his heart wasn't beating on its own?"

"Did the sign back at the roundabout say how far it was to the hospital?" Kayla says.

I shrug.

"Wish Dad's phone still worked, and we could look it up," I mutter. Then—"Oh! His laptop! There's Wi-Fi here, right?"

Five minutes later—after I find the car and figure out how to unlatch the trunk—I have Dad's laptop set up and I'm peering at Google Maps.

"It says it's only ninety-seven meters from the roundabout to the hospital," I tell Kayla. On the computer, I convert the metric. "That's not even a tenth of a mile."

"But look at the map—that's only to the *driveway* to the hospital," Kayla says. "It felt more like ninety-seven miles."

"I don't think we were thinking clearly," I say.

I don't feel like I'm thinking clearly now, either. I start a different search: "heart bypass surgery."

"The surgery could take three to six hours?" I moan to Kayla. I start typing in "survival rates of . . . ," but Kayla stops me.

"Don't," she says quietly.

"What else am I supposed to do?" I ask. "That's all I care about!"

"Those won't tell you if your dad is going to live or die," Kayla says. "Just the possibilities. Probability. Chance."

She takes control of the keyboard.

"How about . . . Do you want to read the rest of my mother's e-mails with me?" Kayla asks, her fingers poised over the keys. "Mom said when I wouldn't answer, she just kept writing more and more about why she did it, what it was like to be pregnant with you, how it felt seeing you and me playing together, all those years ago . . ."

"But you got so mad when I read your e-mail before!" I protest.

"Now I'm inviting you to," Kayla says. "That's different."

We bend our heads together and start reading, and it's like seeing my entire life in another way.

I learn that Kayla's mom has prayed for me every single day I've been alive. The same way she's prayed for Kayla every single day Kayla has been alive.

I learn that when the doctor put me in my mother's arms, my mother cried and cried and cried and everybody thought she was sad, but she said, "No, no! It's joy! I didn't know it was possible to feel this happy!"

I learn that Kayla's mom felt horrible and wonderful all at once, watching my parents walk out of the hospital with me in Mom's arms, Dad's arm around her waist.

*Some emotions are just braided together too tight to know what exactly you feel*, she wrote.

And that makes so much sense, because it's so nice to read about how much my parents wanted me back then. It's so nice to lean against Kayla and have her arm around me, holding me together.

But what about my parents *now*? What's going to happen now?

It starts getting dark outside, and I have to squint at the screen.

"Do you realize we never ate lunch?" Kayla asks. "Do you want me to go look for a vending machine, or a cafeteria, or—"

"Don't be away long," I beg, "in case someone comes back with news. . . ."

Kayla goes and asks the woman at the desk something, and then she disappears down a hallway. She comes back with bags of chips and cookies, and cans of Coke Light.

"I know you like healthy food," she apologizes. "But this was the best I could find in the vending machine." She holds up a red bag. "They even had Doritos. Like it was the most ordinary thing ever. Do you suppose there are Doritos all over the place in Spain, and I just never looked in the right places?"

"We've only been in Spain for three weeks," I tell her. "There are lots of things here we never saw."

I open a potato chip bag and feel eyes on me. It's like

everyone in the waiting room is watching us, even though their eyes dart away when I gaze in their direction.

"*¿Quereis esto?*" I ask, holding out an unopened bag, offering it around.

I see a lot of shaking heads. A little kid—three years old? Four?—starts to reach for it, but his mother pulls his hand back and whispers in his ear.

Okay, that was probably a cultural no-no. I was too much of the eager-beaver *Americana*, acting like we're all in this together, instead of a bunch of strangers in the same room pretending not to notice each other.

The haggard-looking woman even stalks out through the glass doors. I see her drive away.

But then she's back, holding out Styrofoam containers of real food to us: *papas bravas*, and thick slabs of meat . . . Maybe it's even beef tongue, one of those weird things Europeans eat but Americans mostly don't. But I don't care.

"*Gracias*," Kayla and I say, over and over again. "*Gracias.*"

We *are* all in this together. Everyone in this room is either sick or hurt, or waiting and worrying about someone who is sick or hurt.

I do feel a little better after eating real food.

We wait some more. The room starts to empty out, one cluster after another called back. New people arrive. But nobody comes for Kayla and me. Hours pass. Lifetimes. Eternities.

And then a man in scrubs steps out from behind a screen and says, "*¿Familia de David Armisted?*"

He motions us toward the screen, but I've lost the ability to move. I think if I tried to stand up, I'd only fall over.

"*¡Digame!*" I beg. "*¡Por favor digame ahora! ¡Aquí!*"

He has to tell me here and now.

"*La operación fue un éxito,*" he says.

I look to Kayla to see if she understands, but her face is blank too.

The man pulls a Spanish-English dictionary from under his arm. The paperback is so battered, it looks like it's been hanging around this hospital since before the Internet was invented. The man starts leafing through it slowly, searching for the right word.

But it doesn't matter, because the people around us start cheering: "*¡Que bien!*" "*¡Buenas noticias!*"

And then the man in scrubs is pointing to two words paired together:

Éxito—*success.*

The operation was a success.

## Kayla, Drained

**We wait and wait and** wait some more, and finally we're allowed to go see Mr. Armisted. I hang back, walking into his room, but Avery tugs me forward, whispering, "We both saved his life. He's going to want to thank us both."

I bet Avery will never, ever, ever let her father forget she saved his life.

I bet he won't mind.

Mr. Armisted's face is almost as white as his pillow, and the hugs we give him have to be very, very gentle. But his smile is broad.

"I think it was a really good idea, bringing you both to Spain with me," he murmurs groggily.

"Me too," Avery whispers back.

Avery and I fall asleep in chairs on either side of Mr. Armisted's bed. At three a.m., I wake up when a nurse comes in to check on him, but she pats my arm and puts a finger to her lips, like everything's okay and it's fine to go back to sleep.

Then she leaves, and I'm still awake. And I remember that the rental car that's sitting out in the hospital parking lot was supposed to be turned back in six hours ago.

None of us thought about that before, when we didn't know if Mr. Armisted was going to live or die.

I pick up my purse and creep out into the hallway, so I can

go someplace where I won't disturb anyone if I call the rental car company and explain for Mr. Armisted. But when I pull out my burner phone, it's dead too. And of course I don't have the charger, because when we left Madrid, I thought we were only taking an afternoon trip.

*Like the three-hour tour from Gilligan's Island,* I think, and giggle.

It feels okay to giggle again.

In the darkened hallway, I can't read any names on the patients' doors, and the hallway curves enough that I can see only the barest glow of an exit sign—I can't make out the red letters that spell out "*salida.*" It feels like I could be in any hospital, anywhere in the world.

I think about my mom staying with my dad at the hospital after his accident fourteen years ago. There must have been nights like these when she wandered the halls, wondering what was going to happen next.

My dad had some operations that were successes. But he never got the news we heard the doctor tell Mr. Armisted, right before we all fell asleep: "Once you heal, you'll be able to resume all your normal activities."

My dad never got to be normal again.

I don't have any memories of him before his accident, and yet it's him I ache with missing right now, as I stand here in this dark hospital corridor in the middle of the night.

There's a special wink he has, whenever I walk into the room, that lets me know he's glad I'm there.

My mom said in one of her e-mails that every time she goes

to see him this summer, he looks around and looks around, and she has to explain that I'm still not back from Spain. And then he looks sad but not too sad—as Mom put it, "He's also happy you're getting opportunities he and I never had."

I think Mom wants to think that's how Dad feels.

But, for all that my father hasn't been able to speak to me in fourteen years, I still feel like I know him. And I love him.

A lot of kids do worse in the parents lottery.

I'm thinking about Avery's mom, who hasn't called her even once since Avery found out she had a surrogate mother.

Then I think about my mother fourteen years ago, giving birth to Avery right after finding out my father was never going to be normal again. My mother was so sure that Avery's life would be charmed and perfect—so much better than mine.

But . . . maybe I was the luckier one, after all?

I think about how Grandma and Grandpa and Mom were always there for me. I think about how just a few phone calls can get all of Crawfordsville to pray for me, just like that. Probably, my classmates at Crawfordsville High School will go back to making fun of me after they pray for me, but there are worse things.

And the world is a lot bigger place than Crawfordsville High. My classmates don't get to define who I am and what I can do.

Neither does the fact that Mom was a surrogate mother. I can be impressed or dismayed or just in awe of the choices she made. But those choices were hers, not mine.

I have a life of my own, choices of my own.

I go back into Mr. Armisted's room, and even though I'm

still tired, I just can't find a comfortable position, back in my stiff chair. I don't think I'll be able to go back to sleep. But the next thing I know, there's bright sunshine in my face, and a woman runs into the room crying out, "Avery? David? Are you in there?"

It's Mrs. Armisted.

## Avery, Astonished

**"Shh, you'll wake up my** dad," I snap, before it sinks in that this is *Mom* stumbling to a halt before me, staring and staring and staring into my face.

Mom, who is still supposed to be in Ohio.

Mom, who didn't call back—but came all the way across the ocean to Spain instead.

I brace for her to say, *What have you done with your hair? When was the last time you combed it?* Or *You look like you slept in those clothes.* I'm braced to snarl back at her, *I had to sleep in my clothes. It's not like you were here to bring me pajamas. You didn't even answer your phone!*

But there's none of the usual dissatisfaction and disappointment in her expression.

Oddly, there doesn't seem to be any makeup on her face either.

I'm not sure I've ever seen her without makeup.

And her clothes look as thrown together and wrinkled as mine. Not only do her shoes not match her purse, they don't match each *other*. They're not even the same shade of brown.

Mom reaches out and wraps me in a big hug, and I'm so startled, I let her. I even hug back, a little. And I don't burst out with, *You think showing up* now *is going to make up for ignoring me for two weeks?*

"You came," I whimper. "You do love Dad."

"I came . . . ," Mom whispers into my hair, "because I love you. I had to be here for you. You only have two parents, and if . . . if your father, well . . . . I thought you needed me."

It's on the tip of my tongue to snap, *You know what? I was doing fine. I had Kayla. And a waiting room full of Spanish people.* Or, *Only two parents? That depends on how you count it. The woman who gave birth to me was actually willing to talk to me last night, when I didn't know if my father was alive or dead. That's more than you did.*

But Mom pulls back a little, like she knows I'm about to explode. And I catch a glimpse of her face, and . . .

*Oh, crap. Now I see why Kayla keeps saying she can't stay mad at me when she looks at me and sees how I looked as a five-year-old.*

It's not like Mom has drunk from any fountain of youth. She still has the wrinkles of a fifty-three-year-old woman, no matter how much anti-aging skin cream she uses. And she's just gotten off a red-eye flight, which would age anyone.

It's not even that she looks so much like me—I've got a lot of my father's features. Only my hair is exactly the same color as hers, and that's because she dyes hers that way on purpose.

It's more that her thoughts are written on her face, like a little kid's. And she's clearly thinking, *What you're about to say is going to hurt me. And I can't protect myself. Please, please, please don't hurt me.*

"Where were you the past two weeks?" I ask. But I keep my voice gentle.

Mom lowers her head in a humble way I've never seen her use before.

"I fell apart," she says. "I had to get help. I'm still supposed to be getting help, but . . . as soon as I heard the voice mail, I had to come. I had to think about you, not me."

She does look fragile, like it wouldn't take much to break her.

Like maybe the news about Dad and the flight across the ocean did break her.

"Then you and Dad aren't getting divorced," I say. "You'll patch things up, because he almost died, and that made you realize how much you'd miss him."

I could go on talking this way forever. But Mom glances toward the bed, where Dad is still sleeping. Then she puts her hand on my arm.

"Avery . . . ," Mom begins. "I don't know what's going to happen next. But I don't want to give you false hope."

"But . . . but . . . you love him!" I burst out. "Or you used to! You *can*."

Mom winces.

"I do," she admits. "But is it for the right reasons? I don't love some of the things he loves about himself. That's a problem. And . . . I have enough other problems of my own. We haven't been good for each other lately, and a lot of it was because I was too miserable to care about anyone but myself. . . . I haven't been fair to you, either, Avery."

Mom is admitting this? Mom?

Mom is accepting blame?

I'm crying again—I am so sick of crying. There should be a way to switch off the tears when you don't feel like sobbing anymore, but you keep getting more reasons to cry harder and harder and harder.

And then Kayla's crouched beside me, with her arm around me, murmuring, "Shh, shh, it's all right."

Mom looks down at her.

"You're Kayla, aren't you?" Mom asks, as if she really isn't sure.

If Mom says anything about how Kayla's too fat or has a bad haircut or shouldn't wear the color tan with her pasty complexion, I'm going to punch her.

But there's no judgment in Mom's expression.

"I'm so sorry, Kayla," Mom says. "I'm sorry I was never a good host when you and your mom came to visit Avery, all those years ago. I'm sorry I wouldn't even meet you. I'm sorry I didn't come to say good-bye at the airport. I just . . . I just couldn't bear to see your mother. I was too jealous."

"Jealous?" Kayla repeats numbly. "Of *my* mom?"

"Because she could have a baby, and I couldn't," Mom says.

"Dad said . . . ," I begin, but Mom shakes her head.

"I probably deserve anything bad your father said about me," she says. "But I can't hear it right now."

"It wasn't bad," I mutter.

Mom stares at me, wide-eyed and sad.

"Oh," she says. "I just . . . That's where I always go now. Thinking the worst. It's perfectly normal for a fourteen-year-old girl to push away from her mother. It's perfectly normal for a couple who've been married for twenty-three years to have an argument every now and then. But I couldn't let go of any of it. I started thinking that you sensed somehow that I wasn't your real mother, and that's why you liked your father better. I even . . . secretly hoped that you'd hate this summer, so you'd be angrier with your dad than you were with me."

She looks so shamefaced, I have to tell her, "Mom, that's crazy. Of course you're my real mother."

Do I believe that?

I do. I really do. The way I was born doesn't matter.

Mom blinks back tears.

"But I didn't think I *deserved* to be your mother," she says. "Not unless I was perfect. And . . . I couldn't be perfect."

*Mom, you are seriously messed up*, I want to say. But I think about what she's told me about her childhood: how she had to practice the piano over and over and over again, for hours, until she could play every song without a single mistake. How she had to sit at the dinner table with the grown-ups, and never spill anything, and never interrupt the conversation. How her parents cared more about her looking pretty and not mussing her clothes, than listening to her ideas.

Maybe Mom has good reasons for being seriously messed up.

"You're meeting Kayla now," I tell Mom, and there's nothing I can do to stop the fierceness in my voice. "You can be nice to her from now on."

Mom lowers her head, almost as if she's agreeing. And she hasn't agreed with anything I said in the past two years.

"Thank you for calling me yesterday," Mom tells Kayla. "The hospital never called—when I checked with them just now, it turned out that they were one digit off on the number they wrote down, and they kept leaving messages for a total stranger."

*It figures.*

"Wait a minute—then how'd you find us?" Kayla asks. "My phone was dead, and Mr. Armisted's phone was dead—"

"And I left mine back at the apartment in Madrid," I chime in.

"And your voice mail clicked off before I even said the whole name of the hospital," Kayla finishes.

"Let's just say it's a good thing to know an identity theft expert," Mom says, "who could help me track the GPS coordinates on your father's phone."

"You mean Lauren's mom?" I ask incredulously.

Mom nods.

My mother is not the type to track GPS coordinates. Half the time she can't even figure out Netflix.

She's also not the type to fly across the ocean without months of planning, without spending days coordinating outfits and figuring out the best way to pack the prettiest shoes.

I mean, she might chip a nail doing something like that.

But here she is.

"Really, it would have been okay just to call the hospital," I say grudgingly. "And then they could have asked me to—"

Mom's shaking her head.

"There were complications with the tracking," she says. "Something about a cell tower being down? I couldn't just wait and do nothing. I got on the plane, and then I talked to Lauren's mom when I got to Madrid this morning, and she finally had the information. I did call the hospital then, but they were speaking Spanish, and I didn't understand very well, and I couldn't get them to understand me, and—"

"It *is* Spain," I say.

"Also . . ." Now Mom is whispering. "I wasn't sure you would talk to me. And I didn't want the hospital to know that."

Still with the shame. And the secrecy.

I open my mouth, and I'm not even sure if I want to criticize her or comfort her. But then Dad stirs in the bed behind us, and all three of us snap our attention in that direction.

His eyelids flutter open. His groggy gaze takes in all of us, and then his eyes travel back to Mom's face. And I wish I could say that my mother goes running to his side, and clasps his hands in hers, and tells him that seeing him just now in that hospital bed has changed everything, and she's so glad that she came, because now she knows now how much she loves him, how much she wants to stay married to him forever.

But that doesn't happen.

Instead, they stare warily at each other, as if Mom is just waiting for Dad to start yelling, and Dad is just waiting for Mom to start yelling. But then Mom whispers, "I'm so sorry . . . about everything. I wanted to be here . . . for Avery. We both want what's best for Avery."

And Dad nods.

It's a start.

And—I know it's true. Whatever they feel for each other, they both love me.

And they're both here. They're both alive. All three of us are here in the same room, together.

Last night, that was more than I thought I would ever have again.

## Kayla: How It Ends/How It Begins

**It's our last day in Spain.**

We've waited four weeks for Mr. Armisted to get clearance to fly. I overheard a few whispered conversations—I think Mrs. Armisted suggested sending me back on my own, now that she was here, and Avery scolded, "You want to make Kayla fly across the ocean *all by herself*? Who's the one with the heart problem in this family, Mom—you or Dad?"

It was almost enough to make me feel sorry for Mrs. Armisted.

The thing is, I think I could actually handle flying alone. And I do miss my family and the Autumn Years residents. But I've been Skyping with everyone again. I even had a private conversation with Grandma and Grandpa about how they'd known all along that Mom gave birth to Avery.

"I know Mom was sworn to secrecy, but why didn't one of you tell me?" I asked.

"It wasn't our secret to tell," Grandma said. On the iPad screen, her face wavered, the Internet cutting in and out as if to remind me how far away she really was.

"Bet you were surprised we *could* keep a secret," Grandpa joked.

"But did you approve of what Mom did?" I ask. "Or were you upset? Or—"

"We love her," Grandma says. "We love *you*."

And somehow I know that's all the answer I'm going to get from them, on that topic.

It's the right answer.

Another day, Mom borrowed an iPad from the Crawfordsville Public Library and took it to Dad's nursing home so I could Skype with him.

This may sound weird, but I told Mom to leave the room for just a few minutes so I could talk to Dad in private. And I told him I forgive his friend Lester for causing his accident, and I hoped Dad was able to too. I told him that being with the Armisteds this summer has made me realize that nobody has a perfect family or a perfect life, and I'm not jealous of anybody anymore. Not even Stephanie Purley.

I told him that being able to give Mr. Armisted CPR and drive him to the hospital had made me sad all over again, because there's nothing like that I could do to help my own father.

"But for a moment, it almost felt like I *was* helping you, Dad," I whispered. "Does that make any sense? Like, I wanted to save Mr. Armisted even more, because I knew exactly what Avery would lose if he died or . . . stopped being himself. Like that made me try harder, because of you."

Was I trying to say that helping *anyone* would be like helping Dad? Was that why Mom was always trying to help people at the nursing home, as a replacement for helping Dad?

"It's like what Mom said in her one e-mail about watching the Armisteds carry Avery away as a newborn," I told Dad. "It does feel like being happy and sad can get twisted together so tight that you feel both at once. And . . . that's how I feel about leaving Spain and coming home, too."

I finished by telling Dad I loved him, in English and then Spanish, too. Just because. And then he winked at me.

I'm not sure if he understood anything I said, but it sure felt like he did.

When I was done talking with Dad, I really wanted to go back to the blue room at the train station one last time. But it was too late in the day.

This morning is my last chance.

But as soon as I turn the doorknob to leave the apartment, Avery comes sprinting out of the kitchen after me.

"Can I come too?" she asks, and before I can answer, she shouts over her shoulder, "Mom, Kayla and I are taking a walk—don't worry, we'll be back in time to go to that lunch place you want to try. . . ." And then, under her breath, she mutters to me, "We will, won't we? Where are you going?"

I could say, *Oh, over to the Gran Via one last time to try that fro-yo place the kids from our class were talking about*, or *Back to the Prado*, or *To check out the tourist shops to get more souvenirs for my family*. I could totally change my plans because of her.

But she has such a frantic look in her eye, I tell the truth.

"I'm going someplace that helped me when . . . well, you know. The day we both found out my mother gave birth to you. When I was upset."

I could add, *and the day you said, "Is Kayla Butts my sister?" like that would be the worst thing in the world*. But it's almost like I want to see if Avery remembers that, if she'll apologize without me having to beg for it.

She doesn't apologize.

"Honestly, I'd go anywhere, to get away from my mother right now," she said. "You'd think I was the one who had the heart attack! She acts like I can't cross the street without holding her hand!"

"She's going through a tough time," I said mildly. "And she feels bad that she wasn't there for you before. And . . . she's here now. She loves you."

"Yeah, well, she's going to make me hate her. *Again*," Avery groans. Then she stops in the middle of the stairs. "It's okay if I say that to you, right?"

"Avery, what *haven't* you said to me this summer?" I ask.

But Avery's phone buzzes, and she's distracted. After everything that happened, her mom threw away Avery's burner phone and insisted on unlocking Avery's iPhone for international use, no matter what it costs, so Avery is fully connected all the time now.

Actually, Avery's mom wanted to get me an iPhone too, for while I was with Avery, but I said that was silly for just a couple weeks.

Avery looks at her text and mutters as she texts back, "Yes, Mom, I do have my phone with me. Yes, you can reach me if our lunch plans change. Or if something else happens."

Her voice dips on the *if something else happens*, and I can tell she's done bad-talking her mother. For now.

She tucks her phone back in her pocket and glances my way as we continue down the stairs.

"Where we're going—is it that church by the churro place?" she asks. "That's a place you went when you were mad about things, isn't it?"

Sometimes, Avery amazes me.

"How did you know?" I gasp. "Did you follow me, or—"

"No!" Avery insists. "I just saw how you looked at that church when we were eating churros. . . ."

"I went to that church the day you made fun of me for using white bread for the grilled cheese sandwiches," I say.

"I didn't—" Avery begins. She stumbles on a step and has to grab the railing. "Ohhh . . . . I guess you probably did feel like I was making fun of you. But I didn't mean to. I was upset over everything that night."

"Yeah, me too," I admit.

We reach the bottom of the stairs.

"But I'm *not* going back to that church today," I say. "It was kind of too frilly and fancy for me. I'm going to the train station."

"You're taking a train?" Avery asks, giving me an *Are you crazy?* look.

"No," I say. "Just visiting the station."

"Oh-kay," Avery says.

I expect her to ask a lot more questions, but she doesn't. We're both quiet as we pass the eighties music nightclub and head out of our neighborhood. Everything is so familiar now that it's weird to think that I'll never see any of it again after tomorrow: not the wrought-iron railings of all the balconies; not the bright yellow and red flowers in the window boxes; not the one neighbor's door with the crack in the wood. I even feel nostalgic for the little cubbyhole at the end of the street where we take the trash and recycling.

We turn onto Calle de Atocha, and everything's familiar

here, too. There's the grocery store. There's the Museo del Jamon, which I really did think was a museum for ham until I saw the stores in other parts of Madrid too. There's the memorial that looks like a circle of men in trench coats with their arms around each other—the monument honors a group of lawyers killed during the transition to democracy back in the 1970s. I finally looked it up just last week.

We're closing in on the train station, and I almost chicken out when we pass the sculptures of the giant baby heads, and Avery starts talking about how creepy they are. I could tell Avery that I just want to see the area on the lower level of the train station that's like an indoor tropical rain forest. It's actually more impressive than the blue room.

Instead, I turn to Avery and say firmly, "There are rules for where I'm taking you."

"Rules?"

"You can't make fun of anything while we're there," I say. "I don't care what you think, but don't ruin it for me. If you don't like the room, save your opinion for later, when you talk to your friends back home. Just don't ever make fun of this place to *me*."

"Okay," Avery says meekly.

The people streaming into the station around us have backpacks and rolling suitcases; they call out to each other about when the train is leaving for Barcelona or Bilbao, and do they have time to buy a sandwich first?

I get a little jolt when I realize that all the conversations I'm eavesdropping on are in Spanish, and I still understand.

But the travelers head down toward the train tracks, and Avery and I turn toward the blue room.

There's an attendant standing there, like before, and Avery gets a mocking smirk on her face when the woman goes through the long explanation about not opening one set of doors until the other closes behind us.

*This was a mistake*, I think.

Then we're in the blue room, all by ourselves. Avery looks around, and . . . she doesn't laugh. She doesn't even look like she wants to laugh.

"This," she says softly. "This is what I needed at the hospital, when we were waiting to hear if Daddy was going to live or die. Or if he was already dead."

"Then you don't think it's creepy that you can look out, and everyone else is living their ordinary lives—going places—but they don't even see you?" I ask.

I wait for her to remind me that I didn't want to hear her opinion. But she's still peering around, breathing in the stillness of the place.

"I think it's a good creepy," she says. "Eerie, but . . . it feels right."

"Exactly," I say, relief flowing over me. "Sometimes, you need to get away from people who are just living their ordinary lives. Because you don't belong with them. Because your life is too strange. Or you need to figure out some things."

Avery goes and stands under the cone of words, under the one shaft of bright light in the room. She turns slowly, as if reading the spiral of lamentations and hopeful prayers, spun together.

"*Who* is this a memorial for?" she asks.

"The victims of the worst terrorist attack in Spain," I tell her, because I've looked it all up now. "It happened in March of 2004. It was kind of their September eleventh. There were bombs on trains, and a hundred and ninety-two people died. Just ordinary people, going about their ordinary lives . . ."

Avery gazes up again.

"There are a lot more bad things that happened in the world than I ever knew about," she says. "I thought it was mostly just, I don't know, the Holocaust, September eleventh, a war here and there. Homelessness. Drug addiction. I thought, otherwise, everyone's life was pretty good. Like mine."

I don't say anything. I look away, just for an instant, and suddenly Avery's got her head down.

"Daddy could still die," she whispers, and it feels like she's been carrying those words around for weeks, afraid to say them. Until now.

"You mean, because he had one heart attack, he could have another?" I ask. "Don't you remember what the doctor said, how—"

"I know, I know—they fixed all the blocked arteries," Avery says. "But even if he goes to all his doctor's appointments, and does everything he should—and lays off the Spanish ham and the stress . . . Regardless. Someday, he'll die."

"So will you," I say. "So will I. So will your mother and my mother and my dad and my grandparents and all my friends and all your friends. . . ."

And in spite of myself, in spite of everything I know about death that Avery doesn't, I get a lump in my throat thinking about the people I love who are probably going to die much, much sooner than Avery's dad.

Grandma.

Grandpa.

My dad.

"So that's it?" Avery asks, slashing her hands through the air. "We're all going to die someday, so why bother? Why not just . . . What's that awful country song? 'Live Like You Were Dying'?"

"*No,*" I say. "I hate that song too." I just never quite knew why. But suddenly I do. "It's not about skydiving or riding bulls or taking stupid risks, because you're going to die anyway. You can't just give up. Or constantly pray just to accept things as they are. That doesn't leave room for taking the time to learn Spanish. Or making new friends. Or learning CPR. Or learning to drive a stick shift. Or standing up for yourself. Or . . ."

Was I lecturing her or me?

"Or because you're afraid your husband is going to die in a war, you agree to have a baby for total strangers," Avery says softly. "Like what your mother did."

*Oh, Mom.*

I get a lump in my throat thinking about her, too.

Avery keeps her gaze on me. It's a little too intense.

"Would you ever do what your mother did?" she asks.

"You mean, get pregnant and have a baby just to give it to someone else? Would you?" I counter quickly.

Why should I have to answer that question, and not her? I have angry words rushing to my tongue: *Do you think I'm the only one who would ever have to consider that, just because you're rich and I'm poor?* But I hold back and wait for her to answer.

Avery's eyes dart to the side.

"I think I would always be too selfish," she admits. "And . . . right now I can't imagine having a baby, period. For anyone." She grins. "Or *with* anyone."

"Yeah," I mutter. Because we're in the blue room, it feels okay to go on. "And I keep thinking about my mom lying in the hospital watching your parents take you away. When she knew you were the last baby she'd ever have . . ."

"That wasn't my parents' fault," Avery says. She crosses her arms and shivers, even though the sunlight is beating down on her. "It wasn't my fault either."

"I know!" I say quickly. "I know it's just how things turned out, but . . . I don't think I could be a surrogate mother. Er, a gestational carrier, I mean. It's too hard. Even Mom only did it once."

Avery frowns, and the corners of her mouth tremble. But it's our last day in Spain, and I'm not going to make this easier for her. I don't care if her father almost died a few weeks ago and her parents might still get divorced. She needs to understand exactly what my mother did for her. She needs to understand that it wasn't just an implantation and a legal contract and all those other sterile, empty terms. For my mother, bringing Avery into the world was heartache and pain.

*And love and joy and something to hold on to and hope for during a dark time . . .*

I sigh, but Avery speaks before I have a chance to soften my words.

"Your mother was really young when you were born, right?" she says.

"Yes. Twenty."

"Then she's only—what? Thirty-six now? That's young enough to have another baby!"

"Avery, remember my dad—"

For a minute I think she's going to suggest that my mom should divorce my dad and marry someone else. Or find a "baby daddy." Ugh. Now I'm really going to have to yell at her.

But she waves a hand like none of that matters.

"Remember, the egg and sperm that made me came together in a test tube, so there are lots of possibilities," she says. "Artificial insemination. Donor sperm. Or . . ."

"All that costs a lot of money, remember?" I practically snarl. I could go on: *Raising a baby takes a lot of money too. Don't you know how poor we are? Haven't you noticed how most of my clothes come from the thrift store or Walmart?* But I surprise myself by saying, "Anyhow, I don't think my mother wants another baby anymore. That's just what she wanted when she was twenty-one or twenty-two. When her life was different."

"What does she want now?"

I've never thought about that before. Mom is my mother. My father's wife. My grandparents' daughter. It feels like her having the right to want anything for herself ended with Dad's accident.

*Because she's been praying like an old person for the last fourteen years: Please help me gracefully accept this life I've been given. Please let me not want anything else.*

I think about how excited she was, telling me about the chance to go to Spain, how I'd have opportunities she never did.

I think about the ordinary things she wanted for me before: a chance to get my driver's license. A job at the Crawfordsville Dairy Queen. Those were the only kind of things either of us dared to hope for.

I think about something I only heard her say once, to another aide in the staff room at the nursing home.

"Honestly? I think what she wants is to go back to school and get her nursing degree," I say. "So she knows more about how to help her patients. And . . . so she'll get paid more."

"Well, that's *easy*," Avery says. "It'd take—what? Just a couple more years of school?"

"And a lot of money, remember?" I say.

"Aren't there student loans for stuff like that?"

*Do you even understand what the word "poor" means?* I want to ask her. *How is Mom supposed to pay back those loans?*

But then I remember that an aide Mom used to work with actually did go back to school and became a registered nurse. It took her six years of part-time classes, and she complained all the time about how tired she was.

But she did it.

And now she is making more money and helping people more.

I still make a face at Avery.

"Remember how my grandpa lost his farm just like, well, like your grandfather did?" I ask. "That kind of made him allergic to debt. He'd have a heart attack if Mom told him she was taking out loans for school!"

Then I wince, because I should have picked some other catastrophe besides a heart attack.

But Avery shrugs.

"You're pretty good at doing CPR," she says.

And somehow, because we're in the blue room, it's okay for us to say these things to each other.

Avery is still looking around.

"Does anybody else ever come here besides you?" she asks, because we've had the room to ourselves the whole time.

"Not very often, I don't think," I say. "Maybe this was really important to everyone when it first opened, but then the survivors needed it less and less."

"I wish I had a place like this to go at home, when my parents drive me crazy," Avery says. "Or . . ." Her voice gets very soft. "When I'm worried about them."

I think about how pale her dad still looks. I think about how her mother gets tears in her eyes over the smallest problem—when a restaurant doesn't have the exact kind of salad she wants, or when a shop clerk doesn't understand her asking for something in English. Or when Avery tells her to calm down in a tone that really seems to be saying, *Mom, could you just shut up? You're bugging me!*

"Oh, my parents!" Avery says, jolting upright. "We're going to be late for meeting Mom!"

And then we're in such a rush leaving that I forget to give the room one last look around. One last thank-you.

It turns out that the special restaurant that Avery's mom wants to take us to is actually a 100 Montaditos.

"My friend Linda said when her twin daughters were studying in Spain in college, they loved this place," Mrs. Armisted says. "I thought you'd be really excited to go where college students go!"

Mrs. Armisted's eyes glisten. She's trying so hard. I have to grip Avery's arm hard and whisper in her ear when Mrs. Armisted's back is turned, "Don't tell her we've been eating here all summer. Don't tell her we've been hanging out with college students ourselves. Let her think this is a big deal! Let her be happy!"

After lunch, Mrs. Armisted wants to take us shopping. We go into ALE-HOP, a European chain that has a life-size cow in the front of every store. Avery rolls her eyes but starts methodically pulling out clothes to try on. Mrs. Armisted works just as quickly, and when Avery heads back to the fitting room, Mrs. Armisted hands her pile of clothes to me.

"These will look good on you," she says.

I look at the price tags.

"No, no, I already have too much to fit back into my suitcase, going home," I say.

"We can buy new suitcases, too," Mrs. Armisted says. "Please. It's the least I can do after everything your mother did for us. And everything *you* did for Avery and David."

"Come on, it makes Mom happy to buy clothes for people," Avery says, a wicked twinkle in her eye.

The thing is, the clothes actually do look good on me. They aren't anything that I'd wear back in Crawfordsville—one's a red shirt with an uneven hemline; one's a purple dress with little cutouts on the sleeves.

*But maybe I would wear them back in Crawfordsville*, I think. *Maybe I'll just be that girl who looks different—I look different, anyway. Why not look different and feel good about it?*

Who knows? Maybe it will end up being Stephanie Purley who's jealous of *me*.

Even if she makes fun of me, I still like these clothes.

By the end of the afternoon, we're weighed down with shopping bags.

Avery goes to hang out with her dad for a little bit while I call Mom one last time. All she wants to talk about is meeting me at the Columbus airport tomorrow night: "Your grandparents have invited everyone they know, so it might be kind of a big crowd," she apologizes.

I picture how Avery and her parents will see all the gray-haired people: the women with their tightly curled beauty-parlor perms, the men with their sagging pants held up by frayed belts and suspenders. The Armisteds will see that I don't have any friends in Crawfordsville under the age of seventy.

*Or will they just see that I have a lot of people who love me?*

Avery and I leave early for the last event of the day, our last official event in Spain: dinner with our Spanish class. Everybody else has two more weeks before their official good-bye dinner, but Dragomir argued in class on Friday that we needed a big send-off as well.

We get to the restaurant, and even Señora Gomez is there.

"We will miss you both," she says solemnly, after she air-kisses us. It takes me a minute to realize she's actually spoken in English. Her "miss" sounds like "mees," and everything is so heavily accented, I would have understood her better in Spanish.

"Wait—you actually know English?" Avery asks in surprise.

Señora Gomez raises an eyebrow and switches back to Spanish.

"I have been teaching Spanish to *Británicos* and *Estadounidenses* for years," she says. "You think I did not pick up *something*? But in class, it is better for you to think I only understand in Spanish. So you *have* to learn it to communicate. And I learned English too late in life to avoid having an accent. Would you pay attention to me if I sounded so stupid all the time?"

"But—that's how we always sound in Spanish," I complain.

"Ah, but you are learning," Señora Gomez says. "You have gotten so much better this summer. You will be fluent soon."

I guess I have understood every word she just spoke.

I think about the pathetic Spanish program back at Crawfordsville High School. I won't be fluent in Spanish soon. I'll be forgetting everything I know.

But Señora Gomez has given me an idea.

I sit down beside Avery, and across from Dragomir and Andrei.

"I've mostly just heard you speak Spanish and English," I tell the boys, in Spanish. "And muttering things that are probably curse words in Bulgarian. Let me hear what you really sound like. Speak a whole sentence in Bulgarian. Or two or three."

The boys look guiltily at each other when I accuse them of cursing. But then Andrei begins. The Bulgarian words flow out smoothly, and for the first time I realize what a deep, beautiful voice he has when he's not joking around.

Then Dragomir takes over, and his Bulgarian sounds joyous, like he's constantly on the verge of laughter.

"Okay, now tell us what you both said," Avery demands.

Both boys grin and shake their heads.

"Some things don't translate," Andrei says, in Spanish.

"You just pledged your undying love to Kayla, didn't you?" Avery asks.

Both boys blush, and I complain, "Avery!"

Dragomir switches back to Spanish too.

"Okay, I will translate part of what I said," he tells us. "It is that when we leave tonight, we will not say *adios*. It will just be *hasta luego*. Because we *will* meet again later. And it will be soon. I will go to *los* Estados Unidos to see you, or you will visit me in Bulgaria. Or we will meet again in Spain. But we will not say good-bye."

He's watching my face, and I have to look down at my menu to hide the fact that now I'm blushing.

*None of those things are actually going to happen*, I tell myself. Probably when I'm an old lady in a nursing home, I'll repeat again and again *Oh yes, when I was a teenager I had two boys named Dragomir and Andrei fighting over me. But then I had to leave Spain early, so I never really got to fall in love with either of them.*

But there it is again, me giving up on something I might want. It's years and years and years before I'll be an old lady in a nursing home. I could become fluent in Spanish between now and then. I could go to Bulgaria.

I have all sorts of choices. Ideas start to bloom in my head, as if they've been growing there all day and I never noticed: If I can talk Mom into going to the community college for a nursing degree, maybe I can take Spanish classes there too, instead of at Crawfordsville High School. A few of the really smart kids do that, and the guidance counselors are always saying more of us should take advantage of that—it's free! But it never felt like they were talking to me.

Now, though, if I take more and better Spanish classes, then maybe after I'm done with high school I can get a scholarship and study Spanish in college. Maybe there are even scholarships that would let me travel. And then maybe I could be a translator.

Maybe even at a hospital.

Or a nursing home.

"I'm definitely coming back to Spain someday," I hear myself tell Dragomir and Andrei. "Want to meet up back here in Madrid?"

"Next summer?" Andrei says eagerly.

It's crazy, but that doesn't mean it's impossible.

"*¿Por qué no?*" I say, and I feel like I'm answering about a whole lot more than another trip to Spain.

Why not?

## Avery: How It Ends/How It Begins

***Kayla's had a much better*** *summer in Spain than I have,* I think, watching her laugh and—let's be honest, *flirt*—with Dragomir and Andrei. Tears sting at my eyes. I'm almost as bad as Mom, that I can cry now at the drop of a hat.

It's not that I'm jealous. I'm not interested in Dragomir or Andrei, even though they're both funny and sweet. And now that I know them better, I forget that Dragomir has acne or that Andrei is so skinny he might want to try folding himself into an envelope and *mailing* himself to the United States, if he really wants to go there.

But Kayla got all the excitement and the guys falling in love with her.

I got stupid family drama and my parents planning a divorce and my dad almost dying.

It's funny how the whole thing about my parents using a gestational carrier to have me doesn't seem like such a big deal now. I still feel a little weird about it, but so what? I feel weird about pretty much everything right now.

*If Mom and Dad really do get divorced, will I ever get to the point where it seems like that isn't a big deal?* I wonder. *Will it ever* not *bother me that Daddy had a heart attack and almost died?*

The paella comes, in big round skillets that the waitress leaves in the middle of the table. Kayla and I are sharing a seafood one—*marisco*—and the shrimp on top are still in their shells, with antennae waving and beady eyes peering up at us. Kayla and I both shrug and start pulling off the shells.

*I want someone to notice how much self-control I have, that I'm not jumping back and screaming in horror*, I think.

But I guess everyone else is used to shrimp served that way.

Hugh and Susan walk over to our end of the table, and Susan says (in Spanish, of course, because it's Susan), "Look us up if you're ever in London," and Hugh gazes into my eyes and says, "Especially if it's four or five years from now."

Okay, that was kind of cool. That was one good thing that happened in Spain.

One.

Then the meal is ending, and people are starting to leave, and Dragomir leans across the table and tells me, "I have decided to give you a farewell gift. A farewell *fútbol* gift."

I can't help myself. I gasp.

"You're going to tell me the Bulgarian secret?" I squeal. "The way you could almost always steal the ball from me?"

He nods solemnly.

"Well, sort of," he qualifies. "I think it would be disloyal to my country if I just *told*. But if you look up Bulgarian folk dances online, there is one in particular . . . You will recognize the footwork. And if you practice that—that is the Bulgarian secret."

"You're pulling my leg," I say. Even though, let's face it, that's not actually an expression in Spanish. I try again with the correct phrase, which sounds like it's about hair: *"Me estás tomando el pelo."*

"No, no," Dragomir says. He holds up his right hand. "Bulgarian honor."

He still might be pranking me, but it's worth a try.

It will drive Shannon and Lauren crazy if I've learned better soccer skills in Spain than they learned at soccer camp.

So I guess that's another thing that was good about this summer in Spain.

Kayla's hugging everyone good-bye, so I do too. The other kids and Señora Gomez head for the Metro, which is just a block away.

"Your mom said we should call a cab when we're done," Kayla says. "But I kind of forgot, and—"

"And it's not that far and lots of people are out walking around," I say. "It's perfectly safe."

We turn toward Puerta del Sol, because it's an easy landmark in the maze of twisty streets. Our progress is slow, because it's like there's one huge street party going on around us.

"It's ten thirty at night, and there are more people out than I've ever seen during the day," Kayla marvels. "And, look, there are little kids having dinner at that restaurant over there. . . ."

"And it's a Sunday night!" I agree. "I guess this is what Dad was talking about when he said Spain always stays up too late."

"And we missed it all," Kayla says wistfully. "Until tonight."

I think about how I lied to Shannon and Lauren when I didn't want to text them, and I said I was grounded for sneaking out to dance clubs.

"We should have been sneaking out every night," I tell Kayla. "Or—now! Maybe we could . . ."

Kayla shoots me a sideways look and I shrug.

"Okay, not tonight," I say. Not with my parents already falling apart. Not when I feel like I'm the only glue holding either of them together.

"If I can make it back to Spain someday, you can too," Kayla says firmly. "And then you can see and do everything we missed this time around."

I step on a manhole cover, which rocks under my feet. Kayla points at the word stamped in the metal: BOMBEROS.

"Did I ever tell you the first time I saw that, I thought it had to do with bombs or bomb squads?" she asks. "When, really, *bomberos* are just ordinary firefighters? There was so much I didn't understand at the beginning of the summer! So much I was afraid of that really wasn't scary at all!"

*So much I should have been afraid of, that I didn't even know was coming. . . ,* I think.

A burst of laughter sails up from one of the tables of the sidewalk café we're walking past. It's a bunch of middle-aged people; what do they have to be so happy about? They're old enough they probably lived here when Spain had a dictatorship. Their economy sucks. And they don't even have dryers in their apartments.

But they're still laughing. They're still happy.

My phone buzzes, and I almost don't look at it because I'm sure it's going to be Mom fretting about why Kayla and I aren't back yet.

*But if it's something about Dad . . .*

I pull out my phone, and the text isn't from Mom or Dad. It's from Lauren.

**Shannon and I just decided**, she wrote. **We're not playing soccer anymore.**

"What?" I say out loud.

I send Lauren a bunch of question marks. Her reply comes quickly: **We're sick of soccer after camp this summer. We saw the practice schedule for the fall—too intense. And our moms are making us take hard classes. We want to have fun in h.s.**

I show Kayla my phone. My hands are shaking.

"They can't do this to me," I say. "You saw how I was this summer. I *need* soccer."

"Just because they're quitting, that doesn't mean you have to too," Kayla says.

"They're my best friends!" I protest.

Kayla takes my phone from me. She types: **It will make me sad not to have you on the team with me. But I'm still playing.** Then she hands the phone back to me and asks, "Well?"

I hit send. And it's strange: My hands are perfectly steady now.

A minute later, I get Lauren's reply: **Oh. Maybe we will play, after all. We'd miss you if you were always away at soccer practice.**

"Sometimes, they're not actually very good friends," I admit to Kayla.

"Nobody's perfect," Kayla says.

We're in Puerta del Sol now, which feels like party central. A group of guys wearing fraternity T-shirts are daring each other to wade in one of the fountains.

"Am I the only person who ever went on a Spanish vacation and had a miserable time?" I grumble.

"Hel-*lo*?" Kayla says. She wiggles her eyebrows up and down at me.

"Oh. I kind of meant both of us," I say. "And you had *more* fun. Anyway, you get to go home, and you get your normal life back. For me, it's . . . What am I going to do when I get home?"

"You'll be the greatest . . . wait, what position do you play in soccer?"

"Midfielder."

"You'll be the greatest midfielder your high school has ever seen," Kayla says. She holds her hands near my face, like she's showing off my reflected glory. "Ta-da!"

I shove her hands away.

"I mean with my parents," I mutter.

"They're getting better," Kayla says. We're passing out of the plaza now, and she waits until we've turned down a quieter street before she goes on. "You've done okay with them the past few weeks."

"Because you helped," I say, and I embarrass myself by choking on the last word. "You let me complain all I wanted. I could tell you anything, and you didn't get mad at me—"

"Oh yes, I did!" Kayla protests. "I was mad at you practically the whole summer!"

"Well, I was mad at you a lot too!"

We're glaring at each other, almost nose to nose, and then I start giggling.

"This is how Lauren and her sister always sound," I say.

"We're not sisters," Kayla says, and it feels like she's shut a door between us.

We're close enough to our apartment now that we can hear the music coming from the eighties nightclub. It's that "Don't You Want Me, Baby" song again—are they *trying* to make me cry?

I think about how Dad said he'd always hoped Kayla and I could grow up feeling like cousins, and it makes me sad. I don't have any cousins, and Kayla doesn't either.

But I know plenty of kids who barely even know their cousins. Or the cousins are on the other side of the country or even the world—in Los Angeles or Seattle, Pakistan or India or Japan—and they've only met them once or twice in their lives.

"I know we're not sisters," I tell Kayla. "And I know you've got the whole town of Crawfordsville waiting for you to get home. You don't *need* anyone else."

"I am going to be busy when I get home," Kayla says, almost snippily. "But I'm *not* going back to my normal life. I'm going to get as serious about Spanish as Susan is. Because I want to be a translator someday."

She sounds so sure of herself. She knows what she wants.

And it feels like that's all she needs to get what she wants.

"That's nice," I say. "You have your whole life figured out."

We're walking into shadows now, and I can feel the darkness creeping into me.

Kayla reaches over and grabs my shoulders.

"See what you just did?" she says, shaking me. "You don't even *care*. If we were really sisters, you'd be happy for me, too. You'd listen when I told you what I was excited or hopeful or sad or worried about, just as much as I listen when you tell me."

"I *listened*," I say. "I just . . . have too many problems of my own."

"It's like you're still going around yelling, 'Kayla Butts is not my sister,'" she says.

"I never . . . ," I begin. I look over, and Kayla is holding herself so stiffly. I start over again. "Oh. Are you still mad about that?"

"That night we found out everything. You said, 'Is Kayla Butts my sister?' like it would be the worst thing ever. And now we're about to leave Spain, and . . ."

Is Kayla really going to start crying over something I said so long ago?

"I was upset! I didn't even know you then!" I protest. "I didn't know what I was saying!"

"But I'd kind of felt like you were my little sister, my whole life," Kayla says. "Because Mom had never told me the truth, of course, but . . ."

"But you paid attention," I say. "You were watching. You could tell that . . . that I was important to her."

"And you didn't care about either of us," Kayla finishes.

We're both in the shadows now, but I feel like I can see everything. I'm pretty sure Kayla has the same look I see on my mother's face all the time now: *What you're going to say next could hurt me. And I can't protect myself. Please, please, please don't hurt me.* It's hard for me even to remember how I viewed Kayla back at the beginning of the summer: Did I ever slip and call her a big, dumb ox out loud? All that is gone now. Kayla adapted better to Spain than I did. And she was the one who knew to start CPR on my dad right away. She got me to pray and do CPR myself. She was the one I clung to all those endless hours of waiting at the hospital—there's nobody else I would rather have had there with me that day.

She's strong and confident and capable and smart and

determined, and it doesn't seem like anything could hurt her.

But anyone can be hurt.

And . . . anyone can need help healing.

"I didn't care before this summer," I admit. "But, Kayla, really? You saved my father's life. You've put up with me and my mom and my dad during the worst time of our lives. I'd beg my parents to adopt you, if it would do any good."

I picture Kayla and me walking into status-obsessed, appearance-obsessed Deskins High School together, and . . . yep. I still feel the same way. Kayla would definitely help me navigate high school.

She just did, texting Lauren.

"I already have my own family, thanks," Kayla says, and the stiffness is still in her voice.

"But I think we get to make a choice," I say. "Because of how I was born, our parents made us . . . what would you call it? Womb-mates?"

"That's a ridiculous term," Kayla says.

"Right," I agree. "I won't say it ever again. And most people don't get to decide if they're going to have a sister or a brother. But we kind of do. We could never speak to each other again after tomorrow, or we could stay friends forever. Or we could decide that we have an even bigger link. Like, that we *want* to be sisters. And, Kayla, if you think—"

"Avery," Kayla says quietly. "You were right from the very beginning. We aren't sisters. We can't ever be that."

For a moment, it feels like I've taken a soccer ball to my gut. Is *Kayla* rejecting *me*? Was she just setting me up? Pretending she wanted to be my sister, so she could hurt me?

"I mean, that's not the right *word*," Kayla says, as if she sees how hard I have to try not to double over in pain. Or as if she's just figured out something herself. "It's not as bad as 'womb-mates,' but . . . I don't think there is the right word for us in English. Or Spanish either. It's like we're not even speaking the right language."

"Maybe Bulgarian, then?" I'm mostly joking, but I still pull out my phone and start a search for Bulgarian family terms. "Oh, look—Bulgarian has five different words for uncle. So maybe . . ."

There's only one word listed for sister in Bulgarian: *sestrá.*

*"Sechedka,"* Kayla says decisively as she looks over my shoulder. "It's like a cross between the Bulgarian word for sister and the Bulgarian word for cousin. It's perfect."

"Nobody else would ever understand that," I grumble.

"So?" Kayla says. "Who needs to understand besides us?"

She has a point. Still, I lean back my head and yell up at the Spanish sky, "Kayla Butts is my *sechedka*! Isn't that great?"

"Shh," Kayla says, putting her hand over my mouth. "You'll wake up the whole street."

"This is Spain," I say, pushing her hand away. "It's not three a.m. yet, so nobody's sleeping. And who can hear us for all the partying?"

Kayla surprises me by throwing her head back, cupping her hands around her own mouth and yelling, "*¡Mi sechedka está embarazosa!*"

She never would have done that at the beginning of the summer.

"There," she says, looking back at me. She drops her hands. "Satisfied?"

"Yes," I say. "Because you said *está*, not *es*. That means you don't think I'll *always* be embarrassing."

"Right," she says. "Because sometimes you'll just be difficult. Annoying. Bothersome. Bossy. Demanding."

She's grinning. I can tell, even in the dark.

"Or sympathetic," I counter. I loop my arm around her. "Understanding. Listening. Helpful. A shoulder to cry on, when that's what *you* need . . ."

With each word I say, it feels like I'm making a promise. Or saying another prayer.

So many things broke this summer. There's so much more for me to worry about and fear. I found out secrets I never wanted to know.

But it is possible to feel whole and happy again. It's possible to giggle only moments after being on the verge of tears. And it's possible for me to peer at Kayla on this dark night and feel like this is one of the sunniest moments of the entire summer.

Because we *are* connected. By more than our parents, by more than this summer. By our own choice. And we both know it now. We may never use the word *sechedka* again, or we may use it the rest of our lives. But we'll always have the feel of it, the meaning we gave it on this night of shouting at the Spanish sky.

And there can be more.

"When you come back to Spain next year," I say, "can I come too?"

# Acknowledgments

Some books, like some kids, have more "parents" than others—or, at least, more godparents and midwives. I think this marks the first time I've needed to thank people from four different continents for their assistance with a book.

First and foremost, I want to thank my family, and particularly my daughter, Meredith. I started thinking about this book during a family trip to Spain with her, my son, and my husband, and the sense of discovery we all felt is embedded in this book. When Meredith went back three years later to spend part of her junior year of college in Madrid, she agreed to scout around for some of the information I needed to make the book happen. A year and a half later, she accompanied me to Spain once again to act as tour guide and translator for a more concentrated research trip. She managed not to cringe too much over my rusty, mispronounced high school Spanish, and she humored me going to see landmarks that I wasn't even sure would end up in the book—even when it meant walking long distances in 90-degree heat. (However, given the trouble we had finding the 11-M memorial at the Atocha train station, I'm not sure she would have ever forgiven me if that *hadn't* played an important role in the book.) Later, she proofread the book for me to watch for mistakes about Spain or Spanish translations. (This worked much better than relying on Google Translate!)

I also owe thanks to several people who either gave me specialized information or went above and beyond helping me find experts to interview:

Thanks to my friend and fellow writer Jo Schaffer, I was able to interview her niece, Jessika Stephens, just as Jessika was embarking on plans to become a gestational carrier. Jessika was very generous in explaining both the process and her reasoning about wanting to help another family. She also told me how she answered people who didn't see her decision in the same light.

When I wanted more information about psychological issues related to gestational carriers, the children they carry, and the intended parents, my friend Dr. Colby Srsic, who is a psychologist, kindly put out a request for me on a listserv of Ohio psychologists, and so many people responded offering help that I couldn't interview them all. Kathleen M. Payne, Ph.D., of Royalton Psychological Associates in Royalton, Ohio, gave me a lot of information about kids dealing with family situations that mirrored some aspects of Avery's situation. Allison Fagan, Ph.D., who is a member of the American Society for Reproductive Medicine (ASRM) and the mental health professional group within that, talked to me about a range of issues related to what Avery, Kayla, and their parents would have faced all along. She also suggested an important change for the ending of the book.

My friend Dr. Tim Richards answered many of my questions about heart patients, CPR, bypass surgery, and emergency room procedures in the United States. When I needed more specific information about hospitals and medical protocol in

Spain, my friend, former college roommate, and fellow author Christy Esmahan—who lived in Spain for many years, and got her Ph.D. there—swung into action. Juan Asturias, PhD; Carmen Guerrero, Ph.D.; and a cardiologist, Dr. Francisco Martín Herrero, all gave me invaluable information thanks to Christy's assistance (and in some cases, her translation assistance as well).

When I needed to doublecheck to make sure I correctly represented the information provided on a California birth certificate from 2004, my cousin Jamil Tahir kindly sent me a copy of his oldest son's birth certificate—from 2004. (I joked that that is true family loyalty, that Jamil and his wife had their first child the exact right year, even though that happened thirteen years before I needed the information!)

And when I found gaps in my own knowledge about the difficult economic situation American farmers faced in the 1980s, my father answered numerous questions. This also reminded me how proud I am that he succeeded in navigating the challenges of those years as a farmer.

Also, even though I just called her out of the blue and I had no friend or relative to introduce us, Michelle Steele, veterans service officer at the Ohio Veterans Home in Sandusky, Ohio, was very helpful in giving me information about what medical care someone like Kayla's dad would receive through the Veterans Administration based on the details of his accident.

As with any of my books, any mistakes that might remain even after all that expert help are my responsibility, and nobody else's fault.

Some of the other help I got with this book was a little

more serendipitous. While I was in the middle of writing, I took several weeks off to visit China and speak at the Shanghai American School. Obviously China and Spain are very different countries, but the school staff, students, and parents gave me a lot of insight into living abroad, and what it's like to be in a foreign country as an expatriate, rather than just a tourist. I'd particularly like to thank the librarian who originally invited me—Beth Rohrbeck—as well as the librarians I spent a lot of time with while I was there: Kathy Lynch, Marie Slaby, Barbara and Tim Boyer, and Kimbra Power. (And Kimbra is actually from Australia—so there's my fourth continent!)

I also went on a two-week book tour for one of my other books, *Children of Exile*, while I was revising this book. I'd intended to take a total break from *The Summer of Broken Things* during that time period, but a conversation I happened to have with my media escort in Kansas City, Cathy Boyle Basse, ended up redirecting some of my thoughts about a particularly tricky issue I was trying to resolve. So, thank you, Cathy, for helping me even when we both thought we were just talking about life and families in general!

And as always, I'm grateful to my agent, Tracey Adams, who was very patient listening to my fretting about this book. Thank you also to my editor, David Gale, and his assistant, Amanda Ramirez, for the questions they asked that helped me hone my view of this book. I appreciate all the support I've gotten as well from others at Simon & Schuster. I am particularly grateful to Lucy Cummins, who designed the beautiful cover, which may be my very favorite cover I've ever had on any of my books.

And finally, I am grateful to my two local writers groups

for their continued encouragement and support. One group we've never bothered to name, despite more than a decade of meetings: thank you, Jenny Patton, Nancy Roe Pimm, Amjed Qamar, and Linda Stanek. And thank you as well to the writers of OHYA: Jody Casella, Julia DeVillers, Linda Gerber, Lisa Klein, Erin McCahan, Edie Pattou, and Natalie D. Richards.